# GLASS ISLAND

by

Gareth Griffith

www.GarethGriffithAuthor.com

# Contents

# Map

## South-West Britain in the Sixth Century

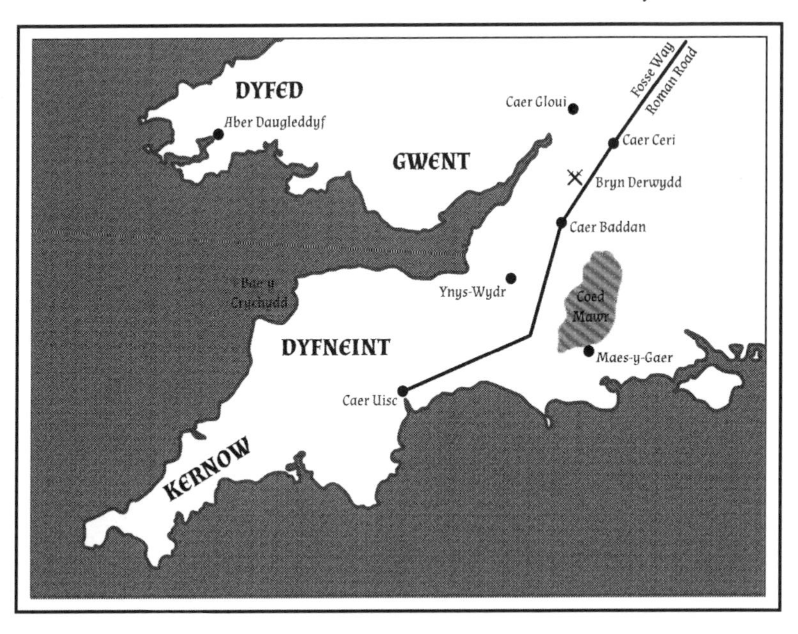

# Glossary

| | |
|---|---|
| Ætheling | prince, male youth in line of succession |
| Caer | fort |
| Cantref | division of land, literally "cant" (a hundred) and "tref" (town in modern Welsh, but formerly used for smaller settlements) |
| Gesith | elite warrior and member of King's war band |
| Gewisse | West Saxons |
| Seax | knife with a large, single-edged blade |

# Place Names

Listed are the place names used in this novel and their modern equivalents. Those cases where no historical Brythonic name is known to the author are signified by an asterisk (*).

| | |
|---|---|
| Afon Hafren | River Severn |
| Afon Pererin/Pilgrim River* | River Parrett |
| Afon Tawel* | River Taw |
| Afon Tafwys | River Thames |
| Afon Toreithiog* | River Torridge |
| Caer Baddan | Bath/Aquae Sulis |
| Caer Ceri | Cireencester |
| Caer Gloui | Gloucester |
| Caer Uisc | Exeter |
| Aberdaugleddyf | Milford Haven |
| Bae-y-Crychydd/Heron Bay* | Barnstaple or Bideford Bay |
| Bryn Derwydd* | Dyrham |
| Cambria | Wales |
| Clyde/Alt Clud | Strathclyde |
| Dyfneint | Devon/Dumnonia |
| Dyfed | South-west Wales |
| Gwent | South-east Wales |
| Kernow | Cornwall |
| Llanilltud Fawr | Llantwit Major |
| Llydaw (Armorica) | Brittany |
| Maes-y-Gaer* | Cadbury Castle |
| Sea of Gaul | English Channel |
| Ynys Wydr | Glastonbury |

# List of Main Characters

## People of the Summer Land and related characters

| | |
|---|---|
| Arawn | Chieftain of the Summer Land |
| Eleri Gwir | Arawn's daughter |
| Gereint | orphan boy adopted by Arawn |
| Mared of the Silver Wheel | seer and cunning woman |
| Cerys | A healer/Mared's daughter |
| Gwion | archer and rival for Eleri's love |
| Meriadoc | Gwion's father |
| Cerridwen | a fugitive/the Dragon Maiden |
| Gronw | Cerridwen's father |
| Gwenda | Cerridwen's mother |
| Olwen | Cerridwen's sister |
| Kado | Arawn's right-hand man |
| Rhian | Eleri Gwir's friend |
| Bryn | a groom |
| Math | a soldier |
| Onnen | Math's wife |
| Idris | son of Math and Onnen |

## Red Cloaks and related characters

| | |
|---|---|
| Ffernfael | chieftain of Caer Baddan |
| Cenydd | priest of the Celtic Church |
| Siriol | a female warrior |
| Branwen | a female warrior |
| Macsen | captain of the Red Cloaks |
| Julia | Macsen's sister |
| Livia | Macsen's sister |
| Riwalus | Macsen's second-in-command |

## Caer Gloui and Caer Ceri

| | |
|---|---|
| Condidan | chieftain of Caer Ceri |
| Conmagil | chieftain of Caer Gloui |

## Ynys Wydr

| | |
|---|---|
| Cynan | bard and chieftain of Ynys Wydr |
| Awen Ysbryd | seer of Ynys Wydr |

## People of Dyfneint/Caer Uisc

| | |
|---|---|
| Erbin | King of Dyfneint |
| Kadwy | Erbin's son/prince of Dyfneint |
| Kelyn | Erbin's son/prince of Dyfneint |
| Marrec | captain of Dyfneint |
| Alun Ddu | captain of Kernow |
| Malo | priest of the Celtic Church |

## Saxons/Gewisse

| | |
|---|---|
| Ceawlin | Saxon king |
| Cuthwine | Ceawlin's son |

# Part One

## AD 576

## "The Hazel Month"

# First Words

My name is Owain. My family were the people of the Summer Land, as they were then. My father was Kado. He died fighting the Saxons when I was very young, at the battle which we call by the name of Bryn Derwydd. My mother was Arian. She was a strong woman of independent mind who went her own way, returning to her own country of the Water Land, which as you must know is a waste of eels and birds, drenching rains and brilliant skies. That was a long time ago – more than fifty winters.

The Summer Land was my first home, yet I have no memory of its last chieftain, a man called Arawn, a good man by all accounts. He had a daughter. We called her Eleri Gwir, the Truth or Plain Speaker. She was one of those who fought at Bryn Derwydd, against the people of the keels who came like sea worms from across the eastern waters. Eleri, my father and the others fought that day in the name of the Summer Land, lest it be lost to us; they fought for our land, for our people, the living and the dead, lest we should be counted slaves and foreigners in our own country. The chieftains of the old cities were at Bryn Derwydd – there was Ffernfael of Caer Baddan who came in company with his Red Cloaks, the last of the legions on British soil; and the ones we called the Irish brothers were there, Conmagil of Caer Gloui and Condidan of Caer Ceri. And a woman called

Cerridwen was with the company, the Dragon Maiden of the Island of the Mighty.

My own life has been eventful enough, although that is a tale for another time. I will only say that the people of the Water Land put their faith in the old gods and it was in that faith that I was nurtured, believing in the thousand gods of that place of marsh and fen, of rising and falling tides. Even today, I keep that faith. Because of it, and because I have studied the healing arts, there are those who say I can tell the future. But that is not true. If I call myself anything it is a writer of history and, as such, if I am permitted to be wise at all it is only about what has already come and gone.

It was my old chieftain's daughter, Eleri Gwir, who gave me the gift of writing. It was she who said I should write down what I know of the history of my people, who are the people of the Island of Britain – *Prydain*, we call it in the old language. Eleri said I should write what I have seen and heard; and what she has seen and heard; and what every sensible and reliable witness I have ever spoken to about these matters has seen and heard. She said she would have done it herself, except that at the end her fingers didn't work as they used to on account of the cold rain, which is a curse that has befallen my people since we deserted the gods of the natural world. But I don't know. Perhaps Eleri didn't want to look too long and hard into the face of the past, finding there all that was lost to her.

You may yet wonder at the truth of what these pages have to say. I can only state that in writing them I have relied on the witness of those who have sworn, before the old gods and the one new God, that their telling is accurate and true. But, yes, some things are of my own imagining, elaborations of the mind, you might call them; yet true enough for all that to the people and their time, growing from their rich soil. I would bring the past to life. I would give it legs and eyes and ears enough to make the people and their time live again.

I should in fairness say that the servants of the new God have been good to me at this time of my life. I write this in the holy house in Llanilltud Fawr, a place of quiet prayer and scholarship where even now the old devotion to the sacred wells and groves and to the world of our fellow creatures lives on after a fashion.

For now, I too live on.

As for this document, if it should survive the trials of this world, it will reach out from my time and place to yours, touching your minds and your hearts.

Like melting snow, like a fox running into long grass, I will say farewell to you now as I melt into the turbulent waters and run into the high reeds of my telling.

# Chapter One

It was a day like any other.

There was rain and there was sun, clouds marched in high dudgeon across the sky, making shadows on the green land below. People went about their business. There was weaving to do, there were children to care for, there was broth to stir. The men tended the sheep and the red cows of the Summer Land; they stood about and watched the blacksmith at his work, bending the hot iron to his will; they thought about women and they talked about the uncertain times they lived in, its trials and perils. "It can't be long," they said; "The foreigners will be upon us."

They came from the east, the home of ill winds; eight lives-of-men ago the storytellers said, a flood rising, retreating, rising again and again. The Saxons were on the march, their name a sword, the vicious *seax*.

"Caw, caw," said the crows in the beech wood, a long cry that echoed across the countryside.

The land was old. "It was old when Belin was a child," the women said. For these people the Summer Land had its own voice, rich and red, and a language made from the texture of the seasons, its secret words, its deep syntax heard in the branches of the big oak that ravaged the air on days of wind and storm. *Henaint* they called the speaking tree, a word that means Old Age in the British language.

"What does it say?" the people asked, hearing the commotion of branches high above, to which old Mared of the Silver Wheel always had an answer.

"Iron and blood," she told the man who asked, imperious in her manner. "What else is there to say?"

"They're coming!" a boy shouted, running headlong up the steep rise that brought him to the village gate.

"I see their trail!" a man shouted from the palisade.

From high in the summer sky a hawk, watchful, dangling, considered the possibilities as it followed the band of horsemen, the dust rising, the serpent line of life and death.

"They're coming!" the boy shouted again, not to be outdone by hawk or lookout. "They're coming, Eleri!"

Small for his age, his hair a mess of curls, he came in a rush right up to the young woman he had addressed. "Eleri Gwir," he said, "they're here."

"Thank you, Gereint," the young woman said, speaking more calmly than she felt.

Where he was small, she was long limbed. There at the threshold to Tre Wyn, in the shade of the rowan tree, she stood tall and fair, her long hair the colour of fall leaves, russet and golden, a faint line of thought working its way down her high forehead.

"My father should be here," she thought. Then, bringing the worry line down between her eyebrows, she wondered where he could be. "He should be home by now." A week ago he had gone to Caer Baddan, to attend the high chieftain's council of war. Where had he got to?

Beside her was a young man, as dark as she was fair; as dark as Brân, people said of him – the gods, the old gods that is, never far from mind or speech.

"Gwion," Eleri said, turning to the young man, her hazel eyes looking for support.

"You'll do fine," he assured her, his words bringing his face to life, his dark eyes shining and intense.

He was used to her taking the lead, speaking up when she had something to say, her voice confident and clear. They didn't call her Eleri Gwir for nothing – Eleri the Plain Speaker, the one who would tell you what she thought of you to your face. That was how her friends and neighbours saw her: clever; inquisitive; as curious as next door's cat. "She's been here before," they said of her, even when she was a young girl, always asking "why", stopping to think before answering a question, watchful, missing nothing.

The sight of her on edge like this was something new to Gwion. He thought he liked it, this vulnerability in her make-up. He wasn't sure, he'd have to think about it. At any rate, he smiled to see his chieftain's daughter in a bit of a muddle for once, a place he knew well enough.

"She'll be fine," Gwion thought. "Of course she will."

All his life he'd been at Eleri's side, watching her grow from girl to woman, his heart full with love for her. All his life he'd wanted something more from her, something different to the rough-and-tumble friendship they'd always shared, the chieftain's daughter and the son of the head cowman of the Summer Land.

"The palisade," he said. "We can see them better from there."

"Yes."

For her part, Eleri could see how it was for her friend Gwion. She felt the aching need, the hunger inside his body. She saw the doubts and uncertainties that plagued him, the feeling that he wasn't good enough, that despite everything, he wasn't the one for her. Eleri felt that need in Gwion. Didn't her own body speak in the same tongue, whispering to her at times, shouting, yelling at others, telling her to get on with it? Didn't she have doubts and uncertainties of her own? And then there was her father. She could feel his restraining hand on her shoulder, kind and firm.

It was complicated.

She was complicated.

When Eleri was fifteen summers, there had been the festival at the Great Circle. They had gone through the Great Wood and across the windy plains to be blessed by the dawn sun. The bard Cynan had been there, in good voice, his words a river of spells and incantations. That night the horned god had made her his queen. He had taken her in his arms, pouring the secret names of the old gods in her ear; she had danced for him and chanted the words of faith and power.

Yet she knew some frowned on this, saying she was born in the hawthorn month, a sign of bad luck that would cast a shadow over the year to come. "The girl should not have been chosen," they said.

Others said different, Mared of the Silver Wheel among them. This Mared, blustering and cantankerous, a seer to her clan all her long life, said that Eleri was a child of the foxglove and that she foreshadowed healing for the Summer Land after years of suffering. Old now, becoming forgetful and hard of hearing, there were times when Mared could still find a way through a thicket of ideas, coming out on the other side and heading in the right or most convenient direction. Most saw the choice of Eleri as a mixed blessing, true to the uncertain times they lived in. Her friends and neighbours had wished her well, at the same time touching wood for luck. There was something about her, something true yet less than straightforward, a complicated inheritance that seemed at once both right and wrong in the circumstances.

If she chose Gwion would it be a blessing or a curse – for him, for her, for the people of the Summer Land?

Climbing to the palisade, Eleri looked out across the familiar face of the rising, falling land. Every place was named; there was a story to everything, one that tied present to past in a long string of memory, stories that gave her goosebumps when she thought of them, stories of love and sacrifice as old as the land itself.

"Caw, caw," said the crows, marking the passage of the horsemen through the Great Wood, a trail of dust their place mark.

"It's all mixed up," Eleri told herself. "Everything in a jumble – me, this place, the whole world." Fear ran down the spine of the country, fear for the old and weak, fear for the future of her people, for the Island, for everything that was dear to them. "How long before the Island that was once whole is broken?" people asked. "Who will put the pieces back together again?"

Gwion was with her, close, his fingers finding hers, telling her it would be all right.

For each and every one of her seventeen summers the war had been drawing closer, a black cloud spreading across the land. Sometimes her people won, but only sometimes, and those times seemed to be getting fewer, bringing the darkness into their hearts, making it grow. Even the great yellow plague that had visited Eleri's people had done nothing to diminish the black spreading cloud. Eleri's father said that the momentum of war was with their enemies. He said it when they were alone, watching shadows in the firelight. He had never sounded so sad or so contemplative.

"I hear them," a watchman shouted. "They're close."

"Round the hill, coming to the willow trees at the river."

Eleri's people had won a great victory at Mount Badon, with the one they called Arthur, where the Saxons were cut down like corn. For two generations that victory had brought a measure of peace. The Saxons had licked their wounds in their ramshackle halls, their numbers growing year upon year. More and more foreign men, their language like a spear in the throat, had come from across the eastern sea, consolidating at first, now expanding, stretching out like a hunting dog ready for the chase, working on its big jaws, showing its teeth. "May Belin shine on us," the old people said, hoping to ward off evil.

Without thinking, Eleri held on to Gwion's arm, children again for the moment, scared of the dark shadows that slithered out from under the tongues of the storytellers to haunt the living night.

All the tales now were of this Ceawlin, the murderous king of the West Saxons – the Gewisse – and his son Cuthwine. There was nothing between her people and these foreigners, no common ground; there never could be, Eleri told herself. Their gods were not her gods and not even the one God, the Christ God that people spoke so much about.

"They're here," people called.

"Over there," they pointed.

In a line of life and death, the horsemen snaked out of the Great Wood, urging their mounts on up the rising ground to the gates of Tre Wyn.

# Chapter Two

For Eleri, it was her first sight of of the Red Cloaks of Caer Baddan. Her heart lifted to see them. All around there was pride and hope. She could see it in people's faces, their eyes lighting up. Eleri saw her friend Rhian waving and calling out.

Riding from the east under the standard of the cross, Eleri counted thirty-one of them, two abreast, in the lead a white stallion, a war horse, bold and headstrong, ebullience in its every step. The distinctive cloaks the riders wore were carried on the wind, proud banners in their own right. Unlike the men of the Summer Land, these warriors wore helmets that caught the sun, as did the mail they wore, glinting like jewels. In fact, there were thirty-three riders in total, with what looked like two women at the very back of the column. Eleri assumed they were hangers-on of some sort. Only when the horsemen drew nearer did she notice that the rider carrying the standard of the cross was dressed in priestly brown.

In her father's absence it was Eleri's place to welcome them across the threshold where the rowan tree stood, heavy with berries at this time of year. There was no reason to be nervous, for something to be niggling at her in the pit of her stomach. "They're with us," she told herself as she made her way to the gate. As Mared of the

Silver Wheel would say when she could think of nothing better: "There doesn't always have to be a reason."

On they came, pounding towards her.

For years Eleri had heard about the Red Cloaks of Caer Baddan; the last of the legions on British soil, people called them. Everyone in the Summer Land, Eleri included, was dying to get a glimpse of this rare breed of warriors, to see if they matched up to the stories that were told about them, to see if they were indeed the inheritors of the glory of Rome and of Arthur all in one.

They came in a great wheel of horse flesh, grey and black and red-brown – the coppery chestnut colour of Eleri's hair, or near enough. At their head was the white stallion, its power and its pride captured in its massive flanks.

Instinctively, Eleri looked for Gwion at her side, only to find that he had held back. Standing amongst the people of the village, he nodded to her, his black eyes speaking encouragement.

The war horse would not be ignored, snorting its arrival for all to hear. Its rider was of the same mind.

Unaccountably, shockingly, it took only an instant.

When the rider on the white stallion dismounted he landed with a thump directly in front of Eleri Gwir. Even before she had the chance to welcome him, the warrior had removed his helmet from his sandy hair and, bowing slightly, he had swallowed her whole with his dangerously playful pale blue eyes.

It was that need, that hunger again.

Eleri in her turn acknowledged the young warrior, remembering and forgetting everything she had been told about men by the women in the weaving room, every detail of every warning. She had always marked herself out as different from her companions – like her friend Rhian who seemed to be a slave to her unpredictable feelings, defining her very existence around whether this or that man had smiled or winked at her over the mead cups. Now here she was, the rational, sensible Eleri Gwir drowning in a sudden flood of feelings, all hot inside, another slave to nature's urges. Everything fled from her heart, or so it felt in that instant, to make space for the captain of the Red Cloaks.

"His name is *Gwalchwen,"* – White Hawk – the warrior said, referring to the stallion, his hand caressing the horse's mane, the warrior bending towards Eleri, as if telling a secret, every bit as familiar as the horned god.

Speechless for a moment, a thing unknown to Eleri Gwir, she had to take a deep breath before she said: "On behalf of my father Arawn son of Edern, I welcome the men of the Red Cloaks to Tre Wyn." Although whether the words were said in that order or in some other, she couldn't say.

Then, bringing her to her senses, she heard someone call out: "There's a man wounded. Get help."

"My healing bag," she called to the curly-haired boy. "Fetch it, will you?" The order was no sooner given than the boy was haring away in the direction of the chieftain's hut. Seeing him dash off, the Red Cloak captain laughed and Eleri laughed with him, in danger of losing herself again.

It was just as well that Cerys, the healer, was there organising matters, showing where the wounded horseman was to be taken.

"Come on, Eleri Gwir!" she called, not one for formalities. "There's work to do."

"I have to go," Eleri told the Red Cloak, pointing needlessly in the direction Cerys had gone. Again, she looked for Gwion, but he too was gone.

"It's all right," the Red Cloak captain said, a wicked, hungry smile in his eyes. "Go with the healer. You have a wounded man to attend to."

Walking away, Eleri imagined those hungry eyes fixed on her, which made her horribly self-conscious. She felt her insides burning up. She was glad to see the boy Gereint running to her, the healing bag in his arms. She thanked him for the second time that morning.

Across the yard she saw Gwion with his father, heading for the slaughterhouse. There was work to do. There was a red cow of the Summer Land to be butchered if their guests were to be feasted.

*

"What have you been up to?" Cerys asked the wounded man once they had him settled.

"A skirmish," the man said. He had a deep wound to his thigh where a spear had found his flesh – a Saxon spear, it turned out. A piece of leather had been tied around his leg to staunch the bleeding. It was covered now in thick, sticky blood.

Luckily, none of the big coils of blood that run down the leg had been severed and his bones were unharmed. He would live, for now at least, until the next encounter with the Gewisse.

"Your name?" Eleri asked, her busy hands finding a clean piece of leather for the man to bite on.

"He's Peris, the son of Cadfan," an authoritative voice from the door of the hut said. "And my name is Macsen, the son of Emrys."

Eleri had no need to look back; she knew as well as she knew the contours of the landscape of the Summer Land that it was the captain of the Red Cloaks. He'd followed her. He said he'd come to check that Peris was in good hands, which seemed reasonable enough. Eleri did her best to ignore him as he stood there, sweat on his brow, his helmet under his left arm, his right hand on the pommel of his long sword, the scabbard decorated with an intricate pattern of silver crosses.

"We ran into a Gewisse war band," Macsen said, watching as Cerys and Eleri tended to the wound, washing it out, getting ready to sew it up. "That doesn't look too bad," he observed. He came over to the wounded man, placing a reassuring hand on his shoulder, a gesture that showed another side to his character; not softer exactly - warmer, giving. He kept his hold as Peris' body contorted in a spasm of pain.

"Keep that needle steady," Cerys said to Eleri, giving her a knowing look.

"I am!" Eleri retorted, doing her best to keep her body from melting in a sticky puddle on the floor of the hut.

"And stop wriggling," Cerys ordered the wounded man. "Bite on that leather."

Perhaps to distract Peris from his pain, Macsen explained to them in his soldierly fashion how the man had come about his wound. "We'd been ordered to ride to Maes-y-Gaer," he said. "A fat lot of good that was. We were sent to see if the lord of that ancient hillfort would join our alliance against the Gewisse. He wouldn't," Macsen snapped. "He's gone rogue on us, attacking our own people."

If there had been something to kick he would have kicked it, Eleri thought.

"And…?" Cerys said, liking digressions about as much as she liked formalities.

"Coming from there, we came across the Gewisse," Macsen continued. "They were camped at the edge of the birch forest under Dolmen Fawr. It wasn't long after dawn, and we had the advantage of surprise. There was no time for them to bring their shields into a wall. They lost twelve warriors, maybe more, before scattering back into the woods."

'Did we lose any men?" Eleri asked, her questioning nature trumping her confusion.

"We lost two men and two horses with them," Macsen answered, seeming to regret the losses in equal measure. "They were good horses," he said with feeling, "but horses we can replace. The men we can't replace. They were good men. Men worthy of the legions."

When the Romans had left the Island many families had remained, some out of choice, some because of family ties that had grown up over generations. Macsen's people had served as officials in the towns and as soldiers in the military zone; they were high ranking enough to own a villa on the outskirts of Caer Baddan, which was where Macsen and his sisters had spent their childhood. In the time of the legions they had been a cavalry family, serving all over the Island, from the wall in the North at the very edge of the civilised world to the port towns on the South coast, for hundreds of years the haunts of Saxon pirates.

His great-great grandfather was Marcus, a horseman without equal, companion to Ambrosius Aurelianus, the one they liked to call Arthur, the one they called the Bear of the Island. If in the intervening years Macsen's family had forgotten their Latin, they had not forgotten their horsemanship – and they had not forgotten Ambrosius. The cavalry had been the key to the great victory of the Britons at Mount Badon. "Always remember that, Macsen," his father had told him. "If the invaders can't be defeated on their terms, they must be on ours."

Macsen had grown up hating the Gewisse and loving the idea of the legions and their cavalry. Horses were like family and friends to him. There was no freedom or joy in the world to compare to that he experienced on horseback. Riding with the Red Cloaks, fighting the Gewisse, he was exactly where he wanted to be. Others might doubt their place and purpose in the world; not Macsen.

Horses weren't the only things Macsen liked. He took the opportunity to take a long second look at the tall, lean young woman with the fire-god hair. He liked what he saw. The way her hazel eyes found reasons to glance in his direction was not something that went unnoticed. The slender line of Eleri's body, the curve of her breasts and the flat of her stomach, were pleasing to dwell upon. He saw the cleverness in her shapely hands and more besides. His sex was stirred.

Macsen would have enjoyed the sight of Eleri longer except that one of the women who had been at the rear of the Red Cloak column appeared at the door of the hut.

Looking up from her work, it was Eleri's turn to observe. She saw that the woman was around her father's age, strongly built, her hair coal black and decorated with what looked like three eagle feathers.

"I wanted to check on Peris," the woman said, very matter-of-fact. "We patched him up as best we could."

"He'll be fine," Cerys reassured her. "No permanent damage."

The woman carried a short sword at her side, a lethal *seax*, the very weapon that gave the Saxons their name. Eleri wondered who and what she might be. Noticing Eleri's interest, the woman said that she was Siriol – a name that means cheerful in the British language.

"You don't look it!" Eleri blurted out.

"And you must be Eleri Gwir," the woman said, amused. "The Truth Speaker."

"That's some name to live up to," Macsen observed, his blue eyes smiling with mischief and intelligence. "I suppose it means you have a big mouth."

Eleri wanted to say something in response – a clever retort, even to ask how she was known to this woman – but she was lost for words, and before she had the chance to recover her equilibrium Macsen and the woman had left, Siriol telling him: "You're needed."

"He certainly isn't needed here," Cerys said to no one in particular. She wasn't one for interruptions from any quarter, dashing young warriors included. It was part of what Eleri had always liked about her, this self-contained nature that didn't need or care to explain itself or to perform before others. Some people found her difficult, because she didn't join in – she didn't gossip with the women in the weaving room, she kept to herself. Eleri had no problem with that. Indeed, she found in Cerys the kind of integrity that she admired, a strength of purpose that wouldn't be swayed by any distraction, not even one caused by a man in a Red Cloak that fell down his back, as far as his shapely hips.

"There," Cerys said, admiring their handiwork, the stiches a crooked purple smile on the man's thigh.

"That's neat work," Eleri said.

"And that's a neat young man," Cerys commented in return, that knowing look again in her eyes.

They worked in silence, clearing up, washing the fine bone needle they had used, checking from time to time on the wounded man. They worked as a team; one teacher, the other pupil in the healing arts.

Inquisitive by nature, for years Eleri had followed on Cerys' heels, forever asking "What does this do?" and "How does that work?"

'Come on then," Cerys would say, glad to see the clever girl taking an interest. "Let me show you what those are for," she'd continue, a handful of leaves in her sun-browned hand.

She was the best kind of teacher, sharing and encouraging. They had grown to like one another. Although Cerys had brought enough children into the world to fill a *cantref*, as she explained it, Eleri was the nearest thing she had to a daughter of her own. Not wanting to interfere and wanting to at the same time, Cerys worried over Eleri's future. It was apt to make her a little spiky, the thought of that handsome young man in a red cloak buzzing around in her head.

"Get that jar, will you?" she snapped, plain and to the point.

Daughter to Mared of the Silver Wheel, Cerys was a small woman, far from young, nothing like her mother in character; unselfish, more thoughtful of others, without pretension to inspiration or pretensions generally, except that Cerys shared her mother's temper on occasions, taking people by surprise when she let that black cat out of its bag. As healer and midwife to the people of Tre Wyn and beyond, Cerys was important in her own right, respected for her knowledge of the properties of the natural world, as well as for her common sense.

"A *very* neat young man," she said now, the buzzing in her head turned down a notch or two.

"If you say so."

They laughed, not out loud, somewhere deep under their skins and in their bones.

# Chapter Three

Eleri's father didn't arrive home that morning or that afternoon either. Instead it was Mascen who called the people of Tre Wyn together, taking charge as if that was the natural order of things. Mascen had twenty-five summers on his back. His voice was firm, a blade tempered in the fires of conflict. Men listened to that voice and followed its lead; they knew that his courage and resolve had been tried and tested. In his youth they found a beacon of energy and hope.

"Where's the priest?" he asked, not pretending to hide his exasperation. One minute the man was there, the next he'd disappeared.

"Praying, I imagine," the Red Cloak at his side said drily.

"Or shitting, or sniffing around, sticking his nose where it doesn't belong," ventured another.

At Caer Baddan the high chief, Ffernfael, had worn the priest like a hawk on his arm. Clearly, he wasn't just any priest. "He's Father Cenydd," the high chief had told Macsen. "The son of Gildas no less. Saint Gildas, some call him." This Gildas was the lettered priest whose Latin was said to be as good as the emperor's and who had used that language to tell the story of the coming of the Saxons as mercenaries when the legions departed, a cancer in the body of the Island, sprouting, spreading. Gildas had not spared his own people, saying their lives had become too easy under Rome, and a lot more else besides.

"You'll be pleased to hear he's going with you," Ffernfael had told Macsen, a touch of humour in his powerful face.

"Christ's blood," Macsen had said, swearing in the new way.

Now, at Tre Wyn, far from Caer Baddan's fading glory and miles from Ffernfael's hall with its sculptures and figures, a mixture of impatience and humorous speculation was taking hold.

"Where is the man?" Macsen asked again, his patience wearing thin.

Eleri was there, missing nothing, letting the young captain run the show for now, amused by the disappearance of his star performer. Behind her stood Gwion, every bit as watchful, amused in his own way to see the belligerent look on the face of the Red Cloak captain.

"Well, what are you waiting for?" Mared of the Silver Wheel shouted, her belligerence an equal to anyone's. "I've been leaning here on my stick all afternoon."

Mared had come by her exotic title as a young girl. Waking one morning, she had gone to the weaving room and told the women there of her dream. In it the goddess she called Rhiannon, the one who went by many names, came to her bedside carrying a silver wheel, the spiral of life and death. The goddess had placed it in Mared's hands. So light was it that it carried her up into the night sky, flying towards the full moon; but then, as Mared reached out her hand to touch the moon's face, the wheel grew suddenly heavy, sending her hurtling down to earth. In her bed again, the goddess Rhiannon had taken the silver wheel from Mared's grasp, carrying it into the darkness, taking with her the power of life and death; only leaving behind the whirring voice of the wheel in Mared's head – or so the girl said. At first many were doubtful. But in time, as the girl's power of inspired thought was revealed, her story was accepted and she became a seer to her people. She'd carried it off; the trick of cunning thought.

That had been many years ago. In old age, her character had become more exposed, her manipulations more transparent. It wasn't just that Mared was getting older, she was ageing, her mind growing inwards, losing the width and perspective it had once had. Always argumentative, she had become aggressively quarrelsome for its own sake.

"Find her a bench, will you?" Eleri Gwir ordered a young man.

"And speak up," Mared said. "Everyone mumbles into their beards."

"Old women included," someone said under their breath.

"What did he say?" Mared asked Cerys.

"Never mind," Cerys answered, doing her best to deflect her mother's belligerence.

His patience used up, Macsen shouted: "Priest!"

As if on cue, Father Cenydd appeared, whether in answer to a call of nature or a summons from his God no one cared to ask and he did not say.

"Here he comes," Mared of the Silver Wheel said, laughing her belligerent laugh.

Dressed in brown, the priest wore a plain cross at his neck made of ash wood, and his freckled forehead was shaven – that morning, it seemed from the bloody nicks and cuts. To Eleri, his long thin face had that fanatical look about it that had come to infect the

Christians since the visitation of the great yellow plague, their peculiar faith feeding on suffering.

"Do we really need this man in skirts to give us heart?" she wondered.

"Father Cenydd will speak," Macsen declared. "What he says comes with the authority of the high chieftain. And that of your own chieftain, Arawn son of Edern," he added.

The words made Eleri wince. Turning to face her, Mared of the Silver Wheel treated her to one of her more mischievous grimaces.

Father Cenydd came forward. He let the crowd settle, his silence carrying an authority of its own, bringing everyone to attention. His right hand clutched at the cross about his neck. They expected him to talk about sin, the Christ God, or even the wrath of an angry God. Instead, he spoke as a prince of this world, not as a champion of the next. He pointed out that the people of the Island, instead of meeting their enemies as one, had perpetuated petty rivalries and age-old clan divisions. "That must end," he said. "If we are not to be slaves in our own land, that must end now."

The priest gave his words time and space in which to do their work. With his hand holding tight to the cross at his neck, he looked over the crowd, seeming to see into their souls. Some took a step back, fearing he would cast a spell on them, his magic something to be reckoned with. Others waited on his next move. Although he had not mentioned his God as yet, Eleri knew it was but a matter of time; first this world, then the next; as sure as swallows fly south in winter, from unity in arms he would progress to unity in religion.

But the priest wasn't done with this world yet. Aiming to shock and startle, speaking loud and plain enough for everyone to hear, Father Cenydd sent a wave of dread through the people of Tre Wyn. Striking a sinister note, he had a rhetorical question to ask. "Do I need to persuade anyone here about the gravity of the situation we face? I think not. On our way here from Maes-y-Gaer we encountered a band of heathens, not twenty miles from this village, on your doorstep no less." The tale of the skirmish was recounted in considerably more gory detail than Macsen had managed.

"Their leader is a vicious brute," the priest declaimed. "A huge warrior, his arms covered in the rings he has earned from his murders. His face is a page of markings, the evil markings of the heathen gods. There he is!" Father Cenydd shouted, pointing for effect to the east. "At Dolmen Fawr, a few miles down the Fosse Road, an arm's length away from your children and your wives."

The fact that the enemy was right there, on their doorstep, was shocking to everyone. Instinctively, they drew closer together, needing to be comforted; fathers placed protective hands across their children's chests; mothers cursed under their breath.

"The priest speaks nothing but the truth," Macsen confirmed, in case anyone doubted Father Cenydd.

Macsen paused, letting the gravity of his words sink in.

"As commander of the auxiliary forces of the high chief," he pressed on, "I'm ordered to patrol the ragged border lands during these months of the hazel and the blackberry when Gewisse war bands are likely to test our resolve. More than that, I am to bring together all the resources, warriors and material from the outlying lands. When we march against the Gewisse we must do so as a single, coherent force, taking our lead from the legions."

"So you expect the Summer Land to save your bacon?" Mared of the Silver Wheel called out, making trouble for the fun of it, always insisting on having her say.

"The Summer Land will do its fair share – no more, no less," Macsen replied.

Father Cenydd took up the argument again, saying: "No one here can be in any doubt that the time has come to stand and fight and to do so in company, under one banner."

"The high chief's banner!" Mared said in her sharpest tongue.

The priest allowed himself a discreet smile, more in the eyes than in the mouth, gratified that the elder woman had walked into the trap he had set for her. "Under Ffernfael's banner, that's right," he said.

Eleri Gwir knew what was coming. She turned towards Mared of the Silver Wheel to see her reaction.

"Under the banner of the cross," Father Cenydd continued. "I bring you the word of the one true God. I bring you the promise of salvation and of life ever after; I bring you the gift and blessing of baptism into the community of our blessed Lord, Jesus Christ."

Tough old Mared, the survivor of a thousand arguments, didn't so much as bat an eyelid. Eleri was impressed.

It was the way now with the priests of the Christ God. In Roman times it had been different; everything had been different. Then the new God was the official god, worshipped in the towns, even in some forts in the military zone. It was the god you had to believe in, or say that you believed in, if you wanted to get on. But the Christ God wasn't compulsory. He wasn't evangelised from one end of the Island to the other; and never to the exclusion of the old gods. In the towns the nailed one was worshipped. Outside, the balance was reversed. In the Summer Land the deities of rivers, trees and stones lived on, as did Belin of the sun, Sulis of water and wisdom, and Rhiannon of the red earth and war, life and death. But even there, in the outlying regions, the ways of the new God were seeping in. To be on the safe side, many prayed to all gods, old and new.

"I know how it is and how it has been," Father Cenydd addressed the assembly, a softer texture to his voice. "I am my father's son, after all." The softness leeched away. "The heathens are upon us and yet we too tolerate heathen worship in our midst. We divide among ourselves, the people of the Island, across boundaries of petty power and false gods. Even in this chiefdom there are a hundred gods, perhaps more, a god for every tree in the forest."

"Don't you know, priest?" Mared said. "Gods grow on trees."

"I know all too well, Mared," he answered, pointedly omitting any reference to her title, refusing to acknowledge her status as seer to her clan.

"I don't come here to uproot and divide," he pressed on, softness evident again in his voice if not in the lines of his thin face. "But I do come with the high chief's authority, to voice Ffernfael's decision. I come to tell you that we fight under one banner, the banner of the baptised, and I come too to tell you that everyone is to be brought into the community of our Lord, that we will go to war as a single community in Christ our Saviour."

At the council of war in Ffernfael's hall in Caer Baddan there had been general approval. Conmagil of Caer Gloui and Condidan of Caer Ceri – the Irish brothers as people called them – were believers. For them, bringing everyone under the banner of the one faith was a matter of tidying up, like mending a frayed hem. Only one note of dissent had been struck. Black-haired Siriol was the one who had spoken against it, the sun-inscribed brooch at her shoulder adding to her eloquence.

"People will resent being told what to believe, they will convert in name only; and this at a time when we all need faith, a true faith in whatever gods are ours."

"There is but one God," Father Cenydd had declared. "If He is with us, if He knows of the love we bear Him, our way will be clear. The sinful ways of the past must be set aside; we go to meet our enemies with the light of Christ, the fire of his gospel, at our head."

"Father Cenydd speaks for me in this," the high chief Ffernfael had said. A man of compromise when compromise was called for, Ffernfael would not budge on this for anyone. Not particularly religious himself, he saw the advantage in bringing the people under the faith of Christ, a faith that was especially strong and meaningful to his fellow chieftains, Conmagil and Condidan.

At Tre Wyn dissent struck a louder note. There were murmurings of disapproval, from the older women mainly. "The Christ God speaks of love, not war," their spokesperson Mared said. "Isn't that right, priest? What good is such a god to us at this time? We need battle gods – not men in skirts preaching sin and love. Besides," she added, "I've seen these baptisms; I'll catch my death of cold."

"You will be reborn; you will have the promise of life eternal in God's company," Father Cenydd responded passionately. "Christ's love is many things – a mother's love and a father's love, forgiving and militant, yielding and all-powerful. It is the way of truth, the truth of the one God."

"And you say my father agreed to this?" Eleri Gwir spoke up at last.

It was his chieftain's daughter that Gwion saw there, tall and confident, speaking on behalf of her people. He saw the Red Cloak leader, the one called Macsen, take a good long look at her. He saw Father Cenydd do the same.

"Yes," the priest answered coldly. "It was agreed by the council of war."

Eleri had a mind to argue the point, except that Mared of the Silver Wheel intervened. "Then I suppose we'd better get on with it," she said, no less pugnacious than usual, yet knowing this was neither the day nor the ground for this particular battle.

It was the day of Eleri's baptism; and Gwion's.

Initiation into the cult of the horned god had been very different; drier for one thing.

# Chapter Four

No time like the present – with the chariot of the sun-god riding into the west on that summer afternoon, the priest led the people of Tre Wyn down to the pool in the bend in the river, in the shade of the willow trees, a place of ancient sacrifices and blessings. Consistent with her status, Eleri Gwir was at the head of the procession, the first to be baptised and the first to find her solitary way back to the village cursing under her breath, shivering and dripping wet.

Sitting on a stone, on a track leading up to the village, was the black-haired woman with her eagle feathers and silver sun brooch, and her cheerful name that didn't appear to suit her warlike character. At least now she had an unmistakeable smirk on her strong-boned face. With her was the second woman who had accompanied the Red Cloaks to Tre Wyn. Like Siriol she was dark-haired, but the likeness stopped there. More slender, more beautiful, her eyes were velvet green, her cheekbones high and fine; a woman for the bards to write about, for princes to fight over, delicate yet strong.

"Branwen," she introduced herself, evidently not one for wasting words.

And with the two women was the fast-running boy, Gereint, his hands and face purple from eating billberries. Eleri recalled that he was an orphan, left to be brought up and cared for by the whole community.

His mother had died young, in childbirth; his father six summers ago in the wall of shields at Beran Byrig. The boy would only have been three of four years of age then.

"The boy has no need of this silliness," Siriol said dismissively, as if making a statement of axiomatic certainty.

"No more and no less than the rest of us," Eleri retorted, not sure why the boy should be standing there bone dry when she was soaked to the skin.

"Come on," the woman called Branwen said to the boy, taking hold of his hand and leading him out of range of any further questioning.

"Why him?" Eleri asked.

Instead of answering, Siriol said to Eleri: "Here, let me help you dry your hair."

Along with the short sword at her belt she carried a woollen cloth in her big, bony hands. Indicating Eleri's coppery tresses, she said: "Your hair still looks like it belongs to the sun-god."

"Perhaps it does."

"And my hair belongs to Brấn, I don't care who knows it," Siriol said, as belligerent in her way as Mared of the Silver Wheel. "I think we'll get along, Eleri Gwir."

"How did you know I'm called that?"

"I met your father at the war council in Caer Baddan. He talks a lot about you."

"Have you been with him?" Eleri asked, very direct, leaving no room for misunderstanding.

Living up to her own name for a moment, Siriol laughed. "Have I been with him? No, I haven't."

"I've heard the women say that he's worth having."

"So he may be, for a man," Siriol answered. "But my heart belongs to Branwen – the fair raven. Unlike mine, her parents knew what they were about when they named her – don't you think?"

"She doesn't have much to say for herself."

"She says enough and does more," was the curt reply. "Sit still and shut up for a minute while I dry this hair of yours."

It was like asking the sun not to rise. Eleri couldn't help herself. "And you ride with Macsen and the Red Cloaks?"

"We do."

In her young life Eleri had known plenty of women of a warlike nature, not least among them Mared of the Silver Wheel. This was the first time she had met a woman who actually rode with the men to war, shield and spear, bow and knife. The old stories were full of such women, warrior queens in chariots and on horseback, a host of deadly spear maidens, breasts bared, death dancing in their eyes. This woman looked the part. She was tall, lean and strong looking. You could almost reach out and touch the wildness in her nature. *Siriol Wyllt* she'd heard a Red Cloak call her – Siriol the Wild. Eleri was excited by her presence. It was like standing in a storm, the thunder and unpredictable lightning. She felt the woman's touch on her hair and head, vigorous and firm, yet curiously gentle too, the woollen cloth like an instrument of war and peace in her hands.

"What do you make of this Father Cenydd?" Eleri asked.

"I can tell you he fights like a bear when he's cornered," was the answer, one that took Eleri by surprise.

"In arguments, you mean?'

"With words and with spears," was the response. "He fell on the Saxons we encountered more like a warrior than a priest. His spear was as bloody as any other."

"They say he comes from over the water, from Llydaw," Eleri said.

"Don't I know it," Siriol declared, a remark that caused Eleri to shake herself free to look at this strange woman.

"You're not the only one with a big mouth," Siriol told her. "I'm afraid we nearly came to blows over it in Caer Baddan."

"Over what? Your big mouth or the fact that the priest comes from the other Britain?"

"Both."

"You're nothing but trouble. Should I even be speaking to you?" Eleri teased.

"Probably not," Siriol said, resuming her hair-drying duties. "I was angry. I couldn't stand to see the old gods thrown over like that. I wanted to get at Ffernfael, so I attacked his pet priest. I told Cenydd that his famous father had taken refuge in the other Britain, fleeing from the war he would have others fight on his behalf. I wasn't very complimentary."

Eleri laughed. She could imagine the effect Siriol's remarks would have had on Father Cenydd, the accusation of cowardice banging about in his heart, working his temper up, his thin lips drawn in a line of anger.

"It gets worse," Siriol said.

"You really are a troublemaker."

"Actually, I'm not proud of myself. It nearly wrecked the whole alliance, everything Ffernfael had worked for," Siriol said. "When the priest told me to shut up about the other Britain, saying it was a subject for another day, the Irish brothers leapt into the argument. Condidan is half mad at the best of times. Then he was really mad, saying he and his brother had five seaworthy vessels ready to sail for Ireland or for Llydaw. Are you calling me a coward, priest, he was yelling like a bull. Conmagil his brother joined in, shouting, his hand on his sword."

"Belin's arse," Eleri said.

"Exactly. Conmagil was shouting that only a fool or a fanatic would deny the possibility of defeat and refuse to make any preparation. You're breaking your word already, Father Cenydd yelled back at them. It was mayhem. By this time the brothers were on their feet, swords half out of their scabbards, threatening to kill the priest for doubting their word, for questioning the courage of their conviction. Do you imagine our enemies contemplate defeat, the priest was yelling. I think not, he said. They trust their vicious gods to bring them victory; they trust in their own strength of arms. It went on like that."

As abruptly as she'd started, Siriol stopped rubbing Eleri's hair. "There," she said. "That's dry enough."

"What happened?" Eleri asked, not content with half a story.

"Ffernfael stepped in. He didn't want his plans scuppered by some stupid misunderstanding. In these dark times we speak from the heart, he said, or something like that; sometimes we agree, sometimes we don't. He managed to calm them down. He has a way about him; people listen."

Eleri liked the sound of that.

"Oh yes," Siriol concluded wryly. "And I apologised."

The truth was that the alliance with the Irish brothes hung by a thread, a spidery thread of words and vows that threatened to snap at any moment. With their gingery hair, painted faces and distinctive clothes, the brothers made a colourful and fearsome sight. They were the sons of an Irish woman captured from a band of Hibernian sea wolves, one of the many that were forever raiding the coasts of Cambria, the water and river lands in the kingdoms of Dyfed and Gwent. A captive at first, one of the unfree, the woman had come to the notice of a chieftain of Caer Gloui, in the lands on the coiling noose of the River Hafren. One thing followed another and here they were, Conmagil and Condidan, pledging allegiance to a grand alliance of the three strongholds, fighting over every bone that was yet to be gnawed clean.

Luckily for Siriol, at Caer Baddan swords had slid silently back into wool-lined scabbards. Quarrels were kept for another day. Eyes that burned with loathing were left to simmer.

Simmering at Tre Wyn were conflicts of another sort.

*

"Father!" Eleri shouted, fighting back tears of gladness.

There he was, standing at the door to their mud and wattle hut, a large man of forty summers, lines of laughter and lines of worry on his long, open face, the leather helmet and the leather jacket he wore were thick and strong, made of the best hide and stitched tight and true by Eleri's own hand. With him was his right-hand man, Kado. And there too was Gwion, still soaking wet, arguing with his chieftain.

"Father," Eleri said again, coming to stand directly in front of him, "what's this about?" She looked from her father to Gwion and then to Kado. "Where have you been?" she asked.

Gwion was the first to speak. "I'm telling your father I must go with him and the Red Cloaks."

"I thought you were asking, not telling," Arawn responded, his manner easy with long-worn authority.

"I am, yes. I'm asking. But I'm also saying that I'm the best bowman in the Summer Land."

"What about me, father?" Eleri interjected. "Were you going to tell me that you'll be going with these men to die in a ditch with a Saxon blade in your back?"

"I'll leave you to it," Kado said to Arawn, trying but not quite able to repress a smile.

"See you later," Arawn replied, the tiredness in his voice audible. "And thanks, Kado. You two," he said, looking at Eleri and Gwion.

"Us two, nothing," Eleri snapped back; "What's going on?"

By way of answer Arawn took his daughter in his arms and gave her a crushing hug. "Baptism suits you, girl; you really do look like a woman reborn."

"Rubbish."

There was a pause while all combatants considered their positions, their strengths and weaknesses.

Now Eleri was the first to speak, saying: "I don't know about Gwion, he must plead his own case, but I'm coming with you. I can use a bow, and you'll need a healer by the look of you." Without pausing, she concluded: "There are other women in the company. I'll ride with them; with Siriol and Branwen."

"Don't rush me, girl," Arawn answered. "And don't you rush me, Gwion." Turning from them, he said: "I have things to do. And so do you. We have guests."

"But where have you been?" Eleri shouted after him.

"Your mother's father," Arawn said, stopping in his tracks. "He's old. At Caer Baddan I was told that he's dying. I went with Kado to pay my respects."

"All that way?" Eleri said, her eyes looking westwards in the direction of the far mountains of Gwent.

"All that way," Arawn confirmed.

When feeling uncomfortable or embarrassed, not knowing quite what to say or do, Gwion had a habit of putting his hand round the back of his neck, dropping his head as he did so, as if searching for something he'd dropped.

"Your father will be looking for you, Gwion," Arawn said, understanding the young man's awkwardness. "Eleri, come with me."

*

Simmering between Macsen and Father Cenydd was a cauldron full of personal and other differences.

His day's work done, a very wet and shivering Father Cenydd came into the village roundhouse in search of warmth, drink and food in that order. Fired by faith, he felt the cold nonetheless, his skinny body standing for hours in the cold river water. Offering him a beaker of hot mead, a woman said playfully: "You'll catch your death of cold standing all that time in that river. Belin himself would need warming up after that."

He knew of course that for many the act of baptism meant nothing much, an extra safety blanket at best. Cenydd believed as fervently as any priest, but he wasn't a zealot exactly; there were soft edges to him, as his wife Ceinwen knew well enough. He had left her behind in the north, in the safety of the kingdom of Alt Clud on the

River Clyde, far from Saxon hordes, close to their son Devi.

"If I don't return," he'd told her at his leaving, speaking into her ear and down into her soul, "know that I love you as much as I love my God."

"You will return," she'd said. "God blesses your mission; He will go with you."

"Well, priest," Mascen said now, approaching him. "Are you done with soul saving for one day?"

"I rest, as Our Lord rested at Jacob's well," Cenydd said, sounding more pompous than he felt. "But the thirst to save men's souls never rests."

The woman gave Macsen a beaker of mead, although she looked as though she would have gladly given him a lot more. Not to be diverted from his course, Macsen said: "We've not spoken properly before, priest. I want you to know that, because Ffernfael decrees it, your work must be done – but I will have you know that it can't be permitted to hinder mine."

When Macsen spoke in this tone, you could hear clearly the confidence born of generations of Roman power and privilege.

His own power deriving from another source, Cenydd was no less self-assured. "I think you're in danger of seeing the world from an upside-down position," he replied, looking over the captain of arms, a man of around his own age but whose mission in life was seemingly very different from his own. "Or should I say that you just haven't understood that our work is ultimately one and the same. We're doing the same work only in different ways."

"That may be so, but from now on we go at my pace not yours; at a gallop, not a trot."

"A people armed with faith will be stronger for it, more resolute," Cenydd said. "You will reap the reward of my work, soldier."

"Maybe, priest. As long as our people believe in something, in something that will bring us victory, that's what matters. That's what Ffernfael cares about."

An awkward silence followed, out of which a note of reconciliation emerged.

"You fought well this morning, priest," Macsen acknowledged, genuinely impressed.

"God's work," was all Cenydd said in response.

For all that, he could not disguise from Macsen the warrior's pride in his sharp eyes.

# Chapter Five

The black cloud that advanced towards them could not be completely forgotten; it was too threatening, too real, too large a knot in all their hearts. But with a red cow slaughtered and butchered ready for the spit, with beakers of fine mead on hand and with Macsen's warriors present, bringing with them conversation and a feeling of safety, there was at least a semblance of secure normality. The young and some not so young women, those not in established relationships, didn't wait to be introduced to a man of their fancy, but went up and introduced themselves, flirting for all they were worth. Baptism or not, there was a carefree attitude in the air, devil-may-care. There hadn't been this many eligible men at Tre Wyn for who knew how long, men with dashing war helmets and daring red cloaks. Frugal in all things, the women knew better than to waste good men with danger and excitement stamped on their faces. "Now that would be a sin," the women joked. Who knows if they would ever see their like again?

As for the Red Cloaks, their thoughts were always running in the direction of women. Even in the best of times they never knew if this day would be their last. Any one of them could have died at the hands of a Saxon that very morning. It was something they didn't want to know about. Better to think of women, the pleasures of the here and now.

Eleri's friend Rhian was with a red-cloaked warrior, asking where he came from, sizing him up for later. She even inquired about his horse, which was not a regular topic of conversation for her. The man laughed, knowing full well and enjoying the game that was being played.

In amongst the flirting adults, children ran about, boys and girls alike fascinated by spears and shields. Seated in a corner, being ignored for once, was Mared of the Silver Wheel. "Tell Arawn to come here," she ordered a young girl, who only ignored her. It was not a time for the old. The summer night was warm and stirring with hot life, butterflies and midges, ants going about their business with the same determination that the young women of the village were going about theirs. The beech wood was alive with birds in the long evening.

"My daughter, Eleri," Arawn said to Macsen, attending to social niceties. "You've met already of course."

"We have indeed," Macsen said, his eyes smiling, hungry.

She came up to his nose, she reckoned, which made him about the same height as her father, taller than Gwion but not by much. But where Gwion was dark, this man was fair; even his eyebrows and eyelashes, Eleri noticed on close inspection, which made her think that he was born of the sea, whereas Gwion belonged to the rich dark red earth of the Summer Land. The heretical thought that he had a Saxon look about him she kept to herself. She found him looking intently at her, his eyes challenging and questioning, disturbing the composure she thought was hers.

"So Eleri Gwir, we meet again," Macsen said; "The girl with the interesting name."

"She says what she thinks," her father said in explanation, not without some pride. "And usually what she says is worth listening to. Mind you," he added, "her tongue may get her into trouble one of these days."

"A girl with strong views," Macsen said, his eyes on her lush auburn hair. Opinionated, his mother would have called it. "Watch out there, my boy," she would have said. "A girl like that is sure to bring trouble across the threshold."

Macsen's mother had died five summer's back; yet her words were never far from his mind, as if she lived on inside his brain. His sisters said the same, that their mother was a spirit inside their heads, alive with sayings and warnings.

Twice now Macsen had referred to Eleri as a girl.

"*Woman,*" Eleri corrected him, trying to make it sound as neutral as possible and feeling a shiver of excitement rush up through the length of her entire upper body and into the pores of her scalp.

"Ah."

"Belin the Great, don't let me blush," she told herself, forgetting everything the priest had said and done. She didn't want to compare Macsen with Gwion – she certainly hadn't intended to do so – yet the impulse to weigh the one against the other pulled at her with irresistible force. Older than Eleri by two summers, Gwion seemed a hundred summers younger than the red-cloaked soldier, young and untried; whereas Macsen's experience of the world of men and women, of blood-taking, of the messy realities of life in an uncertain age, was plain to see in his bearing. He too was young, but far from untried, in war and lovemaking alike.

Eleri loved Gwion, her friend through all her girlhood years. She was at that moment in danger of being in thrall to Macsen, this fair creature of the sea who made her body blush. For the second time that day and for her entire life she was lost for words.

With Macsen was his second-in-command, a seasoned campaigner called Riwalus, a man with an iron countenance that settled on one woman and then another. He raised his cup to Eleri, thanking her for tending to Peris' wound. "As good as new," he said, speaking as an undoubted expert in the giving if not healing of wounds.

There were songs. The children of the village sang about the sun-god and his love for the moon, a performance which brought out the more tolerant aspect of Father Cenydd's character, although admittedly he was not entirely sober by that time. A country bard took up the theme of love, which was to everyone's liking. No one wanted to hear of war; that would come soon enough and of its own accord. When Siriol kissed first Arawn full on the lips and then Branwen there was a loud cheer and laughter.

Gwion came at last. Busy helping his father, he'd missed the early part of the feast.

That morning it had been Eleri Gwir who had been on edge; now it was his turn. He was unsure suddenly of everything. At first, he couldn't see Eleri. Then he found her long sun-god hair surrounded by attentive Red Cloaks. She was tall; they were taller. Big men, all of them, the circle they made was a barrier not easily broken, as formidable in its way as a Gewisse shield wall, something Gwion had heard a lot about but could only comprehend by an act of imagination.

Sensitive as a roe buck, Gwion knew that these men were everything he was not. He knew he had everything to prove in life. He knew the life path of these men was not his path. As he looked at Eleri, his heart shrank inside him, dying a degree or two, it seemed. He wanted to break through the wall of men, to wrap Eleri in his arms, to hold her close and tight, to claim her for his own.

Macsen noticed Gwion hovering at the edge of the circle. With the ease that comes from superiority of birth and experience, the kind of ease that makes you mad with love or hatred, or both, he invited Gwion to join them. "Let the young man through," he said. "Give him some room there, Riwalus."

Macsen didn't mean to smile that satisfied smile of his, but there it was. Gwion felt it like an arrow in his heart.

Holding out her arms, her eyes sparkling with excitement, Eleri said: "Come here, Gwion. I'll introduce you."

"No," Gwion said more abruptly than he'd intended, feeling horribly awkward. "My father; I have to help him. I only came to tell you that."

He was not high born. His father was the head cowman of the *cantref*, an important and honourable position but not one that you would brag about in front of a crowd of smiling Red Cloaks. The smell of the byre and the spit were on his skin, his shirt, everywhere. He liked the smell, the warm smell of the red cows, and wouldn't have exchanged his life for anything or anyone. At least that was what he'd always assumed. Self-consciously, shamefully, cursing his stupidity, he turned away, intending to leave Eleri to her own devices and those of the attentive Red Cloaks.

Macsen's strong hand landed on his shoulder, twisting him round. "Join us. Don't be foolish," his assured, well-meaning voice said, as commanding as it was condescending to Gwion's sensitive ears. One of the Red Cloaks laughed. Gwion imagined it was at him.

Gwion's expression darkened; his eyes erupted, throwing long sheets of black fire; his wiry frame tensed and coiled. "Get your hand off me!" he shouted, loud enough to bring everyone to attention. Not only did he brush Macsen's hand away, he shoved the Red Cloak captain in the chest, sending him sprawling to the sawdust floor.

Quiet.

From raucous laughter the place had turned to deathly quiet.

No one moved.

Rising slowly, murder in his eyes, Macsen came towards the young man with the smell of the byre on his skin. "You'll answer for that," he said.

Gwion stood his ground.

Pulling a knife from his belt, Macsen appraised his adversary, giving Gwion time to arm himself; either that or beg forgiveness.

"A knife!" Gwion shouted, holding out his favoured left hand.

Instead it was Arawn who came forward. He didn't need to say anything. His intention was clear. He would stand with Gwion.

For a moment they were like hawks suspended in the air; time stopping; the world on hold.

The man called Riwalus came between them, veteran of a thousand brawls. "A misunderstanding," he said. "Why don't we drink to that?"

Calmer now though no less lethal, Macsen said: "I would have an apology or I will have his blood on my hands."

"Let it go," Riwalus urged. "There's no harm done. The boy acted without thinking."

At this Gwion pushed at Arawn's arm, ready to meet his fate, about which there could be no serious doubt.

Eleri wanted to intervene. She wanted to tell them to stop behaving like idiots, except that, with the faintest touch on her elbow, her father warned her off. It wasn't the time for plain speaking, not now, not yet.

Riwalus stood in front of Mascsen, blocking his way. Older than his captain by ten years, he had the authority of experience and the latitude that is owed to friendship.

With neither advantage to protect him, Father Cenydd joined Riwalus, his usually bell-like voice muddied by drink. "Fight only the good fight," he slurred.

It was enough for Macsen to see the absurdity of it all. Not that he budged; not that he said anything for a moment, letting matters weigh in the balance: his bruised pride; the priest's reckless courage; Gwion's rash bravery.

"Very well," he said quietly, and the knife went back into his belt, slowly, reluctantly.

"He's a good bowman. He's our best," Arawn said of Gwion, speaking directly to the captain of the Red Cloaks, trying to ease the tension. "We'll need him. We'll need every man we've got."

With cool sea-creature eyes, Macsen judged Gwion's value as a fighter, recognising that he might yet be of some use. "God knows," he thought, "we really do need every man we can get, cowmen included."

As for Gwion, he turned and walked away before Eleri could reach him, his heart, his spleen, every bit of him boiling over in a mess of anguish and regret.

# Chapter Six

The long, warm hazel-month evening wore on. Dusk brought a flurry of bird chatter as they settled in for the night in the tall beech wood. It brought too a flurry of human chatter and other related activity.

Tired though he was, Arawn knew he wouldn't sleep, not with the hot words spoken between Gwion and Macsen running through his blood, not with decisions to be made, about his Eleri's future, about the future of the people of the Summer Land.

Alone with his daughter, he was content to sit and talk, enjoying the last of the year's brew of elderberry wine, letting his blood settle, giving his mind the time to work over the problems and dilemmas of this and other days.

They were close, these two. You could hear it in their conversation: its playful ironies; its nuances of mutual understanding; its shade and colour that could change from light to dark, altering course from fun to serious in the blink of an eye; and you could hear it in the breadth of their conversation which ranged far and wide, across the mysteries of the gods and into the still deeper mysteries of human nature, from the affairs of power to matters of the heart.

"I suppose you took up with some woman in Caer Baddan," Eleri said, playful, nosey, wanting to know the ins and outs of a donkey's bottom, as the saying goes.

"Wouldn't you like to know."

Eleri's mother had died when Eleri was young, too young for Eleri to have any recollection of her. She was used to women taking an interest in her father and he in them, for a time at least. "None of them get under his skin," she thought. "They don't make him itch when they're with him and they don't make him scratch when they leave."

"So what *did* you get up to?"

"This and that," Arawn answered, evasively enough to tweak at Eleri's ingrained inquisitiveness, the hint of a smile on his lips.

Eleri knew to be patient.

"What's Caer Baddan like?" she asked. It was the old Roman civitas of Aquae Sulis, with its baths and columns, things Eleri had heard about but never seen.

"It's not good," was her father's laconic answer. "It's seen better times."

"Do the walls still stand?"

"Yes, and there have been repairs in places. But it's a mess really. The whole place is a mess."

"What about Ffernfael, Father? What's he like?"

It wasn't that he didn't know or that he was unsure of where he stood in relation to the high chieftain; still Arawn paused to consider his answer. He knew that Ffernfael's authority derived not from heredity or other right, but rather from a combination of character and luck. For Arawn, it was a question of arranging his ideas and impressions into a semblance of order. Any old account wouldn't do for Eleri Gwir.

"I like him," he started. "He's a kind of bear of a man, short and powerfully built. And he's clever. He thinks things through. There's more to him that meets the eye, I'd say. When it suits him, he's every bit as aggressive and belligerent as any other chieftain. But he also knows how to pull people together. He can sit the other leaders down and convince them of the need to set petty arguments aside. He makes them see that we're all in this together."

Draining his beaker, Arawn went off on a different tack: "And he has the Red Cloaks at his back, which counts for something, a lot I'd say. Luckily for him there's some family connection with Macsen; on Macsen's mother's side I think."

Arawn paused, reviewing what he'd said. "A lot of character, a bit of luck and the good sense to make the best of it about sums it up," he commented.

"I think I like him too," Eleri said.

"More than anything, he understands the dire position we're in," Arawn went on.

At the council of war, Ffernfael had declared that the time for decision was upon them. "I don't have to tell anyone here of the peril we are in from these Gewisse," he had said. His dark look had scanned about the hall, testing, searching out the resolve of his companions. "The evidence is all about us," he had pressed on. "They advance relentlessly up the valleys, village by village, stronghold by stronghold. The danger now is that, if we cannot hold the ground that is left to us, we will be cut off from the men of Gwent and Dyfed. We will be alone, assuming we are here at all."

The very thought of it sent a cold hand over Arawn's heart.

"What about the Irish brothers, what are they like?" was Eleri's next line of inquiry. "People say they argue about anything and everything, Condidan especially; they say he's mad for fighting."

"He is," her father said. "But his brother reins him in, or tries to. There were a few skirmishes with Ffernfael and others; nothing too serious."

"That's not what Siriol told me," Eleri interjected.

Her father didn't respond directly. "The truth is a deal had already been made. People like me were only there to witness it. You'll find that's the case. The big decisions and a lot of the small ones are made behind closed doors."

"They are here," Eleri pointed out.

"True enough," her father acknowledged, laughing. "Still," he said, looking up into his daughter's eyes, making sure she was paying attention, "always be wary of power and those that wield it. Keep your distance if you can. Remember, to them you're only a means to an end, if you're lucky enough to be that much."

Arawn made an odd sort of leader: too honest and outspoken as a rule for his own good.

Father and daughter talked on, Arawn unwinding, warding off a wave of fatigue, eager as ever to feed his daughter's insatiable curiosity; Eleri liking nothing more than to hear her father explain the ways of the world of power and politics.

"Will the alliance hold?" she wanted to know.

"It has to," Arawn answered. He shrugged his big shoulders. "I don't know," he answered truthfully. Warlike by instinct, the Irish brothers belonged to the messy pattern of things in these days of strife and chaos, stitched into its weave. "We have to trust the brothers," Arawn said. "There's no alternative. The talk is that Ceawlin, the Gewisse king, will march in great force after the winter months. That's what our spies tell us."

"They mean to catch us out, sleeping like bears in winter," Eleri observed.

"Just so," her father agreed. "We have to be ready for them, Eleri. For now, Ceawlin sends the odd war band to test our resolve, snapping like a cattle dog at out heels. But in the spring he'll come with his army. The spies say that his son Cuthwine will join him then from the Saxon homelands across the eastern sea. Ceawlin would have his son at his side."

"He doesn't want him to miss the fun," Eleri remarked ruefully.

"That's about the size of it," Arawn confirmed. "And this Cuthwine will not come alone, we're told, but with fifty keels. In the spring they'll come, with the daffodils or shortly after; just as soon as they can put to sea."

"I hate the sound of them, Ceawlin and Cuthwine," Eleri said, chewing the names over like indigestible cud in her mouth.

"Mind you, they say Ceawlin had a British mother," Arawn said out of the blue.

"Really?" was all Eleri could say. She hated the idea. It was something she didn't want to think about.

"It happens," her father pressed, needing his daughter to understand the untidy ways of the world.

"I know it happens," she said. "I'm not a fool."

Voices were heard outside their hut, only to die away again.

Finally, they got around to the subject of Gwion, every bit as difficult in its way as the Gewisse were in theirs. Testing the water, Arawn started by asking a question to which he knew the answer: "What was Gwion playing at?"

Eleri pulled a face at her father, as if to say: "As if you don't know."

Her father pulled a face back. "Well?" he insisted.

"You know as well as I do."

The truth was that Arawn liked Gwion. What wasn't there to like? He was a kind and sensitive youth and thoughtful with it. "Good eyes," that's what Arawn's mother would have said about him. Gwion and Eleri had always been great friends, since childhood days, seeming to share a language and understanding of their own. They were obviously fond of one another and well matched in looks. What if Gwion asked for a trial union with Eleri? What if Eleri did the asking? What would he say in reply?

It was the one subject father and daughter had always avoided; until now.

"We're friends," Eleri insisted; "We always have been."

"*And* a bit," her father commented, not so old as to have completely forgotten the youthful urge to sexual experimenation.

"A bit; but not much," Eleri conceded.

"Not much for you, perhaps."

He was a fair-minded man. He gave Gwion his due. Only, he worried that his clever, beautiful daughter might settle for the only man she'd ever known, the first pick of the bunch. A part of him said she should wait a few years, to get to know the world and its ways; another part of him worried that the world they knew might not last that long. And was Gwion the man for these dangerous times? He was no warrior; he wasn't cut out to meet the Saxon shield wall, no match for their heavy frames wielding their big linden shields. Willowy and lean, Gwion was a bowman, a fine one at that and a hunter without equal in the Summer Land. Was that enough to protect Arawn's precious daughter? And she was a chieftain's daughter after all. He saw the way the Red Cloaks looked at her, with hungry eyes, ready to devour her. He saw the way Macsen looked at her. What was Gwion but the son of Meriadoc, Arawn's head cowman; a good, steady man holding an important position in the community admittedly; but not a chieftain, not a man of real consequence in the world; whereas in her father's eyes Eleri was fit to be a queen;

and of more than the Summer Land; of the whole of the Island of the Mighty.

"He was in the wrong," Eleri conceded, referring to Gwion.

"He's lucky to be alive."

"It's not easy for him." A statement that encapsulated a thousand and one thoughts and feelings.

"No."

The night was warm, the light dying only now in the long evening of the hazel month.

There was a knock at the door of their hut and a woman's voice calling for Eleri Gwir.

A woman was in labour. Eleri was needed.

# Chapter Seven

In these days of danger, the Gewisse on the doorstep with more than one foot inside the Summer Land, the palisade around the hill top of Tre Wyn was patrolled by guards, day and night. It was one of these guards, a small, sturdy man called Math, who brought the fugitives through the gate to stand under the rowan tree which was the portal into the life of the village. Spear in hand, he kept a wary eye on the group. He didn't want to be the one who fell for a Gewisse trick.

"Find Arawn," he told his son Idris. "Bring him here."

Roused from a deep sleep, swearing in the name of the old gods, Arawn went to see what the commotion was about. He found there a man in his fifties and his younger-looking wife, along with two defiant girls of around fifteen and fourteen years. They were all the one family, they said. It was probably true; the girls had the same look about them, long and thin, their hair breathing red fire.

Arawn would have had them tell their story in front of Macsen, but he was not to be found. Instead it was Riwalus who weighed the truth of it.

"Speak up then," Arawn ordered.

Taking the lead, the woman said her name was Gwenda. "This is Gronw," she said, pointing to the man.

"Can't he speak for himself?" Riwalus said, disgusted.

"I c-c-c-c-c-can," the man stuttered.

"Enough," Arawn commanded, impatient but also sensitive to the man's discomfort. "Speak up, woman."

"We're from the village that lies south of the great dolmen; Dinas Hir, that is," she said.

Arawn and Riwalus knew what was coming next. It was the Gewisse war band the Red Cloaks had encountered earlier in the day. If twelve had died at least the same number had escaped through the birch wood. The leader had been a big, vicious-looking man, long fair hair decorated with bones, a mouth that turned down into cruelty. He'd shouted and guided what remained of his men into the shelter of the trees, leading them in reasonable order to safety, to bring murderous havoc upon these unfortunate villagers. He'd yelled at Macsen and his men in his barbarous tongue, promising vengeance no doubt. The Gewisse were a predictable lot, inclined to violent, not original, thought.

Dinas Hir was known to both Arawn and Riwalus, a prosperous enough place lying in a curve of a river, with good grazing for sheep and cattle, but small and badly defended. Until now it had been beyond the reach of their Saxon enemies, at arm's length as it were.

No longer.

"We were out of the village when they came," the woman Gwenda explained. "There's an old quarry nearby, you probably know it. Just beyond there's a copse of hazel trees. We were picking hazel nuts there. I have them still. Some of them anyway." To prove it she produced a handful of nuts from her pocket. The others followed her lead.

"We heard the screaming," she went on. "Gronw ran back to the head of the quarry." She looked over at her husband before adding with pride: "He can't speak well but he's as strong as an ox."

"And he can run," Riwalus said, disparagingly.

"I'm no c-c-c-c-c-coward," the man stammered, his square chin on the move, rising, his muscular frame taking shape as he said it.

From his vantage point Gronw had seen the Gewisse torch the village. The men that had survived the first onslaught were herded into a circle of jeering swords. Those who tried to resist were hacked down with some sport but no ceremony. The others followed soon enough. The leader of the wolf pack seemed to take particular pleasure in using his *seax* to gouge out the eyes of his victims before killing them.

Murderous and predictable.

And efficient.

The rest of the villagers were brought together, the older women and any cripples separated out and killed, the younger women and children taken crying into slavery, although not before the Gewisse warriors had indulged in some predictable ill-treatment. Hands tied, whips on their backs, the young women walked with blood and semen clinging to their legs.

"We stayed in the hazel copse," Gwenda went on. "What else could we do?"

"Nothing," Arawn said kindly.

"He's a blacksmith, my husband is," Gwenda said.

That brought a smile even to Riwalus' tough face. A blacksmith was a very useful addition to a people at war with swords and spears to make, with horses to shoe, with their lives hanging in the balance.

The minute Arawn had finished hearing the story from the family of fugitives, the skinny, curly-haired boy called Gereint came haring up to him.

"Well, what is it?" Arawn asked.

"It's the soldier."

Arawn waited for more.

"The Red Cloak captain."

"Macsen, you mean?" Arawn said.

"Yes. He wants me to tell you he is seeing to his horse, Gwalchwen that is."

So that was where he was.

"He's there with Eleri Gwir."

'Is he now?'

It occurred to Arawn that on this front at least a decision had already been made, by his daughter Eleri, independently of him or Gwion or possibly even Macsen for that matter. "Desire, like water, will find its way to down to its natural destination," he told himself.

"Yes," the boy Gereint said. "Bryn thought the stallion was unwell, a chill or something, but Eleri Gwir said no and the soldier, Macsen that is, said she was right about that."

The words spilled out of the boy like a river in torrent.

On an impulse, knowing the boy to be an orphan, Arawn told him: "Bryn will ride with us tomorrow to help tend to the horses, and you'll ride with Bryn."

"Thank you, chieftain!" the boy said, a grin as big as a barn spreading over his face.

"Your name's Gereint, isn't it?"

"Yes."

There was something about the boy that made Arawn smile with fondness and foolish hope. He'd be glad of his company.

"Now fetch Macsen here, and that daughter of mine while you're at it."

Off he went.

*

With the fugitives came a real sense of urgency and immediacy of purpose. In no time Kado was on the scene. Macsen was found. With him was Eleri.

"The birth was over in minutes," she told her father. "It was the woman's ninth. It shot out of her."

"And I hear you're a horse doctor now," Arawn commented archly.

"I know as much as anyone," Eleri answered, her face warning her father not to carry the conversation further.

"She really does," was Macsen's helpful contribution.

"See?"

Family issues aside, everything was decided quickly. They would wait until morning. They would pursue the war band, slowed now by their haul of slaves. They would kill the Gewisse. A firm message had to be sent to their king, Ceawlin; that they entered the lands of the Britons at their peril and that, if they chose to do so, they should come in force. Better a proper reckoning than an endless succession of marauding bands, picking off easy targets here and there, sapping the will to fight by slow degrees.

Kado was to stay behind, it was agreed, to organise the defence of the communities of the Summer Land. Gwion's father, Meriadoc, was to oversee the routine life of the village, the harvest that promised to be good this year, the endless round of petty disputes to be settled.

As for Eleri, she would go Gewisse hunting with Arawn and Macsen. Her healing skills, as well as those with a bow, would serve the company well, it was decided. As Kado said: "That girl rides as well as any man and shoots a damn sight straighter than most." Besides, Arawn was glad to have his daughter with him. He was putting her in harm's way; yet at the same time he'd convinced himself that she was safer there, at his side.

The paradox wasn't lost on him. Arawn knew what he was about, of course. A considerate man, he felt sorry for Gwion, but at the same time he was pleased to let his daughter run free in the world, to find her own way and purpose.

Gwion was going nowhere. Discretion the better part of valour on this occasion, Arawn had judged it best not to mention his name in Macsen's presence.

"I have to find him," Eleri told her father. "I can't just leave without talking to him."

"Tell him his time for war will come soon enough," Arawn said. "Tell him he is loved."

"I will."

*

She found him in his father's hut, in a pit of anger and shame. He wouldn't look at her. His face was contorted in a flood of feelings, wounded pride and deep frustration.

"Gwion," she pleaded. "It's all right."

"I'm sorry, Eleri," was all he could say. "I'm sorry."

"Don't be. I know why you did it. I can see what all this is doing to you."

Still, he wouldn't look at her.

"You love me," Eleri said. "I know that. There's no shame in it."

But shame was like a bull kicking inside his chest; shame and the realisation that he'd made a fool of himself before the people that mattered to him most.

"You know I love you," Eleri said. "None of this matters."

"It does," was all Gwion said.

"Can I hold you?" Eleri asked, not knowing what else to say. "Can you hold me?"

"Yes," he said.

He wanted to fight and kill and die, yet here he was holding the most precious thing in his life, something he knew he was about to lose, if he hadn't lost her already.

She had to tell him she was leaving.

"In the morning," she said, "I'm going with my father. We're going with the Red Cloaks," she said, needing all her courage to say it. "The Gewisse are close. We'll hunt them down."

He tried to push her away but she held on to him.

"I'm sorry," Eleri said. "I have to go."

The daughter of his chief was telling him that he wasn't good enough. "A cowman's son," he said, simple words in themselves, the shadows in Gwion's face suggesting the complexity they contained.

"It's not that, Gwion. It's just that my heart, my whole being, my entire life has taken a leap. I must go with it. I'm sorry," she said again.

"I'm sorry too," Gwion responded, regretting at once his peevish words.

Doing his best to shake off disappointment, he got to his feet and held Eleri at arm's length, looking at last directly into the light of her strong face. He was the Gwion she knew, generous and darkly humorous.

"I'll be all right," he said.

It was what she wanted to hear.

"My father sends his love," Eleri said. "He says that war will find you soon enough."

He nodded his head, fighting back tears.

"Whatever happens, Gwion, I'll always love you. We'll always be friends."

"Whatever happens, Eleri Gwir."

He told her she should go. "You've got things to do. Take care. Look after yourself; remember."

"And you, Gwion."

# Chapter Eight

The first light of morning, sharp and clear, found the horses saddled and ready for the hard riding that lay ahead. Arawn's Grey Queen – *Frenhiness Llwyd* – and Macsen's White Hawk – *Gwalchwen* – had their noses to the ground, almost touching, companionable in the fresh morning air. Eleri's horse, a two-year-old mare that went by the apt name of Lightning Bolt – *Melltan* – was there too, pawing the dewy grass.

The sharp-eyed osprey, high up, a trout in its talons, saw it all: the milling horses, the warriors assembling as they shook off the heavy heads of the night before, shields at their backs, swords and spears, and the villagers looking on, reluctant to part with them for the life they brought, the feeling of security, a comfort blanket for all ages. There were embraces, some long. There was sadness and there was pride. And there was Father Cenydd, mounting up with the best of them, his plain cross at his neck, a spear in his hand. On horseback, he looked less pinched and priestly, more like the militant young man he obviously was under the cowl of religion. The standard of the cross was folded on his saddle as extra protection for his skinny rump, an arrangement that did not pass without comment, although not within the priest's hearing.

That morning they rode hard and fast. The land was beautiful; the grass velvet green; the curvaceous hills a sensuous pleasure; the rivers deep and lazy in the dawn light. They rode east along ancient paths until they reached the great Roman road – the Fosse they called it – crossing from one civilisation to another. Going east, they had the Great Wood ahead of them, thick with oaks in some parts, sparse in others. Men, women and horses alike felt the excitement of the chase.

They were a good-sized company, large enough to tackle almost any war band they encountered, small enough to engender a sense of belonging to a picked group, strengthened by personal loyalties to their captain and to each other. "It must have been like this with Arthur," was a thought that sprang up in one mind and jumped effortlessly to another and another. You could see it in their shining eyes.

There were thirty Red Cloaks in their mail vests, helmets glinting in the sun, professional soldiers all of them, sworn to Ffernfael. Father Cenydd was with them, his faith his sword and his shield. And Arawn was there, a hard countryman, with long experience of conflict, feeling invulnerable for a moment in his war gear, with the young captain at their head.

The women of the company rode together – Eleri, Siriol, Branwen and one other. This was Cerridwen, the eldest daughter of Gwenda and the blacksmith Gronw. Like Eleri, she was lean and strong-limbed and her hair had that fire-god look, brighter even than Eleri's, a flame pouring through the morning air. They were like the four queens of the four winds riding to war.

It was her mother Gwenda who had pleaded Cerridwen's case. "She can ride like the wind, that girl, and she loves horses more than she loves her parents. And she's a fighter; I swear it on Belin's shield."

Macsen and Arawn had looked Cerridwen up and down.

"You're a woman?" Macsen asked.

"I am," the girl answered defiantly, looking straight and hard into their faces, her eyes ablaze with a warrior's spirit. "They killed everyone and they took my horse," she added, in a voice that would brook no argument.

Without warning she picked up a spear and threw it twenty paces into the side of a cart, the hard thud it made and its juddering vibration sounding a violent note that made everyone stop and look up. Again she looked at the men, brave and straight.

"Do we have a horse to spare; a suitable horse – *for a woman*?" Macsen inquired of Arawn, his eyes smiling.

"I suppose we do."

"And you're sure about this?" Arawn asked Gwenda. "She'll be in harm's way."

"In company with your own daughter, I hear," was Gwenda's reply. "But she's not to be used, mind," she warned.

"I can look after myself!" Cerridwen said, fierce as a winter storm.

So it was settled.

At the very back of the company rode Bryn, the groom, with the boy Gereint behind him, holding on for dear life. "Doing all right back there?" Bryn would ask from time to time.

"I think so."

"Well, that's all right then."

To retrace their steps to Dinas Hir they had to leave the Roman way that headed north and east. The landscape they rode through was busy with long-deserted hillforts, stone monuments, circles. Eleri thought about the land, its stories and its secrets. There had been order here once, not only in Roman times but earlier, in the time of the tribes of the British people. She liked to say their names – the Dobunni, the Dumnonii, the

Durotriges and the Atrebates. Now, in these Gewisse-cursed days, the old tribal divisions had broken down into petty chiefdoms, into a mess of fugitives fleeing for their lives. Only the Dumnonii in the far south-west of the island, at Caer Uisc in the kingdom of Dyfneint, had retained their shape and organisation. But they were far off and it seemed their king had no intention of coming to the aid of his fellow Britons.

The morning was too fine for gloomy thoughts. Instead, Eleri imagined the congregations that would have come to the Great Circle in the old tribal days, in praise of Belin. She liked it that her father's shield still wore that god's image and not another's.

Their road lay due east, past the ancient fort at Maes-yr-Eos, its ridges cut into a hill from where you could look out westwards onto the flatlands of the River Hafren and beyond to the mountains of Gwent. To the east was the snaking track of the river valley that led through a gash in the Great Wood into the lost lands. It was there they headed, Macsen in the lead, the elation of first light giving way to caution and wariness the farther they travelled.

Confidence is a great thing, for soldiers nothing less than essential; the sense of belonging to a tightly knit group that believes in itself against all others, defining itself as superior, different, a thing apart. Macsen knew this only too well; it was the precious ore that every leader had to find and never lose. But he knew, too, that confidence is only a benefit so long as it's guided intelligently and kept within the defined limits of a leader's own making. Knowing this, Macsen slowed the pace, to let the horses draw breath and for their riders to clear their heads.

"We'll climb to Maes-yr-Eos," he told Arawn. "See what there is to see from there."

They were looking for smoke; any sign of the destructive path the Gewisse had taken. The Gewisse could have headed through the wooded terrain to the plain of the Great Circle that led into the lost lands, keeping to the ridges on the high ground. But Macsen didn't think so, and Arawn and Riwalus agreed. The country up there was too exposed. Wounded, with depleted numbers and captives to herd like cattle, they would travel by the easiest route, along the valley floor, concealed by the thick mass of the great oak forest, searching out any easy targets that might remain in the war-ravaged land.

The company came to Maes-yr-Eos when the sun was starting on its long arc into the west. In the near distance, to the north and west, was Caer Baddan; from the same direction, from the mountains of Gwent, they saw clouds gathering, rain-bearing strands of grey that would soak them through before the day was out. They'd dismounted at the foot of the hill and climbed up and down the deep ditches that ringed the summit of the old hillfort. Bryn, a plain countryman with enough sense to let leaders take the lead, had placed a strong hand on Gereint's shoulder to stop him racing everyone up to the summit. He knew Gereint would have raced Belin himself, given half a chance. *Sgwarnog*, Bryn called him, the Hare.

At the top Eleri was the first to speak. "This would make a good stronghold."

She was standing with Macsen on the crest of the hill, looking down the wooded spine of the great valley. It was the furthest Eleri had been from home. More girl than woman for a moment, she liked the feeling of adventure, scary and exciting.

"As good as any," Macsen commented, his thoughts running along the same lines.

"A good killing place," Riwalus said, joining them.

"As good as any," Macsen repeated.

He wasn't one for wasting words. Gwion came to Eleri's mind, his familiar figure walking straight in without knocking. Given half the chance, Gwion would talk through the day and night and through another day again. It was his way of giving himself, expecting nothing in return, his kindness speaking in every word. Macsen was different, not unkind, yet inclined to snap when he was irritated, showing his impatience, not one to suffer fools. Eleri wondered if he had been like Gwion once, more open-hearted, before war caught up with him. She didn't think so. Plain to see in him were the generations of command and hard duty that were his inheritance. His sea-creature eyes could just as easily breathe fire as dance with charm and laughter.

"Are we too late, d'you think?" Riwalus asked. "Have they got away?"

No.

There it was – the tell-tale wisp of grey smoke in the east, snaking over the forest in a bend in the river.

"So are they running or waiting?" Riwalus asked next.

Macsen thought it over. He went through the options, the scenarios that came immediately to mind. Perhaps it wasn't the Gewisse at all. Perhaps it was just an isolated homestead. He doubted it. Too many war bands of the foreigners had passed this way. Were they just careless? No. Their leader knew his business. He was a worthy enough enemy in his way. Even if they'd paused for some reason – to brutalise their women hostages more than likely – they wouldn't reveal their whereabouts so readily. Perhaps they thought they were in the clear, that no one would pursue them into the border lands. That was plausible enough. The general lack of organisation among the British, their bickering and indecision, would suggest as much. The very thought made Macsen scream inside with bull-like rage. But no, he told himself, instinct and experience speaking. That wasn't it. It was a trap. Slowed by their chattels, human and otherwise, the Gewisse had kept a wary eye to their rear, finding there the company of horse soldiers. As brave as they were brutal, the Gewisse war band had turned to face their pursuers, picking their own ground on which to fight. That was it.

"They're waiting," Macsen answered at length.

Riwalus nodded his agreement.

The morning's hot feelings had turned to cold resolve. Eleri felt the first drops of rain on her long hair as the wind lifted it and blew it about, its fire bright against the gathering grey.

Father Cenydd made the sign of the cross, as if that would turn back nature's purpose. For luck and safe keeping, Siriol and Branwen touched the sun motifs on their rich brooches. All fury, Cerridwen was already running to her white mare, too young for caution, too angry for prudence. Incorrigible, the boy Gereint raced her down.

# Chapter Nine

There was at least one other scenario to contemplate. Cautious, and with sufficient authority and respect to express it without fear of misunderstanding, Arawn put it to Macsen as a hypothetical.

"What if there's more than one war band? What if they've joined forces with a second raiding party? It could even be an arranged meeting place for the war bands that ravage the borders."

What if?

"Perhaps," Macsen said. "But somehow I don't think so. The captains of these war bands are their own men, greedy for themselves, for power and women and for the gold and silver rings that mark their prowess. I don't say it's impossible that they've joined forces, but I don't think it's likely. Besides, our spies tell us that the Gewisse are busy to the north, fighting their own kind, putting their own house in order before turning their full attention on us.Still," he went on, "you're right to counsel caution. We can't afford to lose good men for the sake of a gesture; good women too," he corrected himself when he saw Eleri's left eyebrow rise in disdain, his playful smile returning to his serious face.

Macsen knew that moving through the heavily wooded valley fully mounted would be difficult. He knew, too, that if his suspicion of a trap was right then the Saxons would have chosen ground inimical to cavalry.

More than that, they would have spiked the ground; their slaves would have been put to work sharpening and concealing spikes in the marshy earth, and more besides. Macsen knew he could turn for home and do nothing. A point had been made after all: the Gewisse knew they'd been pursued and that any future incursions were likely to be challenged. But no; that wouldn't do. A more decisive message had to be sent east to the lost lands. The war band could not return. Some of the doubt and trepidation felt among the Britons had to be planted in Saxon minds. They should fear for their lives when venturing west. Their confidence had to be dented.

They entered the wooded valley, not yet far enough for any Gewisse spies to assume that they would move as a single mounted company. What the Saxons didn't know, or didn't know well enough, was that this country belonged to the Britons of the Island of the Mighty. It was their past and their present that was written into its landscape. If the Saxons, the Gewisse, had knowledge of the land, they would have known that the place they had pitched camp was the site of an oak grove, sacred to the ancient tribes and to all the true people of the Island. And if they had known that, there was a good chance they would have known too that a pathway led along the wooded valley ledge, dropping down at the back of the grove. If some or all of that was known to them, they would have comprehended the weak link in their plan. But this was not their land and the Gewisse knew nothing of it.

"Let's assume none of the captives have given us away," Macsen said.

"They wouldn't!" Cerridwen said fiercely.

It was on that assumption that the company divided. Riwalus led a small contingent of seven fighting men leading another seven horses, with Father Cenydd making up the numbers to seem as if a larger company was travelling down the valley floor. Except for Bryn and the boy Gereint, who stayed with the remaining horses, the rest went on foot, shields still on their backs, swords and spears in hand. Up they went through the rich wood, disturbing the residents of the area, the red squirrels lingering on tree trunks until in a triumph of caution over curiosity they were persuaded to make for the safety of the higher branches.

The company moved quietly along the narrow path, first up through the woods and then along the valley ledge. It was the way the victims of sacrifice had been led to the sacred grove, passing the rock face on which a powerful head was carved in rough circles of stone; the head of the King of the Underworld.

"Your namesake," someone whispered to Arawn, with a nod to the carving.

"Aye, good-looking, too."

The rock was said to be a door into the Underworld – into Annwfn – its secret known once to the learned ones but left now in the unsteady hands of wandering bards and the like. As the company passed the spiral head, many of them paused, taking a brief moment to honour the long dead. With Father Cenydd on the lower track, there was no one to speak against the old gods.

They came to the place where the path led down into the valley floor. By then the rain was on them, hard enough to penetrate the sparse covering provided by the oak trees.

"Watch your step," Macsen warned. "Don't slip or fall or make any noise."

The wind had picked up too, racing in from the west, which they took to be a good omen. For his part, Macsen claimed not to believe in nature's signs, that it was all nonsense. Yet, like every soldier before and after him, he found it impossible to deny completely the temptations of superstition. Right behind him, Eleri Gwir whispered that it was a fair wind from the gods. Macsen hoped so.

When she had left her village that morning, Eleri had been dressed as practically as any soldier, her thick hide jacket protecting her upper body. Her one extravagance was the gold torque she wore at her neck, its workmanship fine and delicate. On his return from the kingdom of Gwent, her father had fished it out of his jerkin pocket. "A present from your mother's people," he'd said. "Your grandfather wanted you to have it."

"It's beautiful."

"He said it's been in the family since before the time of the legions, handed down from grandmother to granddaughter."

As they made their way down towards the Gewisse encampment, the rough voices in a brutal tongue rising to meet them, Eleri was glad to have it on her, its cool weight against her skin. She felt the presence of her ancestors in its curving, twisting lines, their lives interweaving with hers in the metal necklace. Cerridwen, she noticed, wore no finery. She'd left her home unexpectedly. Besides, it was doubtful her blacksmith father could offer her more than a brooch hammered in base metal. The thought made Eleri conscious and thankful of her own good fortune.

From the safety of a rock that concealed the track's starting point, Macsen looked into the Saxon encampment. He saw the uneven, rocky ground they had chosen for their temporary home, hopeless for cavalry, and the makeshift fort of rough logs that had been constructed. Fifteen, sixteen, no, seventeen Saxons were inside their barricade, all of them watchful, fully armed. Their leader was unmistakable. His arm rings alone were proof of his warrior status. Most of the enemy were big and blond, but he was bigger yet and more formidable.

Macsen saw that the captives were at the side of the encampment, closest to the bend of the river where the water was deepest, and protected therefore from attack. He assumed they were bound and probably gagged. It was too hard to tell. At least he could see that the barricade had only been built as a shield against front-on attack, leaving the rear of the encampment vulnerable. It made perfect sense, of course. Like the enemy, Macsen could hear the clatter of the horse soldiers coming down the valley, closer and louder by the minute, drawing all the attention in their direction. Much closer, he thought, and the deception would be found out. It was time to act.

When he'd mentioned a diversion, Cerridwen had immediately volunteered herself. Half naked, she stepped now from behind the great rock, into view of the Gewisse warriors. In full sight she removed her ill-fitting jerkin, leaving her young, sleek body exposed to the enemy, pale and beautiful in the soaking rain. For a moment the Saxons just looked, perplexed, dumbfounded.

"Freya's tits!" one yelled on recovering his senses, his eyes transfixed.

Their concentration broken, the warriors gestured and yelled a barrage of obscenities in Cerridwen's direction. Inevitably, accompanied by the jeering of his compatriots, one lanky young warrior, careless of safety, impervious to command, vaulted the barricade and headed for the naked girl.

It was at a distance of no more than a stallion's tail from the girl that the arrow from Eleri Gwir's bow hit him hard and full in the chest, ripping through whatever protective coverings he had, causing him to fall like a felled birch at Cerridwen's feet, the killing tip of the arrow protruding from a bloody tear in his back.

Everything happened then at once. Macsen led his shouting, cursing Red Cloaks, charging into the back of the Gewisse ranks. With surprise on his side, Macsen left any organisation behind, relying on the powerful anger and hatred boiling in the hearts of his men. The exhilarating mayhem of battle exploded before the enemy with sudden force and fury.

"The Island!" the Red Cloaks shouted.

Close on their heels, Arawn crashed into one Saxon, throwing him to the ground and plunging his spear into his exposed neck. He had a narrow escape when a Gewisse spear grazed his left earlobe, his head turning away by instinct at the last moment. The man who had thrown it came lunging at Arawn, spear poised, only to be hacked down in mid-flight by a Red Cloak sword; when he fell, Arawn saw that an arrow was already lodged in the Saxon's back.

Staring defeat in the face, the Saxons, the Gewisse – whatever you called them – fought like men possessed. Keeping their nerve, those that had survived the first Red Cloak onslaught tried to form a rough shield wall, but to no avail. They were under attack from all sides.

From the foot of the great rock Eleri, Siriol and Branwen showered the makeshift wall with lethal arrows. Then from across the rocky riverbed came Riwalus and his contingent, desperate to be in the fight, turning the Gewisse's heads, finally breaking their discipline and order. Their big leader bellowed the names of his gods, his eyes on the thunderous clouds. Like a demon he hacked his heavy sword into his assailants, driving down through the shoulder blade and deep into the body of one Red Cloak, splitting him like a log with a single massive blow. From one side Macsen and Arawn were on him, spear and sword driven into his guts, from the other Siriol's arrow punctured his back, and the thrust of Riwalus' sword finished him off. Not quite dead even now, he fell to his knees, blood pouring from his wounds, gore spitting from his mouth when he tried to speak his last words, his curse on the Britons, his bold contempt.

Naked still, Cerridwen came knife in hand to deal the mortal blow, the knife point driven into her enemy's heart, hatred for hatred, contempt for contempt. Her eyes burned blue flame, brighter even than her long, burning hair.

With heavy raindrops bouncing off his helmet, Macsen turned to observe the devastation that had been made. Two of his men lay dead, one an old friend, a Red Cloak whose name was Madog – Madog the Tall, they'd called him. They had a long history. Madog's father had served with Macsen's; they had been brothers in the blood of war, as Macsen was to Madog. All that was behind them. Lying face down in the boggy earth where he'd fallen, Madog's body was a terrible, fearful sight.

The other man who had fallen was new to the company, coming from among those who had joined at Caer Baddan. He was one of the men who served the Irish brothers; his name was Ifor. Macsen understood from his accent that he came originally from the mountains of Cambria, probably an outlaw from his clan. No matter. His cause and Macsen's had become one.

"Let them lie in the sacred grove," Macsen said. "We'll bury them there." He gave Father Cenydd a stern look but found no argument from that quarter.

Eleri and Siriol said they would see to the walking wounded among the Red Cloaks. Vinegar made from barley was used to clean the wounds, and a sticky coat of good honey. Father Cenydd went to help, glad in his way to be doing more than praying and preaching.

The bodies of their enemies were left where they'd fallen, food for ravens – appropriately enough the birds beloved of their violent god Woden. Spears were used to finish a few of the wounded off, not out of mercy but to shut off their moaning. That was all. Stripped of anything valuable or useful, they were left to rot.

Hatred, contempt, abomination, loathing – call it what you like.

"And you," Macsen said to Cerridwen, sounding harsh for a moment, "come here."

The big Saxon leader had fallen onto his front. Macsen heaved him over. On his naked arms he wore four rings, each more precious than the last. Macsen stripped the finest of these from the warrior's biceps, a ring of pure gold decorated at each end with a dragon head. Carrying it to Cerridwen, he placed it around her slender, pale neck. She wore nothing else; nothing more was needed. Men and women alike of the company looked on, the gladness of vengeance and of victory in their hearts.

# Chapter Ten

There were not so many captives to be freed, young girls mainly, alive because they were ripe and ready for mothering and working. Only two boys remained, both sturdy lads under ten years of age. As for the rest, they'd all perished, for being too slow, too young, too old – whatever reason the powerful find to murder the weak and vulnerable. Free now, their bonds untied, the survivors wept or sat dazed and unmoving, shocked by what had happened to them. Drenched and muddy, bruised and bloody, but alive, they greeted those of the company that fetched them to drier ground. "Thank you," was all they could say.

For Cerridwen, these were her friends and neighbours. Fully dressed again, she embraced one after the other. Her best friend, Eirian, held on to her for dear life, as did the two boys who at that moment were as lost as any two souls can be lost.

"Like animals," Eirian told Cerridwen. "That's how they treated us. My mother they killed because she was too old for them. There's only us left." Neither girl cried. Not then. Their sorrow was too deep for tears. "I'll hate these people as long as I live," Eirian said, her ferocity a match even for Cerridwen's.

"We're losing, aren't we?" another girl said. "We've come to the end."

Macsen knew that she spoke from grief and shock. He knew too that she had to be contradicted. There could be no talk of defeat. He would have spoken if Siriol hadn't beaten him to it.

One for plain speaking, she said: "We'll lose if that's what we say we'll do; we'll win if we believe we can do it. The Island of the Mighty is ours. We are the Island."

They buried their dead and tended to the wounded. It turned out that Father Cenydd had a talent for healing, something Eleri Gwir saw at once, raising him in her estimation. He went a step higher when her father told her he'd seen Cenydd's spear fly into a Saxon back. Then he seemed even more improved when the words he said over the dead were few and simple, only as much about sin and the like as seemed absolutely necessary. As he tended to the wounded he spoke of his family, his son Devi, how much he missed the boy.

"In the morning he would be there, jumping on us, getting us to wake up," he said, smiling. "A good-looking boy too, like his mother in nature, a sweet lad."

Once started, there was no stopping him.

He spoke, too, of his famous father Gildas, who had gone to the other Britain, the land over the water. "I heard from a sea captain that my father died. That was some years ago now, a hard death the man said, some malady eating my father from inside till his stomach swelled up, fit to burst. Later, a godly man brought the news to the north. It was the same story."

For all his stern talk about the evils of the here and now, it was plain that he'd prefer to have his father in this world and not the next.

"My father was a good man, a brave man," Cenydd insisted, ready to take on anyone who said otherwise.

After all that, Eleri was in danger of liking the priest. But with these godly men you could never tell –

likeable one minute, pompous and dogmatic the next. It occurred to her that he was a man of many layers, rigid piety and pride on the surface of his thin, pinched face; the lines of a more caring and humane nature under that; and, beneath it all, at his core, there was a well of ferocity that could be channelled into fanatical faith or, as today, into a warrior's passion. Perhaps even a lover's passion, the thought came to Eleri, only to be drowned at birth. People are complicated, she concluded, priestly types more than most.

The young Saxon who had taken her arrow was the first man she'd killed. She felt nothing for him. Applying a poultice of moss and foxglove flowers, her own concoction, to a wounded man's arm, Eleri remembered the look of surprise on the young Saxon's face. He had no thought of death, his own at any rate. He was just plain thoughtless, in fact. The more of the enemy who were like him the better, she thought. She shared this reflection with her father who, in his usual way, looked at the issue from a different point of view, saying that thoughtless young men made good soldiers, lacking any sense of self-preservation, believing themselves to be protected by a shield of invincibility.

"I'd like to have a thousand of them," he said.

"Young men like Macsen," Eleri ventured.

"Like Macsen five years ago, perhaps," her father suggested. "He's learned a thing or two since then. He's not a *good* soldier, he's the best."

Arawn smiled at his daughter when he said this, his eyebrows rising to the occasion, his playfulness on show. Eleri shook her head. She knew that her father wanted what he said to be taken literally, but also in the language of gentle mockery that the two of them had come to share.

"You did well, Eleri," he said to his daughter, serious suddenly, placing a hand on her arm.

"Thank you, father," she answered, equally serious. It was only now, speaking with her father, that Eleri recognised fully the enormity of what she had done.

By the time they'd made their way back to the forest edge, where they found Bryn, Gereint and their patiently grazing horses, the rain had stopped. After a few false starts a fire was lighted. "We'll risk it," Macsen said. Dried meat and barley bread was passed around. In the sharp air of the evening the oak trees had a defined clarity about them; every feature of their rough trunks was plain to see, as if etched with a monk's quill. In the old days they would have hunted for deer or wild boar and made a proper feast of it. As it was they had to be content with spring water and plain food. Their clothes were still wet from the downpour. The night gathered in.

The talk was of the Gewisse until the beautiful, soft-speaking Branwen said she had a story to tell. Glad to be freed from the shackles of their own concerns, the company gathered round. The tale she told was an old one. There was a magician called Gwydion, the son of a god, who made a beautiful woman out of flowers. Everyone knew it. On that day, in that place, its very familiarity was right and comforting. And when the woman proved unfaithful and plotted to kill her husband, the magician turned her into an owl, to live as a creature of the night forevermore.

"Which is why Blodeuwedd gave her name to owls, and we call them flower face," Branwen said.

Father Cennydd insisted on telling a story of his own God, where water at a wedding feast had been turned to wine. If there was magic to be had, it belonged to his God and no other.

"Where is he when we need him?" one of the soldiers shouted.

"He's here," Father Cennydd answered, certain of that one thing. "He was here earlier when we defeated the Gewisse; he's here now. His power is our power."

"Will you tell us another tale, Branwen?" the boy Gereint asked, his face full of wonder.

Not even Father Cenydd objected, which made Eleri Gwir wonder about him more than ever.

Usually quiet and reserved, her life appearing to be tucked under Siriol's broad eagle wing, Branwen was happy to oblige the company with a second story.

"In the middle of Lake Tegid," she started, "there lived the lord of Penllyn and his wife, whose name was Cerridwen. They had two children, one a beautiful girl, the other a boy, the ugliest boy in the whole world, and his name was Afagddu. Ugly he might be, Cerridwen thought, but I will make him clever and wise. She had in her possession the cauldron of wisdom and, with it, a potion of knowledge and inspiration that was to be boiled in the cauldron for a year and a day. As the seasons passed, so she added to the boiling mixture one herb after another, according to the phases of the moon. And she asked that a boy be sent to stir the magical potion, and that boy's name was Gwion."

Branwen stole a look in Eleri's direction as she said that name, and pressed on with the tale.

"Towards the end of the year," she continued, "three burning drops of the potion boiled over and fell on little Gwion's finger. In that moment of revelation, the boy received perfect knowledge of all things – past, present and future. He learned in this way that Cerridwen was planning to kill him as soon as his work was done."

"I like the next bit," the boy Gereint said.

"Gwion ran away and Cerridwen after him," Branwen said, her voice light with movement. "With the powers granted to him by the cauldron, the boy turned himself into a hare; Cerridwen became a greyhound. Diving into a river, he became a fish; whereupon she changed herself into an otter. When he flew into the air like a bird she became a hawk. He turned himself into a grain of winnowed wheat on the floor of a barn; Cerridwen became a black hen and, on finding Gwion, she swallowed him whole, gobbled him up."

Softly she spoke, and yet Branwen's voice was like a bell in the night air, bearing all the drama of the ancient tale.

Her story unfolded.

"In her own shape again, Cerridwen found that she was pregnant by Gwion and eventually a boy was born to her. She would have killed him except that he was too beautiful to die. Instead, she cast him into the sea in a leather bag, and in that way the child was fished out in a net by the magician Merddin. And Merddin named the child Taliesin. Even as a child, the boy could outwit any bard, so skilful was he with words. In time, Taliesin became the chief bard of the Island and the god of all song and riddling. It was Taliesin who explained to the puzzled gods the truth of their own creation. In song, the gods learned from him the true nature of human love and human hatred, unravelling the deepest mysteries of their own making."

There were murmurs of contement around the fire, as if the tale had the power to put things that had been dislodged back into their rightful place. Clouds passed across the face of the old moon. The forest was alive with sound.

The next morning, in a wet drizzle that threatened to linger all day, the survivors from the Saxon raid were taken by Riwalus to Caer Baddan, as miserable as they were grateful. The main company headed north, patrolling the ragged border that led up into the great valley of the Tafwys, ground that was shared now between Britons, the Gewisse and other foreign tribes from far over the water to the east.

In a few days they came late in the afternoon to an escarpment on which stood another ancient hillfort which went by the name of *Bryn Derwydd* – Oak-Seer Hill. From there, Caer Baddan was to the south, the fortified township of Caer Ceri where Condidan ruled to the north and east, Conmagil's Caer Gloui – the fortress of light – almost directly north, tucked into the marshy wooded lands where the River Hafren contemplated opening its mouth into a larger channel. This was it, the edge of their world, defined by a century and more of war.

"Another good stronghold," Eleri said.

Macsen agreed. His eyes followed the great Roman road that led north to Caer Ceri. He decided that was the way they should go. If there were to be any incursions they were likely to come from that direction, where the war bands of the foreigners, the Gewisse and their more northerly neighbours, were fighting for supremacy over the middle and the heart of the Island of Britain. A terrible melancholy struck him at that moment, one that seemed to hover not far from all his companions, leaping like fleas from one to another. "We're losing; we've come to the end," – that's what the girl had said back there in the oak wood.

"Damn and blast," he said under his breath, letting out the bad air from his brain.

He could have said more. He could have said that his own heart was breaking, like a piece of pottery tumbling to the ground. A memory came to him of his mother picking up the shattered remains of a jug from the tiled floor in their villa, his sister Julia crying because it was her fault, their mother angry, saying the jug had come from the other end of the old empire. "*We've come to the end.*" For Macsen and all the other Romans left behind in Britain that was how it felt. They would fight on, but for what? The empire was no more. "Damn and blast and damn again."

Eleri and Cerridwen had become friends. They were young. They had taken a small bite from an apple that ran on one side with the juices of excitement and adventure, on the other with the pus of violence, brutality, murder, loss and exile. They had been on the winning side. This time. They were young, not stupid. Cerridwen had seen how the destiny of an individual and a community could change like the skies over the mountains of Cambria – clear one minute, dark with foreboding the next. She feared that her friend Eirian would never be the same again, that she might even take her own life. She hated the thought and fought it off. She hated the thought that her life and the lives of her people were breaking. Perhaps they were already broken.

"There's work to do." Father Cennydd felt the melancholy of the moment as keenly as anyone. If they climbed this hill in a year's time, in five years, what would they see? Would it be their hill to climb? What name would it be known by? Like the others, pushing the idea down, he set his hardest face to the north and said: "Come on, let's get on with it." The time for thinking was over; doing and believing were what counted now. It was a time for faith.

Siriol added her voice to his. "Let's fly that banner of yours, priest. Let's see what your God is made of."

For the rest of the hazel month the company kept north of Caer Baddan, using the great Fosse Road as a marker. They moved cautiously east, testing the borders, and found little to report. It was true, the Gewisse were settling scores with foreigners of their own kind, securing their dominance of the lower reaches of the great valley and higher up into the heart of the Island. The company did their best to ready the people of the region. Father Cenydd went about his work, preaching more to the converted here than in the *cantref* of the Summer Land, where the old religion had held stubbornly on, in the shadow of the Great Wood and the Great Stone Circle. And Macsen went about his work, sorting out the men of fighting age, making sure they were equipped to go to war, to defend their nearest and dearest. There were a few women, too, those who showed skill with a bow. Mustering points were agreed upon. The air about him crackled with fearful anticipation.

Eleri, too, had work to do. Along with her father, she did her best to prepare those too young or too old, the sick and the infirm, for what might lie ahead. No one wanted to speak of defeat or its possibility. Yet, who could not? If they should lose the alternatives were stark enough – death for many, slavery for some, exile for others. Especially in the isolated settlements east of the great road, in the soft rising hills, the people were told to clear out as soon as winter was over and make for the relative safety of Caer Ceri. "Don't linger; get yourselves and your livestock out of here." The people listened to her father and they listened to Eleri, her bright fire hair and the authority of her voice commanding their attention.

As the blackberry month approached, with the harvest to see to and family matters to arrange, Macsen gave leave for most of the company to return home. With neither harvest nor family duties calling him, of the Red Cloaks, only Riwalus remained. Many duties and many people called to Arawn. Still, with the Summer Land in good hands, he elected to stay a while, to keep a paternal eye on Eleri and Cerridwen.The farrier Bryn was there, as was the boy Gereint – the cheerful hare who wouldn't, or couldn't, stop running.

Father Cenydd said he would stay with the company despite Macsen's not-too-subtle hints about the fine monk's house in Caer Baddan. There was even a bishop there to tell him what to do and how to think; and there were manuscripts waiting to be read by a truly educated man. Father Cenydd had learned Latin from his father, Gildas; but the truth was that he was not his father's equal in his command of the language. People assumed that he was his father's double, which was not the case in this as in other respects. Cenydd felt his own inadequacy deeply, too deeply. He knew it was the sin of pride. He did his best to lock it away in a secret chest. Besides, he found he liked the wandering, evangelising life that had come his way. If he could not be at home with his wife and son, he would be here, under the banner of the cross.

It was near Caer Baddan that the company dispersed. Siriol and Branwen had thought to stay in the town over winter. But when it came time to say their farewells a messenger arrived from Ffernfael. Macsen had new orders – and it turned out that Siriol and Branwen were integral to those orders.

# Part Two

## AD 576

## "The Blackberry Month"

# Chapter Eleven

When Eleri Gwir awoke her head was heavy from sleep and busy with half-remembered dreams. People said that whatever dream you had on *Ynys Wydr* – the Glass Island – was sure to come true. It was a place of prophecy, a spiralling island where the spirits of the dead went from this life to the next. Some people said that the one they called Arthur, the Bear of the Island, was buried here. According to Eleri's father it was a lot of rubbish. "He died a long way from here, fighting against the Franks in the land across the Sea of Gaul. That's what I was told by my father and he said he'd met this man, when he was a boy not much older than Gereint – my father that is, not the one they call Arthur."

At any rate Eleri hadn't dreamed of Arthur or of anything particularly momentous or even clearly defined. She'd been running and someone had been with her, a man she thought, although it was hard to be sure because her companion wore a horned mask. They were running for hours, it seemed, through doors, into closed rooms, over Cae Fawr near their village. It was a muddle of images. If Mared of the Silver Wheel had been around Eleri might have asked her what it all meant. On the other hand, did she really want to know what all this running was about? Was she running from herself, from her old life, from the Gewisse? At least she didn't need Mared to tell her that the long series of dreams had left her feeling rough and exhausted, as if she'd drank a jug of mead and more.

She looked at Macsen, still asleep by her side. Was this what she wanted? He was beautiful and everything a man should be; he was her own creature of the sea, washed pale and golden, brought to her on the big tides of the Hafren. The sex they had was as strong as they were themselves, physically powerful and satisfying. Like wrestling with a sea serpent, she thought to herself as she dressed. It was good, overwhelming in a way; a drowning of the heart and soul. She had fallen for him; she was falling; the maid and the woman in her together.

But was that what she wanted? When Macsen stirred and called her over to him, the answer was "yes". The shift she'd put on to cover her nakedness was at her feet on the earth floor. She was again ready to devour and to be devoured; to make and to be made.

There was someone calling. Slowly, reluctantly, she uncoiled the sea serpent from around her body and went out into the morning, the taste of their lovemaking on her skin.

They had come to Ynys Wydr on Ffernfael's orders. In company with Eleri and Macsen was Eleri's father, Arawn. Riwalus and Cerridwen were also there, along with the she-warriors, Siriol and Branwen. Running in rings and other shapes around them was the boy Gereint, the Little Hare, to the amusement of Bryn, who saw to the horses with as much regard as if they were made from his own seed. With them and yet apart, casting a separate and longer shadow, was Father Cenydd, a warrior for his faith.

For Eleri it was her first time in this curious place, where land and water come and go like a ritual exchanging of gifts between kings of equal majesty. The company had come down into the wetlands to find there a curious light, the air shimmering with imaginings. Leaving their horses in Bryn's care on higher ground, they had found their way through the waterlogged country to the relative dry land that was the tor of Ynys Wydr. All about them was a shifting landscape, jewel-like in the sunshine, a wet diamond carpet through which ran a few wooden pathways of uncertain tenor, dipping down in places under the surface of the water.

Like Eleri, Cerridwen was new to Ynys Wydr. For the first hour she'd just stared out at the curious air, amazed, discovering suddenly what appeared to be long-concealed visionary powers. It felt to her like the middle of the world, the tor the earth's navel, the pathways running like birth cords through the watery mass. How odd. It was like finding your true mother at the very moment of your own birth.

Cerridwen had thought of wintering with Siriol and Branwen in Caer Baddan, until plans were changed and they found themselves on the Glass Island, sailing on a sea of transient spirits. Odd wasn't the word for it.

Eleri found her looking out across the watery plain. They stared out together, both in awe of the place.

"My father wants me," Eleri told Cerridwen. "And you too, I think."

"Is he going to speak sternly to us?" Cerridwen asked, not too seriously.

"It could be anything. This place is so strange I don't know what to expect next."

Eleri hadn't expected Ynys Wydr to make her feel like she did – like what exactly? A neophyte perhaps waiting to be inducted into the mysteries of a secret cult? Or was it a sacrificial victim? Or was it like a girl taken out of bondage and released into the wilds of her own imagination for the first time in her life? Was that the story of her dream?

"Come on," she said to Cerridwen. "I bet you haven't eaten yet."

"I'm coming."

Ynys Wydr held another surprise for Eleri. Questioning and direct as she was, she hadn't investigated Siriol – how she had come to live this life of soldiering, or where she came from. In this one case Eleri was content to assume that the woman Siriol had emerged fully grown into the world, from a Druid's egg, from the world that had already passed from them. She was a thing apart, a living mystery, something belonging entirely to the past yet existing completely and intensely in the here and now. It hadn't occurred to Eleri that Siriol might have parents living somewhere in the world, still less that she had a man of her own, so to speak.

The only other person she'd met who belonged equally to a category of life all of their own was the bard Cynan. Eleri had seen him at the Great Circle, in the oak month, at the New Year. The idea that he had a home to go to seemed too bizarre to contemplate. He appeared at certain times and left to appear again when he was needed. Who would have thought that he, too, was a chief of a kind, admittedly of the people of the Water Land, a people who would only acknowledge the authority of someone with more than one foot in the next world. They were not a people to be ruled as others were; their true lord was the water itself, its tides and moods. Of where else but Ynys Wydr could the bard Cynan be chief?

When they had first arrived at the palisade at the tor's height and entered the bare hall to find Cynan seated, welcoming them in, Eleri had been more than surprised, shocked rather. Her father Arawn had turned to her, his dancing eyes telling her that he had kept this hidden from her, as something to show her how unexpected the world could be. But then, when Cynan and Siriol had embraced, not as friends exactly and certainly not as brother and sister, she had been shocked beyond belief. Her father's face had by this time creased with smiling. Laughing, trying not to, he had embraced his daughter and said into her ear: "You don't know everything, Eleri Gwir."

Cynan's hall was small and poor, bare of hangings, stripped down like the bard's words.

"Here you are," Arawn said, seeing the girls enter.

By his standards he was very formal now, obviously respectful of Cynan's knowledge and status. Poor though his hall was, the bard was rich in name and reputation.

"Cynan would speak with you," Arawn said to the girls. "He would speak with the Truth Speaker and with the Dragon Maiden."

*Ferch y Ddraig* was what the company had named Cerridwen, more in reference to her fire-breathing soul than either her fire-god hair or the Saxon arm ring she now wore around her neck. She said she was a woman, but for every man in the company she was their maiden charm-bearer. If she kept to herself and to the other women that was her business; she had earned the right to choose or not to choose as the case might be. The men of the company were ordinary enough, with the usual fault lines running through their characters; for Cerridwen those lines were redrawn; for the Dragon Maiden an exception was made. Since the day she had walked naked toward the Gewisse camp she had embodied for the company the struggle that was unfolding between two peoples and two ways of living, the yielding curving lines of one and the harsh and ponderous straight marks of the other.

"Come closer; let me see you," Cynan said to the girls. "I would speak with the most renowned women of the Island of Britain."

"I don't know about that!" Eleri blurted out, forgetting to be nervous.

Cynan laughed.

If he was Siriol's man in some guise or other he was an odd choice; on the small side and a bit old, nothing much to look at, with only his voice marking him out as special in some way. When Eleri had met him at the Great Circle it had been in a crowded frenzy and it was his voice that had declared his identity, a bell across dark water, a guide to the journeying soul, clear and true. Now he used that same voice to laugh, merry as a child. When Eleri asked: "Are you really Siriol's man?" he laughed louder still, tears in his eyes.

"Where did you get her from?" Cynan asked Arawn.

"I think her mother had something to do with it," Arawn responded, any pretence at formality dropping away.

"Excellent!" the bard said. "And this is the maid," he added, turning to Cerridwen. "I know," he said before she had a chance to say it. "You're a woman."

He didn't laugh so much at this as cackle. Seeing Cerridwen fixing him with her hot eyes, the blood coming to a boil in her heart, Cynan retrieved his equilibrium enough to say: "Cerridwen, your name is honoured among those of my kind; the bards of the Island are yours to command. As for the Dragon Maiden, she too is honoured by all those who would resist the spread of the foreign folk who have come among us. I'm pleased that you're here, in Ynys Wydr; and Eleri Gwir too, the healer and the archer; welcome to you both."

# Chapter Twelve

Ffernfael had wanted them to come on this detour to Ynys Wydr. It was not that he expected the men of the Water Land to offer him military assistance of a significant kind. They were too idiosyncratic to form part of a regular cohort of troops. Some would join him of their own accord, archers with the long, curving bows they used to bring down water birds, but not enough probably to make a real difference against the disciplined Gewisse. No, that wasn't it. It wasn't even that Ffernfael had expectations of finding immortality in the words that Cynan would write of him. Unlike other chieftains and the like, petty and otherwise, the high chieftain didn't appear to see himself in an heroic light. The last thing he wanted was a verse celebrating an honourable defeat; he wanted only to win and if anyone, Cynan or some other scribbler, cared to set that to music – all well and good. In Ffernfael's experience victories had a way of taking care of themselves.

So that wasn't it either.

The reason for the detour had to do with religion. Ffernfael was determined to ride under the one banner of the cross. What he didn't want was for the dissenters to rally to Cynan and for that voice to speak on behalf of division instead of unity. Cynan could believe what he liked, as far as Ffernfael was concerned; but for the time being at least he was not to act or speak on behalf of that belief. To Ffernfael, the prospect of Father Cenydd persuading the bard to this course of action was something like a recipe for disaster; put any two men of religion in the same room for an hour and sure enough, be they of the same or different faiths, they were certain to come to blows; men who lived by words, Ffernfael found, were apt to fight over them. "Useless bastards," he called them, although that didn't stop him from trying to make use of the men of faith now. The trick, he thought, was to pick the right horses for the race of life and death that was upon them all.

The horse he'd backed for this particular race was Siriol. She disliked the new religion of sin as much as anyone; she'd spoken out at Caer Baddan; she'd said a lot more besides, calling the Christ God a leech on the old faith, a beggar and a thief. But if Siriol disliked Christianity, she positively hated the Gewisse. And she was smart, sharp as a knife. If anyone understood the need for unity at this hour it was Siriol. She could be relied upon to set aside her dislike of one thing for the sake of her hatred of another. She would counsel Cynan, leading him in the direction Ffernfael wanted him to go.

In his way Ffernfael knew as much about Siriol as she knew herself. She had come to Ynys Wydr as a girl, a maid of seven summers. That had been thirty and more years ago. Her father Melvas had fallen in battle against the Gewisse, a chieftain and more, a warrior worthy of the bards; her mother Fionn had been of the royal house of the people of the far west of the Island, the Kernow, a woman known throughout the Island for her beauty. After the battle she had been taken captive by the king of the Gewisse, a man called Cynric, the father of Ceawlin. It seemed, so the stories of the spies had it, that she was too beautiful and that, for her beauty, she had been poisoned by Cynric's jealous wife. But not, it was said, before she bore him a son, a half-brother to Siriol. As for Siriol, she had been brought west, to safety in Cynan's hall. Her looks, it must be said, favoured her father's bloodline, dark and untamed – *Siriol Wyllt* – Siriol the Wild.

Twenty years her senior, Cynan had formed an attachment to the rough-and-tumble girl, and she to him in her fashion. "He's as good as any man I've met," she'd say. "Better than most." He was kind; and she knew what she was to him. In time, Siriol had sought him out and gone to his bed, without ceremony, with not a syllable spoken. Some nights she would lie with him, some not. She was his wounded bird; he was her thought fox, his mind always on the scent of an idea or a rhyme. That was how it was until Siriol, every bit her father's daughter, left Cynan's hall, the stairway into life in death, to seek revenge on the Gewisse, to bring death in this world to her enemies.

On the company's arrival at Ynys Wydr, they'd embraced, the twinkling bard and the tall, powerful woman, reunited after many years. But Siriol hadn't gone to Cynan's bed that night; he hadn't expected it. She and Branwen had made their own arrangements, the people of Ynys Wydr more than happy to find accommodation for the Lady Siriol. Comfortable, too comfortable perhaps, it was late in the morning by the time Siriol made her entry into the hall.

They were waiting for them, Cynan and his seer, a woman of about twenty summers whose name was *Awen Ysbryd* – Spirit Muse – a slight thing, raven dark, light enough to take flight on the next breeze. And Mascen was in the hall, eating, barely listening, his appetite seeming to increase with every day he was with Eleri Gwir – something Siriol and Branwen had remarked upon, telling him he was a growing boy in more ways than one. For her part, Branwen had said she'd leave them to it, her patience for politics having worn out long since. But Arawn and Riwalus were present, as were Eleri and Cerridwen, the last two at Cynan's special invitation. The boy Gereint was running about the place, but in his case that signified more of a permanent state of being than any particular connection to the proceedings at hand. And of course Father Cenydd was there, wearing his quarrelsome face, ready to take on the world.

"This place," he started, "is a disgrace."

This made Cynan laugh. Eleri had never realised before just how prone he was to laughing.

"Well it is," Cenydd continued crossly, diving recklessly in to the deepest water. "Not a church in sight, not a single convert to our Lord; all of you strangers to the light of the one true God; nothing but a lot of dangerous superstition. This woman, this girl," he said, pointing at Awen, stumbling over his words in his disgust. "This witch; this work of the Devil."

Cynan said nothing in response, seeming to enjoy the outburst. Looking over at Siriol, he indicated that it was up to her to bring the priest under control. The girl Awen cawed like a crow, in mockery of the evangelist of the crucified God.

Not one to suffer fools gladly or for long, Siriol reprimanded Father Cenydd, telling him to remember that they were guests in Cynan's hall and to remember too the purpose of their visit to the Lord of Ynys Wydr.

Then Cynan added his own mischievous contribution, asking the priest why his church showed the sun on its cross, the face of Belin he called it, the light of the world.

"Don't answer that," Siriol ordered the priest. "We'll be here all day arguing about a lot of silliness."

"Your church borrows and steals like a starving beggar," Cynan added, warming to his text. "Your God is a piggy-back god, riding on the shoulders of the old ones, owning nothing of his own except a soppy tale of love that none of you truly believe in."

"Cynan…" Siriol said sternly.

"Well, if I am to be usurped I might as well have my say," Cynan said. "Who else will speak for the gods of our people? Not you, Siriol, it seems."

In his beautiful voice, its many chambers, there was anger and sadness, and with them something of the same resignation Eleri had heard in Mared of the Silver Wheel when she consented to be baptised. They spoke for a world that was already gone, a world that would exist now only in the cracks and gaps of the new faith, in the long memories of the everyday lives of the common people. Cynan was fighting a battle he had already lost.

It was Awen who spoke up, bird-like, her black eyes as sharp and piercing as a crow's. "We won't speak *for* you, if that is what you're asking; we won't speak for the nailed one and his cause." She paused, like a thrush hovering over a worm it was about to stab, certain of its quarry; then looking up, its head tilted to the sun, thinking of something else. "Nor will we speak against you. We know what Ffernfael wants of us."

That was all she said.

Cynan nodded his assent.

"Then I may preach the word of God to these people of the Water Land," Father Cenydd said, not insensible to the hurt his words would give at that delicate moment of flight and departure. It couldn't be helped. His mission was to prosecute the militant cause of the one faith irrespective of the bruises his words would leave on human sensitivities.

Seeing the arrogance in that thin face, Eleri reverted to her first impressions of the priest.

"Fat lot of good it will do you," Siriol answered. She'd played her part in Ffernfael's political game; she would do no more.

Into Arawn's ear Riwalus whispered: "I'm in love." It was nothing but the plain truth. The sight and sound of Awen Ysbryd, her heron legs, her blackbird voice, had turned the soldier's hard bones to lard and jelly.

# Chapter Thirteen

For two weeks and more, through the ripe middle of the blackberry month, they stayed in the Water Land. Father Cenydd went his own way, doing God's work as he called it. Macsen, Eleri and Cerridwen went about together, a bond forming between them; the boy Gereint would tag along. Some days Awen joined them, glad of the company of those her own age and glad to put off her seer's mantle for a time. She seemed almost ordinary until one or other of them caught a glance from those clever bird eyes. The distance between her and the others was never less than the wingspan of a crane, the bird of the wheel of Belin; except that is for Gereint, who formed his own bond with Awen; they would always sit in the same boat, her shapely bare feet in his lap, this being the only time Gereint was known to sit still, under the spell of the seer girl.

With the local people as guides, they explored the marshlands in coracles and flat-bottomed boats, discovering settlements hidden deep in the reeds of the fens; the whole lives of these places seemed to rest on fish and water birds. The people they met were watchful of strangers, exchanging few words and sharing what little fresh water they had with understandable reluctance. They were all small and underfed; when Eleri and Cerridwen stood amongst the girls of their own age they were like creatures from another species.

In Awen's case the people of the Water Land were fearful and curious. The women would approach her first, asking for charms against unwanted children, wanting to know if they would die in childbirth or of hunger or of war. "Tell us what you see," they'd insist. "Not war; not here," Awen would reply. "But die you will, and you don't need me to tell you that." Cautiously, the men would ask her for weather spells and for spells to keep them from the joint pains they suffered and a thousand other ailments. The children, ragged, wild, would stare and point. "Are you her creature?" they asked Gereint, some touching him to make sure he was flesh and blood. "No," he'd answer. He didn't know what else to say. He found them scary, weird, belonging more to nature than to human nature.

News would reach them from Ffernfael. Preparations were going well; the alliance with the Irish brothers was holding; the Saxons were busy murdering Saxons, which had to be a good thing. Ffernfael was pleased to learn that they stayed in the Water Land, making sure that Cynan kept his word. Like all political leaders, Ffernfael relied on trust and trusted no one. He thanked Siriol for her help, which had cemented her loyalty to his particular cause. He inquired about Father Cenydd, whether he was getting anywhere with the heathens of the fens. It wasn't hard to imagine the discreet smile forming on Ffernfael's full lips.

One day, Eleri and the others travelled as far as the coast of the Channel of the Hafren, beyond where the great river emptied into the sea. Macsen had seen it all before and Awen didn't count when it came to such things. For Eleri, however, as for Cerridwen and Gereint, it was new and exciting, to be this close to the big water of the Channel and to look out on its islands and beyond to the rocky coastline of Gwent. They were at the mouth of the Pilgrim River – *Afon Pererin* – which looked friendly enough but was said by their guide to harbour strong and dangerous currents. "And a whirlpool too," they were told. A boatman who knew the river well offered to take them across to the sand spit that fingered farther out into the channel. "We'll camp the night out there," Macsen decided. To their guide he said: "Let them know will you in Ynys Wydr; we'll return tomorrow."

They went exploring. By this time of year, the weather was on the turn. Out on the sand spit they felt a wind blow that rattled their bones. Finding a sheltered spot under a sand hill, secured in place by the hardy marram grass, they settled down to watch the big gulls rise and dip, to follow the corrugated patterns in the sandy beach and to observe the white-capped sea, stirred by the wind yet patiently waiting its time to turn landwards.

Hungry and thirsty, salt in their clothes and hair, sand filling their shoes, eventually they returned to the hollow of a makeshift shelter the boatman and his woman had made – the boat turned on its side for a windbreak, oars planted in the sand for posts, a pelt of seal skin making a roof. Glad of the hospitality, as freely given as a king's, the travellers shared the boatman's meagre food, fish inevitably, and the rough drink the woman served them, which had a powerful effect.

"What is this stuff?" Cerridwen asked.

"Seaweed," the man replied. "Boiled, fermented."

"Now that's evil," Macsen said. "If Father Cenydd was here..."

"Which he isn't," Eleri chimed in. "Thankfully."

"...but if he was here," Macsen continued, his mood lighter than ever.

"If he was he'd be forgetting every vow he ever made," Cerridwen said, laughing.

"That wouldn't take much," Eleri said. "Although to be fair he does seem to be fond of his family."

"Since when is Eleri Gwir fair to priests?" Macsen asked teasingly.

"Since my second drink of this wicked stuff," she answered, holding up her surprisingly shapely wooden cup.

"At least his family's safe enough," Macsen said soberly. "Up there in the kingdom of the Clyde."

"Where?" the boatman asked.

He'd only ever known the Water Land and only then this obscure coastal region that he called home. He didn't care for the people of the interior of the fens, whom he referred to as "them others". He'd heard of Ynys Wydr but that was about it. The pilgrims who had come, generation after generation, to the river, on their way to Ynys Wydr and then beyond to the Great Circle, were no more. Such things were in the past, in the days of the boatman's ancestors. In these times, with Irish pirates prowling the Channel, with the world of faith turning upside down, there was no one to bring him news of the wider world.

"It's north," Macsen said. "A long way from here; where the wall stands and beyond that again."

It was obvious that the boatman had never heard of the wall, let alone of anything beyond it. Like all the people of the Water Land he was small and sturdy, his face and hands browned by wind and sun. Eleri couldn't guess his age or that of the woman who poured out the heady drink from a seal skin pouch. The woman, she noticed, couldn't take her eyes off the Gewisse arm ring that now adorned Cerridwen's neck.

Cerridwen saw it too. It occurred to her that they might be robbed and murdered in this desperate place. Was that why these people were so liberal with their liquor?

Sober as a maid, quick as mercury, Awen said to Cerridwen: "She just wants to touch it. Would you mind?"

Cerridwen let the woman take the precious metal in her hands. She looked spellbound at it, felt it all over with her rough, fish-smelling fingers, a smile of wonder on her face. Holding it up to the moonlight, the woman studied its dragon faces. With great care, she handed the necklace back to Cerridwen.

"Thank you, lady," she said.

Cerridwen would have contradicted her, explaining that she was no more a lady than the boatman's woman, except that Macsen said: "It's the lady's pleasure."

"Yes," Cerridwen said. "It is."

From under his sleeve Macsen pulled out an arm ring of pure silver and handed it to the woman. "It's yours," he said. "In payment for your hospitality."

"Oh, no!" the woman said. "It's too good; what would I do with it?"

"Do you have children?" Eleri asked.

"They're all dead," the woman answered. "The one that wasn't right we gave into Belin's care." Then looking at the arm ring, she said: "There's no one to inherit such a thing, unless it's the fish."

She wouldn't take it.

The boatman apologised to Macsen, who said there was no need. He might have taken offence at the rejection; nine times out of ten he would have done exactly that. Today, he yielded to his better nature. Eleri found that here, in the wilderness of sand and water, the edge to Macsen's character was made smooth; owing no doubt to the effects of the evil brew, but also she liked to think because he was in his true element here, a creature of the sea returning to its place of birth, to its mother and its father.

"Will you take a story in payment?" Awen asked.

"Gladly," the boatman said, relieved to be off the hook.

Making herself comfortable, her bare feet resting in Gereint's lap, the seer of Ynys Wydr told her tale. It was about a hare.

"That's me," Gereint said.

"This is another hare," Awen corrected him.

She told the story of the queen who went to war against the Romans. This queen, Awen said, rode to war in a chariot pulled by four pure white stallions and in her arms she held a royal hare, a jewelled band around its neck from which ran a cord of the finest Cambrian gold.

"We say that to eat a hare is to eat one's mother," Awen said. "We would as soon starve."

Her voice carried up into the night sky, the big moon and the endless, indifferent firmament. She said that when the first foreigners, the Romans, came to the Island, the true nature of the hare was known to the learned ones; the hare was worshipped then for its powers of quickness and fertility, for the fact that it procreates without care in the open, for anyone to see, looking up in thanksgiving at the gods. In those times the hare was one of the royal creatures, taken into the halls of the great ones of the Island.

Her story came around in time to the chariot queen, the copper-haired champion of her people. She went into battle against the legions, preferring this to subjugation. Many thousands of warriors, naked for war, painted, the fury surging through them, were with her. Belin himself was there in the shape of an eagle, looking down on the charging, rushing chariots as they went headlong into the Roman ranks. It was in this form that he saw her loose the band from around the hare's neck, stroking its soft fur, speaking into its pointed ears. He heard the queen say: "Go now, go free; carry my spirit through their ranks; show them to be foolish, show them to be cowards." And Belin saw her let loose her grip on the hare, dropping it down, there amongst the scything wheels of the rushing chariots, placing the hare in the hands of the gods, trusting it into their care.

Gereint couldn't help himself. "What happened to it?" he asked.

"The hare shot through the wall of shields. It ran everywhere about, causing confusion, tickling with its fur the bare legs of the soldiers, running up to their thighs, its big teeth biting. When the queen's chariot crashed into the wall of shields the hare dug its teeth into the sandaled foot of a legionary in the front ranks, making him hop about, causing a weak point for the queen's chariot to smash into."

As she told the story Awen's black eyes dropped into the night darkness, going on a journey of their own.

"The hare lived," she said, her eyes returning from deep space to focus on Gereint. "It ran through row after row of legionaries, right through to the very top of the hill where the pompous Roman general sat on his big horse. There the hare made the horse jump, throwing its rider, who went tumbling down the hillside. Only then did the hare stop running, turning to look over the devastation of the battlefield."

"The queen?" Gereint asked.

"If you look long and deep enough into the night sky," Awen answered, "you'll see that she lives as a star, one of Belin's night brides, looking out for fast and curious boys when they're drinking strong liquor, folding them in her arms."

She laughed; something none of them had seen or heard before. Awen laughed into the hard face of fate.

Under the big sky they slept the sleep of the dead; Cerridwen folded into Eleri and Macsen; Awen with a protective arm around Gereint; the boatman and the woman companionable, side by side in the hollow of their makeshift shelter; fate in the shape of a flower-faced owl keeping a wakeful eye on them all.

# Chapter Fourteen

They put off leaving Ynys Wydr until it couldn't be put off any longer. They were expected elsewhere.

Only Father Cenydd was eager to leave. Even he had to admit that there was nothing for him here; nothing but heathens bound for the fires of hell. Still, he insisted on planting a cross on top of the tor, a beacon of light in a dark place, he called it.

"Do what you like," Cynan told him, knowing full well that other uses would be found for the wood as soon as the priest was out of sight.

"If you tear it down, you tear up your promise to Ffernfael," Cenydd warned the bard.

"Stuff and nonsense," Cynan replied. "D'you think I'd waste my time with the thing when every man, woman and child over six summers in the Water Land can't wait to get their hands on it for firewood?"

The priest was disgusted and genuinely shocked. Standing on the tor's top, visible to the wide heavens, he expected his God to strike the bard down.

Instead, he had to be content to say: "Your time is over, bard; I thank you for your hospitality but I pity you and despise you for your wicked, wilful ignorance."

"Thank you very much," Cynan responded, perfectly affably. "We've enjoyed having you too." He was chuckling again. "You've got to laugh," he said to Awen as the priest headed down the tor, all fire and brimstone.

"It's either that or cry." Tired, hating to admit it, such was the weary summation of a lifetime's study and contemplation.

For the others their leave-taking was long or brief depending on how they preferred to deal with such things. It wasn't only the boy Gereint who had fallen under Awen's spell. Old enough to know better, Riwalus too hated leaving her. His heart was pulled this way and that, in directions and down to depths it had never gone before.

"Goodbye," he said to her, the soldier in him holding back the man; a romantic masquerading as a realist, he was brief and to the point, never expecting them to meet again.

"Goodbye, Riwalus," Awen said, acknowledging the truth of it and knowing all that it meant to the warrior. "I won't deceive you by saying we'll meet in another place; I don't know."

Gereint might have stayed at Ynys Wydr. His leaving was painful to him. Young as he was, he had that feeling that he wanted to die, so deep was his attachment to the place and its people.

"I'll go," he said, for reasons he didn't understand.

"My sweet hare, my love – *sgwarnog, anwylyd,*" Awen said to him. "Run back to me; I'll look out for you."

At the last Siriol embraced Cynan. "Old man," she said fondly, seeing the tears on his cheeks.

"Never forget who we are," Cynan said.

"As if I would; as if I could," Siriol replied.

Over the patchwork of wooden pathways they went, leaving Ynys Wydr behind, making their way to the higher ground where their horses had been stabled. There they found Bryn, fatter than they remembered him. He cuffed Gereint round the ear, not for any particular reason other than he was pleased to see him.

Arawn laughed. Eleri and Cerridwen took it upon themselves to chase the boy around the yard, driving away any bad spirits that might have been lurking in the watery land.

"Mount up," Macsen ordered, instantly older again, in charge and back on course.

*

Returning to the great Roman Fosse Road, they made their way south, joined now by ten Red Cloaks, Macsen's hand-picked men. Only a small company, they found it hard enough to find shelter and food at night, their bodies fighting cold and hunger. They asked the people they met for news. A few stragglers from the east said they'd come into this region over twelve months back, when the Saxons were biting into the south of the Island.

"Will you stay?" Macsen asked them. "Will you stay to fight for this land?"

Even as he asked the question he knew the answer to it. These people were not warriors. A number of them were young and sturdy; given the chance, some of them would throw in their lot with Ffernfael. Many more of them wouldn't. Instead, they'd do their best to avoid the enemy by going deeper west into the kingdom of Dyfneint or, if they were lucky, over the sea to the other Britain.

"I serve Ffernfael at Caer Baddan," he told the stragglers and anyone else that cared to listen. "He has need of men, those who would stand and fight. Go to him there; he'll provide you with shelter and the arms to resist the Gewisse."

Some days he thought he was getting through to these people; other days he felt his urgings to be about as helpful as Father Cenydd's preaching in the Water Land. The ignorance he found, wilful and otherwise, made Macsen mad with frustration. Yet curiously, at some deeper level, he was resigned to his lot. He would shrug his big shoulders and grow thoughtful. Weighing the balance of destiny in his mind, Macsen knew that, win or lose, whichever way the weight should fall, he at least was certain of the part he must play.

To the south and east lay the fortress of Maes-y-Gaer, the place from where the Red Cloaks had journeyed on that first morning. Its rogue lord had refused to come to the aid of his fellow Britons, shunning Macsen and warning Father Cenydd to lay off his meddling. More than that, he was a danger and a menace, sending his horsemen out to terrorise the land about, attacking his own people. Secure in his ancient hill fort he felt safe to do as he liked, turning the place into a refuge for any desperate men that chose to join him, Britons, Irish pirates, Saxons even, oultawed from their own people.

"Watch out for riders," Macsen warned again, on edge, his calm resolve giving way to niggling anger and frustration. The war horse, Gwalchwen, shifted under him, sensing his unease. Man and horse scanned the green country that was before them, the horse inclined to like what he saw, the man not so sure. The Great Wood was close at hand, from where a war band might emerge without warning. A frown settled on Macsen's face.

His frame of mind wasn't helped by the incessant rain that started to fall on the second day. The company pressed on, drying out overnight if they were lucky, getting soaked again within minutes the following day. Drenched, they came to Caer Uisc in the south of the Island. They had come to Dyfneint, to meet with the king of the people who called themselves the Dumnonii, whose lands stretched far into Kernow in the west, where the feet of the Island rested in the lap of the great ocean. Of the company only Riwalus had travelled this way before and then only briefly and years ago, as a messenger for Ffernfael, who was forever sending messages to the Dumnonii. Invariably, it was the same message, one that could be reduced to the single word, "help". It was a word with which Ffernfael's present envoys to Caer Uisc were only too well acquainted.

In its own prosaic way Caer Uisc was as curious as Ynys Wydr. The town was Roman of course, a military camp in origin and purpose. The Romans had built the camp but they had left the administration of the wider region largely in the hands of the kings of the Dumnonii. As long as order was kept and as long as the tin and other minerals that were mined in the country were provided in sufficient quantity, the Romans were content to leave this westerly edge of the Island to its own devices, more or less.

As for Caer Uisc itself, it had been an important military base, the key to Roman power in the region. Nonetheless, the strength of the imperial military presence had varied over the centuries, depending on the politics of the day and the need for troops in those parts of the Island that were yet to be brought under Roman rule. In time the legion departed to more troublesome regions, into Cambria where the tribes were quarrelsome and inclined to resist civilisation. In Caer Uisc only a core of veterans remained; the camp diminished and with it the town declined. Only the walls had been kept in place. Macsen could see through the downpour that they were still in remarkably good shape. Why, he wondered? Had they been rebuilt in later years to guard against pirates, Irish or Saxon? He couldn't say. Probably they'd just been built to the usual high standards in the first place and were more-or-less indestructible.

The curious thing about Caer Uisc was that it was largely uninhabited, except for dogs and for a fishing and boat-building settlement down at the river edge, in the low-lying ground that was presently in danger of flooding. For the rest the town was abandoned. Where there had been a forum and a basilica, even a small bath house, now there was crumbling and decay, far worse than at Caer Baddan, the timber and stone evidently pilfered for other uses. Nothing worked anymore. It never would again. It might have been like this before the Romans departed, or it might have fallen gradually into decay. Again, Macsen couldn't say. Probably a bit of both, he thought.

But the really curious thing was that the camp of the King of Dyfneint was right there, outside the town walls. A simple timber hall had been built, surrounded by a plethora of daub and wattle huts. Macsen, Arawn and the others looked from this muddle of buildings to the walls the Romans had left behind. The contrast was too glaring and too painful to think about. The miserable weather was no help either.

"Unbelievable," was all Macsen said; there was no need to elaborate.

In the late afternoon, spear points down to indicate they came in peace, the company entered the encampment of the King of the Dumnonii. Wet and disgruntled, rain bouncing off their leather caps, the people of the camp stopped to take a look at the strangers. The company's exotic female warriors were of great interest. Off-colour remarks were made along the lines that not all the spear points hereabouts were pointing downwards. Macsen held his temper with help from Eleri, who made a face in his direction.

The king's hall was built on the highest point to the north of the town walls. From there the river was clearly visible, a torrent racing south, as unstoppable as an arrow in flight, or a fool's tongue. Farther out was a stretch of white-capped water, where the river flowed in a wide channel out to the Sea of Gaul. Beyond that again and a long way beyond human sight was Llydaw, the other Britain.

The only other structure of any size in the encampment was a Christian church, made of wood and thatch, its cross with its sun face taking precedence over all else. Evidently, the Romans had taken their knowledge of hydraulics and engineering with them, but left their curious faith behind.

"You're going to like it here," Macsen told Father Cenydd.

The priest didn't seem so sure.

"Why not?" Macsen asked, sensing the priest's lack of enthusiasm.

"History," he answered.

"Words, I suppose," Macsen said. "More trouble than a Gewisse war band."

"Something like that."

# Chapter Fifteen

The king's name was Erbin, the son of Gwynnan; he was the grandson of Constantine who had been the King of Dyfneint in the days of Gildas, that scourge of British tyrants and their lax and fractious ways.

"My father wrote harshly of the king's grandfather," Father Cenydd explained to the company. "Harshly but fairly," he added, sounding almost apologetic.

"You might have told us sooner," Arawn said.

"But didn't Ffernfael insist on you joining us?" Riwalus asked.

"He didn't stand in my way."

"We don't have to tell the king that you're the son of this Gildas," Macsen suggested. "You could be just any soul-bothering priest from the north."

"What did your father say exactly, about the king's grandfather?" Eleri asked, her inquiring mind at work.

For the first time since they'd known him Father Cenydd hesitated.

"Well," he said slowly, "it was something along the lines that King Constantine of the Dumnonii was a tyrannical whelp born of the unclean lioness of this part of the world."

A burst of laughter came from the company. "Oh well, that's all right then," Macsen said ironically. "I don't suppose this new king is one to bear a grudge, priest, so you're perfectly safe on that score."

"Why didn't Ffernfael prevent you from joining us?" Eleri asked the priest. "Surely he would have known this history."

"The high chief has a sense of humour," Father Cenydd suggested. "Besides, he may want to make the present king feel sufficiently uncomfortable to goad him into doing something."

"King Erbin will fear that you may write the same of him as your father wrote of Constantine," Eleri said, "and that's how his name will be known forevermore, no matter what his fawning bards may say about him."

"You're very perceptive, Eleri Gwir," the priest acknowledged.

"Of course, you'll only be able to blacken his name if he lets you live," Macsen pointed out.

"I go where I'm needed, soldier," the priest replied, stoical as ever.

"It should make for an interesting audience at any rate," Riwalus said.

They were waiting. Their horses had been led away, Bryn and Gereint with them. They were waiting for news that the king would see them. The longer they waited the more inclined were they to agree with Gildas' estimation of the Dumnonii. The words uncooperative and inhospitable came to mind. Macsen started stomping about, in danger of letting impatience get the better of him.

All the same, the camp they had passed through had impressed them more than they'd expected. It was orderly enough and, if not exactly bustling with activity on that rain-soaked day, it appeared to be provisioned with all the necessary trades and practices. Clearly, the king's authority meant something here. He ruled in more than name only.

Eventually the door to the main hall opened and they were invited in – Macsen, Riwalus, Arawn and Father Cenydd. Of the women, only Branwen joined them. The rest were told to wait.

Like Siriol, Branwen had her own story to tell; but unlike Father Cenydd's latest revelation this was already known to Macsen and the others. Beautiful as she was, tall, raven-dark, and skilled in the telling of the old tales, Branwen rarely went out of her way to seek the company of others, preferring to keep largely to herself, within Siriol's orbit. At times she joined with Eleri and Cerridwen. Even then she was hardly forthcoming. She would go hunting. Occasionally she would choose a man to lie with. "Odd bird, that one," was what the Red Cloaks said of her. So she was, if odd meant self-contained and self-reliant to a degree unexpected in a woman. She was here now because Ffernfael had insisted on her coming. Like Siriol at Ynys Wydr, Branwen was expected to play her part.

Ffernfael had explained it to Macsen.

"She's the king's niece," he'd said. "Erbin's sister's daughter. She was always like that. Beautiful, mysterious, a kind of island all to herself, a sovereign creature you might say. There's a warning to men in those green eyes of hers."

"Did you love her; did you want her for your own?" Macsen asked. He couldn't help picking up on the way the high chief spoke of Branwen.

"She was already promised." Ffernfael had a way of avoiding making direct answers to the awkward questions people asked him. "Besides, so was I."

"She would have been young."

"Old enough," Ffernfael replied. "In any case she was promised to one of the chiefs of the Dumnonii in the other Britain, a man called Rhun, a chief of some consequence. Their marriage was to strengthen and continue the bonds of kinship between the people of this Island and those already over in Llydaw. The Dumnonii have been over there for generations now, in that bolthole of theirs, taking land when the Romans quitted Gaul, building an empire of their own, so to speak."

"Hardly an empire," Macsen retorted, accustomed to thinking of one empire only and that on the grandest scale. "I hear the soil there is thin and the rain as thick as sticks."

"At any rate that was the plan, hatched in the time of Erbin's father, Gwynnan the Fair, and brought to conclusion in the first years of Erbin's reign," Ffernfael explained. "Not a bad plan, except that things went badly between husband and wife."

"What happened?"

"I can't say exactly. People say he is a cruel man and violent, but I don't know about that. Branwen was in Llydaw a year or two and there was talk of her becoming a nun, throwing herself away like that. The next I knew she was here, in Britain that is. She'd jumped on a ship and jumped off again when she saw the Hafren, or wherever it was she landed. As if you could put a creature like that in a cage," Ffernfael said, his admiration undisguised. "And she landed up in Siriol's arms; can you believe it?" he continued. "With that wild witch-like warrior woman from Ynys Wydr who would slit your throat soon as look at you."

"And Erbin?" Macsen inquired. "How did he take it?"

"Apoplectic."

"And Rhun of Llydaw?"

"Murderous."

"And you want Branwen to accompany me to Caer Uisc," Macsen said. "Are you sure about that?"

"Life's seldom straightforward, especially where blood is concerned," Ffernfael answered, not averse to cultivating a bit of mystery himself.

"He wants Branwen to shame the king," Eleri said when Macsen related the tale to her. "I'm sure that's it. If a woman, a *mere* woman and one of the royal household of the Dumnonii can take up arms against the Gewisse, what cowardice prevents the men of the clan from doing the same? They hide in the vastness of the west, they run to the other Britain when trouble comes calling, they let their fellow countrymen suffer and fight on their behalf; more than that, they let a woman do it, women in fact, which I suppose is the reason why I'm with you and Cerridwen and Siriol; we're there to show them up for the cowards they are."

"Just don't say that, Eleri," Macsen warned.

"Of course not!" Eleri said indignantly. "As if I would."

# Chapter Sixteen

Where Cynan's hall in Ynys Wydr was poor and plain, adorned only with mystery-rags and word-weavings, the interior of the hall of the King of Dyfneint had some semblance of grandeur. Long and colourful hangings decorated the walls, showing hunting and other scenes, lean dogs, dark-browed men and fair women, their dresses blue and gold. A fire burned high, making a show of warmth in that land of coarse rain.

"Welcome to Dyfneint," King Erbin said, formally acknowledging them as Ffernfael's envoys. "Welcome to you, Macsen son of Emrys, to Arawn son of Edern, to Riwalus son of Gwyn and…"; the king paused for effect, "Cenydd son of Gildas, a priest with a lot to say for himself, if memory and my advisers serve me right." He let one eyebrow rise higher than the other in exclamation.

The king's face was big-boned and strong. He was not a tall man; heavy set rather. An impressive gold ring adorned his large, chunky fingers. His black hair was thick and wild, suggestive of an untamed and unpredictable character. A force to be reckoned with, he looked those before him over with dark intelligent eyes, long accustomed to the exercise of power. He knew exactly who and what he was.

The deliberate omission of Branwen from his words of greeting lent a sharp edge to the proceedings. He pondered, or seemed to. His left foot tapped the floor with nervous energy. When it came, King Erbin's greeting to Branwen was separate and distinct.

"And niece," he said, "you are here too, under Ffernfael's protection I understand; Ffernfael who is far off in troubled Caer Baddan."

Branwen made no attempt to reply, knowing none was expected, except perhaps that she bow or prostrate herself before Erbin. Rather, uncle and niece discoursed in silence, in a kind of mute dance of warring blood. If you had met them separately, his bulk, her lean delicacy, you would not have seen the likeness between them; but in close proximity as here it was clear and present. It was in the stubbornness of their demeanour; a likeness more of spirit than looks; a closeness more of reality than appearance. If looks could kill, Erbin would have died on the spot, Branwen with him.

The thinly implied threat in Erbin's greeting to Branwen stirred Macsen to her defence. It was something that could not go unchallenged, and certainly not without remark.

"The Lady Branwen is indeed under the protection of the high chief Ffernfael," he said, his voice steady and determined.

There was a snort from Erbin at the mention of Ffernfael as 'high chief', as if to say, high chief of what exactly?

Macsen felt the loss of the sword and long knife he'd been required to deposit at the door to the king's hall. "She is Ffernfael's official envoy to the Dumnonii," he said. "And the Lady is also under my personal protection," he added with still greater force. Macsen spoke well, just as certain of his place and status as any king.

It wasn't the occasion to conduct a family argument. Erbin might have let it go at that. But he was determined to say more.

"You know that your mother is dead," the king said to Branwen, more statement than question, real feeling and anger still in his voice, the spirit of confrontation evidently alive and well. "My sister Tegid died a stranger to her daughter, unhappy and ashamed."

"My mother would not have me endure abuse," Branwen answered strongly. "You know that, Uncle, as well as I do. If the true facts were related to her she would have understood and supported my actions. My mother would never condone the cowardly violence of men against women. You know that."

She wasn't contradicted by the king. Some of the anger in him seemed to seep away.

"Let's move on from this," the king said.

It had been at least ten summers since Branwen had left Dyfneint. Much had changed in that time, not least her cousins, Kadwy and Kelyn, who had grown from boys of ten and eight into young men. She knew them, of course. Both dark like their father, Kelyn a little slighter than Kadwy, forever the younger brother who would have to try that bit harder to make his mark on the world. After the formalities were done, Branwen approached them.

"Cousins," she said warmly. "Or should I say princes?" She found she was genuinely pleased to see them.

Naturally reserved and a little wary of this woman whose reputation preceded her, Kadwy welcomed Branwen, saying he was pleased that she had come to Dyfneint. He even bowed a little stiffly. Naturally outgoing by nature, without hesitation his younger brother Kelyn embraced his cousin, saying impulsively:

"As a boy I was hopelessly in love with you and now I see why." He didn't stop there. His admiration spilling over, Kelyn said: "And you're a warrior, a true warrior queen."

Siriol apart, no one had spoken so intimately to Branwen for years. She was taken by surprise; she almost cried.

Kadwy maintained his emotional distance, a state of affairs to which Branwen was more accustomed. He gave his brother a cool look. That coolness brought Branwen back to her proper path.

"It's good to see the both of you," she said, trying to seek out the right thing to say, the correct tone, friendly but not overly so, such as to suggest that she had come to beg for help on Ffernfael's behalf, still less to apologise for her own. On her guard again, her natural pride and self-sufficiency would not let her go too far or too quickly.

King Erbin was all business.

"We will provide for the others in your company," Erbin said. "But for now we will get down to the practical matter of your visit. It might as well be aired and done with as soon as possible. Then we can get you dry and have you enjoy the best meat and mead Dyfneint has to offer."

He sat them down and asked Macsen to set out Ffernfael's request.

"I have it in writing," Macsen said, then stopped abruptly, not wishing to embarrass Erbin if he could not read.

"Don't worry, young man," Erbin said almost good-naturedly, "I can read with the best of them. We have more priests and monks here in Dyfneint than you can shoot arrows at and, as you see, we have enough rain-soaked days, when there's precious little to do, for even a lazy blighter like myself to learn the art." He laughed.

"Anyway, I know what Ffernfael writes. It's always the same. I begin to think that he copies out the same words every time." His temper never far from argument, a look of dangerous intent settled in his eyes. "We could always ask Cenydd the son of Gildas here to read Ffernfael's words for us. Are you as good with words as your father? What do you say for yourself, priest?"

Father Cenydd recognised only one sovereign and Erbin wasn't it. His thin face, that could convey warmth and human feeling, could just as readily take on a mask of cold pride and arrogance, the equal and superior of any petty monarch. It was that face that replied curtly: "My father was a master of words and I was his pupil."

More than content, pleased even, with their status as mere onlookers, Arawn and Riwalus did their best to hide the smiles that broadened under their beards.

"Is that so?" the king said coldly, disliking the priest for who he was and what he might do.

Cutting through the game of words, Macsen took it upon himself to explain the position they faced to the north and Ffernfael's request for help from Dyfneint. There was no masking the desperate situation for the three strongholds of Caer Baddan, Caer Gloui and Caer Ceri and their chieftains, Ffernfael, Conmagil and Condidan.

"Those mongrels," Erbin said at the mention of the Irish brothers. "Whose side will they be fighting on when the Gewisse are knocking at the gates of Caer Baddan?"

"They're with us," Macsen tried to assure the king.

"Are they, young man?"

"It is so," said Cenydd, adding his voice to Macsen's. "They have pledged themselves on the Holy Book and they do not take that lightly; they have pledged in their mother's name."

"That Irish whore!" Erbin exclaimed.

"She was a great friend to the church," Cenydd responded. "She was a person of faith. Her sons will not dishonour her name." He spoke like his father's son, with absolute conviction.

The king was half convinced, sufficient to let the dialogue proceed. "Maybe you're right, priest."

"Ffernfael and the other chieftains call on Dyfneint for help," Macsen continued, getting straight to the point. "Without it, I'm not sure if the Gewisse advance can be stopped. They will reach the Hafren. Dyfneint will be alone. The land bridge to Cambria and the north of the Island will be gone. You will be isolated. The fall of Dyfneint will be a matter of time only; of when, not if."

The king held up a hand to stop Macsen's sudden flow of eloquence. "Do you think I don't know, young man? Do you think me a fool? Or worse, do you imagine Dyfneint is too afraid to fight?" His eyes turned to fix on Cenydd. "Is that what you think? Is that what you plan to write?"

"It is not," Cenydd said, with all the sincerity at his disposal. "It is not," he repeated directly into the king's eyes.

"The situation is grim; I know that," King Erbin conceded. "And I know too that more might have been done sooner." He looked at the priest. "And, yes, I know that everything is at stake for you; even the women of the land take up arms again as in the days before the legions came." His eyes were on Branwen. "I know," he said. "The sweet mother of our Lord hears it in my prayers." He brought a cross out from under his shirt and held it firmly in his big hand.

His eldest son, Kadwy, placed a protective hand on his father's shoulder.

"But?" Macsen intervened. "Do I sense a 'but' is coming my way?"

"But," the king said obligingly, "there are many calls on Dyfneint. We are already stretched. Our coastline is long and almost impossible to protect. Already Irish sea raiders have taken control of the two feet of the Island in the land of the Kernow in the far west. To start with I must drive them out. And they grow bolder. We will hear more of that later when my captains return. They will bring news."

"We fight on two fronts, east and west," Macsen agreed.

"And south in the case of Dyfneint," the king corrected him. "The people of Llydaw call for assistance as you do and for the same reasons. They would have me send a force of warriors across to the other Britain to help secure their borders against these people they call the Franks, barbarians dressed as Christians the lot of them. The chieftains of Llydaw speak of hundreds of warriors and in the next breath of thousands."

"But the Island of the Mighty calls to you, Uncle," Branwen said earnestly. "If Ffernfael fails, the lost lands are lost to us forever. They will always be in Gewisse hands. And the Gewisse plague will spread and spread." The king shuddered at the thought of it. "That will have been our legacy to the history of our people. The Island will be broken."

Respecting his niece, in spite of everything, recognising the fighting spirit that informed her life, King Erbin composed his response in careful language. "I know. I know that too." He didn't say that the lost lands were indeed lost forever. He didn't need to. His face was beyond dissembling. His hand folded around his cross. "I don't say that Dyfneint will not come to Ffernfael's aid. I only say that there are other things we are called to do. I will take counsel with my captains on their return."

"When are they expected?" Macsen asked.

"A day or two, no more," Erbin replied.

"They are out hunting for pirates," the impulsive Kelyn volunteered.

"Let's make you and your company properly welcome," the king said, moving the conversation along, playing the perfect host when it suited him. "The sea wolves will do for another day."

The conversation drifted into informality.

"Pirate hunting; I like the sound of that," Riwalus told Arawn. He was looking for something to chase Awen Ysbryd out of his thoughts.

In his own mind, Erbin had called an end to the meeting. Only Branwen wanted, needed rather, to say more – a rare thing for her. "The rumour is that this Gewisse king, this Ceawlin, will come with great numbers. It is rumoured that his son, Cuthwine, is even now in the Saxon homelands in the east, recruiting men for fifty keels. Chasing sea raiders will be child's play compared to what will transpire at the threshold to Caer Baddan. If the rumours are true, even half true, we all know that the three strongholds will be hard pressed and probably outnumbered. It is the time of reckoning, Uncle; be sure of it."

She stopped as abruptly as she'd started. It was the most any of them had heard her say on her own behalf. Her voice carried through the hall, weighty yet soaring, her words like ravens flying into the minds of men, nesting in their imaginations.

The king said nothing, except that his fingers spoke to his precious cross. Seeing this, Father Cenydd said: "Pray my lord; you and I will go to the church; be sure that the Great King will show the way."

# Chapter Seventeen

The captains returned the next day. The rain was still falling; more drizzle than rain, but joined now by a strong westerly wind. The captains on their big, powerful horses and their men mostly on smaller, sturdy ponies entered the encampment every bit as soaked as Macsen and his company had been the day before. They made for the king's hall, a wake of children and dogs behind them. Dismounting, the men led the horses away while the captains shook the wet off their capes and leather caps. As presentable as they could hope to be, they entered the hall without ceremony. At their head was a man called Marrec. They were taken to the king for private counsel.

Macsen and the others watched them ride into the encampment. He'd asked the king why he didn't occupy the fortified town and see to the maintenance of its walls. He wasn't being impertinent, he said, only curious as a military man.

"Have you been inside the walls?" Erbin asked.

"Yes. This morning; we looked around."

"It's a mess," the king commented. "Rubble and filth everywhere. I prefer it where I am." He added without conviction: "The walls are there if we need them; the day may come I suppose."

Macsen had judged it best not to pursue the subject. It was embarrassing to the king. For Macsen, the neglect of fortified towns made him cross, furious even. Others told him that the town had been deserted finally around two decades since, at the time of the plague. It was rumoured that the evil lived and breathed within the confines of the walls, multiplying, growing stronger and more intense. The king, he was told, would not enter the town gates for fear that the evil lurked there still.

"What a place this is," Macsen confided to himself.

Eleri and Cerridwen were with him, watching the captains and their men as they threaded their way to the king's hall. Red Cloaks they were not. Mostly they looked a wild, fearsome lot, black-haired and bearded, but well enough provisioned, a few with helmets and scabbards that suggested good quality swords, many more with spears and bows. Their shields bore the visage of the sun-faced cross that was common in these parts. Their standard bore the same design. "The tin men," Riwalus called them under his breath. But even he had to admit that he would prefer to fight with and not against them.

Eventually Macsen and Father Cenydd, none of the rest, were called to see King Erbin.

"Why the priest?" Riwalus asked, put out.

"For the record, for posterity, for the avoidance of misunderstanding," Eleri told him. "So the world will know what Erbin of Dyfneint pledged to do at this late hour."

"To avoid the fate of his grandfather Constantine," her father added.

"Exactly."

"Clever girl," Arawn said, half teasing, proud of his daughter's sharp mind.

"You are clever," Cerridwen told her friend in her intense way, as if confirming a proposition long disputed.

They were a small, select group in the king's hall. With the king were his sons Kadwy and Kelyn and his leading captain, the man called Marrec. The king seemed not to need or accept other counsel, including from the many churchmen who were to be found in the encampment. Macsen found it interesting that King Erbin appeared to separate political and military matters from those of the religion, to which he was clearly devoted. He liked that. Religion was, or should be, about principle; politics was about practice, doing what was necessary. He had talked this over with Eleri, who could be relied on to have ideas about everything. She had helped him clarify and articulate his instinctive understanding of the issue. She was good like that. "Sharp as a damned *seax*," her father said, the foreign word always sounding odd, brutal.

The man Marrec was introduced to Macsen and Cenydd. The three were around the same age: Macsen tall, fair; Cenydd thin, his freckled forehead shaved in the way of priests; Marrec solid and dark, a warrior for his king. The word formidable came to mind.

Marrec was invited by the king to bring Macsen up to date. "Tell him everything," was Erbin's command.

Like Macsen in many if not most respects, on his day Marrec could be spurred to eloquence. However, his usual style veered towards the taciturn. This wasn't one of his loquacious performances. He was wet through from his long journey. As he sat next to the fire that blazed in Erbin's hall, the steam rose from his damp clothes. The mug of hot mead in his hand was some solace, no doubt, but hardly the equal of a clean shirt and breeches and a good meal. Macsen had admired the powerful black stallion Marrec rode and he suspected that the horse was probably faring better than its rider at this moment.

"As I told the king," Marrec started, "we had reports of sea raiders from the west sailing far up into the Channel waters. Some reports said ten ships, others more; the number multiplied with every telling. They were said to be at the estuary that flows into a bay that lies to the north-west of here, at the mouth of the Tawel River, where it meets Heron Bay – *Bae y Crychydd."*

"Isn't it a bit late in the year for sea wolves?" Macsen asked. "With the weather on the turn and the month of the ivy upon us?"

"It would be if they were sailing out of Ireland," Marrec explained. "But in the last months they have secured a foothold in the west of Cambria, in Dyfed. They've taken possession of the great harbour at Aberdaugleddyf. From there they sail directly to our coast; a short voyage and relatively safe even now that the falling month is upon us."

A moment of intense silence followed. The steam rising from his body seemed an outward expression of the steam coming off Marrec's boiling blood.

"I don't think they mean to stay on the Tawel," he said when he'd composed himself. "They're testing us; testing our resolve; will we, won't we take them on? If we don't, of course they'll be back with an even greater force. In the meantime they kill, enslave, the usual things."

"And did you take them on?" Macsen asked gingerly.

"No," was the reply, said with eyes that looked directly into Macsen's, daring him to say: "Why not?"

"No. They were too many and too well entrenched," Marrec said, clearly frustrated, hesitant to say more.

"My captain's orders were to ascertain the strength and disposition of the intruders," King Erbin explained. "That was all. I won't lose good men in risky escapades," he added, a sentiment that was dear to Macsen's own heart.

"So how many?" Macsen inquired.

"Three boats with full crews; sixty men or so in total; enough to overwhelm the small settlement on the Tawel," Marrec replied. "My guess is they'll stay a week, maybe two, then get out with all the plunder they can carry, women mostly."

"Unless you have something to say about it," Macsen interpreted.

"We'll be there in under three days," Marrec confirmed fiercely. "We'll drive them into the sea, every last one of them." He was not a man to contradict.

"Did they see you?" Macsen asked; "Do they know they're found?"

"No. We were careful. We observed, no more."

"But they must know that word will have reached the king one way or another," Macsen said.

"They'll be ready to sail the minute we show ourselves in force," Marrec agreed. "But show ourselves we must."

Macsen felt it was like talking to his long-lost brother.

Warming to his subject, the mead working on his tongue, Marrec explained: "The real difficulty is the land; the geography is complex and the Irish have chosen their landing spot well. From where we stood, on the big dunes across from the settlement, we were a long spear throw away. But crossing by water at that point is risky, especially with a welcoming party of hairy Irishmen waiting on the other side. The landward journey on the other hand is long, taking a loop south, crossing by the ford downriver, then heading due north again to where that spear would have landed in the first place. Surprise is out of the question. By the time we're in striking distance of them, they'll have set sail and be making down the channel towards Heron Bay." Marrec paused, resetting his fierce face, his mind trained on his enemies.

"But as I said," he continued, "we must challenge them and in force; a statement has to be made."

"Tomorrow, then," young Prince Kelyn said, speaking for the first time, obviously excited, heedless of inconvenient detail. "We ride tomorrow to kill pirates."

His brother Kadwy remained silent. He liked to think before speaking, exercising his brain before his tongue.

"Those girls you brought with you, Macsen," Kelyn said, just as excited as before. "I would sit between them at dinner."

"Those girls as you call them, Prince," Macsen said, as respectfully as he was able, "have killed grown men. They're warriors. It's as well to remember it."

"Before we eat or anything else, an answer must be given to Ffernfael's request for help," King Erbin said, his rascal eyes shifting from Macsen to Father Cenydd. "My captain Marrec and I have discussed your proposal, and I have consulted my sons, of course, who must learn the art of leadership sooner rather than later, and what better way than by advising on the strategies of war." He settled deeper into his big chair. "Unlike your Eleri Gwir and the Dragon Girl Cerridwen, neither Prince Kadwy nor Prince Kelyn have killed in battle. They're virgins both in that respect. But kill in battle they will, be sure of that."

The king's words were spoken in a flat, toneless voice. They might have been a rebuke to Macsen, telling him to remember his place; it was hard to tell with Erbin, whose moods and meanings had a liquid quality, as weirdly uncertain as the unnerving air around Ynys Wydr.

"They will fight the good fight in the Lord's name and for the glory of Dyfneint," Father Cenydd observed, trying to be helpful.

"Mmm." King Erbin didn't seem to be absolutely sure about the validity of one or both limbs to that proposition.

"Marrec advises me to assist Ffernfael," the king said, changing tack. "His advice is an echo of the pleadings of my wayward niece, Branwen. I almost think they have had congress together. What else is there to explain such proximity of thought and speech?"

No one cared to solve the conundrum. Marrec put his back to the fire, seemingly unconcerned by the false trail set by the king, evidently accustomed to his style of discourse.

"I know," the king said, solving his own puzzle. "It's the only thing to say and do. The Island of the Mighty calls to its sons and daughters; they speak and act on its behalf."

Macsen found something to cling to in this line of reasoning. Conversely, Father Cenydd, more used to the undulations and hidden traps to be found in rhetorical speech, found his grip on hope loosening.

"My duty, first and last, is to my people; to Dyfneint," King Erbin stated. "Even in the times of the empire we controlled our own destinies in this part of the world. The tribe of the Dumnonii did not dissolve its power or identity in the corrupting wine of the legions."

With some effort Macsen stopped himself from commenting on this latest observation. The Dumnonii did exactly what the Romans let them do, nor more, no less. It was as simple as that.

Father Cenydd found his hold on hope loosening by another notch.

"But we in Dyfneint do not neglect our responsibility to our fellow Britons," the king declared. "We know that duty lies in that direction too."

The restraining hand of Father Cenydd rested on Macsen's arm, the priest sensing that the young soldier was about to tell the king to "get on with it", or words to that effect. "Patience," the hand said. It brought a rich smile to Erbin's face. He would have liked to prolong the game he played, but he knew too that it would amount to rudeness on his part; a game without rules wasn't worth playing.

"We will come to Ffernfael's aid," he said significantly. "Dyfneint will be there for the reckoning," he added, echoing his niece.

Neither Macsen nor Cenydd spoke a word in reply; from Macsen there was a small bow of the head in eloquent thanks; the priest made the sign of the cross and looked up to where his God was perched in the rafters of the king's hall. Erbin's eyes joined the priest's, solemn now, drained of any playfulness.

"Can I report further to Ffernfael?" Macsen asked at length.

It was Marrec who answered the operational question. "As many men as can be spared," he said. "But count on five hundred at the very least."

"And you?" Macsen asked, knowing the value of the man.

"Yes; God willing I will be there."

"Food," Kelyn said decidedly, his youthful intervention a welcome distraction on this occasion, an escape from gravity. "I'll eat the Dragon Maiden," he said hungrily, "and I know where I'll start."

They laughed at that; except that is for his brother Kadwy, who kept his hunger to himself. Always alert, Father Cenydd noted it, expert that he was in man's hunger, of the flesh as well as of the spirit.

# Chapter Eighteen

The rain had finally stopped, chased away by the wind which carried in its fingers the first pinch of winter. The encampment was all activity, running, orders shouted, straps tested, lips kissed; horses stamped the wet earth in anticipation. Spears spiked the morning; standards cracked out a beat. The King of Dyfneint was going to war.

Eleri Gwir looked around, taking in the busy scene. It had occurred to her that the people of this tribe were extreme in looks, dark or blond, made of charcoal or of sand, she thought. She couldn't say she liked the place exactly. It had about it the feeling of impermanence, of a way of life about to be abandoned for something meaner and more inward-looking. The king might not return for months, a year maybe; that seemed to be the way it was with him, shifting constantly, making sure of his authority in every corner of the knobbly, undulating land.

She told herself she was hard to please. The king's warriors were suitably impressive, more than three hundred experienced fighters in total, giving them a five-to-one advantage over the sea raiders. It was a good feeling, to see the men of the Island joined in concerted force. They were all men who served the King of Dyfneint under arms; Dyfneint had not, as Erbin had pointed out over dinner, reached the stage where it had to enlist its women folk. He smiled as he said it, challenging and disarming in something like equal measure.

Siriol couldn't help herself. "If I was a king in such times I'd use every resource at my disposal," she'd said, with that severity that sometimes stole into her voice.

"Fortunately, Lady Siriol, you are not in a position to decide," the king had replied, smooth as velvet. "I rule here, not you."

Accustomed to having the last word, Erbin had not expected this line of conversation to carry any further. He might have remarked on the failure of Siriol's father to protect his own lands, but decided against it, preferring to placate his eccentric guest. He was playing the perfect host.

"Still, I think Siriol has a valid point to make," Eleri had interjected, too loudly to be ignored.

Erbin didn't know whether to shout or laugh into the silence that rushed into the hall at that moment. Something had to be said; a retort worthy of a king. At the same time, however, an odd idea, more of an inkling, graceful as a butterfly, invaded the landscape of his thinking, suggesting something about this young woman and the future of the kingdom of Dyfneint. Then it was gone. Erbin might have aimed his retort at Arawn, remarking on his daughter's outspokenness. But no; that wouldn't do. This Eleri Gwir was a worthy adversary in her own right. Wanting to overpower yet not crush the young woman, he said: "Tomorrow you will see Dyfneint at war; the validity of the argument will be decided in the field, not at the dinner table."

"Nor in the bedroom!" a man called out, breaking the awkwardness.

The temptation Eleri felt to dispute the king's reasoning was only just mastered by the severe look her father gave her, warning her off. Macsen's angry stare she missed, only to see it too clearly when they were alone.

They argued.

"Why did you challenge the king like that?"

It was their first real, major disagreement.

"Because he was talking through his fat arse," she answered.

Their words carried through the thin walls of their room and out into the world of listening ears.

"Not so loud!" a warning voice said at the door.

In fierce whispers they went at it, Macsen saying there was a time and place for cleverness, Eleri claiming that this was as good a time as any. They slept back to back; or rather they feigned sleep while in their heads they raked over the coals of their disagreement.

"What's he got anyway?" Eleri said at last. "A lot of wild-looking tin men."

"Precisely," Macsen hissed. "He has men; it's as plain and simple as that."

Hating this kind of mean confrontation, Eleri turned eventually and said: "Belin's balls to you, Macsen, why don't you give me a kiss and get over it?"

He did so in the manner of a sea creature emerging from the cold watery depths onto dry land, awkward, hesitant, only warming to his task with suitable encouragement.

Now, in the squally morning, there was plenty about the tin men to impress even Eleri's critical mind. She noticed Marrec, tall in the saddle but snapping like a cattle dog at the heels of the mustering troops. Macsen had told her about him, praising him in a way that made her smile, knowing that he found in Marrec the qualities he wanted others to find in himself.

"We're going with them," Macsen had informed Eleri and the others on his return from the king the day before. "He wants the Red Cloaks with him; he says even a few will make the sea rabble think twice about coming back to these shores." The king knew all the right the things to say when it suited him to say them.

"Let's see what these tin men are made of," Arawn had said to Riwalus.

Seeing the pair of them together, her father borrowing a witticism from the soldier, it occurred to Eleri that they were getting to be friends. She was glad for her father, who seemed lighter and happier in spirit than she could remember.

"They look the part, they talk the part, but do the tin men fill it?" Riwalus had asked, stern and sceptical, keeping a soldier's eye on things.

Eleri had to admit that the king certainly looked the part on his powerful charger, his furs flowing over his armour, his sturdy figure looking grander and weightier somehow on horseback; better as a man of action than one playing either the wily statesman or the unpredictable host.

His sons were another matter. She thought Kelyn an immature pest, always nosing around Cerridwen like a hunting dog. He had sat next to her at every meal they shared, quitting his usual position at his father's side, preferring the company of the Dragon Maiden to that of the King of Dyfneint; or perhaps it would be more accurate to say proximity, not company, as the object of his attention chose to treat him with the studied coolness not readily associated with a blacksmith's daughter. At any rate, he made Eleri nervous. The prince wasn't used to rejection; and rejection was just the thing to make some men show the true stamp of their character. Still, in the brisk morning air his horse was fine enough and he had all his gear in place, all new and untried, she speculated.

His brother Kadwy was harder to pick, quiet and thoughtful, observing the Red Cloaks intently, missing nothing. He could see that they wouldn't suffer anyone, prince or no prince, to put an unwanted finger on their talisman; even a wanted finger might be disputed. It occurred to Eleri that the older brother might make a good king one day, if he got the chance. If he wasn't always just, he would at least be careful; if he wasn't brilliant, he could probably be relied on to be sensible. Wasn't that as much as anyone could reasonably ask of a king, or of any leader for that matter? Sometimes over dinner he too would sneak a look at Cerridwen, which made Eleri wonder what was going on behind those watchful eyes of his. Did he even show some interest in herself? For once in her life she couldn't tell what a man was thinking.

Naturally wary of the powerful, her father had warned her to keep her distance from the princes, to stay close to Macsen and the Red Cloaks. "You never know," he warned. "Their play can turn sour without warning."

Leaving Caer Uisc, its crumbling sadness, the king and his sons were at the head of the retinue, Eleri and the others at the very rear, just ahead of the baggage and the camp followers, a few wives and many more harlots. Next to Eleri rode Branwen. Even by her standards, she had been very private since her meeting with the king. Eleri assumed that they'd met alone to talk over family matters; but she was told nothing and Branwen was still not in a communicative frame of mind; she contrived to be busy with her cap in the squally wind, trying to capture and keep under guard the long tresses of her black hair. Siriol was with them, quarrelsome for no obvious reason, the flying eagle feathers in her hair making a warlike standard of their own. She was telling the boy Gereint to take better care of the fine, pale mare she rode, saying he should brush her down more thoroughly. "I will," the boy said, although in as dreamy a way as he'd answered anything put to him since their departure from Ynys Wydr. He seemed to have slowed down, as if spellbound; or was he saving his energy for a particular and secret purpose? Was Siriol trying to snap him out of whatever lovesick mood he was in, Eleri wondered, or was she just plain crotchety on this chill day?

Eleri was glad to be left with her own thoughts. Her bleeding had started in the early hours. Thankfully. The women in the weaving room knew everything that was worth knowing about and were not afraid to discourse at length on any subject, be it men, sex, parents, children or the state of the world and the place of women in it. The benefit of their advice, they would say to the young girls, was free and not to be sneezed at. On the subject of bleeding their expertise was without equal. From what they said it became clear to Eleri that its effects could vary greatly from one woman to another, depending on age or just the luck of the draw, it seemed. "You have it easy when you're young," some would say. "Not me," the mother of Eleri's friend Rhian would pipe up, and off they'd go. Eleri felt heavy with it, as if her insides were being pulled down into the deep earth, like roots reaching through the warm body of her horse into heat and darkness.

"I'm over it, thank the gods," an older woman would say.

"You're dried up," another would comment.

"I don't know if I'm better with it or without it," the first woman would say, revising her position.

Today Eleri was glad of it, unequivocally so. She wasn't ready to be a mother. The weaving room had a lot to say on the subject of pregnancy generally as well as all the sub-categories it might be broken down into; how not to get yourself pregnant was a specialist subject all to itself. "Don't fuck," was the first line of argument; "Fat chance of that," was the next.

They all had their ideas, and Mared of the Silver Wheel had a concoction of her own that made the rounds; with dubious success it had to be said, considering the conversations about unwanted pregnancy Eleri had heard over the years. Her big ears took it all in. With Macsen she'd been careful when her womb was in flood, inviting him to try it another way, which he was happy to do, admittedly after some insistence. With Gwion it had been different, like an exploratory exercise involving two wills of more or less equal strength, something less urgent, not so overwhelming. Eleri had always felt in control; she was the one with the upper hand. Whereas with Macsen it was more complicated; he was older, more experienced, and she found herself pushed by a gale of her own desire, pulled headlong into dangerous waters.

On the long ride to the north coast of Dyfneint, Eleri's mind turned compulsively to Gwion. She missed him. She could say anything to him. He would say and do things that amused her. Kissing her shoulder, taking the tiny hairs on her arm in his mouth he would say: "Your flesh and skin smell like the sharp, salty sea."

"How would you know?" she would say, laughing. "You've never seen the salty sea, let alone smelt it."

"But I've smelled you, Eleri Gwir," he'd say. "Inside and out, and in my sleep I have sailed across the oceans to lie at your side."

"I suppose you think you can get around me with those fine words of yours," she'd say.

"I certainly hope so, Eleri Gwir."

What a funny sort he was. He had his own smell, something comfortable like a blanket, cows and cooking smells in his thick black hair. Macsen, on the other hand, smelled like a wolf in spring, like a powerful drug you try to give up but can't stop taking.

"Something troubles you," Awen had said to her at Ynys Wydr. "I hope you don't mind me remarking on it."

"I want to kick myself sometimes," Eleri had answered. "Literally kick myself. I don't suppose you ever feel like that."

"You'll fall over."

"Perhaps I already have."

"I don't think so," Awen said helpfully.

Standing on the tor's summit, looking out over the eerie Water Land, Eleri had told Awen about how she'd left Gwion all in a rush, dumping him in a stew of shame and disappointment. "The thing is, I feel bad about it but not as bad as I should feel. I always saw myself as a loyal friend, as someone you could rely on. But now? I must be a very shallow person. I don't know what to think; and the longer I'm away from Gwion the more I think about him."

"That doesn't sound shallow to me," Awen commented.

"But it is. I want to kick myself but I get over it. At least I get over it more than I should."

Needing to be hard on herself, Eleri compared herself to Cerridwen. "She doesn't talk about it, but she told me that the boy she was with was killed by the Gewisse. He'd tried to fight them. It was no good. It fuels her white-hot anger. If she can't have that boy she won't have anyone."

"Whereas you're a trollop," Awen remarked, straight-faced.

"Don't spare my feelings," Eleri said, falling back on the prickly comforts of irony. "Cerridwen's different anyway. She's not the sort to want men gawking at her. She isn't looking to be praised for her beauty. She hates the way men paw at women. This weird, untouchable status she has among the Red Cloaks suits her very well. It lets her be alone."

"We are all of us alone," Awen said. "Whether we know it or not."

Refusing the solace of philosophy, Eleri said: "Gwion may not be. I can see my best friend Rhian making eyes and more at him as I stand here."

"A nest of trollops, then," Awen said, smiling.

Eleri had laughed. "In my case a trollop caught between two stools, if that doesn't sound too ridiculous."

"Don't worry; we're all ridiculous."

"Even you, Awen Ysbryd?" Eleri asked seriously.

"Especially me," the seer had answered, her voice small and trailing into watery nothingness.

Eleri thought now about what Awen had said to her at their parting. "At Ynys Wydr," she'd said, "there are two thrones, one for water and one for the earth. We honour them equally. In our hearts we find a place for both of them."

"But does it help?" Eleri wondered as she rode across the rough land of Dyfneint. The aching in her insides had spread up into her stomach and her heart. She ached all over and wanted to kick herself again, literally.

"You all right, girl?" her father called to her. "You're very quiet for a chatterbox."

He knew, of course. That was the nice and annoying thing about her father. He could look into her head and down into her bowels, it seemed. He could see Gwion there, a black lump in her intestines, something she'd swallowed and which was too big and solid to ever pass from her body.

"Regrets, Eleri Gwir?" he asked.

"Why can't we live two lives all at once? It would make things much easier," Eleri answered.

"But then we would want three; and then four and five."

"Two would do for now, Father," Eleri said.

And she in turn looked into her father's head and down into his heart and stomach where he still grieved for Eleri's mother, regretting the years they'd been apart, waiting for the time their spirits might rise together from Ynys Wydr into the light of the next life. "He's marking time," Eleri thought. "He's been marking time all these years."

She thought too about Ynys Wydr itself, how its odd light shone into them all, making them transparent somehow, preparing them for the journey they must all take.

# Chapter Nineteen

It was pathetic to look at, this settlement at the mouth of the River Tawel, now fallen into pirate hands. This tiny place of rude buildings and dishevelled, cowering people, its wharf a muddy outcrop, little better than a dung heap. Only the three sea raiders' ships – their *curraghs* – moored alongside looked sleek and predatory, ready for action at a moment's notice.

It was pathetic to think about it, that in these days of falling and breaking a band of sixty men, brave enough in themselves no doubt but undisciplined, foul-mannered men all the same, might constitute an army that could terrorise and even conquer an entire *cantref*. It was pathetic to contemplate such an idiotic state of affairs in anything other than a spirit of detached Stoicism. Such were the thoughts that ran through Macsen's head as he looked out over the scene before him. His father came to mind, and with him thoughts of the legions and how easily they would have swatted such ragtag flies as these. There was no order in them; nothing bigger or grander than greed and hungry opportunism. It was a train of thought Macsen found hard to repress.

Come to think of it, the retinue he rode in now was the largest he'd ever known. Ten summers he'd been a soldier, from his youngest days, glad to be away from home and to be of use to Ffernfael, a man he admired. In all those years the closest thing to an army he'd known was Caer Baddan's retinue, which never amounted to more than a hundred or so regular men, more or less regular, depending on the season, the immediacy of the threat posed by their enemies. In a world of petty chieftains they were among the pettiest in size if not in reputation. The Red Cloaks still carried a weight far beyond their numerical strength, the weight of a brotherhood dedicated to a reality and an ideal. But they were not an army, a legion, whatever you wished to call it. They were a remnant, something left over from an imperial age, a hard core that would not melt. Without Caer Gloui and Caer Ceri they were nothing much; with them they were a force to be reckoned with; then again, with Dyfneint in the mix they were the kernel of a real army, a body that could sweep through *caer* and *cantref*, making them its own.

If Macsen was an arrogant, superior sort, which he was in his way, especially in outward appearance, he was also inclined to be inwardly self-critical, regularly calling himself an idiot; not so much for what he'd done, for his actions, more for the irrepressible optimism that sometimes got the better of him, to which he had to take a firm hand. "Idiot," he said under his breath, submitting his British impulsiveness to Roman order. The truth was that riding in company with the host of Dyfneint, he felt anything but pathetic. Riwalus and the others were the same, filled with that fierce ebullience that carries warriors into battle, blotting out fear and doubt, the knowledge of pain, the possibility of injury. Like Macsen, they were ready to fight, more than ready. It was high time the king got on with it.

"They'll get away," Riwalus said at his side, frustration and disgust in his voice.

"They won't." Marrec's tough face glowed with the anticipation of battle. "They'll try to; but they won't make it; not all three ships at any rate."

'That's good," Arawn observed. "Let one of them carry the bad news to their masters; they'll know then that Dyfneint means business."

In the gathering dusk, the days shortening now, they stood on the sands, in the place where Marrec had come to observe the settlement days earlier. Here the waters of two rivers converged, heavy and high from recent rains, the conflicting rush of waters forming dangerous currents and undertows that would make it extremely hazardous, if not impossible, to cross on horseback. The smaller of the two rivers flowed from the south and that was the direction they must take, making a long loop that would bring them eventually to the gates of the very settlement they had in their sights right now. A big seagull saw them stranded there, these curious flightless creatures.

The king and the remainder of his retinue were already heading directly that way, towards the ford. Only these four had made the detour to this vantage point on the long sands, curious to see the lie of this complex land and to check on the Irish, to ensure they hadn't already decamped. They hadn't. So strong was the westerly wind that voices carried faintly over the engulfing waters, shouts and laughter. Arawn even thought he heard the sound of a harp. "Why are we fighting these men?" he thought, seeming to recognise the song; but of course he knew exactly why – because of wealth and power, the same as ever, the same as any war of great empires or of rival clans or of petty neighbours.

"Well, they don't appear to be in any hurry to leave," Riwalus observed. "Perhaps we'll get them yet."

"They're taunting us, more like," Marrec answered. "Daring us to join their party."

"So let's do it," Macsen said.

As solicitous as a father to his favourite son, he turned the nose of his horse White Hawk – *Gwalchwen* – to the south, resting a caressing hand on the beast's warm neck as he did so. "Let's get to the ford before dark."

The sun was already falling, leaving great streaks of red in the western sky, promising better weather to come. At a gallop, the horses – venting their frustration as much as the men – pelted along the hard sand, riding to the king.

Following the uneven paths that criss-crossed the broken landscape of sand and water, it was well and truly dark before they saw the lights of the king's camp ahead; first the lights, then the sounds of people and horses and above all that the noise, a loud, regal voice venting its anger. The guards they passed said that something had happened, but they either wouldn't or couldn't explain what.

"At least we weren't intending to take the Irish by surprise," Marrec remarked, not sure if he should be worried or amused.

"Just as well," Macsen said.

"Can't find his way out of his breeks, I suppose," Arawn said, disclosing his irreverent turn of humour.

"Or into some woman's breeks," Riwalus said, taking the line of thinking a step further.

Marrec gave him one of his hard looks, as if he was about to take offence on his lord's behalf. Instead, he let his horse walk on, saying to no one in particular, his horse maybe, or the cool night air: "Father Cenydd's breeks more likely, he's that fond of his precious church."

"Idiot!" they heard the king shout. "What an unbelievable idiot!"

Eleri Gwir was there, looking out for them.

Without waiting to be asked, she started to explain the cause of the shouting. "It's Cerridwen, or Kelyn, or both of them I suppose."

"Slow down," her father said.

"There was an argument; it ended in fighting," Eleri said, obviously flustered.

"Was the prince hurt?" Marrec asked, his loyalty to Dyfneint beyond question.

"No; not really," Eleri answered, a slight wriggle in her words. "He was kicked, but not badly; not hurt exactly."

It wasn't like Eleri to hedge what she said, which was all the more reason for concern.

"We'd better go and see the king," Macsen said, "before this gets out of hand."

Marrec agreed.

Following the sound of King Erbin's shouting, they entered the tented structure that had been erected for him. "What a lot of damned nonsense," he was saying. "What a lot of fools."

The young prince was there, no worse for wear apparently, although sitting uncomfortably on the edge of his seat. Inevitably, his older brother was present, observing events, as were Branwen and Father Cenydd. Arrayed before the king, in no particular order of culpability or other significance, were Cerridwen, the boy Gereint and a Red Cloak by the name of Iwan Nânt.

"My lord," Macsen said, his pale eyes full of blue fire at seeing one of his own men in trouble. "What is the matter here?"

"My lord, nothing!" the king said, dismissing Macsen's placatory tone, focusing instead on his fighting looks. "The impudence of it!" he spluttered. "The sheer bloody effrontery; the insult to my hospitality."

It took some time for the newcomers to grasp the full story, which in essence turned out to be another chapter of the oldest and most enduring story of all. When a halt to the march had been called, it seemed that Kelyn had sought out the girl with fire-god hair, the Dragon Maiden, ostensibly to check that she wanted for nothing.

"Is everything well with you?" he'd asked, striding towards her.

"Of course; why shouldn't it be?" she'd answered, her naturally clipped speech exaggerated a little to warn off any further advances on the part of the young prince.

Put out, Kelyn had placed a firm hand on Cerridwen's shoulder and moved her into the shadows. "You dare to be rude to me?" he'd said. "I'm a prince of this land, you are nothing." She had told him to remove his hand from her shoulder. "Stop this," she'd said plainly. "Let go of me."

But Kelyn had gone too far to retreat; his pride was hurt; his reputation was at stake. Instead of letting go, he went to kiss the girl on the mouth. It was then Cerridwen slapped him hard, fiercely even, across the face. They were about the same height, these two, and of similar build. The blow she dealt him wounded more than his pride. His emotions hotter than his stinging cheek, he repaid her blow and with such force that she fell to the ground. From nowhere apparently, speedier than ever, the boy Gereint ran headlong at the prince, and, leaping on his back, he tried to pull him over. Small and skinny though he was, the boy was surprisingly strong, and it took a minute for Kelyn to disentangle himself from the hold his wiry opponent had on him and to throw him off. It was long enough for Cerridwen to recover and to deal the distracted prince a forceful kick in his privates, which made him double over in pain.

"Bitch!" he cried out between grimaces.

Compounding events, it was then the Red Cloak Iwan appeared, sword drawn, determined to defend his talisman the Dragon Maiden, or else die in the attempt. And it was thus that the men of Dyfneint found them, their young prince writhing in pain on the ground, his three assailants standing over him – the boy Gereint, the fierce dragon girl from Belin's chariot, and the Red Cloak, his assassin's sword at the ready.

"They must be punished!" Kelyn asserted. "I won't have it otherwise."

"That's your balls speaking," Branwen said. "Your bruised balls and your bruised pride."

"Who asked you?" Kelyn shouted back, turning on his cousin.

"Kelyn," his father said. "I'm the one who does the shouting here. I'm the bad-tempered one and I give the orders."

Out of nowhere, from innate kindness and a sense of fair play, Arawn spoke up, saying: "The boy is in my care; any man that lays a hand on him will answer to me." No one could doubt that he meant every word of it. For good measure he added: "And Cerridwen, too, she came to me as a fugitive from the Gewisse; she too is in my care."

"Iwan is under my command," Macsen said; "From what I can see he has no case to answer."

"Except that he stood over my son, his sword drawn, intending to cause harm to the prince – and would have done so if my men had not intervened!" the king retorted.

Erbin was in a quandary. On one side, a prince of Dyfneint had been assaulted; on the other, it was as a result of his own impetuousness and no real harm or damage had come of it, saving Kelyn's hurt feelings.

Privately, the king was of the view that an incident of this kind had been a long time in the making and that, if fools had to learn by experience, then his youngest son might learn from this. Publicly, he was outraged. A blow had been struck against the royal house of Dyfneint; a blow *and* a hefty kick, in fact.

It was the king's other son, Kadwy, who broke the impasse. "Time is everything here, Father. If we delay the Irishmen will get clean away. Is this not something that could be left until afterwards?"

"It's all very well for you," Kelyn said, addressing his brother in the same spiteful manner as he had previously addressed his cousin Branwen.

"Kelyn!" the king said, bringing the young man to order.

Cerridwen drew Gereint towards her, placing a protective arm around him. Her mother came to mind for some reason, always at the front of things, speaking on behalf of her father, fighting his causes. Just because they hadn't always agreed on everything there is to agree about, it didn't mean that mother and daughter weren't close, made on the same loom, you might say. She was glad she had such a mother. She was glad she'd kicked the prince where it hurt. She was about to say something that she might not regret, but others would. She was saved by the king.

"Very well," Erbin said, indicating that his reflections had brought him to a point of conclusive resolution. Still, he looked volcanic, as if he was about to blow apart under the influence of his own combustible nature.

For an instant his captain Marrec thought he was about to be told to do something that would not sit easily with his conscience.

"Yes," the king said next, finally convincing himself, it seemed. "Time is everything, as my son Kadwy rightly says. Something will be done; these wrongs against a prince of Dyfneint cannot go unpunished. We will speak of it later, after we have dealt with the sea wolves."

# Chapter Twenty

The landscape was complicated, and the Irishmen knew what they were about. They were sea wolves this season, but they might return as invaders the next. For their present purposes the tiny port, the first settlement from the sea, suited them very well. They had known about it, of course, from their sources in Dyfed. "That's the place to go; very snug and handy." They were told about the wide bay and to look for where a large river emptied into the sea. "You can't miss it; the sand spits on either side of the river mouth are like golden markers." Once inside there's a long neck of water, they were told, easy enough to navigate; the settlement is on the south bank, where the waters of the Tawel and another river meet. Their informant hadn't known the name of the second river, the one that flowed up from the ford where King Erbin was camped. Not that it mattered to the men from Leinster. In and out quick and easy they were told; exactly what you want. The Leinster men had liked the sound of it; a safe haven and an undefended settlement from which to try the courage and the resolve of Dyfneint.

For King Erbin and his troops to approach the settlement meant a long journey north up the western shores of the anonymous river that was in fact called the Toreithiog. The Leinstermen would have to be blind not to see them. Before Erbin was halfway they'd be long gone in their sleek vessels, oars working, their haul of slaves bound fast and tight.

But this was Dumnonii land, since the old gods were young, since Brân had pushed open the door of Annwn, leaving the dark underworld to explore the new world that Belin was making. Perhaps it had not always been theirs. Some said that giants lived here before any man or woman, hauling their great stones from place to place, punishment for killing and then eating the first child of the gods. Who could say for sure? But it was surely the case that if you travelled to the edge of memory, if you peered into its depths, this would always have been Dumnonii land, generation after generation, long enough to know its secrets and its gifts.

Time was of the essence. That night the king's encampment was for show, lights enough to guide a pirate ship by, more than enough noise to wake the Dumnonii's long-dead. The incident was real: Kelyn's aching balls and Cerridwen's blackened eye were testament to that; and there was no feigning Erbin's anger in full flight. As for the rest, the camp bustle, it was there to reassure the sea raiders that the king was settled in and would not be on the march again before first light.

The reality was different. Just as soon as agreement to delay punishment had been reached, the local guides were called for, small, lean men mostly, sharp-minded and quick in step. They were brought to the king, to whom they showed no obvious deference, speaking to him as if he were a fellow orchard man.

"Can it be done?" they were asked.

"Yes."

"Even with the water in spate after all this rain?"

"Yes."

"There's no moon; a sliver only. You're sure it can be done?"

"Yes."

"They're a bad lot; killers; they've taken our girls," the leader of the local men expounded. "We'll get them all right."

He led the way out into the night, followed by Erbin and the captains of Dyfneint; after them went Macsen and the others. Iwan Nânt got a nod of approval from his red-cloaked captain; Arawn gave a nod of his own to Cerridwen and Gereint, more of relief than approval; seeing Kelyn ease out of his seat, it was all Branwen and Eleri could do not to laugh. When they stepped outside Kadwy joined them, going with them into the darkness, serious as ever, a miser with his thoughts, giving nothing away.

The land had many moods and oddities. Into the night they went, the local men in the lead, showing them the way to the place where those moods and oddities could be made to serve their cause.

*

Erbin had divided his forces.

It was light when he mounted up and set off northwards towards the settlement. With him were a sufficient number of warriors to defend him should the sea wolves decide to stay and fight it out. Many however were men from the baggage train, pretend soldiers to mask the fact that the bulk of Erbin's force was with Kadwy and Marrec. With Kadwy were the Red Cloaks and all their unsettling troop, amongst them Erbin's own niece and those two beguiling and troublesome girls, as the king saw them. His younger son, Kelyn, he kept at his side, to keep a watchful eye on him.

Time and risk; they were the keys to it all.

In the first place it was reasonable to assume that word would reach the Leinstermen just as soon as the king was on the march. The risk was that they might go on the offensive, especially if the king's depleted numbers were realised. If so, they would have to make the best of it. Erbin was confident enough on that score. He had seen more fights and skirmishes than there were ponies on the moors. But it was also reasonable to assume that the Irish would not choose this day to stand and fight, outnumbered as they still were by Erbin. The sensible move for them to take was to make for their boats and the open sea.

This was where another factor of risk came into play. Erbin and his council calculated that their enemies would make that move, but only when it suited them, when they were good and ready. The Irish were known to Erbin and his captains; they knew them as risk takers, gamblers, boasters. It would suit the Leinstermen, Erbin thought, to make their move at the last possible moment, rounding the headland as the King of Dyfneint entered the ravaged settlement, taunting him, flashing their bare arses at him from the sterns of their ships. That's what they'd want to do; they'd take the risk of capture for the sake of a mad gesture, more intent on demonstrating their contempt for Erbin than on saving their own skins. "See you next year!" they'd shout, or something of the sort in their language that was at once familiar and impenetrable. It made Erbin laugh to think of it. For him, this was a game worth playing.

"They're a mad lot," Kelyn said, rather impressed. He was standing with his father on the shingle beach, watching the departing ships. "Should we call the bowmen to test their range, Father?"

The king said: "No. Let's not hurry our friends away."

His standards were flying. The day was fine and if the wind was up it wasn't so strong as to knock a man off his feet. "About as good as it gets," Erbin reflected. He felt quite light-hearted, contemplating the pleasure of a well considered and executed plan. "So far so good." Even the jeering of the Irishmen couldn't disturb his equilibrium this morning.

The risk was that they'd get clear away, down the neck of the Tawel River and out into Heron Bay. This was where time played its part; time and tide, to be precise. The Dumnonii had plied these waters more or less forever; its moods and odd ways were second nature to them; they knew them by instinct and these instincts were like acquired habits, passed on unconsciously from father to son, mother to daughter. The local men were sure of it – with the waters swollen with rain and the tide running out to sea, as it would be at this time, the ships of the sea raiders would be driven down the channel on the southern side of the neck of water. Prodigious rowers they might be; but like it or not they would be forced by the power of the current into that channel. And for this narrow neck of water, the men of Dyfneint would make a noose, close and lethal.

It was with that in mind that the bulk of Erbin's men had followed their guides into the night, which could boast no more than a scrape of moonlight. "Keep close and quiet," was the command. Heading west at first to avoid the watching eyes of the Irish, they'd eventually come to a pathway that took them northwards towards the neck of water, downriver from the settlement. They were making for a distinctive landform, a place where the channel on the southern side of the neck narrowed dramatically, between the mainland and a sandy island out in the waters.

"Quickly!" came the command to the already rushing troops.

It was no time or place for cavalry; not in this poor light; not when harness sounds were to be avoided at all costs. Just a few strong and steady farm horses went with them, bare-backed, one guided by Bryn, its hooves muffled. On foot the journey was a long, arduous undertaking over difficult marshy land. If they were not at the vantage point by mid-morning at the very latest they might as well have stayed in camp, under canvas and, if they were lucky, under a woman of their choosing. Men stumbled in the dark, which seemed to intensify as the night wore on. Tempers frayed; curses were uttered, more in the name of the old gods than the new – a fact that pleased Eleri Gwir, who on this one issue was fighting her own rearguard action. The captains were busy, encouraging, threatening: "Get along there; move, you useless bastards!" The responses of the men were left to the indifferent oblivion of the night sky.

Tired, fractious, they arrived at their destination in time to allow a few minutes' rest, in the company of a drink and a piece of dry bread.

"They're coming!" the lookouts shouted.

"To your posts," the captains ordered.

"I have to shit," a bowman said.

"In your breeks, soldier," he was told.

The land they commanded was a high dune from which they could see the three approaching boats, their struggle with the strong currents evident. The sea wolves had wanted to veer to the far side of the sandy island that lay before them, keeping to the broader channel on the northern shore of the neck of the Tawel. As the local men had predicted, the river saw it differently, pulling the Irishmen relentlessly into the narrower channel on the island's southern side. If they had cast off at first light, or even an hour or two later, the Leinstermen would have shown a clean pair of seafaring heels to the men of Dyfneint; as it was, they were about to run a gauntlet of sand and water arranged for them by the very same men.

With their open vessels passing immediately in procession under the shadow of the high dune, they made for easy target practice for the Dyfneint archers.

"Wait for the order," Marrec commanded.

Eleri was there with the other women of her company, the tension of the moment showing in her face, in the firm set of her mouth, in the line of thought that was on her forehead.

"Can you see out of that black eye of yours?" Siriol asked Cerridwen, throwing a dollop of humour on their nerves.

"Well enough," was the answer.

"I bet you can see better than Kelyn can walk!" Branwen said.

Braziers were fired. Half the archers would shower the sea raiders with a deluge of fire; the others with a flood of lethal metal.

"Shoot!" came the order. "Shoot at will."

The lead boat was directly under the dune.

"Aim and fire!" the shout was heard. "The helmsman is your target."

Heedless of orders, needing no encouragement, fire and metal went to work on their victims.

The dune formed a headland, in the lee of which the local men waited in their coracles, safe from the clutches of the rushing current. When the lead vessel came into range – its crew dead, wounded or frantically rushing about, taking the helm, stamping out flames – the men in the coracles let fly their grappling hooks into the boat's chaotic bowels. One hook was quickly ejected, and another failed to take a firm hold. Only one was secured, and this brought the rope taut and firm, a signal for the big farm horse at the water's edge to heave for dear life. It was neatly done, with the vessel dragged over and capsizing. The archers cheered, as did the ranks on the shoreline; only the men in the coracles were silent, seeing among the drowning the prize slaves that had been taken, their daughters and their wives.

The same trick couldn't be played twice. For one thing the local men were busy trying to rescue any of their own people they could reach; for another, they were also busy finishing off any of their enemies that showed the slightest sign of surviving the wild current; pulling up and pushing down was what they were about.

As luck would have it, her helmsman and stand-in helmsman dead, the second pirate vessel ploughed into the upturned hull of the first and from there sped towards the shore, where the men of Dyfneint waited for it. The third vessel followed the same or similar trajectory; it came skidding up the sandy beach like a missile from a catapult.

Swords and axes raised, the Irishmen leapt off their stranded boats and formed up in ragged, improvised formation. With nothing to lose, hopelessly outnumbered, they were determined to die well.

Battle cries were shouted: "Leinster, Leinster!"

"Dyfneint!" yelled the opposing side. Spears sounded on shields.

Battle would have been joined except that the figure of a dark-robed priest emerged from among the Dyfneint ranks, calling a cry of his own: "The last rites," he said. "I will administer the last rites."

From the height of the dune Eleri laughed aloud to see Father Cenydd there on the sands, waiving his skinny arms about, crying: "Wait; hold off."

"Of all the crazy men on that beach, he's the craziest," she told Cerridwen.

"Mad fool," was all Cerridwen could say.

"These are Christian men!" Cenydd was shouting.

Eleri's opinion was very different. To no one in particular, she said: "They're a bunch of murdering cutthroats, for Belin's sake."

Cenydd was indulged, briefly, grudgingly, which meant that the Leinstermen who died on that beach went to the heaven of their choice. Still they died, man by man. They fought bravely, but the truth of numbers prevailed. For Dyfneint, Kadwy was in the vanguard, determined to prove himself worthy of his position. Recognising his valour, his men drove hard into the Irish ranks, sending them back from the sandy beach into the water, step by painful step, their meagre numbers thinning all the time. Their leader shouted for his men to rally; when that failed he yelled abuse at his enemies, insisting on having the last word.

Macsen and his Red Cloaks were there, distinctive in every respect, not least their disciplined fighting style. Pride filled the men of Dyfneint to find them on their side. It was Riwalus who ended the leader's shouting, thrusting his sword deep into his guts with such force that it swept the man backwards, splashing into bloody water.

Arawn was in the thick of it. A big man came charging at him, sword hoisted, slicing through his shield and down into his groin and thigh. Falling to his knees under the ferocity of the blow, Arawn made his peace with his own gods, directing his soul to journey to the spirit house of Ynys Wydr and from there into the world of light. But he was getting ahead of himself. He saw the Irish warrior keel over, as the first vessel had done, and drop unconscious into the shallow water where the fighting had carried them. A missile had struck him, it seemed, and he died there, drowning in a hand's breadth of water, as unlikely an end to his warring life as could be imagined. Arawn looked about to see if, in the chaos of violence around him, he could find a cause for this curious outcome. What he found was the boy Gereint, standing on the prow of one of the beached vessels, catapult in hand and a big grin on his daft face.

From somewhere Arawn found the strength to say: "Lucky you didn't miss."

"I usually do," Gereint answered cheerfully.

With only a handful of sea wolves remaining, all of them knee-deep or more in water, Kadwy called off his men, ordering them to take position on the sands, archers to the fore.

"I offer you safe passage out of here," he said, with the confidence of a Caesar. "I have a message I want you to deliver to your chieftains: tell them that the men of Dyfneint will fight for every inch of our land; tell them that." He looked at the Irishmen there in the shallow water, their eyes squinting into the midday sun. "Do you understand?" he asked. Grimly, one or two said they understood well enough.

There were only five of them. Kadwy got it into his head that one of them was not squinting at all but, rather, smirking, as if in mockery of the young prince.

"You," he pointed. "Step forward." When the Leinsterman refused to quit his watery toehold on life, Kadwy said: "Very well; you will all die."

At that, the man's companions propelled him forward onto the sand where the order was given to the archers to shoot him. For her part, Eleri would not admit to pity for a man who was a sea wolf, a slaver, a murderer. Yet she chose not to obey the order – after all, Kadwy was not her prince; her loyalty was to Ffernfael.

"He didn't have to let any of them go free," she pondered. 'So why should I find this unjust and unworthy of him?" There were questions about Kadwy she couldn't answer; and those questions, she found, reflected back on her own hot-and-cool nature.

Not to appear weak to his enemies, Kadwy ordered the amputation of the index and middle fingers of the right hands of the remaining Leinstermen, a physical reminder to anyone who cared to look of Dyfneint's power and justice. Eleri had no argument with that; slavers, killers had to be dealt with by their own ruthless standards.

It was truth for truth, plain and simple.

# Part Three

## AD 577

## “The Ash Month”

# Chapter Twenty-One

Every morning, upon waking, the women of the village of Tre Wyn trembled for the thought of it, the dreadful possibilities that might befall them and their loved ones: exile, death, slavery. You didn't need a seer to tell you; there was nothing Mared of the Silver Wheel or any other know-it-all could say that wasn't already known. Not everything is complicated. Indeed, it was the sheer starkness and simplicity of the situation they faced that cut so deep into their insides, churning up their bowels as much as their minds. They might run; they might die; they might serve foreign masters. What wasn't on offer to them was to remain as they were in the place and with the people they had always known. Such were the bleak reflections of the women of the village, as they rose in the cold, still dawn, the world quiet enough to hear the drop of their heavy thoughts. Later, with the bustle and noise of the day, children crying, husbands moping about, such sombre reflections would be driven away; only to return like thieves in quiet moments, with children sleeping and husbands about their business. The fear that takes physical hold of the body was never far off.

It was the same fear that woke their menfolk from deepest sleep, sitting them bolt upright, their hands reaching out for wives, lovers, children, checking that they were alive and warm; making sure their lives had not dissolved away during the hours of sleep.

"Try to rest," their wives and lovers would say. "Worrying won't help anyone." Yet worrying was the common lot of the women, moving silently about in the first light, dressing, their chores ahead of them, their stomachs grumbling with concern.

It was on such a morning, frosty, breath like dragon breath in the still air, that Eleri Gwir settled to her work, trying to set aside the avalanche of doubt and worry that had come her way. Out in the yard she found Cerys looking up at the fading sickle moon, the outline of its full body lighted by the planet Venus. Eleri had always liked Cerys; she was the nearest thing she had to a mother. She was different and apart from the women in the weaving room, always herself, never playing a role. She was private and honestly straightforward, unlike her own mother, the force of nature who was Mared of the Silver Wheel. Cerys had none of Mared's tendency to performance and manipulation. All the vanity had been poured into Mared's insatiable soul, leaving just a dash for her daughter, only enough to make her think once or twice a month about how she looked.

"I was speaking with the gods," Cerys said, seeing Eleri approach. "I was asking if Llew, the Lion with the Steady Hand, might lend me some of his resoluteness and steadiness of purpose."

Standing beside the older woman, Eleri took her hand in hers. They looked up together into the mystery of the dawn sky, the sun-god stretching out his limbs as he climbed over Bryn Taran, the fading stars stark and cold.

"And how are you, Eleri Gwir?" Cerys asked, kind and thoughtful.

"I don't know."

It was true. For the first time in her life she was at a loss, her usually clear mind a muddle, her own steadiness gone, all at sea. She hadn't seen her father fall. "Too busy thinking about myself," she told herself later, trying to wound her own spirit, finding fault where there was none to be found. How could she have seen when, in company with the other archers, she was making her way from the headland down to the beach where the battle had been fought and won? She wouldn't have it. There was the business with Kadwy. Instead of looking to her father, she had puzzled over the prince's command, wasting her pity on a sea wolf. "I should have known," she told Macsen. "I should have felt it; we're closer than anyone. I'm him and he's me."

If the boy Gereint hadn't jumped from the prow of the Irish boat and splashed through the bloody water to hold Arawn by the armpits and to heave him somehow to dry land, he might have met the same drowning fate as his assailant, the big Leinsterman. As it was, Gereint stood guard over Arawn until the handful of remaining sea raiders had been bundled back onto their boat and pushed out into the torrid current that had them speeding through the neck of sand and out to the bay and channel beyond. "Help!" he cried. "Arawn my chieftain is wounded!"

Those few simple words were a massive blow to Eleri, striking her still and silent for a moment, before sending her rushing to Gereint and her father. She could see at once that it was serious. Not knowing what else to do at that moment, Eleri threw her arms round Gereint, whose face was covered in tears. Siriol joined her there. Inspecting the wound more closely, she asked for fresh water to clean out the cruel gash that ran down the side of Arawn's stomach to his thigh.

"Let's get this sand and filthy sea water out of the wound," Siriol said to Eleri.

"Come on Eleri Gwir, jump to it," Arawn managed to say.

"Yes, Father," she said, the shock of what had happened thick in her voice, her hands reaching into her healing bag.

It was the bleeding she had to stop. If it had just been his thigh she might have improvised a tourniquet. As it was, the wound gaped large and fleshy, blood seeping out of it. If it had been anyone else her mind would have worked in its methodical fashion to solve the puzzle that was before her. As it was, the sight of her father lying there, falling out of consciousness, filled her with dread and panic. Eleri stopped, took a deep breath, told herself to calm down. She watched as Siriol cleaned the wound as best she could, flooding it first with water and then sprinking it with vinegar from the healing bag. By then Eleri had a compress of leaves and moss ready to staunch the flow of blood, enough at least to let her work with a fine bone needle on the butcher's gash. Pressing down on the compress hard enough to bring Arawn back to the world with a kick of pain, she threaded her needle through skin and flesh, easing the compress out as she went, making sure nothing was left behind to rot and fester in the wound. The work took time and a steady hand. Throughout, Eleri did her best to control her loud-beating heart, putting all her concentration into the needle and its thread, blotting out everything and everyone.

"Well done," Siriol said.

"It's pretty crude," Eleri commented. "What would the women in the weaving room say if they saw stitching like that?"

"They'd say well done," Macsen said at her side.

"Yes," Riwalus said, fighting back his feelings. For something to say and do, he went over to Gereint. "Well done, boy," he said, his voice heavy with emotion.

They took Arawn by hammock over the uneven, marshy land to the small settlement at the ford where the king had made camp the night before. Fortunately for Arawn he was unconscious for much of the journey, his mind and body in shock.

King Erbin was there waiting for them, full of congratulations; the good news had run ahead of them. A smile lighted his dark, unpredictable face, coming from a pleasure deep in his entrails. He was happy and buoyant, perhaps dangerously so; it was hard to tell. He embraced his eldest son Kadwy first, and next his captain Marrec. The Red Cloaks were singled out for praise. Becoming animated, Erbin even had a good word for the she-warriors, as he called them.

"Father," a discordant voice said, pulling Erbin's attention in another direction. "There's unfinished business, Father." Prince Kelyn was not one to be ignored for long.

"Later, Kelyn," the king said. "Leave it be for now."

"I insist," Kelyn said. He was a good-looking youth, wiry and vigorous. By his own estimation, he wasn't born to be overshadowed by anyone, least of all his slow-thinking older brother. "They can't be allowed to get away with it; they must be punished," he said. "You said so, Father," he added, striking a note that was almost as childish as it was churlish.

His mood changing, Erbin looked murderous.

"My lord…" Marrec began to say.

"No," Branwen said, placing a restraining hand on the captain's arm, knowing that if he spoke out now he would be condemned in Kelyn's eyes as a traitor; perhaps he already was. At that moment, reluctant as she was to embroil herself in family politics, Branwen knew that she alone could say without fear or favour what had to be said.

"My lord king," she said, as formal and deferential as it was in her to be, "surely the price has been paid; the Red Cloaks, Iwan Nânt among them, have done everything you asked of them; they have done more; they have put the fear of any god you care to mention into the sea raiders." She let the thought sink through her uncle's thick hide, taking stock of his storm-dark eyes as she did so.

"They've done their duty; that's all!" Kelyn interrupted, stamping his foot on the ground.

"It was a misunderstanding," Branwen continued, not to be deflected from her purpose. "That's all, Uncle. I'm sure everyone regrets the incident," she added, pointedly looking towards her young cousin.

"Regret?" Kelyn shouted at Branwen. "*You'll* regret saying that."

He stepped forward, but stopped quickly enough when he saw Macsen and Riwalus fingering their sword hilts. He saw too that Marrec had come towards Branwen, presumably with the idea of defending her, which led Kelyn to an idea of his own, that something would have to be done about his father's precious captain.

"Besides," Branwen went on, doing her best to ignore the movement around her, fixing on the king alone, "Arawn the son of Edern lies sorely wounded. He may not live. He stands guardian over the girl Cerridwen and the boy Gereint and he has paid in blood to Dyfneint whatever was owed." Trying to placate Kelyn a little, she said: "I know that an error was made but let us not compound it with another."

Uncle and niece squared off. “I could make you stay, Branwen, here in Dyfneint,” he said. “I could even send you back to Rhun, your lawful husband, if it comes to that; it’s within my power and I have the right.”

It was his turn to test and probe. A few moments ago he had been all cheerfulness and congratulation; now his playfulness had a menacing edge that could cut and wound. With the full force of his nature, as powerful as the big waves that swept down the River Hafren, he observed the effect of his words on his niece, watching the cloud that passed across her beautiful face.

“I’d be nothing but trouble, to you and to that cowardly husband of mine,” Branwen responded, as coolly as she was able, feeling the rush of the king’s strong will pouring through and over her.

Erbin pondered that observation until Kelyn said: “Arrest her, Father; this is the second time she has betrayed Dyfneint.”

Luckily for Branwen and the others, the interruption seemed to annoy the king to the very core of his mercurial being; he shuddered under his furs. “Arawn is wounded, you say?”

“Yes.” It was Father Cenydd who answered, the scribe who might seal the king’s reputation forever. “It’s bad,” he said.

Seeming to be genuinely sorry, his powerful nature suddenly shifting direction, the king nodded his assent to Branwen. “Let that be an end to it, then,” he said, turning meaningfully for the first time towards his youngest son; as if to say: “And that means you, too.”

“We shall see about that,” was all that Kelyn said.

Followed by a few of the younger captains he went out into the night, under the watchful gaze of his brother, Kadwy.

Not much escaped Kadwy’s notice.

# Chapter Twenty-Two

Eleri saw none of this. Her father was gravely ill.

Standing now in the cold light, Cerys beside her, the village stretching its sinews and its bones, she reflected for the thousandth time on what she might have done differently. Nothing ever came to mind; nothing sensible at any rate.

The king and his retinue, the princes, Marrec and all the captains, young and not so young alike, had left the following day for the west, where there were more sea raiders to be defeated. Erbin's allies and under-lords, the men of Kernow, had asked for his help, and he would provide it before winter set in and thoughts turned to warm hearths and long tales.

For hours that night the king had discussed with Macsen what was to be done the following spring. It was all about timing again; there was no need for the men of Dyfneint to arrive too soon in Caer Baddan, where they would become bored and fractious, and no point in them arriving too late, when the battle was done one way or another. Regular updates would be sent from Ffernfael, it was agreed, sent along a long line of riders that would carry news from the north to Dyfneint, so that Erbin would never be more than a day or two behind events at Caer Baddan. The same arrangements would be in place for Caer Gloui and Caer Ceri, except that there the lines of communication were shorter and more easily managed.

"We have our informers in the Gewisse camp and other spies on the roads leading into the lost lands," Erbin was told. "We should know in good time when they are on the march."

Afterwards, Macsen had sought out Marrec and confirmed with him the arrangements that had been made.

"Nothing can go wrong, then," Marrec had remarked ironically.

"Nothing at all." Macsen had agreed. "And remember to wash the feet of the Island clean of Irish sea wolves for me. I hate nothing more than to have dirty feet."

"I'll do that," Marrec replied.

"And watch your back, my friend."

"I'll do that too."

Marrec had left with the king.

For Eleri there was no leaving. She knew Macsen must: Ffernfael called; war; the Island of Britain. Her own immediate imperatives were less grand and reducible to a single cause: her father.

"I'll stay with him for as long as it takes," she told Macsen. "But you must go; you're needed by Ffernfael."

Macsen didn't argue. "Whatever happens, you can't travel alone at this time," he said, the statement sounding like an order. "The roads are too dangerous, filled with stragglers from the east and littered with those brigands from Maes-y-Gaer."

"I know."

"And your father will not be able to protect you."

"Even if he lives, you mean."

"Even if he lives," Macsen agreed, his sea-creature eyes steady. He had seen too much of death and dying in his young life to dissemble. "Riwalus has spoken to me about this," he went on. "He will stay with you."

"But you need him, Macsen!" Eleri protested. "He's your most trusted man."

"Riwalus is staying," Macsen said. "Do as you're told for once in your life, Eleri Gwir." If it was an order, it was said with more kindly feeling than Roman imperiousness. The playful humour Eleri had found in his eyes the first day they'd met was there again, winning her over.

"I'll miss you," he said.

"Not tonight, you won't," Eleri told him, pushing him down with her two hands, climbing on top of him, feeling the tenderness of his hands on her needy body.

When they were done, she shook him to stop him from falling asleep. A thought had come to her, fast as an arrow. "Cerridwen," she said into his ear. "She must go with the Red Cloaks."

But that wasn't what she had wanted to say.

"Yes," Macsen agreed sleepily. "That's all right; the men love their Dragon Maiden."

Eleri sat up, one hand on the blanket that served as their bed. The darkness around her was absolute; her only sure knowledge of Macsen was the touch of his strong hand and his wolf smell.

"I wanted to say that she must go with you," she said, speaking to the limitless dark.

"Meaning?"

"You know exactly what I mean, you awful Roman," Eleri said, sensing the smile that had formed on his lips. "That's assuming she wants you, of course," she added. "You may not be good enough for her."

"Like you, then," he said, squeezing her hand.

"Be serious, Macsen," Eleri said.

Would she regret this? She didn't know.

The layers that she found in others, priests and even soldiers, were there in herself; looking into her own nature was like digging into a thick layer of peat and finding there a hidden life of plants and animals, lives and souls. What was she doing anyway? She was helping her friends, providing them with gifts. She was also setting herself free. For all her supposed cleverness, she found that she was acting on instinct, taking a path that she had only just stumbled upon and running down it into the darkness of the future. She didn't know what she was doing; only that she wanted Macsen and Cerridwen to be happy and safe. It wasn't complicated: his wolf smell and her dragon fire. If it had been her friend Rhian, Eleri would have been jealous and possessive. With Cerridwen it was different; a sister, a sufferer, a warrior. And Macsen wasn't Gwion; they were the restless sea and the deep, rich earth.

Eleri laughed. "If anything, I'm too good for you."

"That's not how my mother would have seen it," he answered.

"Your mother had a lot to say for herself," Eleri said.

"She's not the only one." Macsen gave her a playful pinch. "Go to sleep, Eleri Gwir; turn that mind of yours off."

But Eleri wasn't ready to sleep; not yet.

Before he was finally allowed to close his eyes, Macsen said: "I'm sorry about your father."

"I know," Eleri answered, turning over to stare into the blackness. "Whatever happens," she said in a whisper, tears in her eyes, "I'll be there at Caer Baddan; my bow; my healing bag."

✲

For almost four weeks of cold, drizzling rain and mad winds from the west, she watched over Arawn, the eternal struggle between life and death. Riwalus was with her, as was the boy Gereint, who had announced that he was staying.

"Of course you are," Eleri said to him, glad for her father's sake and her own.

People from the settlement provided them with shelter, food and drink; they were very kind, giving whatever was theirs to give. One local woman, the cunning one of that place, offered to help tend to Arawn's wounds. "Thanks, but I think we're all right," Eleri answered, taking note of the thick crust of dirt under the woman's nails. If the woman took offence, she didn't show it, not then and there at any rate.

Over all that time Arawn came and went through the door of life and death. "Eleri Gwir," he would say on regaining consciousness; squeezing her hand. Once Eleri opened the big wound, cutting away the rough stitching to inspect the raw flesh beneath, making sure it was clean, pouring honey into the gaping hole. There was nothing more to do; still, her father seemed to be burning up, the sweat thick on his pale face, the shock to his body too great. With a damp cloth, she moistened his lips. He couldn't even eat the herbal broth she made, which dribbled aimlessly down his chin.

When he wasn't sitting beside her, Riwalus went hunting with the men of the settlement, and he and Gereint would walk or sometimes ride out to the sea, like father and son, exploring the world together. They never talked openly about Awen Ysbryd; she was there with them, of course, a sticky paste, a light, a binding oath between them. Gereint ran about, his old self restored, it seemed. Following Riwalus' lead, everyone in the settlement referred to him as the Little Hare – *Sgwarnog Bach.*

When Arawn went at last across into the world of light, his spirit making its journey to Ynys Wydr and onto the spinning, dreaming island in the far west, beyond the sight or reach of man, a grave was made in the old way, a beaker of mead placed at his head and a pouch of barley; his spear rested at his right hand; his sun-god shield at the other. A bonfire was lighted to tell the gods that he was on his way. A circle was made around the fire and the old songs of the tribes of the Island of Britain were sung. There were no priests to interfere. Arawn was sent off in the proper manner of his people. In celebration, the strong apple brew was drunk in sufficient quantity to help him along. In the grey dawn they welcomed the coming of Belin as Arawn would have wanted them to, giving thanks and praise.

Eleri had seen her father walk the slow walk through the door into the other world. She had seen him go to meet her mother. She cried and she sang and she cried again.

Wonderfully, as if by the power of Cynan's chanting, Gwion was there. The reality of his sudden appearance was more prosaic. A messenger had been sent by Macsen to Tre Wyn. "Arawn's dying and the chieftain's daughter is with him," the rider in a red cloak said. "But where exactly?" he was asked. The answer was complicated, a combination of Roman milestones on the Fosse Road and landmarks leading west to the place where the two rivers spilled into the sea. "Just ask along the way," they were told. "We left a long trail of signs and guides behind us."

Arawn's right hand man, Kado, had wanted to leave at once.

"And who will defend us from the Gewisse while you're galavanting about?" Mared of the Silver Wheel had asked him.

Kado had felt the weight of her words and that of the responsibility that was on his shoulders, put there by Arawn himself. Instead it was Gwion, determined to make amends, to redeem himself, who saddled a horse and was gone before first light and before his father could miss him. The guards on the palisade waved him off. He was treated to a big bear hug from Math, who commanded him to: "Look after that young woman."

"I will."

And there he was, raven-haired, black-eyed, dishevelled from the long journey, the smell of the red earth and the red cows of the Summer Land on his skin; on one side holding the hand of Eleri Gwir in the circle round the fire; on the other the hand of the Little Hare.

# Chapter Twenty-Three

There was work to do.

The women of the village were going about their business. "Good morning," they said, seeing Eleri and Cerys standing there, as if under a spell.

"Is it a holiday or something?" Rhian asked in her cheeky way.

Then Cerys' mother came up behind them, indomitable on her stick of yew wood. 'The oldest tree in the forest' was one of the names she liked to call herself.

"Good morning, Mared."

"Is it really, Eleri Gwir?" Mared fired back, never one to miss an opening for disputation.

The day had arrived. They were to abandon the village, for now at least until the outcome of the inevitable battle was known. The talk at the roundhouse had been of nothing else, ever since the news had come from Caer Baddan, that Cuthwine, the son of the Gewisse chieftain Ceawlin, had crossed the narrow sea from the Saxon homelands, bringing with him fifty keels full of hungry, violent warriors. Their enemies had taken advantage of the unusually calm seas and the relatively fine weather. The Saxons were mustering their forces. For the Britons, the reckoning was upon them.

By this time a core of the best men in the *cantref* had been trained by Kado for war. They would join Ffernfael at Caer Baddan. Spears had been newly pointed; shields mended; axes sharpened. Cerridwen's blacksmith father, Gronw, had been kept busy. He had, too, a project of his own. Metal helmets were a rare thing, the preserve of Red Cloaks and high chieftains. Soon after his arrival in the village, as a thanksgiving, Gronw had set about making one for Arawn; that he might ride out to meet the Gewisse in proper style. Some days after Eleri's return he had presented it to her, his stammer making him fall over his words. On this occasion, his wife Gwenda let her husband speak on his own behalf, knowing how much it meant to him and certain of Eleri's understanding.

"It's beautiful," Eleri said, her hands running over the helmet's smooth, high dome with its sun motif, over the shapely silver dragon-form above the eyes. A few months back she would have interrogated him about the origin of the silver, but not now; she was learning a thing or two about what was appropriate to time and place.

"I'm s-s-s-sorry about your father; he was a good man."

"What should I do with it?" Eleri asked.

"Try it on," Gwenda suggested, with the same forceful nature as her daughter.

"No, I don't think so," Eleri said. "It doesn't seem right somehow." She felt suddenly like the boatman's woman out in the Water Land, unable to accept Macsen's offer of his arm ring. The poverty of the woman's life in that windswept place came to mind, as did her innate dignity, her understanding of what was the right and decent thing to do.

"Take your time," Gronw said, clear as a bell.

"I will."

Since her father's death, Kado had assumed leadership of the fighting men of the *cantref* of the Summer Land. It was what Arawn would have wanted. A few of the leading men had dissented; one had even quit for the Water Land after the consesus in favour of Kado was reached, taking his family and possessions with him.

When Eleri had showed Kado the helmet, he'd said in his rough and ready way: "I've got a big head; it won't fit."

It proved to be the case.

"It's like a huge turnip," Eleri commented, noticing the rounded shape of Kado's skull for the first time.

"I'll take that as a compliment, young lady."

"It wasn't intended as one!" she answered, laughing.

"Hold on to the helmet for now, Eleri," Kado had said. "You never know."

Without Arawn's firm guidance, the voices in the big square at Tre Wyn were like geese at their morning meal. "What are we to do?" was the question, to which there were any number of discordant answers.

The fighting men would go with Kado to Caer Baddan; but what of everyone else? Too old and too deeply planted to be uprooted, Mared of the Silver Wheel was for staying put. Her daughter Cerys wasn't so sure. Some argued for going south to Dyfneint; others for the Water Land; some for Caer Baddan and its Roman walls. No one seemed to want to rely on the mercy of the Saxons; they were not known to have a better nature.

Standing at the centre of the square in the middle of the muddle of voices were Kado, and Gwion's father Meriadoc, both sensible and well-respected men in their own spheres but lacking the authority of their old chieftain.

Not waiting for an invitation, Eleri joined them, by an act of will setting aside the self-doubt and uncertainty, the dark thoughts that had lodged like a low mist inside her body since her father's death. More than the first blood of womanhood, more than the first blood of battle, that one event felt like a watershed in her life: the person she was before and the person after. People around her, mothers who had lost children to accident or plague, fathers who had seen their sons fall in war, assured her that time would help to ease the pain. They didn't lie; they didn't pretend that they were over it, that the wound would ever heal, that the door to grief would ever close. "But it will get better, Eleri Gwir," they said. "Keep going; keep busy; we need you."

Yes, they needed her; and she needed them, her friends and neighbours. She would try; she would walk up and out of the mist; she would help herself and those she loved. There were days when she believed it; there were days when the enveloping mist would fall again, blocking out the sunlight. Walking into the centre of the square, she willed her spirit to rise into the full light of day.

"Now we're for it," Mared of the Silver Wheel said, her deaf ears adding tone and volume to her naturally strident voice. "Are you going to order us about like your father used to?" she asked, quarrelsome to the last degree.

"Yes, I am," Eleri responded. "Somebody has to."

Eleri had the floor, quiet for now, although likely to erupt with noise at any minute, as she knew too well. "As I see it," she started, "the best option for those who will not go with Kado is to find shelter in the Great Wood. It's close by and dense enough in parts to conceal an army of Rome; it might even be thick enough to hide Mared of the Silver Wheel."

"What did she say?" Mared asked.

"Nothing, mother," Cerys answered.

"It was something."

"The Great Wood, Mother; Eleri says that's where we should go."

"The ghost wood?" Mared cried out. "Is that where you're sending me, Eleri Gwir, to live with the dead souls of murderers and brigands? I suppose you think I'll be right at home there."

Others saw the sense in it, reluctant as some were to venture far into the Wood, the subject of stories recounted to misbehaving children, who were told of the evil giant Cawr who lived there, waiting to imprison and devour them, flesh and bone. "And around him swirl the spirits of the restless ones," the young ones were told. "Unable to find their way to Ynys Wydr and so barred from the spiralling island of souls that is Caer Sidi."

Some of the people, a few, those with family in other parts, chose instead to go to the Water Land, among them Kado's wife, a stern-faced and strong-minded woman by the name of Arian.

"If he lives, he'll know where to find me," she told Eleri Gwir, who knew better than to try to change Arian's mind.

"Good luck," was all Eleri said, placing her hand on the shoulder of the young boy at Arian's side, a kindly act he remembered all his days.

Most took Eleri's advice, and so for weeks preparations had been made to shelter the bulk of the women and children, together with the men who were either too old or infirm to fight, under the eaves of the fabled Great Wood. Gwion's father Meriadoc would take charge, the heavy limp he had received years back from an angry bull no recommendation for a warrior. Second in charge was Cerys – good-natured, able, the burning embers of her quick temper a reminder that she was nobody's fool and no one's doormat. And Cerridwen's parents would be there, strong and steadying influences.

"I don't suppose you'll be joining us in the Underworld, Eleri Gwir?" Mared had remarked.

"I've given my word," she said. "I must go with Kado to Caer Baddan."

Mared of the Silver Wheel didn't seem to think much of that, saying it was the weakest excuse she'd heard in many a long day. But Mared was getting old and people had stopped listening to her, or listened less attentively and only to those things it suited them to hear. Once Mared had been a seer; now she inhabited a middle ground between seer and selfish old woman. Nothing she said could break the trust the people had in Eleri; needing someone to believe in, they believed in her and so made ready for the migration to *Coed Mawr* – the Great Wood.

And this was the day.

Now that it was here, Eleri could only hope that it was the right decision. One by one, family by family, the people of the village congregated around her and Cerys to watch as Great Belin climbed out of bed and into his chariot of fire. For that moment the women set aside their worrying and, in company with their menfolk and children, lifted their arms and voices in thanks and in praise. They were alive; today, they were alive.

Then it was time to go.

Kado led the way, providing an escort before peeling away, heading north to join Ffernfael. Mared of the Silver Wheel rode like a May queen in a wagon drawn by two bullocks, which she rather enjoyed. Contradictory to the last degree, she was one of the few who had shed no tears when passing the rowan tree at the gate to the village.

Among those who waved them off were Arian and her young son, her stern look kept in place by an act of will, his face a picture of desolation.

# Chapter Twenty-Four

Her horse *Melltan* – Lightning Bolt – was as glad to be back on the road as her mistress. Through the country in rebirth she went with a spring in her striding step, enjoying the freedom that was to be found in movement. Horse and woman alike let their cramped thoughts race away from them, blown clear by the fingers of the still chill wind in their long coppery manes.

Ever since she could remember, Eleri had wanted to see Caer Baddan. Her father had said he would take her one day, but that day never came. With Macsen and his company she had skirted around the stronghold without ever entering its gates. Messengers would come out from Ffernfael directing the company here and there, but in all that time not even Macsen had entered Caer Baddan, keeping to the ragged borders and going wherever he was directed to go.

It wasn't Macsen who rode beside her now. Gwion was with her. When he'd appeared in that distant settlement in Dyfneint, as if conjured by the magician Gwydion from sticks and leaves, they had held on to one another as tightly and for as long as could be. But for all that, they had not recovered their old intimacy; not really. During the long ride from Dyfneint to Tre Wyn there were occasions when Gwion's flow of words buzzed around Eleri like a bee in summertime. Then he would fall silent, self-conscious as never before; never quite able to reach all the way back to their easy companionship of old. Both felt it, the slight awkwardness between them. Something like a lump of clay, cold and damp, obstructed the path leading from one soul to another.

In all that long journey from the wastes of Dyfneint to the Summer Land, it was Riwalus who had taken the lead, riding his horse hard up the tracks and roads they travelled. At his back was Gereint, less at ease racing along on top of a warhorse than on his own two feet. With them were Gwion and Eleri, all four of them going with heads down into the wind, their grief as heavy as their own weight and more besides. For days they'd journeyed without incident, reaching the Fosse Road on the third day, making camp in the shelter of an abandoned Roman quarry. It was there, in the small hours of the night, that Gwion had prodded Riwalus awake, saying: "there's someone there." With that, Riwalus was on his feet, sword drawn, Gwion with him, then Eleri and Gereint too.

"Show yourself," Riwalus ordered.

In the light of a half-moon, a child of no more than ten approached, a small rock in its hand, aimed at the soldier. A second child and a third came forward, barefoot and hopelessly ragged, one carrying a stave, the other a knife.

"What's this?" Riwalus asked. "Are you robbers? Are you alone?"

'Food," the first child said, coming closer.

A girl's voice declared they were alone, which seemed to be the case.

"You're welcome to some smoked fish," Gwion spoke up. "It's all we have."

It turned out they were from the east, from beyond the Great Wood. Their people were dead. They were heading for Dyfneint where they hoped to find passage across the Sea of Gaul. "My uncle is there," the girl said. Her thick hair sat like a crow's nest on her head. Even in that dim light Eleri could see the hardness that threatened to settle in her wounded eyes.

'Why don't you come with us," Eleri told them, her mind pondering the fate that awaited these children on the Fosse Road - bondage, slavery, slow or sudden death. Dark with her own grief, Eleri could see no light at the end of that road.

"No." They were determined to find their uncle in faraway Llydaw. There was no persuading them.

"We've killed men," the girl told them defiantly. "We can look after ourselves." As she said it, she gave Gereint a hard look that seemed to say, "I bet he hasn't done anything like that."

In the morning Eleri asked again, only to receive the same answer.

"Certain?" Riwalus inquired.

"Yes."

There was nothing to do but wave the children goodbye, stopping to watch as they disappeared up the Roman road.

The incident had left its mark. The disturbing memory of the children – small and vulnerable and yet brave and unyielding too – was impossible to shake-off or push aside. Now, as Eleri and Gwion headed for Caer Baddan, it was something to talk about, a shared experience that led them away from the difficult intimacies of their own relationship.

"I wonder what became of them?" Eleri asked. "She was a tough girl and clever with it. Do you think they made it, Gwion?"

"I don't know. I hope so."

Glad as he was to be talking about this and not some other subject, one in particular, in the end of the day there was nothing much Gwion could say. He relapsed into awkward silence, the topic that buzzed in his brain refusing to sound on his tongue. Not quite redeemed, in his own eyes at least, he couldn't bring himself to talk about Macsen and the Red Cloaks. It was something that would have to learn to lie still and quiet between him and Eleri.

Trying to lighten the air around them, she rather carelessly asked him about Rhian, saying: "She's been making those eyes at you, I suppose."

"Is that what you think?" Gwion said, his open nature closing by degrees, his black eyes making for a deeper darkness.

"I don't know; you tell me," Eleri answered, a bit shirty, regretting what she'd said and wanting to start again but not able to find a way back to the beginning, to the strong roots of their friendship.

"*A bit; but not much,*" she'd said when her father had quizzed her about the sexual nature of her relationship with Gwion; and it was true enough – they'd messed about, hands going here and there, holding back ultimately when it would have been easier to go right ahead.

"Oh, Gwion," Eleri said. "I want us to be friends. If I die I want you to think well of me; as well as I think of you."

He smiled at last, his dark smile.

"The same goes for me."

Eleri might have said any number of things. She brought the chestnut mare she rode a fraction closer to Gwion, enough to let her leg rub against his, which brought that smile out again.

"Gwion," she said, intending it to carry its weight and more in meaning.

"Eleri Gwir," he responded, glad to be riding alongside her, some of the many tangles in his heart unravelling.

Still coiled inside him was the knowledge that he would never get everything he wanted: they were friends; he would have to make do with that. Weighing on him, too, was the thought of that first difficult conversation with Macsen that was sure to come, those pale blue eyes of his summing Gwion up and finding him wanting.

Riding through the waking land, she smiled at him; setting the complications of life aside, letting her grief go as far as it wanted. The helmet she carried on her saddle was his for the taking, but Gwion had said that he would feel a fool and a fraud in such a fine thing – a novice soldier, a mere archer, a cowman's son. "My leather cap will do."

They approached Caer Baddan from the south, crossing the curling river into the old Roman civitas. From what her father had told her, Eleri went there with expectations of crumbling magnificence. What she found was far better and a lot worse than she'd imagined. Even now, broken, dilapidated, buildings in ruins, it was as beautiful in Eleri's eyes as it was strange. The statues, some disfigured, were so exquisite they took her breath away. The baths were something from another world and yet, when she looked at the fabulous carving of a great and powerful head with coiling hair, there was also familiarity to be found, something of her own world. She was in awe and wonder. And in despair too, from the moment the first ragged mother and child came to them begging for food. They rode on through the mess of displaced people, dribbling in from the lost lands to the east, seeking refuge. She saw that some work was underway, repairing and reinforcing the walls to the city's north. Otherwise, rubbish lay in the streets unattended, set upon by dogs and dirty children, the town's authorities long gone, or swamped it seemed by the influx of newcomers. Some people had found shelter with relatives and friends but many more were living under rough canvasses, or else under the uncertain shelter of the delicate birch trees that lined the streets. The river bank was full of stragglers in makeshift homes, crouching under upturned coracles or sheltering under hides suspended from the branches of the willow trees. "It's not good," her father had said when questioned about Caer Baddan; but then he had never been one to overstate his case.

One thing she found there was the boy Gereint, running about after Riwalus, who seemed to have adopted him. He dashed up to Eleri, saying: "All the Red Cloaks are here, Eleri; you should see them all together, their swords and their shields."

He had always brought a smile to her father's face and now she found he had the same effect on her. "It's good to see you, Little Hare," she said. "Have you seen Cerridwen? Is she with you?"

"She's with the Red Cloaks, I think. They're very busy; the war is here."

Seeing the helmet that was tied to the pommel of her saddle, he asked in his high-spirited, chirping way: "Is it my chieftain's helmet?"

"It was to be his; now it's looking for a new owner," Eleri answered. "I'd gladly give it to you, but it's too big."

"The other Red Cloaks all have a proper helmet; only Cerridwen doesn't have one," the boy said, with such complete conviction that Eleri knew for certain that it could only belong to her friend.

"Then it's hers," she said. It was, after all, her father's own handiwork.

At the centre of Caer Baddan was the great bath house, in working order still, with its columns and statues, among them a figure in bronze of the water god Sulis whom the Romans had made their own. Not easily impressed, Eleri wondered about the simple spring that would have been here before, the people of the Dobunni worshipping the hot red juices gushing from the earth. Even in disrepair, the baths were fabulous; yet she wasn't sure she liked them exactly. They oozed not mystery but organisation and control; the Romans, she reflected, were like tom cats marking the territory they conquered, even the ground belonging to the gods.

Eleri preferred the wild places. The night before they'd left Tre Wyn the people had gathered at the water pool in the river bend. At that holy place tokens had been left to the god of life and water who dwelt there; curses had been made against the Gewisse; words had been spoken for the dead.

"May the generations to come hear the secret names of the gods," they had chanted.

You couldn't say such a thing, not with proper conviction, Eleri thought, with a roof over your head.

To one side of the bath house was the ruined temple. Eleri assumed it had been destroyed by zealous Christians, which made her wonder why, in their magpie way, they hadn't requisitioned it for their own use. Was it too corrupted even for the Christians?

Near that was Ffernfael's hall, made of wood not stone, the work of her own people. Kado led them in, more than fifty trained fighters, the best men of the *cantref* of the Summer Land. Neither Eleri nor Gwion had ever seen so many people in one place, not under cover at any rate. This wasn't like the Great Circle where the congregation of people was always tiny compared to the host of stars that looked down on them. In here it was close and crowded with men; it was mostly men Eleri observed; she saw no trace of Cerridwen, or of Siriol or Branwen for that matter.

The mustering of the southern *cantrefs* had brought to Caer Baddan every able-bodied boastful man who could shout for a drink from the servers who rushed about the hall; all of them women, Eleri noted, most of them young and comely. She saw too that many of those raucous men had wandering hands that explored the women's thighs and private parts without invitation, which made the maids move even faster, swivelling as they went, trying to avoid unwanted contact. Eleri saw many things and many of the things she saw she wanted to change.

Kado had known her all her life; he knew that if anyone in that bustling hall could land him in a fight with some brutish farmer-turned-warrior it was Eleri Gwir, her fire-god beauty and her straight-talking mouth. Even if the rich torque at her long neck marked her out as separate from the maids in their plain shifts, it was no guarantee against her being propositioned by the first half-cut stranger who caught sight of her. A calculating man in his way, Kado gave it five minutes at most. Listening to Arawn's voice in his head, he pulled Eleri to his side, taking hold of her sleeve and giving her a long, knowing look.

She trusted Kado. He was plain and strong and constant; he had fought shield to shield with her father against their enemies. "I know," she said. "We're not here to fight one another, even if half of this lot could do with a good kick up the arse."

"Out," he said. "Take Gwion with you; find Cerridwen."

They found her at archery practice in company with Siriol and Branwen, a group of Red Cloaks looking on, betting on the flight of every arrow, the old coins of the empire, snipped and rough-sided, still in use.

When the three women set down their bows a Red Cloak shouted: "Hey, I'll never get my six coins back if you leave now!"

"There'll be plenty of gold and silver in those Gewisse arm rings to make you rich!" Siriol shouted back.

After Cerridwen had asked about her family, Eleri showed her the helmet. "Your father made it for my father; I'd like you to have it."

"Thank you," Cerridwen said, taking the helmet in her hands. As Eleri had before, she ran her fingers over its smooth, sun-adorned dome, peering into its deep, warlike eye sockets. She took hold of its long nose guard. "I like the dragon," she said, looking at the fierce worm that wriggled over the helmet's front. "My father made this?" she asked, a little incredulous, as if doubting his ability and skill.

"There's more to him than meets the eye," Gwion said. "Everyone has come to respect him."

That pleased Cerridwen. Pulling back her burning forest hair, thick and long as a dragon's tongue, she tried the helmet on for size.

"Perfect," Branwen said.

And so it was.

Seeing Macsen appear, striding purposefully towards them as if about to order them to clean their weapons or to get about some chore or other of a military nature, Gwion took a step back. Eleri saw it. Some things she preferred not to think about; and this first meeting between Macsen and Gwion was one of them. There were times when Macsen could be a terrible pain in the neck – superior, a cut above his surroundings; a bit too Roman was how Eleri thought about it.

This wasn't one of those occasions. Today he was at his forgiving, generous best.

"Eleri Gwir," he said, deliberately cool, a little distant, like a planet acknowledging the return of a wayward moon back into its orbit. "And Gwion," he said, positively warmly by the standards of a pale-eyed creature of the restless sea. Extending his hand to the young man in an act of reconciliation, he said: "It's good to see you; your spear and your shield are welcome." He could think of no higher compliment to pay any man, from Arthur to Caesar. "Eleri has told me all about you," he went on. "Good things all of them."

"Thank you," Gwion said. He didn't know if he wanted the earth to swallow him up or for the sky to fall on his head. Through his discomfort he managed to give Mascen his hand, strong from the tending and the slaughter of the cows of the Summer Land.

The firmness of his handshake pleased Macsen, which he made known by the merest hint of a smile.

Happy, relieved, unable to contain herself, her ebullience and amusement spilling over, Eleri blurted out to Macsen: "Normally, it's the helmet you'd be drooling over, not Gwion."

"Well, I am pleased to see him and any other man with a spear in his hand," Macsen said.

"In case you haven't noticed," she said, "he doesn't have a spear in his hand. He's carrying a bow."

The normality of the exchange, the cheek of it, made even Gwion feel more relaxed.

"It's like your father used to say, young woman," Macsen said – mocking, scolding. "You don't know everything, Eleri Gwir."

She didn't even know where the battleground would be; not for certain.

"Bryn Derwydd," Macsen said. "You remember the old hill fortress to the north? We go there tomorrow. Ceawlin is marching his Gewisse up the valley of the Tafwys; we'll meet them there at Bryn Derwydd."

That was the last they saw of him that day.

"There's a lot to do; I can't be standing around all day talking with the likes of you, Eleri Gwir," he said, his rougishness and the eagerness for battle written across his handsome face.

# Chapter Twenty-Five

From the vantage point of the summit of Bryn Derwydd you could see far and wide. Three comrades-in-arms – Macsen was there with Cerridwen and Eleri Gwir. They watched from their crow's nest the ribbons of fighters marching under the standards of the cross – north up the great Roman road from Caer Baddan, south down the same Fosse Way from Caer Ceri, and in a south-easterly direction from Caer Gloui, the last contingent picking their way through the watery low-lying lands of the River Hafren. Were there a thousand in total? It was hard to say. More probably, if all the promises had been kept.

The mustering of so many men from three different strongholds had been no mean logistical feat. Much of it had been Macsen's doing. Throughout the winter months, on his return from Dyfneint, he had liaised between Ffernfael and his fellow chieftains, the Irish brothers as people called them, Conmagil of Caer Gloui and Condidan of Caer Ceri, as quarrelsome a pair as Macsen had ever come across.

Backwards and forwards from one leader to another he'd gone, some of his Red Cloaks with him. Father Cenydd would invariably join him, partly because the church liked to meddle in everything and partly because the bishop at Caer Baddan got on Cenydd's nerves more than he cared to admit. For his part, Macsen had grown used to the priest, almost liking him, recognising that in another life he would have welcomed his fierce commitment into his company. Then again, like every churchman Macsen had met, Cenydd was a nest of contradictions: desire against abstinence, humility against pride, faith against reason.

"It keeps me busy, all this toing and froing," Cenydd had told Macsen once, almost in the manner of a confession. "Otherwise my mind is always on my family. I know it's wrong, but I don't like to be parted from them for so long."

"It's all God's work," Macsen told him, adopting what for him was an unusually religious turn of phrase, an echo of something Cenydd had said to him once. "Your family; the church; the war against the Gewisse."

Another constant was Cerridwen. Her presence was always welcomed among the Red Cloaks. From them, by word of mouth, down the tributaries of human communication, her fame grew, the story of the Dragon Maiden unfolded along the ragged borders and from there carried to the strongholds and settlements of the disputed land. Riding into Caer Gloui or Caer Ceri, people would come out to stare at the passing Red Cloaks; but it was Cerridwen they went to, touching her as she passed. As for the Irish brothers, she held them like playthings in the palms of her hands. It wasn't intentional or planned. There was no artfulness to it. True always to herself, Cerridwen never put on a show for anyone; she never set out to impress, still less to beguile. These she accomplished by the simple force and truth of her character, becoming a talisman for them all, chieftains and common folk alike.

For the Irish brothers, their fascination with her was deeply felt, absolute even. It carried them back, beyond the Christian God of their mother to the horse goddess,

Rhiannon, who like Cerridwen was said to ride a white mare.

Her unyielding spirit on show, Cerridwen said it was all wrong: "Don't you know my name is associated with the sow goddess; the one who devours her husband-kings," she told Macsen. "That's what the bards say. I rather like the idea," she added, letting a flake of humour float out into the world.

"We'll leave the details to others," Macsen told her, always the pragmatist. "Anyway, all those old gods were doing things like that; behaving badly."

He would say nothing to disturb whatever view or understanding the Irish brothers had arrived at regarding Cerridwen. She had become the seal to the oath they had given, the best assurance Macsen had that they would come when asked to Bryn Derwydd to live or die in the company of their Dragon Maiden.

It was obvious to everyone that Conmagil of Caer Gloui treated her with great respect and even something more, perhaps. For that reason Macsen would always make it clear that Cerridwen was with him in every sense, no questions asked. And it was true enough; although for a time only in the way that an acorn contains the true promise of the oak tree.

Like most things in life, everything but soldiering in fact, it was complicated. His men loved Cerridwen, but that didn't mean they wanted to see their captain in bed with her. His sisters were suspicious by nature. When he'd taken Cerridwen to his family's villa on the edge of Caer Baddan their distrust of the blacksmith's daughter had shown in every look they gave her. As for strong-willed Eleri Gwir, she'd given her blessing, so to speak; but blessings can sometimes be curses in disguise, compelling a person towards a mistaken course of action, a wrong turn in this one life that is granted to us. Being told you can do something and doing it are two different things.

Never shy, Cerridwen told Macsen that she and Eleri had talked it over, the whole relationship thing. For months it remained at that, a brief conversation, her forbidding solitariness a warning against intimacy, his diffidence born of many things, the most unusual for him being a tantalising fear of rejection. Eventually, at winter's end, from her own desire Cerridwen came to him, stepping into his room in the cold light of morning. Her nakedness, the pearl brilliance of her skin was striking, irresistible to his starving flesh.

"Move over," she said, a lover's command, an order a queen might give to her humblest servant.

Like Eleri, Macsen found her long and lean and every bit as bossy in bed; like her godly namesake, Cerridwen had a devouring presence that brought him to the razor-sharp edge of what it meant to be alive. Was Cerridwen with him? More accurately, he was with her.

"That's it," he'd said to himself. "We're with her: me, the Red Cloaks, Ffernfael, the Irish brothers, the lot of us."

At the summit of Bryn Derwydd, Macsen took a long look at the trails of fighters heading his way and took an even longer look at Cerridwen, her newly acquired helmet hanging from the saddle of her white mare, ready for action. He liked what he saw. Then he caught Eleri's eye. She was her old watchful self; missing nothing as usual. Up here, the mist that had hung about her for so long was lifted. At this time of reckoning, she was where she wanted to be and with the people she wanted to be with.

The three trails of fighting men converged at the base of the hillfort, half a mile or so from its steeper western edge. A camp was forming, cooking fires were lighted, men grouped together according to their districts and loyalties. The shape of the alliance was there on the ground to see – Ffernfael's followers to one side, Conmagil's at the centre and Condidan's to his brother's northerly flank.

And Dyfneint? Where were the men of Dyfneint?

Macsen didn't know for sure. "You don't know, or you're not saying?" Eleri quizzed. He didn't know. As arranged, riders had been sent south just as soon as he had news of the Gewisse mustering. None had returned. There were no messages; no explanations. There was time yet, but not much; a day perhaps, two at the most. Macsen tried not to dwell on it, but as the hours passed, he could think of nothing else.

"They're not coming," Eleri said.

Macsen didn't answer.

Coming down from Bryn Derwydd, Macsen, Cerridwen and Eleri walked over to where the Red Cloaks had made their camp. A trestle table had been set out for the leaders under a canvas cover. Walking directly in Macsen's footsteps, Eleri and the others came within sight and hearing of the three chieftains. It was the first she'd seen any of them. The Irish brothers were gingery by looks and temperament, big men the two of them, warriors, their features solid and bold, lean and ink-stained. Ffernfael, the high chieftain, was of a different stamp. He was shorter, darker; the first impression he gave was of quiet, brooding authority. Remembering what her father had said, Eleri thought he seemed bear-like, his shapely hands like claws waiting to pounce, his mind of a similar shape and disposition. The Irish brothers were more like feral ginger cats on the prowl, Condidan the more feral and prowling of the two.

Making sure Cerridwen was at his side, fully visible, even now enjoying the effect she had on the brothers,

Macsen reported to Ffernfael, telling him that all was in place and in good order. He knew Eleri was behind him and very deliberately drew to one side to afford the chieftains a better view of her. He didn't want to distract them from the business at hand, just enough to stop them from dwelling on the absence of Dyfneint, trying not to let that overwhelm and discourage them and so fracture the fragile alliance he had worked so hard to establish.

Rising to greet her, Ffernfael welcomed Eleri and said how sorry he was to hear of her father's untimely death. "A decent man," he called him. "He'll be missed." In an unexpectedly mellow voice, suggesting there was more to him than met the eye, Conmagil said he was sure that Arawn was with the one true God and all his saints.

"Possibly," Eleri said in as neutral a tone as she could manage, not wanting to offend the chief of Caer Gloui, yet more determined still to honour and stay true to her father's memory.

Condidan looked her over critically, approvingly. "Where d'you get them from, Macsen?" he asked rhetorically. "Are you hiding them away in that villa of yours?" He laughed, a quieter, softer laugh than Eleri had imagined. His brother laughed with him.

"So, Red Cloak," Conmagil said, angry and harsher sounding, "Dyfneint has let us down; that fat worm Erbin, that saddle sniffer, has betrayed us."

"And don't say *possibly*," Condidan warned; "Or we may come to blows."

Before Macsen could answer, Condidan got up and kicked over the bench he'd been sitting on. It was only then that Eleri realised just how large a man he was and just how much violence lurked in him, ready to explode at any minute. Whereas his brother Conmagil seemed relatively contained and controlled, a man who would use violence in a calculated way to achieve defined goals, the violence in Condidan was waywardly, frighteningly unpredictable. Outwardly, the difference between the two brothers was fleeting and subtle; even the heavy inking on their cheeks and hands was similar. Inwardly the difference was stark and obvious. Conmagil looked at Cerridwen with the eyes of a lover; whereas Condidan looked at her with the eyes of a rapist. He was the kind of man who thought that women were good for one thing and one thing only.

"I hope he rots in hell," Condidan said, referring to Erbin.

"Your scouts tell you nothing?" Conmagil asked Macsen, calmer now, as if his own anger had found an outlet in his brother's violent outburst.

"None have returned," Macsen answered. "We can speculate, I suppose, but I don't know the truth of it."

"You promised, Red Cloak; you gave your word," Condidan said threateningly. "Have you walked us into one of your traps? Is that it?"

"Whatever Macsen said, he said on my behalf," Ffernfael intervened, his body hunched over where he sat, intent on its own purpose, like a bear waiting to pounce on a salmon.

Not listening, Condidan waved a large dirty finger in Macsen's direction. "If we get out of this alive, Red Cloak," he said, his murderous eyes looking from Macsen to Cerridwen and back again, "you and I will have our own reckoning. And so will that witch woman of yours," he added for good measure.

By instinct, Macsen's hand moved to the pommel of his sword.

"No," Cerridwen said, her one word seeming to carry more authority than all of Condidan's blustering vehemence. The helmet she carried in her arms seemed to speak along with her, another more ancient voice concealed within its deep eyes.

"Sit down, brother," Conmagil said. He motioned to a serving man to right the bench. Changing the subject, he said in his mellowest voice: "That's a fine helmet, Dragon Maiden; will you try it on for me?"

She thought about it.

Slowly, deliberately, Cerridwen pulled the helmet over her burning hair and stood there before the men, tall, iconic, a warrior queen, a horse goddess, a talisman for them to believe in and to die for.

"Dragon Maiden," Condidan said simply, his fury gone, for now at least. It was as much an apology as it was a declaration of faith.

# Chapter Twenty-Six

For four days Macsen's scouts had tracked the Gewisse army as it rowed and marched up the valley of the River Tafwys. Their orders were to watch and report only; they were not to challenge or engage under any circumstances. "No skirmishes; nothing," they were told. "Let them think they have a clear passage right up to the battleground itself." Macsen wanted to spring at least one trap on his enemies. "We can give them something to think about," he told Riwalus.

His scouts told him that Ceawlin was twenty-five miles or so away, moving steadily, deliberately westward, his troops and camp followers making a long, snaking trail behind him. The scouts estimated that at least three thousand were on the march, although how many of them were front-line fighting men was hard to say.

"If that estimate is about right, I'd say over two thousand men," Riwalus said. "Two and a half, perhaps."

"Give or take a hundred here or there," Macsen said.

They were standing on the hilltop in the late afternoon, the wintry sun disappearing fast behind them. Nothing was to be seen to the east, nothing untoward at any rate: no fires, no telltale signs of smoke. The land before them was heavily wooded, oak trees mostly. If you had a mind to, you could hide an army in there. But that wasn't Ceawlin's game. He knew full well that the

Britons would be waiting for him; he almost certainly knew the exact spot. Signs of his approach would strike fear into his enemies' hearts. Of that he was certain. He didn't care if they saw his camp fire; he was more than happy for them to see a thousand camp fires, the more the better. Ceawlin wasn't hiding from anyone. He was marching, conquering in arrogant pomp. Another tom cat on the prowl, he would want to be seen, for his presence to be felt. Give it another hour and there would be fires and smoke aplenty, enough to satisfy any number of lookouts on any number of hill tops. Macsen only had to wait.

There they were, the smoke trails, just visible in the fading light.

Now the enemy was this close, Macsen had withdrawn his forward scouts. There was nothing more to know. Besides, with so many Gewisse in such close proximity, the danger of capture was too great. Ceawlin might know where the battle would be fought. What he might not know was the configuration of the British forces; in particular, news of Dyfneint's treachery, if that was what it was, might not have reached him. It would only take one captured scout to let the cat out of the bag.

"Will it rain?" Macsen asked Riwalus. He wanted it to rain or even snow, anything to make the ground wet and treacherous for men trying to advance in formation up the slopes and through the ditches of Bryn Derwydd.

"No," was the answer. "I don't think so."

"Pity."

Bryn Derwydd wasn't the largest or highest hillfort in this part of the world by any means. Still, with the number of fighting men at his disposal, it was large enough and with something to spare. All of Macsen's planning had included the contingent of five hundred men from Dyfneint; without them, his forces were too thin on the ground for comfort.

"Think," Macsen told himself.

That was what Ffernfael would be doing; he must do the same.

The mass of the Gewisse army fought and travelled on foot. This wasn't a war band, agile and fleet. Like all armies it was slow and cumbersome.

"Could we hit them somewhere?" he asked Riwalus. "Just enough to hurt, without compromising our own numbers?"

Riwalus wasn't sure. Any action would be risky, in his opinion. Older than Macsen by ten years, Riwalus had been fighting all his life. There was no doubting his bravery. But he wasn't one to throw away his life on some foolhardy venture, on something that might amount to no more than a pinprick for Ceawlin and his men. Macsen had learned a lot from Riwalus. If a risk was to be taken, it had to have a reasonable chance of success and it had to count for something.

"Our minds must be on the battle itself," Riwalus warned. "And not on peripheral actions. Small victories count for nothing against big defeats."

They'd climbed Bryn Derwydd, taking the steeper ascent on its western edge, to check on the lookouts and to clear their minds. The next morning the full British force would take up position on the hilltop, ready for the battle that would almost certainly begin on the following day. They'd come up alone, except for the boy Gereint, who was always at Riwalus' heels.

For reasons best known to himself, Gereint had climbed down to the big defensive ditch that ran around three sides of the hillfort. It was deepest on the eastern side, where the ground sloped upwards in a gradual incline. Macsen had discussed with Ffernfael the possibility of reinforcing the ditch with obstacles, a wall of spikes that might impede the enemy's advance. Ffernfael had vetoed the idea. His view was that such things rarely, if ever, impeded a truly determined enemy and tended to be used as cover for the men advancing up the final and steepest bank of the hill. "No," was his decision. "Let our archers go to work on them as they negotiate the ditch. Give them nothing to hang on to and nothing to hide behind. That's a steep bank they have to climb. Even if it's dry, it'll be hard going for them and easy pickings for us."

Macsen wasn't really convinced. He'd argued his case. Still it was no. But Ffernfael had happily agreed to the erection of a vicious line of spikes at the very top of the last bank on the eastern wall of the fortress, to provide a final obstacle to the enemy and cover for the archers, which was where Macsen and Riwalus were standing now.

"That boy really is a Little Hare," he said to Riwalus, as he watched Gereint run about. "Hey, Gereint," he called. "Will you run down the wall of the ditch for me and up here to where I stand? Let's see how you go."

The boy stood at the top of the ditch at its deepest spot.

Macsen and Riwalus played the battle out in their heads, seeing the Gewisse wall of big linden wood shields forming where Gereint stood, the Saxon warriors preparing for the most dangerous and least controlled aspect of the ascent. They would have had a drink or two that morning, to build them up and to push down their fear. By this point the effect of the alcohol would be wearing off. They'd be left with the raw reality of war, like coming out into the bright sun after hours in a darkened room. Their captains would urge them on, and down into the hollow of the ditch they'd come, many of them to die, many of them to suffer from terrible wounds, and some to advance to the last stage of their climb, up the imposing grassy bank, their shields the only material things between this life and the one that supposedly awaited them in Woden's hall. If you wanted to conquer this hill, this land of the Hafren, the Island of the Mighty, that's what you would be called upon to do.

"From here?" Gereint asked.

"Yes!" they shouted.

They watched him run – small, nimble, unencumbered by shield and sword. Down he came into the ditch, quick as a river in torrent. The ground at the foot of the ditch was uneven; holes had been dug into it for the unwary and the preoccupied to stumble into. Ffernfael had come up with the idea of concealing short, vicious spikes, no bigger than a man's thumb, in these cavities, capable of piercing through leather, skin and flesh. With no one around him, no fallen bodies or men desperate for cover, none of the chaos of war, the boy ran on, picking his way stealthily over the spiked and pitted ground. Then he faced the steep climb up the grassy bank, at the top of which was the large spiked wall, jutting out at 45 degrees. Even with no shower of metal raining down on him, not wounded, with no cause to be afraid, still Gereint slowed down. To make quick headway he had to cling on to the tufts of grass and still he slid about. At last he was at the top of the bank. His smallness a disadvantage now, only with some difficulty did he manage to get his hand on to the spiked wall, which he clambered over hesitantly, slowing down, taking good care not to injure himself.

He wasn't out of breath. No one had ever known Gereint to be out of breath. But it hadn't been easy. Macsen and Riwalus were both satisfied with what they saw. Of course, the Gewisse attack would be different, slower, more deliberate, taken stage by stage. Their best men would lead. Any hint of hesitation or outright cowardice would be dealt with by the sword. Their captains would be as ruthless with their own men as with the Britons. There would be chaos and there would be order. The expected and the unexpected would be in play. It would be nothing like this.

"Thank you, Little Hare," Macsen said. Even he had adopted the sobriquet, the invention first of the farrier Bryn and adopted later by Riwalus. All the Red Cloaks called him that now. Cerridwen was their Dragon Maiden; Gereint their Little Hare.

"What about the surprise attack idea?" Riwalus asked, reverting to their previous conversation.

"Let's sleep on it," Macsen said.

*

They returned to camp, where they found Father Cenydd in conversation with the she-warriors, Siriol and Branwen, Eleri and Cerridwen.

Gwion was there too, standing to one side, letting the others dominate. Used to his captain's ways, Riwalus took it upon himself to say: "I like the young man." He looked over at Macsen, wondering if a knot of enmity was still stuck in that proud head of his. For good measure, Riwalus added: "I hear he's a fine archer, but he's not what I would call a soldier."

Macsen knew what Riwalus was about. They understood one another, as much and more than many married couples. In their way, they were as close any two human beings can be.

"We've made up," Macsen said. "It's all forgotten."

"I'm glad to hear it."

"You know what Eleri Gwir is like," Macsen said. "She told me over and again I shouldn't bear a grudge against the lad. In fact she drove me crazy. She wouldn't shut up about Gwion, itemising all the good things about him. He's generous. He's this, he's that. If she'd told me he was a better lover than I am I would have hunted him down and killed him on the spot."

"She was sparing your feelings," Riwalus said, laughing into his beard.

"You speak from experience, I take it?" Macsen fired back.

"At least she didn't say he's a better soldier than you."

"I've seen him use a bow, Riwalus," Mascen said seriously. "He's good. He's very good."

"That's something."

"He'll give what is his to give," Macsen said. It was all he could ask of anyone, soldier or cowman.

Entering the circle of talk, switching his thoughts in another direction, Macsen jokingly said to Cenydd: "Once again we find you sweet-talking the women, Father."

"And all the best-looking ones at that!" Riwalus added.

None of the women laughed, and Father Cenydd obliged Macsen with one of his intense, thin-lipped stares. He seemed genuinely embarrassed. It occurred to Macsen that he might even be blushing. It was hard to tell in the light of the fire, and with Cenydd's freckled face.

"Don't worry, Father," Macsen said, intent on compounding the mild offence he had intended to cause. "Your wife won't hear about it from us."

"Actually, we were talking about religion," Siriol said, trying to resume the serious nature of their conversation.

"I suppose you lot have converted the poor man to heathenism," Macsen volunteered, plunging deeper into controversy.

"It wouldn't occur to us to want to convert anyone," Eleri said. "That's for Christians, with all their talk of the one God."

Before the conversation could go any further down that track, Ffernfael joined them, alone and unannounced.

"I'll murder them; I'll drown them in a vat of mead," were his first words. No one had to ask who he was referring to.

"What now?" Macsen asked.

"They're arguing over the battle order," Ffernfael said. "They insist on fighting side by side, which means that one of them and not Caer Baddan must hold the centre."

To Eleri, he seemed more like a dark bear than ever, round and big-shouldered, brooding and powerful. "Is that so bad?" she dared to ask.

"The Red Cloaks must hold the centre," Ffernfael stated. "That's where the main thrust of their attack will concentrate. We must match our best men against theirs."

It could have been Eleri's imagination, but she thought she heard him growl with displeasure. "I won't argue," she told herself. "I'll keep my mouth shut."

"Perhaps that's not how it will be," she heard herself say. "The Gewisse may see things differently."

She felt the light but distinct pressure of Gwion's hand on her arm. Her father would have done the same, she reflected.

Ffernfael looked her up and down. He'd already been shouted down by the Irish brothers that evening, and now this. "Are you telling me my business, girl?" he asked.

Her father had warned her about challenging leaders, saying: "They might claim that they want to hear what you have to say. What they really want, most of the time, is to be told how right they are. That's even the good ones. Be careful what you say around them, Eleri Gwir. Pick your moment." He spoke to her now, his voice in her head, pulling her back.

"No, my lord," she answered.

"Has anyone told you that that mouth of yours will get you into trouble one day?" he asked, still cross, his big hands like bear claws.

"Yes, many times."

"And so it will."

"If I live long enough," Eleri said, the need to have the last word leaping up in her.

Macsen wanted to intervene on Eleri's behalf, but he didn't know what to say exactly. It was Gwion who spoke for her, putting himself in harm's way. "Her mouth is big, my lord, but so is her heart. She will fight for this land as bravely as any man."

A leader with the foibles and sensitivities of a leader he may have been, but Ffernfael wasn't a small-minded man. Unless it served a particular purpose, petty vindictiveness wasn't in him. As an example of his type he was better than most. For the present he was the still centre of the storm, battened down, silent.

Into that silence the others – Siriol, Branwen, Macsen and even Father Cenydd – spoke all at once, defending Eleri. Cenydd named her a healer, which for him was a compliment of a high order: "A heathen, my lord, but a healer also." Eleri was amused, which always put her in a dangerous frame of mind.

Saying nothing, her silent authority as palpable in its way as Ffernfael's own, Cerridwen stepped closer to Eleri, so that they both faced the high chieftain directly. They were like two embers from the furnace of the fire god. Even Cenydd saw it, briefly, before by an act of will he pushed the heretical image as far away as it would go. "*Get thee behind me.*"

As if riding the fire chariot of Belin, completely unexpectedly – as a dare to himself, or was he just showing off? – the boy Gereint ran into their hot circle of words and jumped over the camp fire and out into the dark.

They laughed; Ffernfael made a sound between a chuckle and a growl.

"Tomorrow first light, Macsen," he ordered and turned on his heels. "And bring those two with you," he shouted over his shoulder.

No one doubted that he was referring to Eleri and Cerridwen.

# Chapter Twenty-Seven

As Riwalus predicted, the weather stubbornly refused to cooperate. The one time they actually wanted it to rain, for the skies to open, there was nothing but wan sunshine; even the winds had fallen still.

"I bet it's raining in Dyfneint," Macsen complained to Riwalus, as they made their way to Ffernfael.

"I hope its pouring a plague of evil dogs on them." Riwalus said.

They'd talked about Dyfneint into the night. What could have happened? It was one thing for King Erbin to change his mind about coming to their aid. If that was it, why hadn't at least one of the many riders they'd sent returned to tell them the bad news? Why had they been killed or imprisoned? It was too much to believe that misadventure had befallen all of them. There were fugitives and stragglers on the roads, it was true, some of them intent on robbery and worse – but surely not all the riders could have met that same fate? If Erbin and his sons had perished driving the sea wolves from the feet of the Island in Kernow, they would have heard about it.

"Are they at war with one another, d'you think?" Siriol had asked.

"I hope not, for their sake and ours," Branwen said. After the battle with the sea wolves, she had offered to stay behind in Dyfneint with Eleri. "To help look after your father," she had said. Everyone had counselled against her staying, including Siriol, who was adamant that Branwen was safer away from the complexities of her tribal homeland.

"Get her out of here," Eleri had told them.

More than anyone, Macsen trusted his brother soldier Marrec. If it had been possible to send news, he was confident that Marrec would have done so, always assuming he still lived.

Bringing their nighttime deliberations to an end, Macsen had said, "I'm sorry, Branwen, but it doesn't look good."

"Not for them, and not for us either," Eleri had chimed in.

For Ffernfael and his allies the immediate issue was that their battle order was predicated on Dyfneint's participation. The original plan was for the brothers to stand together on the fortress' northern flank, placing Ffernfael and his Red Cloaks at the centre and the forces of Erbin of Dyfneint on the southern flank. The archers of all the contingents were to be deployed primarily in the centre formation, on the front line initially and falling back as required, with the probable advance of the Saxons to the brow of the hill. These arrangements were thought to work well. The discipline of the Red Cloaks would permit the archers to advance and retreat through their ranks as required. To ensure the plan's relatively smooth operation in the panic and mess of battle, the Red Cloaks were to have had command of all the bowmen.

That was the theory.

As for the flanks, with the combined forces of Caer Gloui and Caer Ceri to the north and Dyfneint to the south, it had been reckoned there would be sufficient numbers to cover any outflanking movements the Gewisse might attempt.

That was the plan.

"Without Dyfneint it's dog shit," Condidan said at their morning council of war. "Without that fat arse Erbin and his turd droppings nothing adds up."

It was hard to disagree.

Without Erbin their numbers would be stretched thin across the flanks of the hillfort. There was simply too much ground to cover. If the flanks were pulled into the fighting at the centre, the rest would be left exposed. For Macsen, it was like the mathematical problems he'd been set by his tutor; either the numbers added up or not; you couldn't invent a solution of your own. Four plus four never made nine, let alone ten as was required here.

Macsen saw Condidan look at him as if this was all his doing. It wasn't rational, but then neither was Condidan. "That mad bastard," was what Ffernfael had taken to calling him. "I can handle Conmagil, but his brother is another story. There's something missing in that head of his."

Famous for his persuasive gifts, for finding a path through the most difficult conflicts, Ffernfael was at a loss when it came to Condidan. He knew him to be ruthless. His power and position in Caer Ceri had a firm foundation in murder and intimidation. Whereas Conmagil had inherited the command of Caer Gloui from his father, Condidan had taken possession of Cae Ceri from another chieftain who had also killed his way to the top, a story that was only too familiar. In the ten years or so that Condidan had been in charge, nothing had been done to repair Caer Ceri's defensive walls. For Condidan, power was an end in itself, to be used for personal gain and enjoyment. The only restraining forces on him were his brother, when it suited him, and the memory of their devoutly Christian mother, to whom Condidan was mawkishly attached.

As Ffernfael recognised, another potential source of influence was Cerridwen, although as the events of the previous day had shown, her authority over Condidan was far from certain or consistent.

To speak for the church, Father Cenydd had been asked to attend the council of war. Cerridwen was there and, on a hunch, the wily Ffernfael had also wanted Eleri to be present. Macsen and Riwalus completed the group. The brothers had come alone, disdaining advice from anyone.

There were times when Conmagil took the lead, smoothing over his brother's very rough edges. Then again, there were times when he was happy to let the more unpredictable and volatile Condidan make the running. This was one of them.

"So let me get this straight," Condidan said now, belligerently loud, addressing Ffernfael and Macsen. "You don't deliver Dyfneint and you still want to hold the centre. I don't think so, *high chieftain*. I think you and your precious Red Cloaks should move over and let me and my brother fight alongside one another. That's what I think."

"And you agree?" Ffernfael asked Conmagil.

"I don't disagree," Conmagil said.

"This is an alliance of equals," Condidan argued. "In fact, the last time I counted, we're contributing the lion's share to it."

Both Ffernfael and Macsen felt that anything they said was likely to inflame the situation. What Condidan asserted was true enough. It was those intractable numbers again. Instead of responding to Condidan, they let the problem boil and bubble like a pot of murky broth in the early morning air.

Father Cenydd looked pinched and tired. He had been with the brothers for hours the night before, trying to soften their position, tiptoeing around their protruding sensitivities as he did so.

"It's vital that we stick together," he said. "We come here under the one standard of the cross; this isn't about us, it's about the very survival of our faith and our way of life."

His words fell a little flat. No one carried the argument further.

For the first time in her life, for the first time she could remember at any rate, Eleri Gwir asked permission to speak.

Two gingery heads turned to inspect her. The brothers seemed amused at the prospect, but even they were pleased to have some respite from male contrariness. Besides, curiosity was working its subtle way through them, like water through rock. They'd assumed that Eleri was only there to keep Cerridwen company, or as something easy on the eye, a distraction, never expecting her to speak up on her own accord.

"Well, let's have it then, girl," Conmagil said in his smooth voice. He very nearly referred to her as Macsen's whore, until a restraining voice in his head advised against it.

"Make it quick," Condidan snapped.

Her heart was pounding. She tried to control her breathing. Glancing at Macsen, who seemed to be inviting her to speak, she said: "I just wanted to say that the Gewisse might do something unexpected, and that perhaps we should think of doing something unexpected ourselves."

"And what would that be?" Conmagil asked brusquely.

"I don't know; I only thought that we should try to think about it in a different way."

Condidan scoffed.

"That's useful," his brother said ironically. "Even if it is a bit late in the day."

"But if we do stick to our battle plan," Eleri ploughed on, "my lord Ffernfael is right. Only the Red Cloaks have the training and discipline to hold the centre. It's what they do."

"Did you put her up to this?" Condidan barked at Ffernfael. "Or you?" he said aggressively to Macsen.

"No one put her up to anything," Ffernfael sought to assure them. "I don't think even God himself could put her up to something. But what she says is true. The Red Cloaks belong at the centre. Unless of course we decide to do something unexpected," he added without conviction.

She didn't know it then, but Eleri was to learn that once the military mind gets a plan or idea fixed in its head, getting it to change its course, persuading it to look at the problem differently, presents one of life's most intractable problems. It isn't intelligence that's at issue but imagination. Even Ffernfael and Macsen, neither of whom was wedded to dogmatic habits of thought, could not make the leap of imagination needed to adopt a new perspective. They kept on thinking, but in a straight line. For them, it was the plan and battle order as originally conceived or nothing. Admittedly, the hour was late to change tack. But, then, if as they said the hilltop fortress now presented an apparently insoluble problem of scale and numbers, why persevere with it?

"Why not abandon the fortress?" she asked.

"And lose the high ground?" Ffernfael said. "I think not."

They all found that amusing, except for Cerridwen, who said: "She may be right; she often is."

Not even the prestige of the Dragon Maiden could deflect the men from their course. On the other hand, the diversion created by Eleri had given Conmagil the opportunity to reconsider his obstinacy over the battle order. “Very well,” he said reluctantly. “If my brother agrees, the Red Cloaks can have their glory.”

“Much good it will do them,” Condidan said, by way of indicating his approval. “For the sake of the one true God – let’s get on with it before Ceawlin is shitting on our heads.”

“I suppose that’s something,” Eleri told Cerridwen privately. “But I don’t know what exactly.”

“We’ll have to trust to our own courage,” Cerridwen said. “At the end of the day it’s all we’ve got.”

“The land is ours, Cerridwen,” Eleri said fiercely. “It’s always been ours. I just can’t imagine it otherwise.”

Her own imagination was not without its limits. More accurately perhaps, where this particular subject was concerned she only cared to exercise her imagination selectively, and to a limited extent.

# Chapter Twenty-Eight

By the time the council of war was concluded Macsen had given up any thought of mounting a surprise attack of his own. There was too much to do. The fortress had to be secured; there were manoeuvres to practice. Patrols had been sent out to ensure that the Gewisse didn't try a surprise attack of their own. They were very close now. The smoke from their fires coloured the sky and filled the air with the smell of burning.

The whole British camp was already on the move, men and equipment. Conmagil's Caer Gloui would take the northerly flank, Condidan's Caer Ceri the southern end. Caer Baddan and its allies, the men of the *cantref* of the Summer Land among them, would hold the centre, facing eastwards, the home of all ill winds. Horses were making their way gingerly up the slopes to the summit of the hill, which was large and flat enough for cavalry, should the need or opportunity for cavalry arise. Always solicitous about the welfare of the horses, Macsen went to supervise their progress up the steeper western ascent, where there were no ditches or other obstacles to negotiate.

Eleri found Kado organising the men from the *cantref* of the Summer Land as they waited for the order to march up to the fortress top. They would be positioned at the centre, immediately to the rear of the

Red Cloaks. The only exceptions were those who would join the brigade of archers, Eleri among them.

Gwion would be with her. As Kado said: "That lad couldn't spear a virgin at two paces but he could put an arrow into her father's eyeball at a hundred."

For Gwion it had been a hard pill to swallow, to be told that he was not cut out for shields and spears, the more so because in his case he had known it all along. He felt his inferiority keenly and would have done anything to contradict it.

On the other hand, Kado had made a great play of his skill as a bowman. "We must have the right men in the right places," he insisted. "You just have to accept it, Gwion."

Accepting his lot was made easier by the contrary Eleri. This was the Eleri who had fallen instantly for Macsen, the burly military man. And it was the same Eleri who didn't seem at all judgemental about men's physical prowess or the relative lack of it. It would never have occurred to her to find fault with Gwion on that score. When he raised the subject, she'd said playfully, looking him up and down: "Don't worry, whatever Kado says your nice arse makes up for it."

There was the subject of sex again. They hadn't avoided it exactly. Eleri wasn't one for avoiding touchy subjects. "I'm not with Macsen anymore," she'd told Gwion. She wasn't with anyone. Still, the subject of sex would not go away; its cunning insistence worked its way through her young body, into the pores of her grief and out again.

For his part, Gwion was like a cat in a tree, hopeful, waiting for a sign, for an invitation to pounce on his preferably willing prey. The previous night they'd lain side by side, friend by friend, comrade with comrade. For Gwion it was agony; he'd squirmed about and tossed around, unable to stop the itching in his body. "I'm sorry," he'd said to Eleri. "I'll move to let you sleep." Her own body waking from the hibernation born of grief, she'd reached backwards, her hand on his thigh, holding him in place; then taking his sex in her hand, she'd held and fondled him until he spurted his seed out onto the red earth.

"I'm glad you'll be with me," she'd said.

"I'm glad too; whatever happens."

They hadn't slept; they'd talked; about the past; about the present; leaving the future to take care of itself. Eventually, in the small hours, sleep had found them, his wiry body curled like a cat into hers.

All that day the brigade of archers and the Red Cloaks practised the manoeuvres they'd planned. There were just over a hundred Red Cloaks divided into two equal groups, one captained by Macsen, the other by Riwalus. The slick precision and speed with which their ranks opened and closed, changed formation and moved to allow the archers to file through them, now to the front, then to the rear, was impressive. The orders were barked out loud and clear; whistles were blown – one whistle for advance; two to retreat. Nothing complicated; keep it simple was the order. Not only the archers but the troops directly behind the Red Cloaks, the men from the Summer Land and others, were trained to obey the ordering calls and to allow the bowmen to pass through their ranks. But that was less impressive. A good deal of strong language was heard from among the ranks. The Red Cloaks watched all this with raised eyebrows, sufficiently reconciled to their fate to find entertainment in the unprofessional mess. Inevitably, some of them fell to wagering on which individuals or how many would head off in the wrong direction. "You have to laugh," they said.

Cerridwen laughed along with them, especially when she saw Eleri going the wrong way. "Even you, Eleri Gwir!" she called.

"Shut up!" was the answer.

"You try it," Branwen called to her, although she and Siriol were like old hands, never missing or taking a wrong step.

Nervousness, anticipation, the fearful excitement of imminent battle were everywhere, making the quiet ones talk, the talkative ones more inclined to contemplation than usual.

Cerridwen would fight with the Red Cloaks. That much was taken for granted. She had acquired from Macsen a short, lethal sword and had long practised how to use it behind the crowded wall of shields, stabbing into the gaps created by the front-line men, going for the groin, the unprotected nether regions of the enemy. She was ready. She would wear into battle the helmet her father had made. The sun-god of her people would be her shield.

A shout came from the lookouts, a horn was sounded; the crows in the high oaks were speaking to them, telling that a host of strangers was nestled there. All that day the Saxons had been advancing from the east through the wooded valley that lay before the fortress of Bryn Derwydd. The hill itself was clear of trees, as was the space around it, cleared many years ago by the people of another age. From the brow of Bryn Derwydd the land fell away, down to the huge ditch and down again until it levelled out and ran eventually into the oak woods, which were coming back to life after the long winter, buds and leaves showing, red squirrels waking up.

By midday the vanguard of the Gewisse army was in place, Ceawlin the king and his son Cuthwine with their sworn earls and captains taking stock of the British fortress. By the time the winter sun had made its low journey to the far side of the hill, the rest of the army could enjoy the same view, the reverse of what the British pickets saw, the gradual and in some places steep climbing land, the man-made ridge about three quarters of the way up, the steeper ascent to the brow of the fortress, capped by its vicious-looking wall of spikes.

The king had seen it all before; he knew its terrors and its rewards. For his son Cuthwine it was new, a frightening dare, an invitation to glory. Ceawlin asked his son what he saw.

"The enemy; a fortified hill, Father," was the answer.

"Yes, fortified," Ceawlin said. "But only to an extent, I think. They could have built higher, more formidable obstacles – a palisade running the length of the hilltop perhaps. They didn't. They want us to attack, to engage them. This is the place they've chosen to make a stand. They don't want us ravaging the land and their precious townships and leaving them all the while sitting up there like spectators at a Roman carnival. For them, it's now or never."

"So they're making it easy for us, Father?" Cuthwine asked.

"I doubt that; just not so hard as to put us off attacking them front on," Ceawlin said. "They're creating something like the illusion of weakness, to pull us in, to get us off our guard."

"It doesn't look weak to me," his son remarked.

"But it doesn't look invincible either," the father said. "It's something between the two, between hope and despair."

Ceawlin had kept his army under the shelter of the trees, letting the crows speak his name, warning of his arrival. Now, in the late afternoon, it was time to show his face to his enemy. Row upon row they assembled under the forest canopy, numbered in thousands, dressed for war. Row upon terrifying row they advanced into the open, swords, spears and axes beating on shields, the shout of "Woden, Woden!" rumbling up the sides of Bryn Derwydd. Out of bowshot but within hearing range, they kept up the thumping shield song and the war chorus of the Gewisse. They had come to intimidate and to conquer.

Ffernfael and the others understood it was a demonstration of strength. As sure as day followed night the Gewisse would attack, but not today. It was late; the sun was in their eyes. They were putting on a show to jangle nerves, to empty bowels and to sow doubt and uncertainty. They were putting the fear of their violent god into the hearts of the Britons.

The black cloud was here and now.

What was there to say or do at this breaking and making time?

Was there an answer to the thousand questions in every heart and mind?

To the brow of the hill came a rider on a white mare. She had many names. She was Cerridwen of the Cauldron of Wisdom. She was Rhiannon the Horse Goddess. She was the Dragon Maiden of the Island of the Mighty; the Spirit Queen of *Ynys Wydr*. She was a blacksmith's daughter and she wore a helmet made by her father, fashioned by his clever hands into an object of violent beauty. From under the helmet her fire-god hair ran down her naked back, a torch in the sun that was behind her. Her breasts were bare and painted in the ancient manner, blue dyed and swirling shapes. In her left hand she carried a spear. Slowly, proudly the white mare walked across the brow of the hilltop, war spirals painted on its side, its long mane flowing, careless of the shouting, shield-beating men below. Slowly, deliberately the rider raised her spear, its murderous point long and bright in the falling sun.

The Britons marched under the banner of the cross, but their cry was: "The Dragon, the Dragon – *Y Ddraig, y Ddraig*!" They came to the brow of the hill, spiked like a crown of thorns, row upon row of them, showing themselves to their enemy, staring them down.

"Woden, Woden!" the Gewisse resumed, after falling quiet at the sight of the Dragon Maiden.

And so it went on into the darkness.

To Eleri's ears the language of the Gewisse sounded like something a wolf had chewed and vomited out. It was just as she'd imagined: there could be nothing between her people and the Saxons. The whole shape and sound of the Gewisse universe was ugly and foreign. She'd heard Conmagil say that, should he live, he had ten ships at anchor in Caer Gloui ready to sail to Llydaw, the other Britain across the water, over the Sea of Gaul. "Anything to get clear of this Saxon curse," she'd heard him say. She knew now what he meant by it. Before, the curse of the Saxons had been for her something between reality and abstraction; now it was reality, terrible unadorned reality, pure and simple. It was the tide of brutality and ugliness rising in the east to crush and enslave her people.

"Gwion," she said. "Hold my hand, will you."

They found Siriol. She was arranging the eagle feathers in her pitch-black hair, preparing for war. She appeared positively joyful that it had come to this at last.

*

That evening, under the stars, with the Moon Goddess in full glory, Branwen told them a tale about

Arthur. The land, she said, was in misery – barren, the crops failing season upon season. Brân, the King of the Island of the Mighty, was in grievous pain. A wound had been dealt him in the groin, leaving him in agony, and impotent. His queen was in distress. She would have cried bitter tears except that nothing flowed and nothing flowered in all the land.

Branwen paused a moment. She listened to the Gewisse shields beating out fear and death in the near distance. She smiled her quiet smile, a princess of Dyfneint, a she-warrior.

"In all the land," she resumed, "there was hunger and want."

"Was Arthur called for?" the boy Gereint asked.

"Arthur was called to the king's hall," Branwen said. "A quest was given him. You must go to the Underworld, to Annwfn, he was told. You must find there the Cauldron of Healing and return it to its rightful place and owner. If you do that, the king and the land will be healed; if you fail, all hope is lost."

As the story unfolded the circle of listeners multiplied. Father Cenydd was seen elbowing his way to the front to hear again a story from his childhood, told to him in secret by his mother in the land of Llydaw over the water. *Cenydd Frych* she'd called him at such times – Freckled Cenydd.

"Arthur set out on his quest with his companions, seven in all, among them his brother Kai and his friend Bedwyr. They set out in Arthur's ship and sailed into the west. Their guide was the eldest of all creatures, the eagle Gwernabwy, who brought them to the entrance to the Underworld, into which they sailed."

Branwen recounted the trials that faced Arthur and his companions in their journey through Annwfn. Two died when the King of the Underworld sent his vultures to bombard them with rocks; two more when the hounds of Annwfn were unleashed on them. At last, they came to the edge of a dark land, to a high cliff into which was cut a deep cave. Into the cave they ventured, down into the Underworld. They came finally to a hall of skin and bones, and there before them, guarding the entrance was the monster clawing cat, Cath Palug. Beyond the monster, at the far end of the hall, was the Cauldron of Healing, and near that a cage which held a child, a boy with burning, fire-god hair.

"Let us pass," Arthur called out to the monster Cath Palug.

The big cat was at its meat. Lifting its massive head, the beast fixed Arthur with baleful eyes. Quick as lightning it sent out its dreadful claws, clawing at the companions, ripping at their mail shirts. One of Arthur's followers died from his wounds. Then Arthur, the Bear of the Island, drew his sword, Caledvwlch, and with a mighty blow sliced the evil monster in two, from snaking tail to the huge whiskers, long as spears, on its nose. From its dead body there poured out the spirits of all the dead the big cat had devoured. Out the spirits went from the hall and out through the cave in search of the world of light that lies through Ynys Wydr.

Taking a giant step over the dead beast, Arthur told Kai to take hold of the Cauldron while he looked to the child.

"No," said Kai. "The Cauldron is your quest."

"Very well," said Arthur.

It was Kai who brought the child out of the cage, but it was Arthur who learned that his name was Prydain – *Britain* – and that he was none other than the son of the great creator – "Whose name I know," Branwen said, "but I will not speak."

Only three companions returned from the quest – Arthur, Kai and Bedwyr. With them they brought the Cauldron of Healing, and with it health and plenty to the Island and its king. They brought, too, a second gift, the true name of the Island of the Mighty, which is Prydain, the name that will live forever.

The silence that met the ending of Branwen's tale was profound. The shield-beating of the Gewisse had ended for now; the horses were still under the eye of the moon; the army of the Britons held its breath in the night cold.

# Chapter Twenty-Nine

The day was raw and grey, the sky low, the land a luminous green. To the west rain fell over the mountains of Cambria.

They were all on edge. For the tenth time Eleri checked her gear, her bow made from the branch of a dwarf-elder, her lethal arrowheads; she went through her healing bag once again, making sure she had everything she needed: needle, thread, moss, vinegar, honey. It was a day for killing and for healing. Gwion was with her, as were Siriol and Branwen. Cerridwen had taken up position with Macsen's Red Cloaks. Father Cenydd had joined Kado's men, spear in hand.

As for the boy Gereint, he'd come by to say hello first thing before dashing off in his unaccountable way. He was to help see to the horses, all of them penned at the rear, on the western side of the hilltop. The last Eleri had seen of him, Gereint had been heading off in the opposite direction, which she had found oddly comforting.

Something told the boy that he should run right the way around the summit of Bryn Derwydd, that it would make a binding circle of the spirit, never to be broken – win or lose, it would always hold. When that was done, Gereint paid a visit to Riwalus, who said: "Remember me to Awen Ysbryd if you happen to see her again."

"I will," the boy said. "But Riwalus, there's no need; by then you will have spoken to her on your own account."

"Watch how you go, Little Hare," Riwalus said.

"And you, Riwalus."

Then it started. Out from under the woodland cover they advanced. The beating of shields had continued through the night, now on, now off, a ritual designed to unnerve the enemy. Now the Gewisse advanced to the foot of the hill in eerie silence, the leaders easily identified by their helmets, the mass of warriors bare-headed, many of them bare-chested, yielding nothing to the grim cold. On and on they came, line upon line. Only when they were all in place did the slow rhythmic beating of shields begin, swords and spears and axes.

"Caw, caw!" the crows called from their ragged nests.

Ffernfael stood with Macsen on the brow of the hill. To their left was Conmagil; his less predictable brother Condidan held the southern flank on their right. The brothers were great fighters. There were no fears on that score. They would play their part to the last man, Ffernfael was sure of that. Looking across, he could see Condidan's gingery violent disdain for the scene before him, the unfolding battle lines of the Gewisse king. Ffernfael caught Condidan's eye and half-smiled, the hunting smile of a bear.

"So here we are, Macsen," Ffernfael said. "The day has come around."

He was calm. Over him fluttered the banners of the cross, catching whatever breeze was to be had at this elevation on this limp, windless day. Father Cenydd had spoken to him that morning and had said what churchmen are supposed to say on these occasions: that God is with you, the truth is yours, the sword of Christ.

Ffernfael had seen Cerridwen walking among the Red Cloaks – stern, beautiful; he'd seen the eyes of the men follow her about; he knew the old gods were here and that, when all was said and done, his fate and those of his people were in their hands.

For Macsen, it was the day for which he had been born into this world. He was exactly where he wanted to be. He couldn't run; it wasn't in him. He was nobody's slave. His lot was to stay and fight. His people had been at Mount Badon where the Saxons had been routed. Macsen honestly didn't know if this was to be such a day: his Roman side said one thing, his British side another. The mystery over Dyfneint niggled away at him. It changed nothing. He saw the smile Ffernfael gave Condidan; Macsen smiled too, his cool sea-creature smile.

Passing in an orderly fashion through the Red Cloaks, a group of archers were ordered to the front. Recognised as their champion bowman, Gwion was there. So, too, was Eleri. Until that moment she'd only heard the sound the Gewisse ranks made. Now she saw them, half naked, fair, tanned even at this waking time of the year; they bellowed like bulls in their foreign tongue; spears and swords and axes raised in demonstrations of courage; the heavy shields sounding in the still air.

She saw the ranks open as a man came forward. The little of the Saxon tongue she knew told her that the cries of the warriors were for their king. Through the ranks he came, impressive in his mail and his fine helmet, but shorter than she'd imagined, unless the distance and the angle of the sloping land deceived her. "Ceawlin!" they shouted, deep and long, when he stood before his men, his sword held high. Eleri got a shock when he removed his helmet to show his long hair, the same coppery colour as her own. She remembered her father telling her that this Ceawlin was rumoured to have a British mother, taken captive by the Saxons. “Odd,” she thought, not knowing what to make of the man’s disturbing familiarity.

“My half-brother,” Siriol said beside her.

“I’m sorry,” Eleri said, taken aback, not knowing what to say.

“Don’t be. I intend to kill him,” Siriol said.

Macsen was intent on counting. “There are fewer than yesterday,” he told Ffernfael. “I counted approximately two hundred barbarians fifteen deep; not exactly but near enough. Now I make around two hundred ten deep.”

“Yes; I see it.”

Eleri’s warning of the unexpected came to mind. Turning to a Red Cloak, Macsen told him to check on the lookouts to the flanks and the rear. “If they see anything, I must be told immediately,” he ordered.

“They might be in reserve,” Ffernfael suggested. “Or they may have been inflating their numbers yesterday with odds and sods.”

“It’s possible,” Macsen said, although the uneasy feeling stayed in the pit of his stomach.

It was starting. The Saxons were advancing up the grassy slopes of Bryn Derwydd. At a point marking the limits of a bowman’s range they halted, shields at the ready. A captain, a Saxon earl maybe, came to the front, a big man wearing a helmet, and mail to his thighs. He had about him an air of invincibility, which he used as much to summon the courage of his men as to undermine that of his enemy. Facing the Britons on the hill, he drew his long sword from its scabbard.

On the hilltop, Gwion was given the signal. “Target practice,” he was told. Taking a deep breath to control his nerves, he took aim and fired. He would never be a warrior like Macsen. His name wouldn’t be honoured in song. But he would give whatever was his to give this day. As he aimed to fire, his left hand close to his face, the sweet scent of the red cows of the red earth was on his skin. The archer found his mark, his arrow piercing the right eye socket of the warrior's helmet and driving into the soft, mushy brain behind. As if struck by a bolt of lightning, the big man toppled over in front of his unbelieving troops, invincible no longer. He might have been born on the Island of Britain, a native you might say; or he might have been one of those who had crossed the narrow Winter sea from the Gewisse homeland, sailing with Cuthwine, the king's son. Unquestionably, he died at the battle of Bryn Derwydd; he was the first to do so on that day of death.

Urged on by its captains, the Gewisse army resumed its climb up Bryn Derwydd, taking refuge under a wall of shields. "Hold," was the order to the British archers. There was no point wasting arrows.

"Hold!" Macsen shouted again.

Eleri felt the temptation to let fly very keenly, but she held on like the rest of the archers, doing what she was told. Then "Fire!" was the order as the front line of the Gewisse advance reached the summit of the great ditch, close enough for the bowmen to take proper aim. *Thud*, the arrows sounded as they bit into the big Gewisse shields. Some found their marks. The front line especially suffered heavy casualties, the bowmen aiming for and hitting exposed feet and lower limbs. Gwion's marksmanship was something to behold.

"Forward," the Gewisse captains ordered.

By this time Macsen was really worried. "These aren't their best men, their *gesiths*," he told Ffernfael; "I'm sure of it."

"I'm sure of it too," the high chieftain said. "Ceawlin's sending his second best to clear the way for his vanguard. They'll walk over these bodies like Romans over coloured tiles."

"Perhaps." Macsen was only half convinced. He couldn't put his finger on it exactly, but something told him that the Saxons were holding something back. He had come to expect from his enemy a combination of control and wild belligerence, order and frenzied spontaneity. It was the last quality that was missing here. Where was that sense of absolute self-belief and conviction? Where was the necessary illusion of invincibility? What he saw was caution, and even respect for the Britons. Macsen reasoned that those in the vanguard should take their superiority as a given, denying their enemy everything other than wholehearted contempt. Where were these men? Were they still breakfasting? But, then, Macsen had never defended a fortified position of this magnitude before. Was he misreading the situation, applying old experience to new circumstances? He didn't know.

"Still no news from the flanks or the rear?" he checked with his Red Cloaks.

There was none.

Cautious or not, according to plan the Saxons were dying in the great ditch. Those at the front found the spiked holes that had been prepared for them and duly stumbled and fell in pain, creating chaos behind them into which the Britons hurled a storm of arrows and spears. It was easy killing and hard dying. Discreetly, the Gewisse captains finished off the wounded to stop their cries of agony from dampening the resolve of their remaining warriors. The Britons, too, were falling. The spiked crown around the brow of the hill offered sparse cover to the defenders, providing the Saxon archers with ready targets of their own. Belatedly, shields were brought to the British front line to provide protection to their bowmen. Gradually, inevitably, the organisation of war was giving way to its messy reality.

Eventually, standing on their dead and dying, the Gewisse regrouped and an imperfect shield wall was formed. Those at the front had indeed been sacrificed to the violent Woden, which seemed to bear out Ffernfael's theory that the best troops had been held in reserve for the second phase of the fighting. He was probably right. If so, there was enough trouble staring them directly in the face; to worry about surprise moves and hidden forces was a luxury they could ill afford.

More immediately pressing was the ill-discipline in their own ranks. In their eagerness to engage the enemy, men from the unruly flanks were crowding into the centre, war fever winning them over, Condidan's quarrelsome voice shouting "Out of my way!" was as loud as any other. By the shape of their attack, concentrated on the hillfort's middle section, the Saxons were starting to dictate the course of the battle. Seeing this, Macsen sent out messages to the Irish brothers and their captains to hold to their own designated positions. "Don't leave the flanks exposed," he warned. "Give the Red Cloaks the breathing space we need."

That was Macsen's message.

Within moments, news of another sort reached him.

The unexpected was upon them.

# Chapter Thirty

"To the ǽtheling; to the ǽtheling!" the Gewisse captains yelled.

There was no need, for the elite fighters of the Saxons were already there, forming a knot of iron and flesh around Ceawlin's son, Cuthwine.

The first wave had come on horseback, charging out from the woods towards the steep western side of Bryn Derwydd, pushing the horses on until they lost momentum, discarding their mounts and then running, shouting, wielding swords and spears and axes, shields at the ready, the illusion of invincibility bright in their hearts and minds. Overwhelmed, the British lookouts and the few troops that had been wagered against this long-odds eventuality were cut down.

Iwan Nânt was posted there. He was the first Red Cloak to die that day. He was not the last.

"Cuthwine!" the Gewisse shouted, in affirmation and defiance now. More and more men were streaming up. There must have been four hundred at least. They were at the western edge of the hillfort, looking out across the flat expanse of grassy land. They cheered to see the main body of British forces turn in their direction, shock and surprise spreading through the ranks.

The news reached the British leaders last of all, spreading down the line from one man to another.

"Shit!" Ffernfael said.

There was no time to think and none to plan.

His helmet discarded, evidently intending to confront the Gewisse force that had appeared at his back, Eleri saw Condidan striding through his men, his furiously gingery head standing out like a beacon. She saw Macsen in heated conversation with Ffernfael. Behind the Red Cloaks were Kado and the men of the Summer Land; they too were turning to face the young ǽtheling and his sworn men, his *gesiths*. From messiness, things were degenerating into chaotic muddle.

There was no time to dwell on the unexpected. Eleri's attention was on the Gewisse warriors in front of her, who were now edging their way up from the ditch. She contributed to the hail of metal that flew at the wall of shields, some arrows finding their mark in flesh and bone, some men collapsing, some stumbling, and others continuing their steep climb up to the fort's summit. Gwion was with her yet, as were Siriol and Branwen, all of them unleashing arrow after arrow into the body of the advancing Gewisse army. And Cerridwen was with them, her spear driving down into the Saxons.

Macsen had wanted to join Condidan and Kado, taking half the Red Cloaks with him against the ǽtheling.

"No," said Ffernfael.

"We're already stretched and they're dicing us up even further," Riwalus warned.

"Where are those Dyfneint buggers when we need them?" Condidan bellowed from a distance.

"Give that young bastard hell!" Conmagil shouted.

"I will, brother."

He was outnumbered and he was pretty certain that he would be outclassed. Still, without hesitation Condidan headed in the direction of Cuthwine and his men. He motioned to Kado to form up at his rear, with the hope of making a tight square of men that might fight as a single unit even if outflanked and surrounded. The enemy waited for them at the hill's western edge, content to stretch the different parts of the British forces as far apart as possible.

Within minutes the two forces clashed, shield meeting shield, shoving, heaving, stabbing, the cries of men in anger and in pain, bones cracking, flesh ripped open. Condidan took the centre against the big Saxons, using all his weight and guile to find and explore the gaps and cracks in his enemy's shield wall. His men gave everything. They had nothing to lose. Condidan would have dearly liked to face the ǽtheling one on one, to show the young upstart how it was done. The sworn men around Cuthwine made certain that didn't happen, keeping the knot of iron and flesh that guarded their prince tightly locked.

As the fighting progressed, the British formation proved harder to maintain. Men were lost. Even with one body replacing another, the flanks of the square came increasingly under pressure. Condidan could hear the Saxon swords at his back slicing through leather vests and helmets. He could hear Kado rallying the men of the Summer Land. "Arawn!" they shouted, recalling the name of their last chieftain at this fatal hour. Father Cenydd was in the thick of it, his spear as bloody as any man's.

Seeing his brother's hopeless plight, Conmagil rushed to his aid. With fifty men at his back he smashed into the Saxon lines, intending to fight his way through to Condidan's side. Like two gingery summits amid lesser peaks, the brothers hacked into their enemy. It was the short stab of a spear that killed Conmagil, the force of its thrust tearing through his mail and into his gut. An arrow found Condidan's unprotected and all too conspicuous head, dropping him quicker than any sword. He would have preferred to go out a different way, something less prosaic; but, then, which of us gets to pick and choose the manner of our dying?

At least Conmagil's intervention gave the surviving British the opportunity to regroup and slowly disengage from the Gewisse who, by this time, had themselves suffered serious casualties. Kado was gone; but not Father Cenydd; ever the frustrated warrior, the thin-faced priest, his freckled head spattered and splashed with red blood, pulled the men back and shouted for the square to be reformed.

The Gewisse held off. It was clear to them that the battle at the eastern edge of the fort had turned decisively in their favour. Seeing this, the ǽtheling's men shouted their war cries. "The Red Cloaks!" Cuthwine called out, his bloody sword pointed in their direction. It was his chance to make a real name for himself.

For the Britons, conversely, chaotic muddle was turning into chaotic catastrophe. With the Irish brothers gone, the flanks to the north and south were left exposed. Cuthwine and his men could see the Saxons pouring over the hilltop from both directions, overwhelming the defenders. Facing attack from three sides, the Red Cloaks at the centre were being pulled in all directions.

It had all happened suddenly, with the instinct of a dog smelling fear and weakness. The minute the Saxons saw defenders were draining away from the flanks, they shifted the focus of their attack from the centre to the exposed southern side first, from where Condidan had gone, and then to the northern side. In no time the hilltop was swarming with the enemy, the sides of the British forces falling in.

In the confusion that followed, bodies everywhere, alive and dead and all points in between, Ffernfael held the central position, while Mascen took control to the south and Riwalus to the north. Outnumbered, their position became increasingly desperate. Ffernfael fell, blood gushing from his mouth as he hit the ground, the spears of the two warriors he'd faced protruding from his bear-like back. Eleri's healing bag stayed on her shoulder. It had turned out to be a day for killing and for dying, not for healing.

Improvising, the Red Cloaks and the other surviving Britons formed a hollow square, into which they pulled any archers that were still alive.

"Get in here!" Macsen shouted to Eleri and Gwion, who were still fighting on the exposed centre of the hill. "And you two!" he yelled to Siriol and Branwen.

Had they heard? If so, they'd chosen to ignore him.

Covered in blood, his own and that of his enemy, Macsen tried to manoeuvre his remaining troops in the direction of Cenydd and his men. The Britons under Father Cenydd had formed a defensive position, with their backs against the enclosure that held the increasingly skittish horses. Even to a priest the hopeless situation of Macsen's men was plain to see. Nobody's fool, not even his own, Cenydd saw just as clearly that his own situation was every bit as hopeless.

Seeing the peril the Red Cloaks were in, Cenydd and his men moved forward to help Macsen, and together they succeeded in pulling back to their original position against the horse enclosure. But it was messy, a confusion of violence and noise, and it was only achieved at great loss of life in the face of the relentless Gewisse onslaught.

The entire summit was a mosaic of mutilated bodies, severed arms and legs and heads; around them the red of blood and the brown and green of trampled mud and grass. The dead on both sides must have numbered over a thousand, considerably more in the case of the Gewisse. But here they were, rampant, victorious, in for the kill, while the Britons were down to their last hundred.

"Dyfneint," Macsen thought, the bitterness of betrayal rising in him. But what was the point? He looked around at those that were left. His friend Riwalus was with him, and twenty or so other Red Cloaks. He saw Cerridwen, her helmet and her spirit bright. Father Cenydd was there, sword in hand. The rest were men from the strongholds of Caer Baddan, Caer Gloui and Caer Ceri, their chieftains all dead. There were, too, some men from the Summer Land. Not enough. "Numbers," Macsen thought; he'd never liked numbers.

"We'll mount up, brothers!" he shouted. "Let's do this properly. Open the gate! Get the horses out!"

When he pushed through to the enclosure he saw Eleri and Gwion, alive yet. Their bows had been discarded for want of arrows. Gwion held a spear, Eleri nothing but her healing bag.

"Get out of here," he said to them, his cool eyes blazing. "Don't waste your lives; your people need you. Go!" he ordered, pointing the way, seeing them hesitate.

With difficulty the nervous horses were led out. One man was kicked in the head. For Macsen, ever since his father had taught to him to ride as a young boy, there had never been any freedom like the freedom he felt on horseback. It was the same now. He mounted his horse *Gwalchwen* – White Hawk – as ever resting a caressing hand on the beast's warm neck as he did so. He was where he wanted to be. He and Riwalus shared a meaningful nod, which said everything there was to say. The Gewisse shield wall was not properly formed yet; this was the moment; a gesture maybe, but one that mattered to the Britons who had fought at Bryn Derwydd in defence of the Island of the Mighty.

Then another unexpected thing happened.

From out between the horses' legs ran the boy Gereint, fast as a hare, running straight at the Gewisse lines. They saw him skip up the shields of the perplexed, shouting warriors and over the wall of men and iron, a Little Hare running through the Saxon army. They saw a ripple forming in the ranks, marking his path. Then it was gone. There was no trace of the Little Hare. He had disappeared into mystery.

"*Sgwarnog Bach* - Little Hare," the Britons said, not loud, quietly, a private reflection. The thought of him brought a smile to all their faces.

Now they were ready.

At a signal from Macsen, the Red Cloaks moved forwards. They rode for joy and in fierce exaltation; their horses as ebullient as their riders, glad to be getting on with it at long last. The shout of all the Britons was "Arthur, Arthur!" They shouted for love and in thanksgiving. They shouted in the sure knowledge that the Bear of the Island of the Mighty was with them.

Macsen and Riwalus were in the lead, swords raised high; the crazy gladness and grim determination of battle was in them.

At the centre, at the very heart, was Cerridwen, her fire-god hair streaming out from beneath her helmet, a banner and a beacon, a statement of pride and defiance. In her burning hair were all the tongues of all the gods of her people; the spirit of the Island was there, merry and wild.

With her was Cenydd, the memory of his learned father Gildas no longer heavy on his shoulders. The priest was light in the passionate embrace of his militant faith, his true course obvious to him at last. He was there, riding with the Red Cloaks of Caer Baddan. This was where he had to be. He would meet his wife and son in another place, of that he was certain.

Seeing the Gewisse shield wall, even the war horses shied and pulled up. It all added to the mayhem and confusion, their massive rumps crashing into their enemies. Some Red Cloaks dismounted, others stayed on horseback. The fighting was fiercer and more reckless than ever. For the Saxons, Cuthwine hacked and stabbed like a man possessed. One by one the Britons fell, the men from the Summer Land and those from the three towns. Cerridwen was the burning core around which they made their stand, the heart of their resistance, their Warrior Queen.

At the last, Cerridwen was cut down, iron from a Saxon forge ending the life of the blacksmith's daughter.

The warrior who had killed her was about to yank the helmet from her head, except that the fatally wounded Riwalus drove his short sword into the man's leg and groin, sending him reeling away in agony. Father Cenydd clutched the simple cross at his neck; his last words were a curse on the Gewisse, darkly rich enough to please a seer of the heathen faith. Pulled to the ground, wounded, on his knees, his red cloak stained and torn, the mischievous light in Macsen's pale eyes went out when Cuthwine's princely sword plunged into the heart of the captain of the last of the legions on British soil.

It was the end. The Saxons cheered and praised their gods. "Ceawlin!" they chanted.

In time, after the victory had been duly acknowledged, the king of the Saxons returned to the brow of the hillfort. There he stood over the bodies of two women. One of them was his half-sister. Her name was Siriol, which means cheerful in the British language. The other was her friend and lover, the fair raven

Branwen. They had stayed behind, ignoring Macsen's call to abandon their position. Siriol had stayed to fulfil her promise of revenge, made to her father's memory, to take the life of her half-brother, Ceawlin. Branwen had stayed with her. In the chaos of battle, Siriol had caught sight of her brother and had sent her last arrow in his direction, only to see a burly warrior get in its way. She had turned to see Branwen cut down, an axe slicing through her body like butter, from her shoulder to her big heart. And then Siriol fell, the eagle feathers in her black hair flying no longer.

"Watch them," Ceawlin had ordered on reaching the summit. He didn't want scavengers stripping the bodies. He'd already kicked one out of the way.

Now here he was in victory, standing over the she-warriors, taking a feather from his half-sister's hair. He wasn't sentimental. He would have killed her himself if he'd had the chance. Nonetheless, he ordered that the bodies be treated with respect. "Build a pyre for them," he said.

The feather he floated into the air, and watched it wriggle and glide on the currents of Bryn Derwydd before falling back to earth.

# Part Four

## AD 577

## "The Hawthorn Month"

# Chapter Thirty-One

For as long as she lived there wasn't a day when Eleri Gwir didn't think about Bryn Derwydd. A part of her said she should have died there; a part of her wished she had. But she hadn't. As her friend Macsen had said, her people had need of her. She lived for a reason.

With Gwion she had headed west. Getting off the hillfort's summit was the easy part. The furious last battle that was fought there captured everyone's attention, giving the fugitives a chance to slide away down the steep-sloping hill. There were scavengers about already, picking over the spoils. One of them studied them from a distance. He shouted something, incomprehensible words that meant in any language: "Piss off, these are our spoils." His companion looked them over suspiciously but did no more than that, preferring to attend to the pickings that lay at his feet. He must have said something that made his companion laugh – a nasty, malicious laugh.

Eleri and Gwion weren't worth even thinking about, not on such a day of comprehensive victory and rich awards. Carrying only her healing bag, her fine torque hidden away, Eleri looked desperate enough to play the part of camp follower and battleground scavenger; and Gwion looked ragged enough, holding nothing but a spear, one of the many hundreds that littered the ground. Playing the role of scavenger to good effect, from a dead

Saxon warrior he took a short sword, which he concealed under his cloak. Following his example, Eleri put a long-bladed knife in her bag. She hated doing it. It was against the order of things, to contaminate her healing plants and poultices with this instrument of death. But this was a day of killing, not healing.

Coming down from the summit, they could see that what remained of the British camp on the low levels had been deserted. Canvasses and wagons were scattered about. Smoke drifted up. The cooks and the farriers and the women must have fled. Hopefully. There might have been a few stragglers left behind. If so, the swarm of scavengers would have seen them off, no quarter given.

The despair Eleri and Gwion felt at that moment, these fugitives in their own land, was too deep for words. Ashen-faced, they made for the safety of the woods to the north. Somehow they had to find a way through the Saxon-infested territory and back to the Great Wood where their people were sheltered.

"May Belin protect them," Eleri said, over and over, compulsively, as she staggered away from Bryn Derwydd.

"Will they call us cowards?" Gwion asked.

"Will there be anyone left to call us anything?" Eleri countered.

When they found cover under the trees she noticed that Gwion was bleeding from his side. She made him lie still on the cold ground while she administered to the wound, which was deep enough but not serious, a lucky escape from something that could have been a lot worse. The work of healing seemed right to her. It calmed her shaking hands; brought her shocked brain to heel. Something good had been done this day after all.

"Keep it clean," she said. "It should be all right."

"Thanks," Gwion said, but his mind was elsewhere, with the men of the Summer Land in whose company he should have died. When Macsen had told them to go, Math from their village had said: "Yes, get out of here; see that my family is safe." It was something; a something to hold onto against the terrors of the mind.

There was no safe route from here. If they went west the Land of the Hafren would be full of marauding Saxons, drunk on victory and greedy for plunder and all the spoils of war. They could strike east, down what had been the ragged border between the Gewisse and the Britons; there the same might apply, but not to the same extent, they reasoned – if only because the border lands had already been stripped bare. It was a matter of degree; the lesser nightmare. East it was.

Sleep was impossible. The big moon urged them to get going. Hungry though she was and likely to be far hungrier yet, in thanksgiving Eleri left a morsel of bread for the Children of the Moon. As her father had used tell her: "There's always something to be thankful for and it's them we should be thanking."

"For you," Eleri said, speaking to the Moon Goddess and to her father at the same time.

Going deeper into the woods, they planned to loop around the Saxons whose land this was now. Noise was all around them, men drinking and singing, very badly and horribly out of tune it had to be said. After all that had happened, it surprised Eleri to find how much the tuneless singing jarred on her sensibilities.

"Listen to that," Gwion said. "To think we lost to people who sing like crows."

"I know."

There was the smell, too, of burning wood and flesh. Pyres had been built by the Gewisse for their dead. Looking back, they could see flames rising in the distance, from the summit of Bryn Derwydd. They stopped to watch, the fires multiplying, lighting up the night. There was chanting, too far off for them to catch the words even if they'd wished to.

Eleri's blood ran cold to think what might have been done to the bodies of her own people. At best, they would have been piled in a ditch and left to rot; the other possibilities were too awful to think about, boars snuffling and birds pecking and gouging at eyes and exposed flesh.

Then she felt it. The full, undiluted, pure and powerful sense of loss came over her suddenly, like a big wave from deep inside her body, an unstoppable force moving through her entire being. Something had caught up with her; call it despair, anguish, grief; whatever words there are for the bleakness that overtook Eleri at that moment.

She cried. She could do nothing else. She sobbed pathetically, for her friends, her people, her broken Island.

It rendered her immobile, rooted to the spot.

Gwion would have embraced her but she held him off, gently but firmly, wanting and needing to experience the complete abjectness and wretchedness she felt. It was part of her now. "This is who I am," she thought. "This is what I must learn to endure."

She was sorry for herself and she was sorry for everything and everyone that was dear to her. It poured through her, the big wave, into every corner, through her nails, her teeth, into the tips of her fire-god hair. And with all that, a countervailing power worked inside her, taking up arms against this unbearable sorrow. She knew that she was strong. She felt that strength pushing back the wave of sorrow that was threatening to overcome her.

"Let's get away from here," Gwion said.

"Yes."

They moved off, keeping silent, checking now and then on the direction they were taking, saying as little as possible. They tried to shut off their thinking, which was hopeless. They gave in, letting a flood of thoughts race through their minds.

Of all the things that went through Eleri's crowded head that night, the one that offered some crumbs of comfort was the thought of the boats Conmagil had prepared to sail from Caer Gloui to Llydaw, the other Britain over the water. Eleri imagined them sailing down the coiling River Hafren and out into the channel, away from all this. She imagined what it would be like to be at sea.

From there her reflections turned naturally towards Macsen, her sea creature from the deep, his spirit swimming like a salmon at this minute, making for open water in the springtime of his other life. She imagined Cerridwen, the Dragon Maiden, coming across the water to the island that lies behind the North Wind, her hair red and golden, her helmet in her hand. She saw Siriol and Branwen there, two more warrior queens. Her thoughts ran on this way, warm and healing. Would Father Cenydd see his heaven, she wondered? Was the Little Hare's spirit running to Awen Ysbryd? Was Riwalus' already there?

An owl hooted nearby.

Looking up, Eleri caught a glimpse of its flower face in the moonlight.

Rain started to fall, the drops heavy on the oak leaves.

# Chapter Thirty-Two

Travelling slowly, mostly at night, keeping to the wooded lands wherever possible, always tired and even hungrier, their sleep fitful and disturbed, Eleri and Gwion arrived in three days at the outskirts of the Great Wood. "Home," they thought, seeing the familiar landscape. It had been their home. It was theirs no longer.

Already the foreigners were everywhere, sorting out who would get what, marking the ground with the scent of their power. Eleri and Gwion had had some lucky escapes along the way, on a few occasions only just avoiding the need to run or fight. More and more war bands and stragglers seemed to be moving in behind the main Gewisse army – at least that was how it appeared to Eleri and Gwion. One time they came across a warrior pissing in the woods. Fortunately for them he had his eyes closed. They were close enough to see the silly smile on his face. On the second night they came across a Gewisse slave camp, the Britons in chains, the slavers at their meat. They didn't hang around. There was nothing they could do.

Picking their way through the Great Wood, which thankfully seemed clear of the enemy, they came at last to the gorge where their people were concealed. They'd been spotted of course, which meant that their arrival into the shelter of the gorge was greeted by a crowd, all of them wanting to hear the news and dreading to hear it at the same time. The fact that they were alone, only two of them when more than fifty had left for Bryn Derwydd, spoke for itself. There was an eerie silence, broken only by sobbing and the questioning words of children.

With all those familiar faces looking at them, Eleri and Gwion felt all their fears and regrets well up. Why were they alive? Where were Kado and all the others? Why wasn't Cerridwen with them?

Brave as ever, it was Cerridwen's mother Gwenda who broke through the awkwardness. Going to Eleri, she put her arms around her and said in a voice loud enough for everyone to hear: "Welcome home, Eleri Gwir, and you, Gwion."

Cerys joined them, holding onto Gwion first and then Eleri. Then everyone crowded around, embracing them, tearful but glad to see them.

Last of all was Gwion's father, Meriadoc, who came to his son and held onto him for dear life. He was a gentle man, firm when he needed to be, especially where the wellbeing of the animals in his care was at issue, but no warrior. For Eleri, he encapsulated the red earth of the Summer Land from where he had never strayed in all of his fifty years. He'd been self-conscious about embracing his son who was alive when so many others had perished. He hadn't wanted to embarrass Gwion who would feel the awkwardness of his situation intensely. But he was glad to hold him, to see his black raven hair and eyes, more like the son of Brân than a cowman of the Summer Land.

"Father," Gwion said.

Fathers and sons can go through life barely or very rarely acknowledging the love they have for one another in words, or by any other means. Those occasions when it is acknowledged, if they come around at all, tend therefore to be special, so much so that they can become the defining moments of their lives. This meeting between Gwion and his father was like that. It had about it that quality of truth and revelation. They'd always been close. Gwion was proud of his father, recognising his skills and the conviction with which he went about his work. This was different, a moment of recognition for them both, a whole that was greater than its parts and at another level of intensity.

"Father," Gwion said again.

"Eleri Gwir," Meriadoc said, turning to her. "I can't tell you what it means to me to see you again."

Eventually, Eleri and Gwion were allowed to sit and to enjoy the first real food they'd eaten in days.

"That tastes good," Gwion said. It was as if he'd never tasted food this good in his life.

"We knew it was bad news," they were told. "If we'd won the men would have been back days ago."

"Back and boasting and getting drunk and jumping on the women," Cerys said.

People laughed. It was true enough.

Tired as she was, almost dropping asleep in front of them all, Eleri noticed two things. One was that Mared of the Silver Wheel was conspicuously absent, the other was that there were far more people here now than when she'd left for Caer Baddan. The encampment appeared to have grown into a sizeable community of many villages and their outlying areas.

"Sleep," Cerys ordered before any serious questioning started, either from those at the camp or from Eleri Gwir, who could always be trusted to have a barrage of questions in that head of hers.

That evening they told the story of Bryn Derwydd to the whole camp, stopping to answer any questions as they went. "Shush," some said, "let them finish." But everyone wanted to know about their loved ones and the flow of desperate questions was impossible to stop. Cerridwen had a sister, a year or so younger than herself. She was Olwen, and she had the same look about her, a fierce burning fire. She said that she knew that Cerridwen would have died well, giving no quarter to her enemies, but she wanted to know if her sister had fallen early or late in the battle. They told her the plain truth, which was remarkable enough. They said about the helmet, which Cerridwen had worn but which was now in Gewisse hands.

"The same must be true of her dragon ring," Olwen said.

"Yes."

It was one of a hundred answers to a hundred questions.

Gwion had already spoken privately with Math's wife, telling her that her husband had fought to the very end and that he had asked Gwion to look out for his family. Math's wife's name was Onnen, a very round woman with bright, intelligent brown eyes and a quick-fire way of talking. She had two boys to care for, although luckily for her they were both sturdy lads and old enough to make themselves useful to her and others. Gwion wanted to assure her that he would honour Math's request.

"Thank you, Gwion," Onnen said. "We'll all of us need all the help we can get, I'm sure. Math was always very fond of you and of that young woman, I must say. He had a soft spot for the pair of you and he wouldn't have you throwing your lives away, I'm sure." Without stopping for breath then or later, she said: "I'm in the same boat as everyone else. But I'm luckier than some, with my boys nearly grown."

Gwion felt very young and foolish, standing there offering help to Onnen. She was a sensible, practical woman, at least fifteen years his senior. It occurred to him that, for all her talkativeness, if Onnen was to fall apart it would all happen on the inside, the walls of her life crumbling privately, hidden from view. But he didn't think that was likely. She'd suffered loss many times in her life, losing two children when they were barely two years of age, and with another stillborn. This was another storm she would have to weather. And for all her loss those eyes of hers were extremely lively yet.

"We'll try to look after one another," Gwion said, trying to strike the right note.

"We will indeed, young man. You look after yourself now, and that father of yours; he's not getting any younger, I'm sure."

"He's an old man," Gwion joked, catching an ember from Onnen's infectious jauntiness.

"Like all these old buggers you left behind with us," Onnen said. "I loved Math, you know," she said seriously, her eyes dimming. "He was a dear man." She tried to fight back tears but failed; Gwion tried harder still.

No one seemed to bear Eleri and Gwion any ill will for having survived when so many had fallen. They were young. They belonged naturally to the future. Not even Mared of the Silver Wheel had anything too waspish to say. She was there in the evening to hear about Bryn Derwydd. Eleri had wondered if something had happened to the old woman. Had the move been too much for her after all? Had she caught a chill as so many of the old ones did at this time of year? Had she died of natural or other causes? The answer to any apparent mystery was simple and straightforward: Mared had been asleep when they'd arrived and nobody had thought or cared to wake her. Let sleeping irascible old women lie was the rule for this and every other day.

Now there she was, perched on a tree stump which she'd commandeered and made into a woodland throne from which she could pontificate and harass at will. To Eleri, she looked indestructible, seemingly unconcerned about anyone's loss, as playfully mischievous as ever.

"If it isn't Eleri Gwir and her friend Gwion," she'd said by way of a welcoming remark. You never knew quite what to expect with Mared, except that it would be something likely to put you on your mettle. "Alive and kicking," she'd added.

"And how are you?" Eleri asked her, as neutral a response as she could think of and one calculated to send Mared off into a monologue about her own trials and tribulations.

"Alive and kicking, as you see," was the pert answer. "Although they've tried to kill me off a hundred times and more," she added for good measure.

"Without success, I see," Eleri ventured. She knew there was a thin line between humouring the old woman and saying something that would offend her.

On the cusp of being offended, Mared said: "I see you and that boy had a bit of luck then."

Eleri was in no mood for this. Fortunately, Cerys came to her rescue, telling her mother to move over and make some room on the tree stump. Nimbly changing the subject, she said to Eleri: "There's a lot more of us than when you left. They've come from all over the Summer Land."

"It's not just Eleri Gwir that has good ideas," Mared commented, like a naughty child throwing in her observation, insisting on being heard and endeavouring to stay relevant.

"We'll have to decide what to do," Cerys said, ignoring her mother.

"Tomorrow," Eleri said.

# Chapter Thirty-Three

The next day started with a head count, a muster. The children were counted; the women above a certain age and those below it; the same with the men. It turned out that they'd acquired over a hundred more people, making a total of two hundred and five, with three more on the way, one imminently. Women outnumbered men by around two to one; and proportionately the men were older, or else had been excused military service because of an existing infirmity. "A sorry lot," was Mared of the Silver Wheel's considered judgement as far as the men were concerned. "I wouldn't trust them to guard a henhouse from a lame fox."

A tally of horses and wagons was made, and of any weapons – bows mostly, but some spears and a good number of shields. The only real sword they had was the one Gwion had pilfered from the Saxon warrior at Bryn Derwydd, and that was more of a short *seax* than a full-bladed sword. The knife Eleri had picked up wasn't much smaller, and there were several others to add to it. Then there were the axes, short- and long-handled.

It was decided that Gronw the blacksmith was to be their armourer, and he was to keep a watchful eye on their supply of arrows in particular. Gwion's father, Meriadoc, would help him; among his many skills, Meriadoc was a talented fletcher.

How many of them would bear arms? Every boy above the age of ten said he would fight. Gwion was put in charge of the bowmen and of sorting out who could and could not hit an oak tree at ten paces. Besides Eleri, many of the women and girls said they would fight and it was agreed to let them prove themselves to Gwion's expert eye. They were all strong, used to the heavy and toiling work and chores of country life. Some were good and some very good; Olwen was the best, which surprised no one; on the other hand Rhian's hidden skills with a bow were a revelation. "You never know until you try," she said.

Young though she was, it was agreed without argument that Eleri, the daughter of their old chief, should take the overall leadership.

"She hasn't killed me yet," was Mared's helpful remark.

Eleri's second in command was to be an older man from another village, whose name was Padarn and who was known to everyone and respected for his good sense.

"She'll eat you alive, Padarn, if you're not careful," Mared remarked, which made everyone chuckle. When she cared to, Mared of the Silver Wheel still knew how to play the game of power and influence, albeit within an ever-decreasing sphere.

The day after next they were on the move.

Deciding what to do had involved an intense but ultimately brief debate. They'd met in the early morning, everyone sitting or standing in the shelter of the gorge in the forest that had served as their encampment. As before, the choices were stark: death, slavery or exile. Of course, some of the younger women might get lucky – if that was the word for it – and win the hearts of some burly Gewisse warriors and so become the heads of their households. It wasn't unknown. Far more common, however, was for a British woman to be picked up and put down again, to be passed around and to be whored. None of the women of the Summer Land wanted to try their luck. They would leave this place, the sacred land of the Dubonni; they would go into exile with what remained of their people. That was the decision.

There were two possible directions for them to go. One was west to the Water Land, which might not be overrun by the Gewisse immediately, there being nothing there but paupers and eels. Who wanted to be a pauper and who wanted to eat eels for the rest of their days? No one. Not the Gewisse and not the people of the Summer Land.

"Funny lot in that Water Land; I never did like them," Mared said, and she was not alone.

"What about Arian, mother?" Cerys asked in a correcting way. "You liked her well enough."

"A bit stuck up, but I suppose Kado could have done a lot worse for himself," Mared conceded.

"There you are, then."

"I don't know – all that water rotting their brains."

The other direction they could go was south, to Dyfneint.

"Never trusted them," was Mared's contribution, which in light of recent events was heard with some approval. "I always said I never trusted them," she added for emphasis. "That king of theirs can't lie straight in bed. Everyone knows that."

But there was no real choice. If not the Water Land it had to be Dyfneint, from where some or all of them might sail over the Sea of Gaul to Llydaw, the exotic land across the water.

"My sister buggered off there years ago," Mared stated.

"You never told me that!" Cerys said, surprised at this piece of family history.

"Well I'm telling you now. She's dead, no doubt. Come to a bad end, I suppose."

"Leave any possessions you don't need," Eleri told them all. "We'll have to move fast; there'll be children to carry. Just the essentials."

The quickest and easiest route was by the Fosse Way. But they couldn't risk leaving the Great Wood, not until they were much farther south and hopefully beyond the reach of any Saxon patrols, or any war bands on a spree of their own. That meant sticking to the smaller pathways, and that meant that the wagons would have to be discarded. They would all be on foot except for the very old, who were put on ponies. Getting them onto the ponies was an exercise in itself, which had the children in stitches of laughter.

"What if I have to *go*?" asked one of the old men, thinking of his leaky bladder, panic setting in.

"You won't," Eleri told him in no uncertain terms.

The effort it took to get Mared of the Silver Wheel on a pony was considerable. Cerys sat behind her mother to make sure she didn't fall off.

"I'll kill her," was the first thing the daughter said at the end of the first day's travel.

"I'll kill her," the mother echoed when she finally managed to climb off the pony, helped by Meriadoc and Padarn and watched by a gang of children.

The next day was the same.

The Great Wood, for so long the subject of fear and suspicion among the Britons, was their shelter. Sprites and monsters were said to live there, the stories told to the young and consumed like mother's milk. But as they knew only too well, other things besides supernatural terrors lurked there. Outlaws infested the Wood, desperate men with no allegiances, not to kings or gods or lands. Scouts had to be sent ahead to watch for these men. Gwion was in charge of this, helped by Olwen, Cerridwen's sister. Six of the older and cleverest boys were sent out in pairs, with strict orders to take great care lest they should be captured by outlaws. The rest of Gwion's archers remained with the main group. Unless called upon to attend to some dispute or other, Eleri walked at the front of the group, taking the lead, while Padarn took up the position at the rear, making sure there were no stragglers.

It was slow going.

On the third day Eleri had to order a halt while she and Cerys saw to the heavily pregnant woman who had gone into labour. Her waters had broken and the contractions were coming close together, doubling her over in pain.

"Oh, no!" she cried.

The privacy they arranged for her was a piece of hide canvas tied between two trees. They kept her standing. Eleri rubbed the woman's lower back to try to ease the hurt. Cerys squatted between her legs, her hand feeling for the infant's head. It was the woman's second child and by the standards of these things the delivery went smoothly enough, without complication. All the same, the woman gave one almighty scream before a piece of leather was found for her to bite on. Her scream was enough to alert every outlaw within a twenty-mile radius, but then her smile on seeing her baby son was as warm as Belin's belly, as people said.

Seeing Eleri again, cleaning her hands as best she could with a pile of leaves, Gwion shook his head, indicating his general view that this wasn't going too well. Eleri shrugged her shoulders in response, as if saying: what else is there to do?

Their relationship was like that: struggling, a bit off course, close but not intimate in the old way, one step forward and two back. Of course it was early days, and the trauma of Bryn Derwydd and the anxieties of the Great Wood had to be factored into any reckoning. Nonetheless, standing there under the oak trees, the ground littered with their sparse possessions, children grumbling that they were tired and hungry, it seemed as if something had gone out of their relationship. Perhaps it was more accurate to say that their relationship had itself evolved into a new creature, friends still, firm and true, but also something more and different. They were leaders now in their own right. The weight of responsibility was too heavy to let them go all the way back to their old intimacy. A cold, damp lump of clay still obstructed the pathway leading from one to the other, taking a new shape now, knobbly with care and concern. But, then, they were bone-tired themselves, and their stomachs grumbled as loud as any with hunger.

There was no time to dwell on matters of either the gut or the heart. A scout, one of Math's sons, a boy called Idris, reported an outlaw camp ahead.

"How far?"

"About two miles."

"How many?"

"I counted ten men. I didn't go close."

"Dogs?"

"I didn't see or hear any."

"What d'you think?" Padarn asked. "Are we close enough to Dyfneint to strike west for the Fosse Way?"

All eyes were on Eleri. She knew no more than anyone else. There was no right or wrong answer. There was just a decision that had to be made and she had to make it.

"Yes," she said. "We'll risk the Great Road."

"Are you sure?" Gwion asked. "If it's ten men we could surprise them."

"Assuming they don't surprise us first," his father Meriadoc said.

"We've made enough noise to wake the dead," Padarn observed.

In no time they'd all come around to Eleri's way of thinking.

"We'll keep a watch on our backs in case they're tracking us," Gwion said. "I'll divide up the scouts and go with Olwen to see what's ahead of us to the west. We can't take anything for granted."

"Trouble," Cerys said. "We can take that for granted."

By twilight they'd made their way to the edge of the Great Wood, from where they could cut across country to the Fosse Way. Gwion and Olwen returned with news that the land ahead seemed clear of Saxons but that it was a matter of luck whether they stumbled across a war band.

"We'll be like a flock of lambs waiting to be picked off by eagles," Gwion said.

"At least we should be clear of any outlaws," Eleri said, looking for a silver lining. "We'll camp here overnight and try our luck tomorrow."

The outlaws came with the dawn.

Fortunately, Gwion had posted scouts deeper in the forest, with strict orders to return to camp if they saw or heard anything. It was Idris again who delivered the message – "They're coming."

Instead of mounting a surprise attack of their own, the outlaws were themselves taken by surprise when they came running and screeching towards the camp only to be met by a disciplined volley of arrows. They tried to retreat, but Gwion had concealed a group of archers behind their lines, led by Olwen. The efficient way Olwen and the others finished off the attackers gave Gwion heart.

"Don't hope," he told himself, which was easier said than done.

They counted seventeen bodies, all filthy, dressed in rags, not one with an ounce of flesh to spare. Badly wounded but well enough to be questioned, one of their attackers told them that more men outside the law were camped to the south.

"You won't get through that way," he warned them. He also warned them to stay clear of *Maes-y-Gaer* – Fortress Field. "They're not to be trusted," he said. "The lord there is no good." Which, coming from an outlaw, was saying something.

"Why didn't you join him?" Eleri asked, remembering what Macsen had said about Maes-y-Gaer, that it was infested with men outside the law, Britons and even Saxons, that its lord used the ancient hillfort as a base to ravage the land about.

"Look at us," the man said pathetically. "We're all old and slow. They wouldn't have us there."

Macsen had left empty-handed from Maes-y-Gaer. He'd called the lord of that place a rogue and more besides.

That was good enough for Eleri.

There was only one course open to them. Like lambs to the slaughter they must head for the Great Roman Road and from there to Dyfneint.

"If there are eagles, let them be ours," Eleri told herself, although who or what exactly she meant by "ours" was far from clear.

# Chapter Thirty-Four

Padarn sought Eleri out early next morning. He came with news of something that was unexpected to her.

"They want to go back," he said.

Padarn must have been in his fifties; what hair he had was iron grey and stuck out in tufts over his head. Shorter than Eleri, there was nothing obviously impressive about him. But he was honest and capable and he had a way of including people that made them like and trust him. His authority had deep roots in his own history and that of his community.

"Who wants to go back?" Eleri said, shocked.

"Those from my village and some others," he said.

She couldn't believe it. Such a thing wasn't within her comprehension. Just as she had come to recognise the limits of the imagination of the military mind, she now had to recognise the limits of her own imagination. She hadn't foreseen this because it was outside the range and scope of her foresight. What were these people thinking of?

"Are you sure, Padarn?"

"They prefer to take their chances back there, where they know."

"It doesn't make sense."

"It does to them," Padarn told her.

"And you, Padarn; what will you do?" Eleri asked.

"I don't think they'll kill me, the Saxons that is; I'm too old. I'll stick with my people," he answered staunchly.

"Slavery," Eleri said, the one word summing up everything.

"If I'm lucky," Padarn said, managing an ironic smile.

It was a morning of cold drizzle, the sky low enough to jump up and grab a handful of grey. Dismayed, Eleri went to speak to those who wished to return to the Summer Land. Would it spread like an infection, she wondered, this yearning for the familiar, for home?

"Are you sure?" she asked them several times over.

No, they weren't sure. But nor were they sure of the alternative that she presented. Their lives, they said, were a choice of evils.

"You'll be shovelling shit for some Saxon all your lives," Eleri said. "And your children will be shovelling shit for some Saxon; and their children will do the same."

"Don't mince words, Eleri Gwir!" someone joked.

"I don't understand," she said. "You've come all this way."

"It's too big a thing for us to do," a woman said, her hungry child in her arms.

At least the infection didn't appear to be catching. The people from her own village of Tre Wyn were with her still and would continue on to the south. At one level the consensus seemed to be that she hadn't killed them yet, to borrow Mared of the Silver Wheel's pithy encapsulation. There was also the feeling that they'd committed themselves to a certain course, one they must see out together and to the end. Cerridwen's father, Gronw, said in his stuttering way that nothing would induce him to turn back, from which others took heart and resolution.

Padarn told her that they'd part company here. Instead of travelling on to the Fosse Way, his people would go north along the western edge of the Great Wood until they arrived in a landscape of ghosts that was their own. "We can't hide from the Gewisse forever," he reasoned.

Of all those who went with him, Eleri was saddest to part with the new baby boy, just a few days old. The mother had asked Eleri to name him. "Arawn," she'd said without hesitation.

"Well, let's get on with it," she said, resigned, simultaneously running up against the limits of her imagination and her powers of persuasion.

"*You don't know everything, Eleri Gwir.*"

With about a third fewer in number, Eleri set off west. "Look out for eagles," the scouts were told. Gwion said that he and Olwen would take their best horses and go as far as the Great Road to try and ascertain its relative safety.

"Take care," Eleri told him.

She couldn't lose him as well. Her mind turned to Macsen and his brave Red Cloaks; the feeling of loss hit her in the stomach again, a physical anguish. It was something she had to ignore, she told herself, pushing the pain away, counting herself fortunate to be so active, to have endless decisions to make, small and great, enough to displace mawkishly depressing thoughts and feelings, for now at least.

The usual morning ritual with Mared and the other old folk over with, they set out, the ponies patient under their loads, the fringes over their eyes concealing whatever scurrilous thoughts were running through their clever heads.

By early afternoon Gwion and Olwen hadn't returned, which made Eleri fidgety, and that made her cross. She snapped at a grumbling child. She told an old man to stop complaining and think himself lucky. There were no eagles of any description; but then there was no Gwion either.

Finally, as darkness fell, Gwion and Olwen returned. Eleri gave thanks to the Great Creator, such was her relief at finding them safe. She noticed that Gwion almost fell off his horse. After days with barely any sleep, he was exhausted. Bryn Derwydd was still running through him; their journey to the Great Wood; now this. Eleri recognised that he'd taken a lot on his shoulders; from a boy not so long ago and an untried young man not so many weeks before, he'd become a figure of authority, the real leader now among the men, supplanting his father without meaning to. People looked to him as they looked to Eleri. Assuming they lived, it was something he'd have to get used to. Already responsibility was changing him. She missed the way he used to rattle on about things, his enthusiasm and his heart worn on his sleeve. But she was proud, too, of the Gwion that he was and that he was becoming; a reluctant leader born of necessity. Sometimes they were the best kind.

"What did you find?" she asked.

"Fugitives, like us," Gwion said.

"Not so many all together like we are," Olwen explained.

"Families; smaller groups of people, all heading south for Dyfneint, hoping to sail to Llydaw," Gwion elaborated, recovering a little.

"No Gewisse?" they were asked.

"We saw none," Gwion said. "We were told that war bands are around, but that the main Saxon army is to the north. It seems they've met with resistance from the three strongholds, from Caer Gloui especially, where the walls are in good order. No one knew for sure but they thought that all three would have fallen by now. No one knows anything really, except that we lost and the Gewisse won and everything else flows from that simple fact."

"What about the war bands?"

"It's hard to say. Ceawlin probably sent them to scout the ground down this way. He'll want to know if there are any centres of resistance, I suppose," Gwion said. "It all seems a bit random and opportunistic. A man told us that if they come across any fugitives they'll either kill them or round them up, depending on how the mood takes them. Mind you, I don't know who told him that."

"Our old friends rumour and hearsay, I suppose," Cerys observed wryly.

"Probably."

"So the Great Road it is," Eleri said resignedly.

"I suppose so," Gwion said. "Unless the eagles come to carry us all to Caer Uisc."

"An eagle can come and take my mother anywhere it likes," Cerys said with undisguised feeling.

No eagles or any other winged agents of salvation came. They saw no one on their slow journey to the Fosse Way, which was something to be thankful for in the scheme of things. Eleri remembered to give thanks, as her father would have wanted. Each stream they crossed was the haunt of a local god whose name may not have been known to these relative strangers but whose presence was to be acknowledged. Their lives, Eleri felt, were in the hands of this sacred land to which they had been untrue, neglecting to defend it to the limits of their strength. If forgiveness was deserved and if her gods had been a lot of weak-minded fools, she might have asked it of them. Eleri Gwir wouldn't insult her gods by asking such a thing; the truth of what had been done and not done was as plain as it was undeserving of forgiveness. It was something else she had to learn to live with.

"Where are we, Eleri Gwir?" a child asked. "How far is it to go?"

"Not far now," she answered, more patiently than the day before when Gwion hadn't been with her. In amongst all the other things she had to think about, she made a note of the fact that Gwion and Olwen were getting to be friends and more than friends, always riding off together, at archery practice, the one praising the other to the skies. The thought produced a sharp prick of jealousy in her side, which amazed her. It made her laugh out loud. Is anything stronger, hardier, more intense and more insidious than jealousy, she wondered? In time, she would learn the answer to that question.

In the meantime, before them was the Great Road the Romans had built, from Caer Uisc in the south of the Island to a place far in the north and east. Even with the rain that was falling, it lifted their spirits. People and horses alike appreciated the level going, the sense that they were getting somewhere. Mared of the Silver Wheel, who seemed against all predictions to be getting stronger by the day, was in particularly high spirits, saying now how much she had always liked Dyfneint people and how much she was looking forward to seeing the country.

"Just as well, Mother," Cerys answered, her bottom sore and her patience worn thin. "Because that's precisely where we're headed."

Like Gwion before, Eleri was allowing herself to hope, enjoying the luxury of it, her mind straightening up, in keeping with the road she was on.

In the meantime, Gwion's state of mind had moved to another level. More nervous than hopeful, the underlying reality of their situation digging into his bones, he told Eleri: “We’re vulnerable.”

“Weren’t we always?” she responded.

“I’ve got a bad feeling.”

# Chapter Thirty-Five

They came across the dead bodies early the next day. As before, Gwion had posted scouts to their rear, to guard their backs should a marauding Saxon war bad suddenly decide to go for a gallop down the Fosse Way. Saxons weren't expected from the south, up from the direction of Dyfneint. Nonetheless, scouts had also been sent that way. To their surprise, it was from that direction that the boy Idris brought the news.

What did it mean?

"Trouble," Cerys said.

They found a copse into which they brought all their people and belongings. Archers were posted around the perimeter. Two scouts went a mile north and two south, with orders to carry any news directly and immediately to Gwion.

"You are not to get caught," he warned them. "Don't take stupid risks; don't take *any* risks."

Gwion and Olwen went to see the fly-ridden bodies for themselves. Birds circled overhead. Majestic-looking crows had settled to their meat and only gave it up when Gwion slashed at them with his sword. All the bodies had been stripped of any wearable clothing and any other meagre possessions they might have had, trinkets and the like, with which they must have hoped to buy their passage to Llydaw. There were nine bodies in all. Gwion and Olwen recognised the mutilated face of a man they'd spoken to a few days earlier. The killing was very recent, therefore.

"We have to get back," Gwion said, feeling that their people could be in imminent danger of attack.

Riding hard, they found Eleri at the head of a straggle of tired and anxious people, looking almost as defenceless as those three children Gwion and the others had met on this same road.

"I don't think it's Saxons," he reported back to Eleri and the others. "They wouldn't bother to take the clothing; they're not desperate enough for that."

"Outlaws, then?" Eleri asked.

"Or a war band from Maes-y-Gaer," Gwenda suggested.

That seemed plausible enough.

"What if it's the people of Dyfneint themselves?" Gwion said. "The local people from this area, I mean. They may not want fugitives streaming into their land. They may be happy to dispose of them and to take all they own."

"They'd be poor enough and desperate enough," Gwenda concurred.

"Would they leave them on the road like that, in plain sight?" Eleri asked, needing to be convinced.

"I don't know," Gwion said. "As a deterrent to others, perhaps."

It was possible; anything within reason was possible.

Everyone looked to Eleri. Tired as she was, her clothes torn and unwashed, her precious torque hidden away, she still had the appearance of a chieftain's daughter, a coppery-haired queen even, tall and brave and proud.

"I won't go back," she said firmly. "We'll meet whoever is out there and we'll take them on. I'm not promising anything. I only know that I want us to stick together and to see this through."

She could see doubt settling in some of the faces in front of her; she could sense despair creeping into their hearts. Why shouldn't the others look and feel that way? After all was said and done, she was no stranger to the same doubt and despair. Her resolve to fight was an act of will, a stubborn refusal to accept the seemingly hopeless facts of their situation.

It was Gronw who spoke again, throwing off his stutter for that instant. "And I won't go back either," he said. "Nothing has changed," he struggled to add, his speech impediment playing him for a fool. "Nothing," he declared, that one word a statement of his resolve.

Eleri could have kissed him. The sound of her own tenacity spoken back to her brought tears to her eyes.

"Aye," one or two muttered in response. Then, putting a brave face on things, others joined in, saying Gronw was right. 'We're not going back," they said. "We're in this mess together."

"Let's face it," Gwion commented, his face dark with foreboding. "There's only one way for us to go."

"What if we stay here and secure our defences like we did against the outlaws in the Great Wood?" someone asked.

"We can't stay here forever," Eleri pointed out.

"Waiting like sitting ducks," Gwenda said.

"We're probably already within the borders of Dyfneint," Gwion observed. "We should just press ahead."

There was no right answer.

On they travelled. The place where the rotting corpses lay came and went. They averted their eyes.

*

It was midday when the shout was heard from the scouts: "On the hill to the left, horsemen!" There they were, riding deliberately into view, their banner showing a black dragon against a gold backdrop.

"Britons," Eleri said under her breath, disgusted.

"It's Maes-y-Gaer," Meriadoc confirmed, the only person there who had had dealings with the rogue Lord of that ancient stronghold.

"Bastards," his son said.

The horsemen moved slowly forward, fearing nothing themselves, letting fear and panic grow in the hearts of the people of the Summer Land. The horsemen seemed as though they intended to charge directly at them, picking up speed gradually, step by step, the thunder of their hooves increasing on the hard surface of the Roman road.

Like an old hand Gwion brought his archers forward, Eleri among them. "Aim for the horses," he said. "Don't hesitate. Follow my lead."

The horsemen of the rogue lord came on.

"Hold!" Gwion shouted.

He sensed the panic rising inside his archers. Boys, girls, young women mostly, a sorry lot that – reasonably enough – the horsemen expected to crumble and run, to be swept aside and drowned by the tidal wave of their violence.

"Hold!" Gwion shouted again, more urgently this time, feeling the instinct to fire in himself, barely able to resist the temptation.

At twenty-five paces he let fly, close enough for the most novice archer to hit something, far enough away for the wounded and dying horses to fall or pull up without trampling and spilling into the defenders.

Legs splayed, eyes flashing, rearing and neighing, the lead horses crashed in a powerful jumble of sweating, steaming flesh, throwing their riders or pinning them to the ground. A few of the horsemen directly behind those in the lead were skilful or lucky enough to pull up before adding to the spillage, many more went down, archers finding their marks, horses stumbling into others, their spindly legs breaking, the whole charge fracturing. Spears were thrown, one finding Rhian's left shoulder. Those throwing them were brought down.

The horsemen had expected old men to kill and boys to terrorise, girls and women to rape and to carry off if they were anything to look at. They'd expected easy pickings, a few trinkets, weapons, anything they could use and trade. They hadn't expected to die.

"Hold!" Gwion shouted again, seeing the wreckage they'd created, the bodies of the lead horsemen mangled and fallen before him, their compatriots to the rear doing their best to get away, moving beyond the modest range of most of his archers.

There were about twenty horsemen remaining, enough to do the people of the Summer Land considerable harm if they went about it in the right way. One man seemed to have taken charge. He walked his mount, a grey stallion, arrogantly forward while he contemplated his next move. He must have seen Gwion draw back his bow. He must have dismissed the possibility of being shot at that distance. He fell like a sack of acorns, surprise on his hard face, his right hand on the shaft of Gwion's arrow, lodged deep in his heart.

"Gwion!" the people of the Summer Land shouted.

They watched as the horsemen turned away. The men from Maes-y-Gaer had suddenly shifted their attention. It wasn't that they were planning to run away. No; they were watching, listening.

Then the people of the Summer Land heard it. There was the unmistakeable sound of more horsemen approaching up the Fosse Way, from the direction of Dyfneint. Their hearts sank inside them.

"Stand back, Rhian!" Eleri shouted to her, seeing that she was wounded.

"I'll do no such thing, Eleri Gwir!" Rhian answered.

"There's too many, whoever they are," Gwion said, as the sound grew, the ground vibrating under them, the noise carried from cobble to cobble.

They were close now. The thunder was deafening.

They saw what remained of the men of the rogue Lord of Maes-y-Gaer scatter in all directions, and with that the horsemen from the south came into view.

"Dyfneint," Eleri said, seeing the standard of the sun-faced cross, a burst of colour against the bleak sky.

"There must be a hundred, at least," Gwion said, standing next to her.

"Are they with us or against us?" people asked.

# Chapter Thirty-Six

"You're a week late, young man," Mared of the Silver Wheel said, her frame shrinking with age, her spirit as large and as pugnacious as ever. "Speak up!" she shouted, her eyes fixed on the young man's lips.

"I know," he said, louder by the slightest degree, his manner a little haughty and reserved, distant enough to make the tiny hairs on Mared's shoulders rise in protest.

"No one speaks up anymore," she said, looking for a fight but not getting one.

The young man was standing in the midst of the bemused and relieved people of the Summer Land. He was *with* them. There was no need for him to win them over, to charm them or the like. The very fact that he was here, that he was a Briton and that his intentions didn't appear to be hostile in nature was enough. Mared of the Silver Wheel notwithstanding, they were more than happy to treat him like a king.

"Eleri Gwir," the young man said, his tone formal, measured.

"Kadwy."

Shock sounded in her voice.

"And Marrec," she said, still nonplussed.

"Yes," Kadwy said. "Dyfneint is here at last. I hope it's better late than never."

Eleri was somewhere between bursting out in tears and slapping Kadwy in the face. She was drunk on thankfulness and sober with recrimination. Suddenly the stress, the exhaustion she felt caught up with her. Her first instinct was to strip naked, to throw all her dirty clothes away and with them the anxieties and responsibilities of the past days, and to throw up her arms in thanks to Lord of the skies, to be reborn, innocent of all the blood and hardship. She was somewhere between falling to the ground and leaping into the clouds. It was possible that she might have done one or the other, or both even, except that Cerys came and held on to her.

"We'll give thanks," Cerys said.

"Yes."

They walked to the low hill from where the horsemen of Maes-y-Gaer had come. Before the men of the Christian host of Dyfneint, in sight of the standard of the sun-faced cross, in that green and grey land, the women of the Summer Land bared their bodies and stood, hands linked, arms held high, and chanted the ancient words of praise to the gods of that place and to the god whose chariot rides the grey sky of the Island of the Mighty. As the chanting continued, the boys and men of the Summer Land and many of the host came to stand with them, their weapons put aside, their clothing discarded, and joined in the song that was as old as the land itself.

Kadwy stayed apart. If he didn't approve, he said nothing. If he was impatient to be off, he managed to keep it to himself. Unlike his father Erbin, he wasn't religious. To Kadwy, all religions seemed equally implausible – *water into wine*; *a woman from flowers*. But he saw that religion was powerful and that it could be useful; so many were believers, even someone as bright as Eleri Gwir. He stayed where he was. He was inclined to think that there could be too much religion and too many beliefs. It was a thought for another day. Indulgence has its time and place, he told himself. After all, with the Island broken, shattered in so many ways, the song would not be heard in this land again.

His captain at arms, Marrec, stayed with him. His duty was to his king.

From the moment the host of Dyfneint had regrouped, after chasing down those horsemen of Maes-y-Gaer who had survived the first onslaught, it was obvious to Eleri that something had changed. The young Prince Kadwy she'd met the year before was no more. In his place was a young man of greater status and authority. Here was the King of Dyfneint.

"So where were you?" Eleri asked, recovered, clothed, cleansed, very much her old self again. "You were needed at Bryn Derwydd."

She might have gone about it differently, less directly, asking Kadwy how his elevation to the throne had come about, for example. She might have praised his good timing or complimented his military exploits. Her father's warnings about leaders jumped around in her brain. "A bit of flattery never goes astray, Eleri Gwir," he'd say. But she was who she was, and she asked what her character said she had to ask.

"Later," Kadwy said firmly. "First I'd like to be introduced to your captain of archers."

"How d'you know it isn't me?" Eleri asked, her tongue working quicker than her judgement.

"I've seen you draw a bow, Eleri Gwir," Kadwy replied. "I've also seen you refuse to draw a bow," he added after a pause, his meaning clear to them both.

Like an alert fox, Kadwy saw everything; missed nothing.

Gwion was introduced to Kadwy, who had high praise for his archers. Marrec chimed in, saying he was impressed.

"I should thank you for coming to our rescue," Gwion said tentatively, not sure how he was to address the two men before him, one barely a year or two older than himself, the other only a few years older again.

Self-conscious, he couldn't shake off the truth that both these men were greatly superior in status to himself. Macsen came into his head. Gwion gave himself a talking to: he had been at Bryn Derwydd, he had no reason to feel inferior to these or any other men. He was cross with himself for feeling awkward, which didn't help to make him feel any less awkward.

"You did a good job on your own account," Marrec said.

"These boys and she-warriors of yours are a dangerous lot," Kadwy commented. He hadn't intended to make them feel ill at ease, but he saw that was the effect of what he'd said. He was a king, and when kings praise the military exploits of others, it means they either intend to co-opt or destroy them. Usually he would have let it go at that, happy enough to create a fissure of doubt in the minds of others. Today he explained himself, saying: "I don't mean anything by it; it's just an innocent remark."

"The innocent remark of a king," Eleri said archly.

"Precisely, Eleri Gwir," Kadwy said, again with unmistakeable firmness.

Eventually Dyfneint's story was told. It was an old story. We are inclined to imagine human affairs to be complex, subtle, a pattern of infinite intricacy made on a vast loom that accommodates a universe of difference. It's true, of course. Yet, the stories we tell about gods and men invariably come down to lust, greed and power.

Some tales may rise or fall above or below these common themes. This wasn't one of them. It was of the same clay as countless others, pointing to the central paradox of human life, which is at once depressingly predictable and horribly complicated.

After they had made camp for the night, Kadwy invited Eleri Gwir and Gwion to join him.

"Bring a few of your people along," he said.

"Gwion's father Meriadoc," Eleri suggested.

"And that young woman," Kadwy said wonderingly.

If there was one thing Eleri enjoyed in life, a pleasure like no other, it was observing the way men went about fishing for information about women they fancied; the cooler the man's nature the better. Setting aside the temptation to play Kadwy along by pretending she didn't know who he referred to, Eleri said: "That's Cerridwen's sister; her name's Olwen."

"Really," Kadwy replied, his tone perfectly neutral.

"Yes, really," Eleri said. "The Dragon Maiden's sister."

"Very well," Kadwy said, words sufficient to constitute an invitation.

They found Kadwy in company with Marrec and one other man, a few years older again than Marrec, as raven-haired as Gwion and every bit as wiry and lithe, but with a wildness in him that Gwion would never own, a broiling sea, piratical wildness of the spirit.

"*Alun Ddu* – Alun the Black," Kadwy said, introducing the man. "The captain of the people of Kernow."

There are some people you take to straight away. For Eleri and the others, Alun Ddu was like that. The wildness of his spirit made you want to leap into a leaky calfskin boat with him and sail off into the limitless west. There was a life-giving ebullience about him, an inexhaustible energy. He had none of Kadwy's kingly circumspection or Marrec's soldierly reserve.

"Kadwy here tells me you were at Bryn Derwydd," he said to Eleri and Gwion. "What can I say?" he added, his passionate eyes clouding with shame. "The men of Kernow should have been there. The king will explain," he said, his attempt at formality every bit as awkward as anything of Gwion's.

Kadwy was no storyteller; still less Marrec, who helped the tale along. They told it straight so that what the story lacked in adornment it made up for in reliability.

"I will start by saying that my father King Erbin and my brother Kelyn are dead," Kadwy stated.

He was sitting on a low stool, which hardly seemed very kingly, yet his stillness and thoughtfulness commanded authority. Like Macsen, Eleri thought, he is young still but old with responsibility. She could see that he was mastering himself and his new role, figuring out the nuances of his own person and deciding whether to adapt these to kingship or to adapt kingship to himself. His reserve was natural to his guarded, watchful nature and also a product of his attempt to make sense of his position in life, a survival strategy, you might say.

"As you know," Kadwy continued, "after defeating the Irish sea raiders in the north, we went west to Kernow. The feet of the Island were infested by the same pestilence and my father was determined to drive them out. A promise had been made to Kernow and we would keep that promise," he said solemnly.

"Even though it was late in the year and winter was coming on," Marrec interjected.

Close though he and Macsen had been, Eleri hadn't had much to do with Marrec before now. He had been important to King Erbin, of course; he seemed essential to Kadwy, a pillar – or was it an arch? – upon which his kingship rested. Macsen had liked him and Eleri could see why.

"The men of Kernow are great warriors," Kadwy said, looking to Alun. "But the sea wolves were heavily entrenched, and with the weather deteriorating..."

"Is it ever good in Kernow?" Eleri asked.

"The sun has been known to shine for at least ten minutes at a time," Alun said.

"Rarely," Kadwy said dryly. "In any case, it proved a long and difficult business. The Irish would have taken flight but the seas were too rough. There was nothing for it but to stay and fight, which is what we wanted, a reckoning that would prove decisive and long-lasting."

"It dragged on to Christ's birth and beyond," Kadwy said. He looked about before continuing, checking on his audience before starting on a difficult part of the tale. "My brother Kelyn had been restless for some time. To be honest, he was born restless. You remember the incident with the Dragon Maiden?" he said, addressing Eleri but also taking a look at Olwen. "That was only the symptom of a larger problem. He wanted things his own way. He wanted power. He resented my father and wanted him out of the way. He wanted me out of the way." Kadwy looked at Eleri. "What was your opinion of my brother, Eleri Gwir?" he asked.

Eleri didn't know how Kelyn had died; whether Kadwy was seeking approval for his actions, whatever they may have been. As an only child, she didn't always realise how thick blood could be and how easily offence could be taken on its behalf, even where a brother agreed with one's estimation of his sibling. She could only be honest, and she told Kadwy that she considered his brother to be exactly the sort of man who shouldn't be trusted with power: vain, impetuous, nakedly ambitious, and a few other things besides.

"That's about the sum of it, I'm afraid," Kadwy said. Instead of taking offence at what Eleri had said, he seemed glad to be relieved of the burden of explaining his brother's failings.

"As winter wore on and the campaign of attrition offered little amusement for someone of his temperament, Kelyn's restlessness grew," Kadwy explained. "He became fractious and openly troublesome. He questioned my father's orders. He made enemies of our staunchest men, like Marrec and Alun, and befriended every captain and chieftain who was out for himself and for no one and nothing else. Kelyn became a real problem for my father. He begged to be allowed to return east to Caer Uisc where he could have oversight of our interests in that region, which on the face of it seemed reasonable enough. Eventually, my father gave in to him and let him go. My father didn't like it, but he was tired of Kelyn's meddling and tantrums. He didn't think anyone would take my brother seriously. I said I would go too, but Kelyn would have none of that. So there it was; my father and I were encamped in Kernow, shepherding sea wolves, while my brother was making mischief in Caer Uisc.

"In the end, hunger and impatience drove the Irish out and we defeated them. But that was towards the end of the second month of the year, and there was still the promise to Ffernfael to be kept."

"Did any of the sea raiders get away?" Olwen asked.

"No. We killed them all," Kadwy told her, liking the question as much as the questioner.

"But we were a long way from where we needed to be," Marrec said. "Right down in the toes of the Island."

"Yes," Kadwy said. "We travelled east towards Caer Uisc. My father had three hundred of his own retinue; another two hundred men of Kernow were with us. News had reached us that all was not well in Dyfneint. All kinds of rumours were spread about, all of them concerning my brother Kelyn. We heard that he had marshalled the forces of several chieftains against us. My father, it was said, ruled on his own behalf, taking little or no advice from his chieftains, relying too much on his sons and on the church, to which he was devoted. The chieftains wanted a share of power and that is what Kelyn promised them, a seat at the table, so to speak."

"As if Kelyn would share power with anyone," Marrec said dismissively.

"I don't know if he used them or the chieftains used him more," Kadwy remarked.

"Perhaps the manipulation was mutual," Eleri suggested.

"Yes; I'm sure it was," Kadwy said, impressed at Eleri's astuteness. "At any rate, the king's retinue came east. We expected trouble but we didn't expect an all-out battle, which is what we got at the edge of the great moorland that lies before Caer Uisc."

"As bloody a fight as I've ever been in," Alun said.

"It was bloody," Kadwy confirmed. "The men on both sides took it upon themselves to disregard any thought of tactics and just launched into one another, as if they were fighting sworn enemies, not fellow Britons. My father died. Marrec was wounded. The slaughter was dreadful on both sides."

Kadwy paused to clear his system of the memory.

"No clear victor emerged," Marrec explained. "Fortunately, we were able to call on more reserves from Kernow. It took time, but eventually we returned to the field and Kelyn was defeated."

"He was killed in that second battle," Kadwy said, disgust in his voice at the thought of his brother's wasted life. "We returned finally to Caer Uisc to find everything upside down. The men my father had relied on for support were dead or imprisoned. The messengers Ffernfael had sent to warn of the impending battle with the Saxons were likewise dead or imprisoned. I think our return to Caer Uisc must have been on the same day as the battle of Bryn Derwydd took place. Can you believe it? We had failed our own people. A king was dead. The Island was broken and for what, the impatience of a young prince of Dyfneint and the stupid machinations of chieftains who should have known better."

He paused again, wanting and needing to feel the full force of his anger and shame, not one to hide from the truth of such feelings.

"What can I say?" he asked Eleri and Gwion rhetorically. "Anything I would say would sound lame and feeble."

"Say nothing, Kadwy," Eleri said. "You're here now."

"Without you, the people of the Summer Land would have perished," Gwion said quietly.

"I don't know about that," Kadwy responded. "The people of the Summer Land are a pretty remarkable lot."

"Pretty *and* remarkable," Alun added meaningfully, his dark wildness like an impending storm.

"Sleep," Eleri said firmly, cutting off that line conversation before it started. "The remarkable *and pretty* people of the Summer Land need sleep."

But this was too sombre an occasion to end on such a note. Marrec inquired about Macsen and Riwalus; Kadwy asked about his cousin Branwen and her lover Siriol.

"And Cerridwen, the Dragon Maiden," he said. "Tell us how she fared in all this."

Eleri and Gwion said as much as they could. The battle was like a dream or nightmare to them, remembered in sporadic images, more by feelings and impressions than by reasoning powers. They found it was not something they cared to talk about in any detail, even if they were able to.

"We lost," Eleri said. "We lost everything and everyone."

# Chapter Thirty-Seven

Cerys was at that time of life when a woman's body is oppressed for no reason by sudden bursts of heat which can make her irritable, uncomfortable and, regardless of the weather, intolerant of clothing. For days, a lifetime it seemed, she had been bounced around on the back of a grumpy pony, holding on to an even grumpier old woman whose days of sudden heat were long behind her and who had gone beyond caring about other people's discomfort. At first light, Eleri found Cerys at the campfire preparing a drink of fennel seed and clover by which she swore as the only thing that helped control the flushing waves that went through her. She was in one of her rare dangerous moods. Her first words to Eleri were: "You can leave me here to rot or you can leave my mother here to rot. The same goes for that evil-minded pony, who does nothing but side with my mother."

Old friends had no need for too many words of explanation. They prepared the brew together and talked about its qualities in a professional manner, as well as about the nature and causes behind this flushing which, like bleeding, affected some women more than others. Gwenda joined them. She was on the cusp of experiencing the problem at first hand, or not, as the case might be. They talked on; other women coming to listen or more commonly to make their own opinion or life experience known. They agreed that Cerys had it bad and everyone was keen to know if the fennel seed and clover potion actually worked or not.

Not the most social of creatures at the best of times, it wasn't long before Cerys informed the crowd of women that she had work to do, even if they had none themselves. Everyone was used to Cerys and they got the message clearly enough. Within a minute or so she was left sipping her brew more or less contentedly with only Eleri Gwir for company – teacher and pupil, mother and daughter almost, but without the intensity that can blight that relationship, during a girl's awkward years especially.

As for Cerys' own mother, despite claiming to be awake before dawn every morning Mared of the Silver Wheel was still fast asleep, safe in the hands of the Moon Goddess. The golden rule about not waking Mared was applied with absolute strictness. Cerys had promised a heap of exotic curses on anyone who failed to follow her orders.

The people of the Summer Land had come a long way. Yet there was still some way to go to reach Caer Uisc. At least now they felt safe and the road was good. Inevitably, people made all too obvious and unoriginal comments about Romans and roads. There was something like a feeling of normality abroad. With nature reasserting itself, the young women of the Summer Land were taking an interest in the more desirable men among Kadwy's retinue, a state of affairs which did not adhere to either a strict age limit for women or any clear standard of desirability for men. Patched up from her close encounter with a spear, her arm in a makeshift sling, Rhian was to the forefront of these proceedings, milking her new-found reputation as a heroine for all it was worth.

"These she-warriors really are a dangerous lot," the watchful Kadwy observed to Marrec.

"They certainly are that."

"But useful for replenishing our numbers," Kadwy further observed, one eyebrow raised, signifying that the comment was of humorous as well as serious import.

"And for replenishing morale I should think," Marrec said, smiling, his own inclinations tending in that direction.

Like dew before the sun, the smile evaporated. On the order of his king, Marrec was about to visit immediate heartache and disappointment upon the sexes. His orders were to divide the retinue in two, one half to be led by Kadwy to escort the people of the Summer Land to Caer Uisc, the other half led by himself to patrol the borders of Dyfneint, discouraging incursions by either Saxon war bands or any from Maes-y-Gaer. Marrec had the amusing idea of sending off the older men on escort duty while the more eligible amongst them stayed with him. The idea, like his smile, faded. The sensible thing was to let Alun and the men of Kernow return south to Caer Uisc and for them to then head for home over the great moorland. The idea of Alun and his wild men from the west escorting all those women made Marrec smile again. There was nothing else for it. He hoped he'd still be smiling on his own return to Caer Uisc.

Marrec went north up the Fosse Way; Kadwy south.

The journey to Caer Uisc took another five days. The pace was slow with old and young in train. Besides, the new king took the opportunity to inspect the land through which they travelled. Diversions from the Great Road were made by Kadwy and a core of his men, leaving Eleri and her people in the safe keeping of Alun and the men of Kernow.

For Eleri, these were days of hard but not unpleasant walking, the rain having turned to a light drizzle and then to something like dry weather, although never actual sunshine. They were days of relief and of trivial and not-so-trivial decisions of a family nature, although not her own, unless she co-opted her friends and neighbours to be her family. She had no other. They were days of curious loneliness when, as if from the earth of Dyfneint, there rose in her a profound sense of her own solitude, even in the midst of so many people, with so much to say and do. They were days of contemplation after the shock and rush of battle and then of flight, a time for loss to settle into the deeper sediments of her being. And they were days of gladness when, in company with Gwion and Olwen, she would walk over the springy heather and feel the wind take her long fire-god hair, shaking out complexity and doubt, making her young again and foolishly hopeful.

Among the many family issues that came her way were disputes two girls had with their mothers about wanting to take up with men from Kernow. The girls were Nest and Enid, two friends who, over a matter of days, had contrived to fall hopelessly in love with two of Alun's men. They wanted nothing but to follow them to the far reaches of the west, where the land of the Island ends, giving way to the limitless ocean. They didn't care if these men had ties and commitments back home. They didn't know if the Kernow soldiers would be able to support them. They cared and knew about one thing only.

Their mothers had been young and headstrong once themselves. For them, infatuation was not an unexplored land. They knew what it was like to be ordered about by their bodies, to think with their skin, to understand with their wombs. Neither mother was foolish or forgetful.

But they had lost their husbands and their home. They didn't want to lose anything else, especially on an impulse that might be regretted, that probably would be regretted when their daughters came face to face with the hard realities of life in Kernow compared to the relative plenty they had known in the Summer Land. All this and more was explained to Eleri, who was asked to intervene in the dispute, to talk sense to the girls, or conversely to make the mothers realise how wrong they were to worry.

Eleri was barely a couple of years older than Nest and Enid. She was the one who had gone off with a dashing Red Cloak, abandoning the man everyone had supposed she would couple with. Who was she to talk?

"You're young; they'll listen to you," the mothers said.

"You're young too; why are you siding with them?" the girls said.

It was another battle of sorts, one in which reinforcements were needed.

Eleri asked to see the men involved. She made inquiries about their situations. She invited Alun Ddu to join them. She made it very clear to Alun that the girls were not to be led on and then abandoned to their own devices once they arrived in Kernow. She asked Alun to vouch for the men. She set out the new life these girls might live in Llydaw, across the water, or even here in Dyfneint.

Every bone in Alun's body was inclined to let his hard-fighting men have their fun. He would do no less himself. But there was more to him than bones. He recognised Eleri's authority amongst these people and he saw the justice in what she said.

"I can't order my men off these girls," he said. "I can't go against nature when they're yowling for one another like cats on a summer's night."

"I don't expect miracles," Eleri told him. "I just want them to be straight with these girls. They need to know what they're in for in Kernow, as do their mothers."

A meeting was called of girls, mothers and men, and held in the presence of Eleri and Alun Ddu. The men confessed to having wives back home; the mothers drew sighs of relief and made "I told you so" faces; the girls looked Eleri full in the face with pure contempt in their eyes. It was another thing she had to learn to get used to.

Eleri was also active, or more relevantly watchful, on another front. All day and every day she saw the relationship between Gwion and Olwen develop into something more than it had been and less than it might become. Others saw it too, of course, but were careful not to remark on it in Eleri's presence.

Only Gwenda – Olwen's mother – spoke of it, saying in her stern way, her arms folded: "Those two are getting very friendly."

Eleri agreed. "It's good to see," she said, surprising Gwenda and herself.

And it was good to see. No one in the world, not in this world at any rate, was dearer to Eleri than Gwion. She loved him. She wanted him to be happy. She wanted him to grow and to flower into the special man he had always been destined to become. With Eleri, he was always in her shadow, even now. "It's time he got out into the sun," she told herself. Her father had worried that she would fall for the first and only man she'd ever known; the same applied for Gwion, falling for Eleri, the girl he'd known all his life, the chieftain's daughter, with her confidence and the strength of character that came with it. Bossy Eleri Gwir telling him what to do; Gwion standing up to her, making her think twice, insisting there was always another point of view.

Before, in Macsen's bed, there had been a part of her that still wanted Gwion for her own. She had been the one to throw him over, and yet she had been the one who couldn't let him go, not completely, not yet.

Now she was ready. She thought of him as a strawberry coming out from under a rhubarb leaf, which made her laugh. He would prefer to be thought of as an eagle flying the nest, or a wild pony, snorting, shaking its black head before running free at last.

Eleri saw their paths diverging. For herself, her life burned by grief, Eleri was coming around to solitude, needing space and time to rebuild the bridges that connected her to the world. Her journey was inward, whereas Gwion's struggles with the same emotions took him outward into the world. It was a relief as much as anything; it made her happy to see Gwion with Olwen. "She'll suit him very well," Eleri told herself, bossy Eleri Gwir needing to approve the direction of Gwion's departure, letting go and not quite letting go, even now.

But what did the gods really have in store for Gwion and Olwen?

What Gwenda didn't see was the watchful way the young king, Kadwy, looked at her daughter. Eleri saw it. In the evenings, after his day's hard riding, Kadwy would ask Eleri and a few others to join him. Olwen was there. True to his nature, Kadwy would listen more than talk, more suited to the role of observer on these occasions. He would take them all in, sizing up Gwion, his eyes on Eleri, his inquiring gaze resting longer on Olwen than any other. He wasn't like Kelyn; he had none of his brother's impulsive and hungry brutality. But he was a king and who knew what he was thinking.

Kadwy asked about their plans.

Eleri took the lead in answering. "The people talk of starting afresh across the water in Llydaw. A few have relations there. They say there's land to be had and that more of our people are needed. They say it's beautiful. It even rains less."

"So that's what *they* say, Eleri Gwir," Kadwy responded quizzically. He seemed to make a point of referring to her by her assumed name.

"*They* do."

"What do you say, my lord?" Gwion asked.

"I say it's probably true," Kadwy responded. "But I also say that we in Dyfneint need good people. If they all sail off to Llydaw what will become of us?"

No one answered that Dyfneint would be conquered, if not this year or the next, then at some point in the future. Such evil thoughts were better left unspoken.

"Will you sing us a song, Alun Ddu?" Kadwy asked. "Make it sad, will you; lift our spirits with a melancholy song."

Alun sang about a curlew that lived on the banks of a river. The curlew saw the river in all its lives, swift and agile at first, a child of the hills, broader and slower in its middle reaches before flowing wide and sluggish at last into the ocean. Like the lives of men, the curlew observed, from youth, to middle age and on to old age and death.

The song was suitably melancholy; they felt better for it.

# Chapter Thirty-Eight

When Marrec returned after several weeks to Caer Uisc, he heard the cuckoo in the woods and he found the people of the Summer Land making ready for their journey to the other Britain across the Sea of Gaul. Arriving with Marrec were more fugitives from the north, escaping from Ceawlin and his Saxons. The Caer Uisc he found was busy with people, some preparing to leave, others considering staying, everyone contemplating their likely and possible futures, weighing up the costs and benefits, reaching into their pockets and bags to see which course was within their means.

Marrec found Eleri sitting apart from the others, perched on the slowly decaying stone walls of the old Roman town.

"Good afternoon, Eleri Gwir," he said. "Do you mind if I join you?"

"Not at all."

"Your people are preparing to leave us," he said.

"Yes. A few will stay. Most want to be on their way to Llydaw. They want to start again in a new land."

"What about you?" he asked.

"I must go with them. It's expected of me," she said, her tone neutral, matter of fact.

They talked on amiably enough about the borders, the problems with the rogue lord of Maes-y-Gaer and the like. Eleri was less forthcoming than Marrec remembered; more inward-looking. He wondered if this reticence was something like a cold that she was catching from his king, Kadwy.

The next day they met again.

More like her old self, Eleri asked: "And is this coincidence, captain?"

"I'm sorry if I disturb you," Marrec said.

"That's all right. I was thinking about you anyway," Eleri said. "I was thinking of asking you a favour."

It was Marrec's turn to be reserved. She looked at him and he looked at her.

"Well, let's hear it," he said cautiously. He was wary of favours.

"I told you yesterday that I must leave with my people," Eleri explained. "Before I do I would like to go to Ynys Wydr."

Whatever for?" Marrec asked, surprised, the hazards of the journey and all the other arguments against the proposal forming in his mind.

"It's just something I have to do," Eleri said.

"But why?"

"I don't know why exactly," she said. "They're all there or they've all passed that way; Macsen, Cerridwen and the others; my father. The spirit of the Island itself is there, whole and strong and beautiful."

"Ceawlin could also be there – and not in spirit only," Marrec said.

"D'you think so?"

"No," he answered honestly. "The Gewisse have enough spoils to occupy them without concerning themselves about the Water Land."

"That's what I thought," Eleri said, looking at him again, challenging him to say what she wanted him to say.

"So I suppose you're looking for some mug to accompany you to Ynys Wydr," he said obligingly.

"The thought had occurred to me."

"And I suppose you have someone in mind?"

"I do in fact. I happen to know someone who has nothing better to do than sit around flirting with young women."

Marrec laughed, but he was serious when he told her he'd have to think it over as well as talk it over with Kadwy.

When Gwion heard about it he said he was coming with her.

"No," Eleri said, her refusal absolute. "Stay here; look after things; look after Olwen."

"We haven't talked about that," Gwion said tentatively.

"There's no need," Eleri said crisply. "I can see she's right for you, Gwion."

There was no place for dissembling between them; there was no need to argue or contradict.

"Make sure you're back in time to sail with us to Llydaw," Gwion said, relief showing in his eyes at not having to plough over the field of his relationship with Olwen. "We won't go without you."

"You can't," Eleri reminded him, fingering the gold torque at her neck as she said it, the very thing she would have to part with to pay for their passage. Before reaching Caer Uisc she hadn't reckoned on the cost of sea travel for so many people, not until the wily sea captains had pointed to her precious torque, demanding it as the price for their services.

As for travelling to Ynys Wydr, when Mared of the Silver Wheel heard about it she said she'd known a lot of clever people in her time and that half of them were not right in the head.

"Take care, Eleri Gwir," she'd said, more like her old self, holding Eleri tight by the arm; "We need you.

And you too, young man," she said to Marrec, taking a close look at him through fading eyes. "Take care of this one and yourself."

Before leaving Caer Uisc, Eleri went to speak to Kadwy. She had already thanked him for allowing Marrec to accompany her to Ynys Wydr. This was another matter. People called her "the Truth Speaker". It was time she earned that name.

The room was small and hot. It was just the two of them, king and chieftain's daughter. Eleri accepted a glass of mead and nervously took a bigger gulp than she'd intended, which sounded at those close quarters in her throat. Kadwy waited for her to settle, his face giving nothing away, the gulp duly noted.

"You want to speak to me, Eleri Gwir," he said when he was good and ready.

"Yes, my lord," Eleri said.

"Kadwy will do; we're old friends."

Another Eleri might have argued the toss about that; this Eleri let it go, thinking more about whether they would still be friends after what she had to say.

"What I have to say may seem presumptuous," she said. "You may laugh in my face or throw me in chains."

"Really" Kadwy said, intrigued.

"Yes."

"I'm all ears."

"It's Olwen," Eleri said, feeling as if she'd dived over a cliff edge.

Her hesitation seemed to amuse the king, who remarked on how unusual it was to see Eleri Gwir tongue-tied. "We should have a scribe present to preserve the moment for posterity," he joked.

"Your brother," Eleri tried starting again on another tack.

"What about him?" Kadwy asked.

"Don't play with me like a cat with a wounded mouse, Kadwy," she said, sounding cross and more like her usual assertive self.

"Why not?" he asked shamelessly, laughing.

"I came here intending to live up to my name by speaking plain and straight, and look what you've made me do," Eleri said, her temper rising into her coppery hair.

Kadwy laughed again. "You want to ask me about Olwen," he said. "What are my intentions? Will I act to her as my brother acted to her sister? Am I seriously interested in her, or is she just a passing fancy? You want to tell me that your friend Gwion loves her and that she loves him. Is that it?"

"Yes it is, Kadwy," Eleri said earnestly. "I don't want to return to Caer Uisc to find Gwion has done something stupid; or Olwen for that matter; or you."

"You're only supposed to assume that kings are inclined to do stupid things when you're speaking *about* them, not *with* them," Kadwy said, enjoying himself immensely.

"I'll remember that when you hang me," Eleri said.

"Look," Kadwy said seriously, "the girl Olwen is everything a man could want, clever, brave, good-looking. If she chooses to stay in Dyfneint of her own free will, so be it. But it seems to me that she has already chosen the path she wishes to take and the man that will go with her. Who am I to contradict that?"

"You're the king," Eleri said.

"But not a tyrant, Eleri Gwir," Kadwy replied. "Besides, kings must think about women in terms of alliances. What is this girl but a blacksmith's daughter after all? She won't do, Eleri Gwir, no matter how much I desire her."

"Not even if she's sister to the Dragon Maiden; not even for a king's amusement?" Eleri asked, fishing for certainty.

"Not even," Kadwy said. "If only out of respect for you."

Eleri said nothing.

"That's got you thinking," Kadwy said mischievously.

The room was smaller suddenly, hotter. For a moment Eleri thought he was going to kiss her. Her skin tensed. He didn't.

"Marrec will take good care of you," the king said. He smiled. "Or you will take good care of him. I'm not sure which. Just be sure to return in one piece, the pair of you."

The usually self-assured Kadwy appeared suddenly vulnerable to Eleri, young even, no more than his twenty summers. She had never heard him speak with such openness or affection before. She liked him for it. The more she saw of Kadwy the more she liked him. He'll make a good king, she thought, not for the first time, assuming he is allowed to learn the craft; if Ceawlin doesn't sweep him away or he isn't killed in some petty squabble among the chieftains of Dyfneint. She didn't envy his position or his power. She didn't envy any king.

# Chapter Thirty-Nine

Eleri found Ynys Wydr as she'd left it, a mystery spread with a gauze of breathing, shimmering light. They arrived on the third day of their journeying. They came with the freedom of travel and movement in their hearts, already set apart from their normal lives, if such a thing as normality could be said to exist for them. For Marrec as for Eleri, the journey was like a cleansing after betrayal, battle, wounding, the death of a king. They came from the west, through the wet lands that spread out from the coast, leaving their horses on firm ground and taking to the flat-bottomed boats that plied these waters. Pilgrims, they came from the Pilgrim River – *Afon Pererin* – guided by the strange people of the country, who knew nothing of kings and everything about reeds and water fowl and eels and fish. They came at twilight to Ynys Wydr – the Glass Island – the sun spreading out on the western horizon, the world of air and the world of water cloaked in light and dark.

They were taken to the bard's hall and asked to wait. Threads of mystery hung about the place; word-sprites jabbered in the dark timbers. Mead was brought. A bed would be prepared, they were told.

"Beds," Eleri said, used by now to firm speaking.

They waited. Food was provided, a simple dish of bread and fish. People came and went. Finally, a curtain to the side of the hall was parted by a young woman, elfin-boned, dark-hued, a bird-wraith and a sight to behold. It was the Spirit Muse – *Awen Ysbryd.*

"Welcome," she said. "Although I'm afraid we have a poor welcome for you this night."

Infatuation is not confined by age or sex, to such as Nest and Enid, young girls at the awkward time of life. Eleri saw it in Marrec, the warrior, the dutiful captain of Dyfneint. She saw it leap into his eyes. She saw it dive into his bowels. She saw its enduring wreckage and its sudden glory strike at the man's heart. Awen Ysbryd, the seer, the young woman was before him; her lithe grace; her drop-dead beauty.

"My lord Cynan is gravely ill," Awen said, sombre and formal. "His time for journeying to the island beyond the north wind is upon him."

"I'm sorry," Eleri said.

"The Island of the Mighty is broken; his heart is broken," Awen said by way of diagnosis and explanation.

"Ynys Wydr," Eleri said softly, tenderly, like a mother thinking of a child she had lost at birth.

"I must go back to him. Words must be said," Awen continued.

"Can we do anything?" Marrec asked awkwardly.

"You have brought the Truth Speaker at this hour; that's enough," Awen answered, her blackbird voice sounding through the shadowy hall. Coming to stand before Eleri Gwir, reaching out to touch her lips and hair, Awen added: "Ynys Wydr has need of the healer and the archer." Without further explanation, holding out her hand, she took Eleri with her through the curtained door, leaving Marrec bereft, with nothing but the moon, the planets and the stars to look at.

Eleri was taken to a plain room – a table, a low bed. She found Cynan lying there, dressed in a white shift, smaller than she'd remembered him, his wispy hair flat on his smooth head. His skin, she noticed, was perfect, without blemish, no wrinkles or the marks that come with age. She saw, too, that his spirit was already departing his body, bound for another place and time.

The names of all the gods were spoken over the dying bard. Taliesin, the god of his kind, was invited to accompany Cynan on his journey to that other island spinning out there in the west, call it Caer Sidi, the Apple Island, Avalon. Hand in hand, Awen and Eleri, seer and Truth Speaker, sat for hours, their heads growing light with the incense they burned, their minds set free of the complexities of this world, the names of the gods repeating, starting over, endless as the sea. With Cynan's last breath his spirit was released into the glistening night sky; the velvet black; the diamond light. The planet Jupiter was the brightest object, perfectly still and fiercely shining.

There was no need for a bed. Eleri slept where she was. As before, her dreams were a muddle, comings and goings, Macsen, Cerridwen, even Father Cenydd. She woke to the sound of a male voice, a boy's voice, the unmistakeable voice of Gereint, the Little Hare. There he was, sitting opposite Awen, her naked feet in his lap, the words of an old verse on his lips.

At first Eleri said nothing. The wonder of it was enough.

"How did you get here?" she asked at last.

"Awen Ysbryd," was the answer.

While it was less than complete as an explanation, the statement appeared to encapsulate the gist of it. It would do for now. Later, Gereint told her that he'd just kept running through the Saxon ranks. A man had taken hold of him, but he let go when the fighting started. Gereint ran off and kept running. The scavengers assumed he was something to do with them. He just kept on going.

*

On hearing of the death of their chieftain, the people of the Water Land came to Ynys Wydr, arriving in coracles and flat-bottomed boats, some coming over the wooden walkways, seeming to walk on water. A pyre was built. Songs were sung, some familiar, some that Eleri had never heard before. The seaweed drink was consumed, the same brew she and the others had shared with the boatman and his woman. There was mead. The old world, the ancient scheme of things, the skin and web of their lives was mourned. The rising sun, the fire chariot of Belin, was worshipped. Thanksgiving was made. Eels were cooked on open fires. The small, dark people of the Water Land came to Awen, asking their seer for words to carry them through their hard, narrow lives. They came to Eleri to kiss her hands, the healer and the archer. They melted away into the air and into the earth and into the water. This being the first day of the hawthorn month, Beltane's day, they had other revelry and lovemaking to attend to.

Eleri saw that Marrec stood apart from the festivities. It seemed the world they mourned and praised had already perished in his heart. Not even Awen Ysbryd could bring it back to life. To the extent that he believed in anything, the sun-faced cross was his religion, still a mongrel faith in Eleri's eyes, miserable in doctrine and ritual. In this as in so many other respects she found him like Macsen, which had its own comforts for her, the thought of a brother in blood who yet lived. But it was a thought and that alone. She wasn't looking for another

Macsen; or for any man if it came to that; she wasn't in the market.

For Marrec, this journey was the first chance he'd had in ten years, since he was a very young man, to stand aside from his soldiering role, to take stock as it were. It was a retreat from the world of the taking and giving of orders into a small, precious space where there was liberty of thought and action. More pragmatically, the wound he had suffered to his left shoulder in the first battle against Kelyn still troubled him, on damp days especially, and there was no shortage of those in Dyfneint. The rest felt good. As for Eleri, he could see that she was working through the huge events that had pulled her life apart. In war as in love, he reflected, timing was of the essence. This wasn't the right time. In any case, Kadwy had spoken to him, saying how special Eleri Gwir was to him, not declaring his love for her or anything of the kind, but suggesting an attachment that had its own intensity of feeling. It was enough to put Marrec on his guard. And then, of course, there was Awen Ysbryd, a spear thrown at his heart.

Marrec was in no hurry to leave Ynys Wydr. It was the place itself. It had its own heathen way with people. Its spells were ingested from air and water; there was no hiding from them; you couldn't harden your heart to the spirit of the place, which even now was more potent that any Christian mass or seaweed brew.

Finding Marrec peering over the airy landscape, his will gliding on the still waters, his warrior heart beating low, it was Eleri who said they should be thinking about leaving.

"Would they come with us?" he asked. "Awen and the boy, I mean."

"I doubt it; but we can ask."

They wouldn't; of course they wouldn't.

"Anywhere else I would be a fish out of water," Awen told them, her roebuck eyes smiling at her own witticism. "I'm needed here, by the people of the Water Land. I'm not needed anywhere else."

"What about you, Little Hare?" Eleri asked.

"I'm needed here too," he said without hesitation, a statement they knew to be true even if they didn't know why.

Like Riwalus before him, Marrec found it hard to leave, yet leave he did. Duty was deeply impressed upon him, down to the last layer of his being.

"You should be safe here," he told Awen. "For some years at least. You've got nothing the Gewisse want and they will have other things to do, Dyfneint to contend with, the men of Gwent, other tribes of their own kind, the Land of the Hafren to divide up between them. Ceawlin will look here last, if at all."

"Thank you, Marrec," Awen said.

"It's little enough," he answered. "But remember, if I live, I will be at Caer Uisc; you can find me there."

"The time will come when *you* will find me," Awen said.

It was the third day of the hawthorn month, Eleri's birthday. Awen found her at first light peering over the eerie Water Land, watching delicate long-legged herons and cranes starting their day's toil and frolic in the crisp air. From the ancient tree that grew on the tor, Awen presented Eleri with a single white hawthorn flower, its sticky-sweet scent erotic and feminine.

"I'll keep it as a treasure," Eleri said. She kissed Awen, breathing in the scent of her skin. "I once told my father that I would like to have two separate lives; that way I could have my meat and eat it, as they say. But standing here with you feels more like the same life repeating, like living the same experience twice over."

"Except that you're a different person now," Awen said.

"Perhaps; I've still got a big mouth; I'm still bossy; am I really that different?" Eleri asked.

"Different enough," Awen observed, turning to look into Eleri's eyes.

In her heart Eleri was overjoyed to be with Awen Ysbryd. It struck her that this was why she had come to Ynys Wydr, just to exchange these few words which meant nothing much and everything as well, to put the world in its rightful place. Sadness and gladness were in equal measure here, air, earth and water, their powers at the same height and volume.

"The boy Gereint is the nearest thing I have to family," Eleri said. "I hadn't thought of it before. My father loved him like a son."

"He runs through all our lives," Awen remarked. "He is close to the dead," she added, heading off on a tangent of her own.

"What do you see, Awen Ysbryd?" Eleri asked.

"Change," Awen said. "Any fool can see change; a foolish seer even."

"Marrec thinks you will be safe here, for a time at least."

"Unfortunately, like the rest of us, soldiers are only permitted to be wise after the event," Awen said, her light laugh forming.

"Let's hope he's right."

"The gods will be here even if we're not."

They left shortly after. Eleri gave Gereint such a hug that it lifted him into the air. She wanted to cry. Instead she laughed. Gereint laughed. Marrec laughed. Awen Ysbryd cried silent, salty tears.

# Chapter Forty

They found Caer Uisc in mess and uproar.

The number of fugitives from the Gewisse had multiplied. People argued over food, over living space, about all the things people usually argue about but with the intensity that comes from fear for the future and present gnawing hunger. At least they had somewhere to go to; they had cause for hope. The tricky part was finding a passage on a boat across the Sea of Gaul to Llydaw, the land across the water, where they were promised a new start.

The people of Britain had been making this journey for generations; with each burst of Saxon expansion and before that even, with the departure of the Romans from Gaul, when the tribes of the Dumnonii and the Kernow had seized on the opportunity to undertake some imperial expansion of their own. They had gone into the vastness of the other Britain, away from the murderous Saxons, marking out a territory, a place where the old ways might endure. For some, like Cenydd's father Gildas, it was a refuge for the new faith; a safe harbour; a seeding ground. Unlike the Saxons, the Frankish barbarians had taken up the new faith; dialogue was possible on the basis of common oaths.

Llydaw was large and its chieftains were always in need of more people – fighting men, fishing men, farming men and their fertile women. Arrangements had been made for ships to carry the latest refugees from the Island of the Mighty. Three had arrived and made sail under a pink morning sky, only to run into a storm that brought huge rolling waves from the great ocean beyond. One ship had been lost. Now another three ships were docked at Caer Uisc, preparing to leave for Llydaw in a few days. On hearing of the hazards of the journey, some had elected to stay put in Dyfneint. Many more were clamouring for berths, arguing, fighting over the limited places on offer. Gold helped, what there was of it. Otherwise the fugitives were left to squabble and shove.

"What a mess," Eleri said, her innate sense of order horrified.

"I'll find Kadwy," Marrec said in his determined way.

Eleri found the people of the Summer Land in a sheltered corner under the old town walls. Gwion was there, his black curling hair peeking out from a scrum of hostile women.

"Here she is at long last," one woman said.

"A bit late in the day," another commented.

"While you've been going about the country, doing whatever you're doing, we've had nothing but trouble to deal with here," a third remarked.

They were in high dudgeon, all fired up and ready to blame someone.

Gwion emerged from the scrum, saying: "Eleri; thank the gods you're back."

She'd never seen him look so tired or so flustered.

"What's going on here?" she asked.

"Its Nest and Enid," a woman said. "They've gone off this morning with that lot from Kernow, men with tin for brains and for bollocks too for all I know, leaving everything behind, throwing their lives away like that," she said, making a gesture with her arm in indication of futility and waste.

In tears, Nest's mother said she hoped that Kernow and everyone in it would sink into the sea.

"Drowning's too good for them," said Enid's mother, her anger and frustration plain.

"And Gwion let them go," Nest's mother said accusingly.

"What else could he do?" Cerys spoke up in his defence.

"I didn't even know they were going," Gwion said, his temper rising by this time.

"Look," Eleri said firmly, every bit her father's daughter, "it's their decision – Nest and Enid's. I'm sorry they're gone and I agree that it's stupid and a waste. But it was their decision to make and they've made it." She gave both mothers her sternest look. "It's not Gwion's fault and it's not yours," she said, although as to the truth of the last part of that statement she wasn't entirely certain.

"He could have spoken to them," Nest's mother said tearfully.

"We all could have done a lot of things," Eleri said fiercely. "I could have been here. Gwion could have said something. You could have said something different. I won't hear any more recriminations. What's done is done."

They seemed to accept that, grudgingly, with mumbled grumbling words that were sure to grow louder when Eleri was out of earshot.

Gwion took a deep breath: "No wonder my father was happy to let leadership fall into my lap." He was learning.

"Cows and sheep are a lot less trouble then people," Cerys remarked.

Eleri was left with Gwion and Cerys, all three of them feeling rather sorry for themselves. "So what are the plans?" she asked, after they'd taken a few moments to recover their equilibrium.

"Nothing definite, still," Gwion said. "Some of us could have sailed before, but I didn't like the look of the weather. The gulls were flying to land. There was obviously something on the way. The captains saw it, of course, but sailed against their better judgement. There's too much gold talking too loudly for anyone to be sensible."

"Common sense has gone out of the door and good judgement with it," Cerys said.

"The ships in port now are spoken for," Gwion continued. "But hopefully we can sail on the next lot."

He looked particularly earthy to Eleri, a creature out of its element talking about the sea and its unfamiliar moods and manners. But he had done well.

"Thanks," she said to him. "For everything."

She didn't ask him where Olwen was; she just looked at him, her coppery head on one side. All his life Gwion had watched her converse in this fashion with her body, without the need for words. He knew the signs and how to read them.

"Gronw, her father," Gwion said. "He was well one day and sick the next. I'm afraid he's dead."

"I'm sorry," Eleri said. "I should have been here."

"There was nothing to do," Cerys reassured her. "It was his heart that gave way, suddenly, without warning."

Life's messiness was all about.

✲

Eleri found Kadwy surrounded by a pack of men, all of them standing except for him, his presence made known by the sound of his calm, firm voice. Marrec was there. He beckoned her forward.

"My lord," she said, thinking it best to keep to the formalities in the company of such angry, hostile-looking men.

"Eleri Gwir," the king said, rising to welcome her, taking her hands in his. "It's good to see you."

Put out, a big scruffy man stared hard at her with a look that could kill a cat at twenty paces. He was a sea captain and he was unhappy and he didn't like to be interrupted by an unannounced young woman, even one as striking-looking as Eleri.

"It's a mess," he said. "The people fight and argue; they promise to pay one thing then they haggle; they put their gold down and then they pick it up again. The chieftains of Llydaw said we would be paid a fair amount for every person seeking refuge. But when will they pay us? Can they be trusted?"

Others joined in. Related and unrelated lines of argument were pursued; complaints were made and made again. The captains and the leaders of the refugees almost came to blows until Marrec's sword was heard to speak in its own whispering voice as it came from its scabbard, telling everyone to settle down and to remember that they were in the presence of the King of Dyfneint. For his part, Kadwy was seated again, holding up his arms, signalling that he wanted quiet and order.

"This is Eleri Gwir," he said, young but authoritative. "The chieftain of the Summer Land. She was with Ffernfael at Bryn Derwydd. She is a truth speaker."

Eleri was dressed in whatever finery she owned; the golden torque which was still in her possession for now; a silver brooch that tied her cloak; a ring of turned gold from the mountains of Cambria. The men took due note and allowed her their grudging respect. The king watched, making his own mental notes. Marrec stood at her side, like a fierce wolf daring any of the pack to break away.

The chaos around Kadwy was real enough. Yet, Eleri half suspected that he tolerated delay the best to encourage some to stay here in Dyfneint and so continue the good fight on British soil. Either way, the time had evidently come to resolve the deadlocks and to clear away obstructions; the time had come for order to be imposed.

"From this hour my captain Marrec will oversee the refugees and all matters relating to them," Kadwy said, an iron edge to his voice. "Eleri Gwir will assist him," he added, to her surprise. "There will be a system and there will be an agreed cost and method of payment. Anyone found cheating or in any way exploiting the misery of these people will be put in chains." Kadwy looked hard at the captains. "Is that understood?" he asked.

It was.

There was another surprise waiting for Eleri that evening.

In Kadwy's private rooms she found Macsen's sisters, Julia and Livia, sitting in relative comfort like members of a protected species. They'd met before, fleetingly in Caer Baddan to where the sisters had come to wish their brother luck, and for safety should fortune fail him. His sisters had the same blondness, the same sea-creature, pale-blue eyes, the same high cheekbones and indefatigable haughtiness that commanded attention. To Eleri, they were pure, clean water from Sulla's spring. Not waiting to be asked, she embraced them. "Thank goodness you're alive," she said.

Julia was the talker. Once news of the defeat at Bryn Derwydd had reached them, she said, they'd abandoned

Caer Baddan. Many had stayed to serve their new lords; not them.

"Christ knows what the Saxons would have done to us."

"I've got a pretty good idea," Eleri said.

"Yes, well, so had we. Our household went into hiding. There was a place Macsen knew, a deep gorge to the west. Of course, we couldn't stay there forever. Eventually we came south. We were lucky enough to come across a patrol from Dyfneint. And here we are," Julia concluded, not one to waste words, disdaining drama and any form of display.

"How many of you?" Eleri asked.

"Five in total. We were joined by two older men and one woman who had served our family all their lives."

"What will you do?"

"If we can, we'll go across the water," Julia said. "We could stay, of course, but what would we do here?"

Eleri wondered what they would do anywhere, except starve or whore or, if they were very lucky, marry. They were older than Eleri, although not by much, and eligible enough candidates in their way for beggary, prostitution or marriage. She feared for them and at the same time she recognised their toughness and resolve. "I'll remember not to underestimate them," she told herself.

To the sisters she said: "Why not join with the people of the Summer Land, for now at least?" It wasn't that Eleri had any need of more difficult young women, or useless old men for that matter; but they were Macsen's sisters; there was a debt to be paid.

She received a suitably laconic answer the following morning: "Yes." By midday a contrary message was brought by one of the older servants, saying that the young ladies had been offered a place in the king's household, which they'd accepted.

"They send their thanks," the man said.

Thinking they might have done a bit more, by way of making a personal appearance, Eleri was inclined to be cross. Then she told herself not to be so petty and, thinking about it a little more, she breathed a sigh of relief. She was carrying enough burdens over the Sea of Gaul without looking for any more.

*

Finally, the day came for the people of the Summer Land to leave Britain, the Broken Island. They went on board three ships, barks they called them. The ships were out of a port in Llydaw, but their captains were men from Dyfneint originally and owed direct allegiance to Kadwy.

Hoods pulled over their eyes, the people tried not to look at the land they were leaving, staring instead at their feet, their grieving kept to themselves. In their arms and on their bodies was all they owned in this world: clothes, a few jewels if they were lucky enough, whatever coins remained after the captains had been paid out. Their bows and any other weapons were with them; Gwion and Eleri made sure of that. "We may run into pirates," they told the others. "You never know." Eleri was their leader on one ship; Gwion on another; Meriadoc and Cerys on the third. As they took their places and waited for the tide, Mared of the Silver Wheel, in her loudest voice, spoke the names of the old gods, all those she could recall and those she was reminded of by others. The drumbeat for the oarsman sounded and the names sounded with it, the chant ending as it started with Llyr, the god of the sea.

Olwen went with Gwion. The night before, her mother Gwenda had said she would stay behind in Dyfneint where her husband was buried; Olwen and Gwion alike pleaded with her to join them and she had come around when Olwen had told her she was pregnant and there would be a grandchild in Llydaw.

"I missed my bleeding," she said. It promised a new start for them all. "My father wouldn't have wanted you to throw away your life on mourning," Olwen had told her mother, which Gwenda knew to be true.

A priest had visited Eleri, asking if he might find passage with the people of the Summer Land. He was from the north of Cambria, a monastic community in a place called Bangor, which he spoke about with great enthusiasm, as if it were the Great Circle or some other wonder of the known world. His name was Malo and he was young and open-faced, with freckles on his shaved forehead, which reminded Eleri of Father Cenydd. She reasoned that Malo would probably do very nicely for one of the many unattached women of the Summer Land; he might have done for either Julia or Livia, for the pair of them if that suited. Eleri welcomed him on board and could only smile at how shocked he looked to hear the holy names chanted in farewell to the Island of the Mighty.

Marrec wasn't there. His king had still other uses for him and he was sent north. There were no frills to him.

"Goodbye, Eleri Gwir," he'd said, plain and simple.

"Goodbye, Marrec."

But Nest and Enid were there, large as life. Alun Ddu had personally escorted them back to Caer Uisc, saying they were more trouble than even the men of Kernow needed in their lives. "Take them for the sake of Christ across the Sea of Gaul," he'd said. "And be sure to keep them on the other side."

Eleri wondered if Malo had made a vow of chastity, and if he had, how long it would last in the company of the dangerous women of the Summer Land. Did the chieftains of the other Britain know what they were letting themselves in for?

She had spoken privately with Kadwy. He fascinated her, if only because she couldn't read him the way she could other men. Perhaps the layers in his being were packed tighter than usual. Perhaps there were no layers, only the fathomless depths of his liquid soul. She didn't know. He was both passionate and reserved, heat and cold, dark and light, always watchful. Eleri supposed people said the same of her, or something like it, which drew her closer to Kadwy, her twin in nature, a sisterly closeness she felt it, a fascination with someone so similar to herself and yet still impenetrable.

As ever on parting, there was a rare awkwardness about their last meeting. What can be meaningfully said? What can be done? Marrec had it right; short and sweet; *let the heart break alone, let it beat out the time of yearning.*

"I hope we meet again, Eleri Gwir," Kadwy said.

"I hope so too."

Messiness and uproar; that was the sum of it.

Waiting to board the vessel, Eleri Gwir pushed back her hood and looked long and hard at the land, its colour, its weather. The last few days had been busy for her, organising, bossing people about, doing a lot and pushing thought as far away as possible. Even so, her heart grew heavier, an iron ball that she dragged about, a weight that sank deeper and deeper into the wet soil of the Island. Today, it felt heavy enough to sink the bark she was about to board. So heavy was it, Eleri could barely drag one foot after the other.

"I'll go to the bottom of the ocean," she told herself. "And everyone will go with me."

Standing beside her was Gwion, bare-headed, looking landwards towards a flock of sheep on a hillside. Like Eleri, not a day, not an hour passed that his mind didn't find itself at Bryn Derwydd, the Saxon host before them, their linden shields, their spears, their axes, their swords; and Ceawlin their king, the ring-giver, the hero, the sound of his name and the names of the Gewisse gods resounding through the land. And like Eleri he fretted about his life when those around him had sacrificed theirs. He knew he lived for a reason; but what does the heart know or care about reason?

They had no need for words. Truth had been spoken. The reckoning was made.

Gwion was to be a father. That was something; a spear thrown from the passionate heart into the ravaging host of messiness and uproar; an arrow of hope to shoot down the eagles of grief and loss.

# Part Five

## AD 578

## "The Oak Month"

# Chapter Forty-One

A year passed.

The people of the Summer Land were lucky; some faltered but most found their way in their new country. Gwion was luckier than most. With his father he farmed a smallholding in the north of Llydaw, the sound of the sea always in their ears, day and night, the wind raw at times, the earth good and welcoming. Gwenda lived with them. Late in the Christian year Olwen gave birth to a boy; they called him Gronw. Olwen and Gwion were well matched, their passions, their desires, the resolve and strength of their characters. Working side by side, they found their new life suited them; and, as they loved and liked each other, so their neighbours liked them in turn and invited the young couple into their society.

Nest and Enid had no trouble finding young men to chase after; their mothers were glad to have them safe and close. Rhian caught the eye of the son of a high-ranking man and set about producing the next generation of chieftains.

As for Eleri, she settled into a quiet life. She lived with Cerys and her mother Mared, an arrangement which for the time being pleased and suited them all. With Cerys, she offered her services as midwife and healer, for which there was always need. At least they didn't starve. At the start of the winter months Cerys started a relationship with a widower, a farmer, whose fractured arm she'd helped to set. He had sons enough. He wasn't looking for a wife who would provide him with any more; Cerys would do very nicely for him; and she had about the same opinion of the widower.

As the year passed, Eleri spent more and more time with Mared of the Silver Wheel, a chieftain with nothing to rule and an ancient seer without a future. They made an odd couple, although snug enough in their way. As Mared's deafness intensified so her voice grew louder; as her eyes faded so her tongue grew sharper with frustration. There was nothing wrong with her mind and her constitution was as strong as ever, strong enough to walk down to the sea shore every day to collect sticks for their fire. Eleri handled her as well as anyone, her firmness undiminished. Besides, they had a common cause in their disdain for the new faith, conspicuously avoiding its rituals and festivities, keeping to themselves after a fashion, which involved Mared telling anyone who cared to listen exactly what she thought of the Christ religion. Eleri kept her own counsel on these and other matters, a red squirrel in hibernation maybe, or a copper butterfly wrapped tight in a chrysalis, her hair the same glorious fire-god colour.

Paradoxically, the young priest Malo was one of the few visitors to their simple hut. He would walk over the headland in the evenings, regardless of weather, and join them for broth and conversation. He was curious to learn more about Father Cenydd, the son of the famous Gildas who was so venerated here in Llydaw. What was he like? Did he speak of his father? Eleri told him what she knew about the thin-lipped, proud and difficult man she had known who was as passionate about his family as he was about his faith. She didn't say it, but Cenydd's religion seemed like an inheritance from his father, one that had never sat altogether comfortably on his shoulders. Being the son of Gildas hadn't been easy for Cenydd.

"He died well," she said, which was the best she could say of anyone.

Inquisitive by calling, Malo asked about all kinds of things, the healing qualities of the natural world, the characters of men and women. More than anything the old religion fascinated him; he was like a child putting its hand into the candle flame, curiosity getting the better of him.

"Of course, what we know now is only the surface of things," Mared would declare. "The real learning was lost when the Romans came. The learned ones were all killed on the Holy Island of Môn, and with them went much of what we used to know."

"I come from those parts," Malo said.

"From where, Rome?" Mared asked him, playing the dotty old woman.

"Ignore that," Eleri said.

"Why don't you get together with this young woman?" Mared confronted Malo. "Look, she's there for the taking."

"And ignore that too," Eleri said, the firmness in her voice intensifying.

Eventually, they'd steer the conversation back on course. Sometimes the two heathens would tolerate a few improving words from the young priest, along with tales of miracles and wonders worked by holy men.

"Gimmicks," Mared called them, and Eleri agreed. "We have our own gimmicks, thank you very much."

All the same they found the stories of the desert fathers inspiring and would have heard more than Malo knew to tell. Malo was also in possession of the gift of reading and writing, which fascinated the two women, Eleri especially.

"Will you teach me?" she asked.

"She'll let you lie with her if you do," Mared said wickedly.

"Behave yourself," Eleri said. "Pay no attention to her Father Malo," she added, preferring not to bring the young priest's vital juices to the surface, assuming they were not already there.

The winter months were spent in that way, talking by the fire, Eleri learning her letters, the priest enjoying her company more than he cared to admit, Mared remembering slivers of knowledge and passing them on, at the same time firing a barrage of mischievous comments and suggestions. Eleri's reading was in Latin, which she found hard going and yet peculiarly rewarding. The months passed; her Latin improved; the gift of reading was a revelation.

The first anniversary of the Battle of Bryn Derwydd came and went. Gwion came over with Olwen and Gronw, carrying the gift of a piglet in his arms. Gwenda and Meriadoc were with them. A fire was made on the headland. Math's wife Onnen joined them with her strapping sons. At fifteen, Idris was serving with the local chieftain, learning about war and women, although not necessarily in that order. Everyone from the district made their way to the headland. The fire burned high and bright; Gwion, Eleri and Olwen sent fire arrows into the darkness.

Arriving late, in company with his war band, was the chieftain of the Dumnonii in the north of Llydaw, a man called Rhun. A volcanic, strongly built man in his forties, he exuded power and violence, his character sounding in the harsh jangling of his horse's harness. It was a reminder to them all that this land, too, had to be fought for and defended, every tree and stone, earth and sky. Eleri knew it better and deeper than most. Still, remembering what Branwen had said about this man's cruelty towards her, Eleri shuddered.

People still called her Eleri Gwir – the Truth Speaker. Would she speak truth to this man, her protector now, the one who had extended the hospitality of Llydaw to the people of the Summer Land?

"You are the famous Eleri Gwir," he said, striding towards her.

"Yes, my lord," she answered.

Their eyes locked, his darkly devouring, hers proudly unyielding. "Is there anything you want to say to me?" Rhun asked gruffly.

"To thank you," she said, "for granting refuge to the people of the Island."

He nodded approvingly. Eleri invariably thought of her father on these occasions, about his advice which was more prudent than his example. Doing what she knew for certain Arawn would have done in the same circumstances, she invited Rhun to send a fire arrow into the darkness, in memory of those who had fallen at Bryn Derwydd.

"Many fell," she said, "many good people; my friend Branwen among them."

"You saw her fall?" Rhun asked, about as curious as he was angry.

"Yes. I looked back. She and Siriol refused to retreat. A Saxon axe cut her in half, from her shoulder to her heart."

Inured to the violence of war, Rhun acknowledged the fact with a cursory nod of his big head. A door, long open, closed in his mind; you could hear it shut with a bang.

"Very well," he said aggressively. "Give me your bow." The fire arrow he shot carried far into the darkness, far out into the eternal sea. Eleri had a mind to shoot Rhun about the same distance, his arse on fire.

There is a saying among the Britons, that spring sunshine is like poison – *haul y gwanwyn fel y gwenwyn.* As the weather improved, with the ash month waning, Mared of the Silver Wheel took to spending more time out of doors, picking bits and pieces of driftwood and then sitting for hours in the warming sun, ignoring the still chilly bite to the westerly wind. It started as a cold, then a cough that went into her lungs and left her gasping for breath. The day Mared died, it felt to Eleri as if a great spirit had left the world; indeed, the old world itself ended on that day. She and Cerys observed the rituals. Following instructions, under a sickle moon a pyre was built. "I don't want to be shoved underground like your poor father," Mared had told them in her loudest, fiercest voice. "I'm not a vole."

For Eleri, Mared's death was the end of one thing and the start of another. When the first boats from Britain arrived, she went to speak to the refugees on board, fewer now than the steady stream of the previous year. The piglet she gave to one of these families along with her hut – the witches' hut, people called it: "Which means it has strong spells around it," Eleri told them. She spoke to the captains and paid for her passage back to the Island with the silver brooch that tied her cloak. Something cheaper would do well enough now that she was nobody special. She inquired about Dyfneint and was told that the young king was going to war, which made her fearful for Kadwy and his people.

"Do you know his captain at arms, Marrec?" she asked. They knew *of* him, that was all.

"You'll write to me, Eleri Gwir," Malo said, as sorry as anyone to see her leave.

"I'll try."

"You'll be missed."

"They have you, Father; they have your god. What more could the people of Llydaw need or want?"

"We won't argue; not today," Father Malo said, the freckles on his forehead like drops of red paint from Belin's brush.

It was the start of the oak month when she packed her few possessions in a cloth and walked across to the next bay to visit Gwion and his family. She would have done so sooner, if not for her promise to Rhian to be there for the birth of her first child – a strapping boy.

"You've come to say goodbye," Gwion said.

"Yes."

"Why, Eleri?" he asked. "Why not stay and make a life here? The earth is good."

"Not as good as the red earth, surely," she said, smiling. "I won't have Gwion saying a thing like that."

"No, not that good; but good enough," he acknowledged, his dark eyes as kind and insightful as ever. "You can't say you miss the weather," he said.

"There's certainly rain enough here to remind me of home."

"But it's not the same," he said sombrely.

"It's the same yet different; like me," she said.

He knew what she meant. They all did in their way.

Once she had wondered if there was anything stronger, more enduring and intense than jealousy, something that eats away at you, corroding your inner life. For some people, she reflected, jealousy was indeed the ruler of their hearts and minds. But not in her case; not now and not ever was her hope. Some other creature of the soul was eating into her, hard to put her finger on exactly, not readily captured and examined, for all that it was common enough among the people of Llydaw, showing in their eyes and speech, in their insatiable need to go out into the treacherous sea. People called it yearning – *hiraeth* in the British language.

For what?

Eleri could only answer for herself. It wasn't for any person or place in particular. She would have given anything to sit and talk over the fire with her father. She would have gladly given her life in exchange for victory over the Gewisse at Bryn Derwydd. The *cantref* of the Summer Land was sewn into the cavities of her body as tight and sure as if it had been stitched by the women of the weaving room. For the special friendship she shared with Gwion there was a locked room in her heart. Yet, her yearning was for none of these, or for none of them singly or in particular. It was for something stupidly vague and horribly real, an idea, a flight of fancy. If she tried to explain it to anyone she would appear ridiculous. Clever Eleri Gwir would be reduced to an absurdity.

She tried it out on Gwion, someone she could trust even with her life's absurdities.

"What I can't stand, what pulls me apart and calls me from sleep and dreams," Eleri said, "is the idea that the land is lost to its stories. These foreigners know nothing of it. For me, the land and its naming are one and all these are lost, irretrievably I suppose." She stopped. "Does any of that make sense?"

"I know," Gwion said, his eyes telling more than his mouth.

"It's stupid, I know," Eleri said. "To walk through that land was to walk with the gods and with the first lords of naming; it was to walk with Arthur and Kai and Bedwyr. And we've lost all that. These foreigners will find their own names in their own ugly wolf-mangled language; they will make their own stories or none at all. The land will be theirs, not ours, in every sense. I can't endure the thought of it. I just can't. We lost and I can't accept we lost. There's this door open inside me that I can't shut. How mad is that?"

"It's mad; but it's real," Gwion confirmed. "It's that layer of sadness under everything else, for something that's real and is unreal."

Eleri had known he would understand, or do his best to pretend to at any rate. She felt him flow like a healing liquid into her body, a feeling to savour and remember, she told herself.

"Goodbye then," she said, embracing him.

"Farewell, Eleri Gwir."

Picking up her possessions, she made for the pathway that led to the harbour from where she would return to what her people called the Island of the Mighty.

"Remember," Gwion called after her, making her turn around, her eyes looking into the setting sun.

"What?"

"You don't know everything, Eleri Gwir."

# Last Words

The older I get the more I think on these things, the people and the places, the world that was ours.

"It's not enough to think, Owain," Eleri Gwir would badger me. "You must write it down."

"I will," I say. "When my research is all done, when I'm ready."

"Don't leave it too late. Time runs away from us, fast as a hare. Look at me," she would say, holding out her hands, her long fingers stiff with the aching illness.

There was a day, not so long ago, a year or two, at the time of the year's giving, when the holly tree flowers. On that bright day, under Belin's eye, we sat in the garden in Llanilltud Fawr – you may know the spot, behind where the blackcurrent trees grow, in the shade of an oak tree. A magpie cocked its eye at us, I remember, before it hopped away about its business. We talked and talked that day. If Eleri Gwir's fire-god hair had lost its coppery brilliance, in her essential self she was very much the same, that fighting spirit of hers, her no-nonsense, caring nature.

"Write it down, Owain," she said. "Before we're all dead and gone."

"Why?" I asked.

"Because if we are to live on, if we are to be remembered, the land and its people, our story must be known," Eleri said. "If we don't make our mark on the page, we'll be lost to history. No one will know we ever lived and breathed. We'll melt away and we'll be gone forever, carried off by the river of time."

'Bryn Derwydd won't be forgotten," I insisted.

'It will if a record isn't made. It has to be worth remembering to someone, Owain. Our story has to be worth remembering. If we don't tell it, who will? Will our enemies? I don't think so. They'll tell their own side of it, if they say anything at all."

I do as I'm told.

With Eleri Gwir it's the only way.

I write these words that our story should be told and that it should be remembered. I write that you should know the history of your land and of your people. If my words survive the trials of this world, you will know how it was for us, how the Island of the Mighty was broken. What was lost was lost with a hard fight. What was kept was kept in the same way. No quarter was asked; none was given. I write that you will know the names of your dead. For Eleri Gwir, for all the people of this tale – Macsen, Cerridwen and the rest – for my father and my mother as much as for the chieftains and the kings, I would bring the past to life. I would give it legs and eyes and ears. I would reach out from my time and place to yours, touching your minds and your hearts.

# Author's Note

Relatively little is known about late 6th-century Britain and much of what is believed to be known is contested. There are more questions than answers, some large, others more specific: *Why did the Anglo-Saxons not become British? What was the scale of the Anglo-Saxon migration to Britain? Is that migration best described in terms of conquest and invasion or more as a transfer of elites with the indigenous population remaining more or less in place?* There is of course a large body of literature relevant to this area. For an excellent overview and encapsulation of the major issues of historical interpretation see – *The Anglo-Saxon World* by Nicholas J Higham and Martin J Ryan (Yale University Press, 2013). The historian Peter Heather has also informed my thinking on this period of history, notably *Empires and Barbarians: Migration, Development and the Birth of Europe* (Macmillan, 2009). The magisterial first volume of the history of Wales by TM Charles-Edwards (*Wales and the Britons, 350-1064*, Oxford University Press, 2013) only came to my notice after I had completed this book.

The broad interpretation I have adopted is based on three key assumptions. One is that the Anglo-Saxon migration was a long-term process, occurring over many generations. The second assumption is that the Anglo-Saxon takeover was messy and that it varied from one local area to another, in particular as between what is now south-east and south-west England. Whereas the elite-transfer model may apply to the south-east where the scale of armed resistance from the British may have been minimal in the aftermath of the Roman departure, the story in the south-west seems quite different, with the Saxon advance being marked by a series of pitched battles until they reached what is now the Bristol Channel. Admittedly, the Saxons may have reached that point earlier, in the 5th century, only to be pushed back east by renewed British resistance. My third assumption may be more controversial. It is that the indigenous population of Britain had a sense of themselves as a "people", as "fellow-countrymen" ("*kombrogi*"), not in the modern sense of nationhood – more, rather, in terms of cultural unity; and with that there was a concern for the "integrity" of the Island of Britain. I find this clearly expressed in the only native voice we have from the 6th century, that of Gildas, a polemical voice no doubt but no less instructive for all that. The case doesn't need to be overstated. The Pictish north was an exception of sorts. Countervailing forces were also at work, not least those of tribalism and localism right across Britain. Further, as things developed the reality on the ground would have been messy, as opportunistic leaders sought to take advantage of the fluid situation, sometimes making alliances across ethnic and language boundaries no doubt. Still, it is worth bearing in mind that the events depicted in this novel occurred over 150 years after the Romans left Britain; if historically accurate, they suggest concerted resistance on a significant scale. Who knows for certain? "The Dark Ages" remain dark to us. In the final analysis, the present work is one of historical fiction, told from the losing side.

The centrepiece of this novel is the Battle of Dyrham, said to have been fought in AD 577 just north of modern-day Bath. The source for it is the Anglo-Saxon Chronicle which records that three British "kings" died in the battle. They were said to be the kings of modern day Bath, Gloucester and Cirencester. The names of these kings are also recorded but these were almost certainly not their actual names but, rather, Anglo-Saxon versions and interpretations. An example of a variation between an original British name and its Anglo-Saxon rendering is that of the 7th-century princess of Elmet – Rhianfellt in her native language, Rǽgumeld in the anglicised version of the 9th-century Durham *Liber Vitae* (Max Adams, *The King in the North*, Head of Zeus Ltd, 2013, p 263).

The entry for AD 577 in the Anglo-Saxon Chronicle reads as follows (Note: The word "and" is abbreviated as "7" – http://www.documentacatholicaomnia.eu/03d/00011154,_Auctor_Incertus,_Anglo_Saxon_Chronicle,_EN.pdf):

Her Cuþwine 7 Ceawlin fuhton wiþ Brettas, 7 hie .iii. kyningas ofslogon, Coinmail, 7 Condidan, 7 Farinmail, in þære stowe þe is gecueden Deorham. 7 genamon .iii. ceastro Gleawanceaster, 7 Cirenceaster, 7 Baþanceaster.

And in translation:

This year Cuthwine and Ceawlin fought with the Britons, and slew three kings, Coinmail, and Condidan, and Farinmail, on the spot that is called Derham, and took from them three cities, Gloucester, Cirencester, and Bath.

For the purposes of this novel I have altered the names of two of the kings, notably changing the king of Caer Baddan's name from Farinmail to Ffernfael, thereby hopefully bringing it closer to its British original. But that may be open to dispute. Relevantly, in chapter

12 of *Wales and the Britons, 350-1064* it is stated that "the forms of the British kings' names are early..." (p 381).

Language is a complex issue in the context of 6th-century Britain. It would seem that for the language spoken by the native British population it was a time of change and transition, with the transformation from archaic usage to one that is more familiar to contemporary speakers of Welsh. There is also the question of the deviation at this time between Welsh, on the one hand, and Cornish and Breton, on the other. Technical issues of linguistics are involved and I can do no better than to commend to the interested reader the work of Kenneth Jackson, *Language and History in Early Britain* (Edinburgh University Press, 1953). Chapter 2 of *Wales and the Britons, 350-1064* should also be noted, where it is argued that "the varieties of British remained dialects rather than independent languages until the twelth century" (p 92). For convenience, I have adopted modern Welsh usage, which I acknowledge is not an exact match for the language of the 6th-century Britons. The association of the name Cambria with Wales is a further anachronism, again adopted for convenience as a means of referring to that part of the country which, in the the 6th century, would have been divided into separate kingdoms, among them Gwent in the south-east and Dyfed in the far south- west.

As any traveller to Wales will know, pronunciation of Welsh names and places is always difficult. The word "Welsh" is derived from the Anglo-Saxon for foreigner and the Welsh language is very much a foreign tongue, often with no exact phonetic equivalents in English. The central character of this book is Eleri Gwir. Basically, "Eleri" is pronounced *Eler-ee*; "Gwir" is something like *Gw-eerr* – with the "r" sounded hard and full, somewhat along the lines of Edith Piaf. I will leave further explanation to the experts, except to say that "C", as in Cenydd, is pronounced as "K" and that a single "f" is pronounced as "v."

In addition to the books already cited I should mention the brilliant novel *Hild* by Nicola Griffith (no relation), which set me off thinking about the "heroic age" of British history. I must also acknowledge the influence on this novel of Robert Graves' *The White Goddess*; my borrowings will be familiar to any reader of that wonderfully eccentric work. Graves posits a thirteen-month Celtic calendar where each month is ruled by a tree (with 23 December as one extra day). The tree calendar is as follows:

| | |
|---|---|
| Birch | 24 December to 20 January |
| Rowan | 21 January to 17 February |
| Ash | 18 February to 17 March |
| Alder | 18 March to 14 April |
| Willow | 15 April to 12 May |
| Hawthorn | 13 May to 9 June |
| Oak | 10 June to 7 July |
| Holly | 8 July to 4 August |
| Hazel | 5 August to 1 September |
| Vine or Blackberry | 2 September to 29 September |
| Ivy | 30 September to 27 October |
| Dwarf Elder | 28 October to 24 November |
| Elder | 25 November to 22 December |

# Acknowledgements

My warm thanks for all their excellent professional help and advice to Llinos Cathryn and Cara Wynn-Jones of Lodestar Author Services. Sam Griffith and Simone van Nieuwenhuizen provided comments on many aspects of the novel. Talina Drabsch, Deryl Mason and Gwyn and Robin Brown read it in draft form. My thanks to them and especially to my wife Sue for her unfailing encouragement and a lot more besides.

Printed in Great Britain
by Amazon